109

W9-BBA-671

Waldwick Public Library
19 East Prospect St.
Waldwick, N.J. 07463

Green

Tor Books by Jay Lake

Mainspring
Escapement
Green

Green

JAY LAKE

A TOM DOHERTY ASSOCIATES BOOK
NEW YORK

Waldwick Public Library
19 East Prospect St.
Waldwick, N.J. 07463

This is a work of fiction. All of the characters, organizations, and events portrayed in this novel are either products of the author's imagination or are used fictitiously.

GREEN

Copyright © 2009 by Joseph E. Lake, Jr.

All rights reserved.

A Tor Book
Published by Tom Doherty Associates, LLC
175 Fifth Avenue
New York, NY 10010

www.tor-forge.com

Tor® is a registered trademark of Tom Doherty Associates, LLC.

Library of Congress Cataloging-in-Publication Data

Lake, Jay.
  Green / Jay Lake.—1st ed.
      p. cm.
  "A Tom Doherty Associates book."
  ISBN-13: 978-0-7653-2185-5
  ISBN-10: 0-7653-2185-8
  I. Title.
  PS3612.A519G74 2009
  813'.6—dc22
                        2008050608

First Edition: June 2009

Printed in the United States of America

0 9 8 7 6 5 4 3 2 1

This book is dedicated to my daughter, whose story it is. Someday she may choose to reveal which parts are true and which parts were made up by her dad.

Acknowledgments

This book would not have been possible without the wonderful assistance of people too numerous to fully list here. Nonetheless, I shall try, with apologies to whomever I manage to omit from my thank-yous. Much is owed to Karen Berry, Sarah Bryant, Kelly Buehler and Daniel Spector, Michael Curry, Miki Garrison, Anna Hawley, Dr. Daniel Herzig, Ambassador Joseph Lake, Adrienne Loska, Shannon Page, Tom Powers, Matthew S. Rotundo, Ken Scholes, Jeremy Tolbert, the Umberger family, the Omaha Beach Party, Amber Eyes, and, of course, my entire blogging community in all their bumptious glory. There are many others I have neglected to name: That omission is my own fault and does not reflect on you at all.

I also want to recognize the Brooklyn Post Office here in Portland, Oregon, as well as the Fireside Coffee Lodge and Lowell's Print-Inn for all their help and support. Special thanks go to Jennifer Jackson, Beth Meacham, Jozelle Dyer, Melissa Frain, and Eliani Torres for making this book possible, and real. Also, I want to thank Irene Gallo and Dan Dos Santos for such a striking cover, which, oddly, very much resembles my child.

Special thanks go to Bridget and Marti McKenna, editors of *Æon* magazine, who first published "Green" in short story form in *Æon Five*. Without them, *Green* would never have seen the page.

Finally, I would like to acknowledge the nameless ox that watched over my younger brother when he was a very small child many years ago in a faraway land of rice paddies and endless sunlight.

Errors and omissions are entirely my own responsibility.

Green

Memory

THE FIRST thing I can remember in this life is my father driving his white ox, Endurance, to the sky burial platforms. His back was before me as we walked along a dusty road. All things were dusty in the country of my birth, unless they were flooded. A ditch yawned at each side to beckon me toward play. The fields beyond were drained of water and filled with stubble, though I could not now say which of the harvest seasons it was.

Though I would come to change the fate of cities and of gods, then I was merely a small, grubby child in a small, grubby corner of the world. I did not have many words. Even so, I knew that my grandmother was lashed astride the back of Papa's patient beast. She was so very still and silent that day, except for her bells.

Every woman of our village is given a silk at birth, or at least the finest cloth a family can afford. The length of the bolt is said to foretell the length of her life, though I've never known that a money-lender's sister wrapped in twelve yards of silk lived longer than a decently fed farmwife with a short measure hanging on her sewing frame. The first skill a girl-child learns is to sew a small bell to her silk each day so that when she marries, she will dance with the music of four thousand bells. Every day she sews so that when she dies, her soul will be carried out of this life on the music of twenty-five-thousand bells. The poorest use seed pods or shells, but still these stand as a marker of the moments in our lives.

My silk is long lost now, as are my several attempts since to replace it. Be patient: I will explain how this came to be. Before that, I wish to explain how

I came to be. If you do not understand this day, earliest in my memory like the first bird that ever grew feathers and threw itself from the limb of a tree, then you will understand nothing of me and all that has graced and cursed my life in the years since.

The ox Endurance bore a burden of sound that day. His wooden bell clopped in time to his steps. The thousands of bells on my grandmother's silk rang like the first rainfall upon the roof of our hut after the long seasons of the sun. Later in my youth, before I returned to Selistan to see the truth of my beginnings for myself, I would revisit this memory and think that perhaps what I heard was her soul rising up from the scorching stones of this world to embrace the cool shadows of the next.

That day, the bells I heard seemed to be tears shed by the tulpas in celebration of her passage.

In my memory, the land rocked as we proceeded, in a way that meant I did not walk. I had eyes only for Endurance and my grandmother. My father drove the ox, so my mother must have carried me. She was alive then. Of her I can recall only the feel of arms as a pressure across the backs of my legs, and the sense of being held too close to the warmth of her skin as I wriggled away from her to look ahead. I hold no other recollection of my mother, none at all.

Her face is forever hidden from me. I have lost so much in this life by racing ahead without ever pausing to turn back and take stock of courses already run.

Still, my unremembered mother did as a parent should do for a child. She walked with a measured tread that followed the slow beat of Endurance's wooden bell. She held me high enough that I could look into my grandmother's white-painted eyes.

Her I recall well in that moment. Whatever came before in my young life is lost now to my recollection, but my grandmother must have been important to my smallest self. I drank in the sight of her with a loving eagerness that foretold the starveling years to come.

The lines upon her face were a map of the ages of woman. Her skin seemed webbed, as if her glittering eyes were spiders waiting to entrap whatever little kisses and pudgy hands might stray too close. I do not suppose she had any teeth left, for her betel-stained lips were collapsed in a pucker that seems to me in memory to have been as familiar as the taste of water. Her nose was long, not so much in the fashion of most of Selistan's people, and had retained a certain majestic force even in her age. She had no hair left but for some errant wisps, though as most of her scalp was covered by the arch of her belled silk, I suppose this knowledge is itself a memory of a memory.

There must have been a washing, a laying out, a painting of the white and the red. These things I know now from my experience of later years, learned upon the corpses of those I helped prepare for the next life, as well as the corpses of those I have slain with my own hands.

Did my father run his fingers across his mother's cooling body to do these things?

Did my mother perform that ultimate rite for him?

Did my mother and grandmother live well together in the presence of my father, or did they fight like harridans?

So much has been taken from me. What has been given in return seems hollow next to the brilliance of that moment—the sharpness of the colors painted on my grandmother's face; the rich, slow echo of Endurance's bell and the silvery ringing from my grandmother's silk; the faded tassels on the ox's great curving horns; the heat that wrapped me like a bright and stifling blanket; the dusty, rotten smell of that day as my father sang his mother's death song in a toneless, reedy voice that sounded bereft even to my young ears.

That brilliance is reinforced by a skein of later experience, but it also stands alone like the first rock of a reef above the receding tide. I wish that the past were so much more open to me, as it is to the blue-robed men who sit atop the shattered heads of ancient idols in the Dockmarket at Copper Downs. For a few brass taels, they will enter their houses of memory to recount the order and color of festival parades and marching banners in decades long lost to dust.

Distant memory is an art that absorbs its followers, immerses them in the mazes of the mind. I am overtaken by recall of more recent times, of blood and passion and sweaty skin and the most pointed kind of politics. For all that was taken from me in the earliest days of my stolen childhood, those distant memories would still be safe and sane compared with what has passed since, if their return were ever granted to me.

It would bring me the sound of my mother's voice, which I have lost.

It would bring me the look of my father's face, which I have lost.

It would bring me the name they called me, which I have lost.

My image of my grandmother is as bright and powerful as sunrise on the ocean. She stands at the beginning of my life. Her funeral marks the emergence of my consciousness of the world around me.

For all that bright and shining focus on my grandmother, she was gone at the beginning of all things. Whoever she might have been to me in the rhythms of ordinary living is buried deep within the impenetrable fog of my infancy. I like to think she held me during the days when my mother must have worked the fields alongside my father. I like to believe she crooned to me songs about the world.

These things are even less than guesses.

My grandmother's last moments aside, what I hold most in my memory from those first days of my life is Endurance. The ox seemed tall as the sky to me then. He smelled of damp hide and the gentle sweetgrass scent of his dung. He was a hut that followed my father but always cast shade upon me. I would play beneath his shadow, moving as the sun did if he stood for too long, sometimes looking up at the fringe dividing his belly where the fur of each of his sides met and a fold of skin hung downward. The white of his back shaded to gray there, like the line of a storm off the hills, but always spattered with dust and mud.

The ox continually rumbled. Voices within prophesied in some low-toned language of grass and gas and digestion that endlessly fascinated me. Endurance would grunt before he pissed, warning me to scramble away from his great hooves and hunt frogs among the flooded fields until he found a dry place to stand once more. His great brown eyes watched me unblinking as I ran in the rice paddies, climbed the swaying palms and ramified bougainvilleas, hunted snakes in the stinking ditches.

Endurance had the patience of old stone. He always waited for me to return, sometimes snorting and tossing his head if he thought I'd moved too far in my play. The clop of his wooden bell would call me back to him. The ox never lost sight of me unless my father had taken him away for some errand amid the fields or along the village road.

At night I would sit beside the fire in front of our hut and stitch another bell to my silk under the watchful eye of my father. My mother was already gone by then, though I cannot recall the occasion of her death. Endurance's breath whuffled from the dark of his pen. If I stared into the shadows of the doorway, I could see the fire's fetch dance in the depths of his brown eyes. They were beacons to call me back at need from the countries of my dreams.

There came a certain day in my third summer of life that, like most days there, was hot as only Selistan can be. You northerners do not understand how it is that we can live beneath our greater sun. In the burning lands of the south, the daystar is not just light, but also fire. Its heat falls like rain through air that one could slice with a table knife. That warmth was always on me, a hand pressing down upon my head to wrack my hair with sweat and darken my skin.

I played amid a stand of plantains. Their flowers cascaded in a maroon promise of the sweet, sticky goodness to come. The fat stalks were friends sprung from some green jungle race, come to tell me the secrets of the weather. I had made up my mind to be queen of water, for it was water that ruled over everything in our village. Warm mud was caked upon my feet from my sojourns in the ditches planning the coming of my magical queendom.

Endurance's bell echoed across the paddy. The clatter had an urgency that I heard without at first understanding. I looked up to see the ox's ears flattened out. His tail twitched as if he were bedeviled by blackflies. My father stood beside his ox with one hand on the loop of rope that served as a bridle. He was talking to someone dressed as I had never seen before—wrapped entirely in dark cloths with no honest skin exposed to the furnace of our sun except the dead-pale oval of his face. I wore no clothes at all six days out of seven, and my father little more than a rag about his waist. It had never occurred to me that anyone would have so much to hide.

My father called my name. A thousand times I have strained in memory to hear his voice, but it will not come to me. I know it was my name, I know he called it, but the sound and shape of the word are lost to me along with his speaking of it.

Can you imagine what it means to lose your name? Not to set it aside for a profession or temple mystery, but simply to lose it. Many have told me this is not possible, that no one forgets the name she was called at her mother's breast. Soon enough I will explain to you how this came to be, but for now believe that the loss is as great to me as it seems incredible to you.

Papa turned toward me and cupped his hands to call out. I know my name hung in the air. I know I ran toward my father with my hair trailing behind me to be tugged by the sun and wind. It was the end of my life I ran toward, and the beginning.

Laughing I went, covered in the dust and mud of our land, a child of sun-scorched Selistan. My father continued to hold Endurance's lead as the ox tossed his head and snorted with anger.

Close by, I could see the stranger was a man. I had never seen a stranger before, and so I thought that perhaps all strangers were men. He was taller than Papa. His face was pale as the maggots that squirmed in our midden pile. His hair peeking out from behind his swaddling was the color of rotting straw, his eyes the inside of a lime.

The stranger knelt to take my jaw in a strong grip and bend my chin upward. I struggled, and must have said something, for I was never a reticent child. He ignored my outburst in favor of tilting my face back and forth. He then grasped me by the shoulder and turned me around to trace my spine with a rough knuckle.

When I was released, I spun back hot with indignant pride. The maggot man ignored me, talking to my father in low tones with a muddied voice, as if our words did not quite fit his mouth. There was some small argument; then the maggot man slid a silk bag into my father's hand, closing his fingers over the burden.

Papa knelt in turn to kiss my forehead. He placed my hand in the maggot man's grasp, where the silk had so lately slid free. He turned and walked quickly away, leading Endurance. The ox, ever a mild-mannered beast, bucked twice and shook his head, snorting to call me back.

"My bells," I cried as I was tugged away by the maggot man's strong hand. So the belled silk was lost to me, along with everything else to which I had been born.

That is the last of what I remember of that time in my life, before all changed: a white ox, a wooden bell, and my father forever turned away from me.

Leaving Home

THE MAGGOT man and I walked the better part of the day. My small brown
hand was folded tightly within his huge pale one. He had looped a silken cord
around both our wrists, lest I slip his grip and flee. I realized he was not a
maggot, but a corpse. This man had walked into our village from the lands of
the dead.

My heart flooded with joy. My grandmother had sent for me!

It did not take me long to understand how foolish that was. The maggot
man smelled of salt and fat and the crispness of his cloth. The dead smelled—
well, dead. If a person had been made ready for the sky burial, or an animal for
the sacrifice, that was one thing—but anything that died under our sun soon
became a stench incarnate.

He was alive enough. He must have been burning with the heat.

So instead I eyed the cord. It was a color of green that I had never before
seen, bright and shining as the wings of a beetle. Women had their silks, but
even my child's eye could see this was another quality altogether. The threads
of which it was made seemed impossibly small.

The cord did not matter so much anyway. We had walked past the huge
baobab tree that marked the extent of my worldly travels up until that day. The
road we followed was a cart track, but the maggot man and I might as well have
been the last two people alive under the brassy sky.

I know now that my father had a name besides Papa, and my village had a
name besides Home. The world is wider than a woman can walk in a lifetime,
perhaps a hundred lifetimes. Every town and bridge and field and boulder has

a name, is claimed by some god or woman or polity or tradition. That day, I knew only that if I turned and ran far enough, fast enough, I would reach the old baobab and follow the hollow clop of Endurance's bell all the way to my little pallet and my own silk beside my father's fire.

The fields around us had changed even with this short walk. They did not harvest rice here. There was no endless network of watery ditches full of frogs and snakes. Fences stood instead, dividing one patch of stone-filled grass from another identical patch of stone-filled grass. Faded prayer flags hung on fence-posts, almost exhausted by wind and sun. A few narrow-bodied cattle with large sagging humps watched us pass. No light stood in their eyes, nothing like the spark of wisdom that had dwelt in the fluid brown depths of Endurance's gaze.

Even the trees were different. Skinnier, with thin, dusty leaves instead of the broad gloss of the nodding plantains at home. I turned, slipping my wrist around within the loop, to walk backwards and look down the long sloping road up which we had been walking.

A ribbon shone in a broad land below us, silver bright with curves like the sheltering arms of a mother. Fields and orchards and copses surrounded it for a distance of many furlongs, punctuated with the rough nap of buildings and little smudges of forge fires. Was that water? I wondered.

The maggot man slowed his stride to allow me my stumbling backwards progress. "What do you see?" His words were thick and muddled, as if he had only just learned to talk.

A land of rice and fruit and patient oxen, I thought. *Home.* "Nothing," I said, for I already hated him.

"Nothing." He sounded as if the word had never occurred to him before. "That is fair enough. You leave this place today, and will never see it again."

"This is not the way to the sky burials."

Something in his words miscarried, because he gave me a strange look instead of answering. Then he reached for my shoulder and twisted me around from the past to face the future once more. The clasp of his fingers ached awhile.

We walked into the failing of the day, sipping every now and then from his leather bottle of water. The road we followed grew stony and thin. Even the fences gave up, the land unclaimed or unclaimable. Dark, rough rocks were strewn about, some so large the track was forced to bend around them. Everything that grew up here was dusty green or pale brown. Each plant wore a crown of thorns where in my home they would have borne flowers. Insects hummed loudly enough to pierce my hearing before falling stone-silent at the sharp cry of some unseen hunting bird.

The shadows of the few remaining trees grew long about the time their numbers began to strengthen. I stumbled in my fatigue. Recovering my step, I realized we were heading downward for the first time since setting out.

Before us, at the foot of the slope, I could see an iron-gray plain gathering darkness onto itself.

"This is the sea," the maggot man said. "Have you ever heard of it?"

"Is it stone?"

He laughed. For a moment, I thought perhaps I heard the true man within the cloak of black cloth and muddled words. "No. Water. All the water in the world."

That frightened me. A ditch was one thing, but enough water to cover all the land like a rice paddy was another. "Why do we walk there?"

"To see how strong you are."

"No, no. Why do we go to this water?"

"Because the sea is the next step on the journey of your life."

The immensity of it was beyond description. I saw how the far edge of the water faded into the distance. "I cannot swim so far."

The maggot man laughed again. "Come. There is a house farther along our way. We can eat there. I will tell you of . . ." He paused, grasping for a word. "Water houses," he finally said, and looked embarrassed.

Young as I was, I knew perfectly well that no one built their house of water. Either the maggot man was an idiot, which did not seem likely, or his words had failed him again.

"I am hungry," I told him politely.

"Walk," he replied.

We ate stew that evening in a wayhouse. I now realize how small and mean the place must have been, especially by the standards of my captor, but he'd had his purposes. It was much like my father's hut—mud walls set with beams to make the frame of a thatched roof. The room was larger, though, so big that four tables could fit within and there still be room for the cook's fire and her black iron kettle.

I had never seen such a great building.

We sat on a bench at one table. A few other folk were around. All glared at the maggot man. No words were said, but I knew even then that trouble followed him, that he was seen as a curse. He'd slipped free the cord. In memory

I cannot say whether that was more to ease his dining or to make less of a show of his trade.

Our stew was served within shallow bowls of earthenware. I peered at the outside where it angled away from me. A pattern of lizards and flowers chased one another around the curve. The lizards I could understand in this sere, hard place, but the idea of flowers must have come from my home, for no one born here would see them among the thorns and rocks.

The dark brown stock filling the bowls was almost bitter. It had been made with some small polished nut that split neatly in two beneath my spoon. Instead of homey rice, grains floated in the broth. A few leaves swirled loose, along with chunks of pale meat that tasted like ditch frog.

"Fish." The maggot man smiled. The effect was ghastly on his pale face. "It is always good to fill your belly after a day."

"Fish," I said politely. I wished I had a plantain.

When he was nearly done, he pushed his bowl between us. A dark green mallow leaf floated in the brown puddle at the bottom. "I have asked the word of the house woman," he told me, almost proudly. "Boat. See this mallow leaf? It is like a boat."

"There is mallow growing in your sea?"

The maggot man sighed. "I am trying to tell you why you will not have to swim."

"I never swam because of mallow." I poked his leaf. "Taro tastes better anyway."

"Wood floats," he said.

"So do I."

"We will travel on a boat of wood, which floats like this mallow leaf in your stew."

"I thought you said the sea is made of water."

He threw up his hands and muttered at the rough ceiling of the wayhouse. He then looked at me with a frown. "You will be fearsome once you speak Petraean."

I'd never realized there were more kinds of words in the world. "Will my father speak Petraean, too?"

A shadow clouded his eyes. "No," he said in a clipped voice. "We must go. It is another few hours' walk to the port."

I followed the maggot man into the deepening gloom of night. My feet began to get in each other's way. Keeping my pace was especially difficult when the road made a sharp bend or wound through a steep drop along some gully.

The maggot man walked on. His stink had blown off with the evening breeze. Instead my nose was tickled by the scent of salt, and a rot I'd never smelled before.

I was ready to go home. The next time I stumbled, I let myself fall to the ground. The green cord slipped from his wrist. I bounced up off the road and sprinted away.

The maggot man was faster than I might have credited. He was upon me in a dozen steps, grabbing me up into his arms while I kicked and screamed, then working one hand free to slap me very hard across the mouth.

"Do not break from me." His voice now was stone, hard and unforgiving. "Your path is set. The only way forward is at my side. There is no way back."

"I am going home," I shrieked at him through the taste of blood in my mouth.

"You are going on." A rueful smile slipped across his face. "You have . . ." He reached for a word a moment, then gave up, instead saying, "Fight. You are strong in body and spirit. Most girls would have run at the first, or fallen crying later in the day."

"I don't want fight. I want to go home."

He still held me in a very tight grip. Together we turned, looking back up the road. "How far do you think you could find your way across that wide country of rocks and thorns? If I had not carried water, what would you have drunk?"

I would lick the sweat from my hands, I thought, but the sting of his blow was a sharp, hard lesson that warded my lips. "I will go to your sea," I told him grudgingly. "But then I am going back home."

"You will come to my sea," he agreed. He said no more than that.

Quite late in the evening we found an inn. I had finally collapsed of sheer fatigue. I made the last part of this journey slumped across the maggot man's shoulder. The moon gave the night land a sheen like silvered tears. I wondered if it would polish me bitter bright as well.

He had a little room already taken, I realized much later. At the time, we walked through a huge kitchen and up what I later understood to be a flight of stairs to a high room with nets draping from above. A hutch stood within, a thing of bars and boards. Alongside it was a bed and a rough table, all beneath a sloping roof with an inset window tightly shuttered.

Before I knew what he was about, the maggot man dumped me into the hutch and slid the latches across the door.

"You stay there," he said. "No running. I must do things, then sleep."

I howled, screamed, hurled myself against the bars, raged at the top of my lungs. The world did not hear. The maggot man sat at his table with a carefully trimmed candle and for a long time poked a narrow stick into a little packet of papers sewn together within leather sheets. Every now and then he smiled at me, somewhere between indulgence and mirth.

My bell for the day was unsewn. I did not have my silk or my needle. I knew then that I was little more than an animal to him. Caged, kept, to be taken over the mallow-filled waters of the gray sea to whatever dead land the maggot called his home.

I cried until sleep claimed me, though his candle flickered and his stick scratched and scratched against the paper. In my dreams that scratching became the claws of a mangy wolf, pale as death, jaws set to drag me away through a frog-filled ditch the width of the world.

I was awoken by words I did not understand. The maggot man had opened the door of my cage and held a plate with fried dough twists and slices of yellow fruit I did not recognize. He spoke again.

"You utter the tongue of demons," I told him.

"Very soon I will speak to you only in the language of your new home," he said in my words, "except at extreme need." He shook his plate at me, then repeated whatever he had said before.

I did not want to come out within reach of his hard slap, but my stomach had other ideas. The dough smelled good, and the fruit looked sweet enough. I followed the growling of my hunger from the cage.

"Eat," he told me. "Then we will go find our boat."

The dough tasted every bit as delicious as it had smelled. Likewise the fruit—sweet and fleshy and sour all in a single mouthful. This was as fine a morning meal as my father had ever made for me.

When I had finished my food, I looked to see that the maggot man had gathered up a fat leather satchel. He held out his hand with the green twist of silk already around his wrist.

I could have fought harder. Perhaps I should have. I do not know what good it might ever have done. I am still fighting even now, so perhaps I only began the resistance slowly and never stopped. That day my curiosity overtook my anger as I willingly bound my hand to his. Decent food and a weariness of struggle were all it had taken to break my young spirit to the maggot man's desire.

"Come," he said, "let us see to our boat."

"I do not have to swim?"

"No, you do not have to swim. We shall sit easily as we pass across the sea." He added something in his words, which I of course could not then understand.

We set out into the bright morning along a muddy street in a village larger than I had imagined could exist. We passed amid a cacophony of men and horses and dogs and ox-carts as we headed for the water's edge. I even heard the clop of ox bells, but none were the tone of Endurance's. No one remained to call me back, while this strange, pale man continued to push me forward on the path he had chosen for me.

I followed him into the future.

My memory is a curious thing. Though I was quite young, I clearly recall these early conversations. They were of necessity in the tongue of my birth, for I spoke no Petraean yet. I even recollect Federo—and how young he was then—looking for words he did not know, such as *boat*. I did not know what a boat was either, not in those first days. My memory supplies the substance of the conversation rather than the specifics, so as I think back to that time, it seems to come back to me in the language of my enslavement rather than the language of my cradle.

Likewise with the memory of my first ship. I know from recalling those days that she was named *Fortune's Flight,* for those are among the first words of Petraean that I learned. Years since, I have looked in the ship books at Copper Downs, and so I know that *Fortune's Flight* was an iron-hulled steam barquentine. She was built on the shores of the Sunward Sea, where the princes of the deep water have foundries to make such things. This knowledge fuses into my memory so I can recall the arrangement of her masts and sails and smokestack as she rode at anchor offshore, even though at the time they must have seemed to me nothing more than strange trees, while the mysteries of steam would have passed beyond any understanding I could have summoned.

Fortune's Flight rises white-hulled and gleaming on the waves of recall. A cloud of gulls circles her fantail, crying their soulless lament. Swabbies move about her deck, and whistles blare orders in those codes that all sailors know. She is lean and beautiful, her narrow stack streaming pale smoke. She is a house upon the water, a hunter's courser set to carry his prey back to the manor hall to be dressed and hung.

I must have then seen her as a white building with a treed roof, for I cannot imagine another view to my youngest eyes. Now that I know her power and her purpose, I cannot look back on the ship of my captivity with less awareness than I possess today.

How we were transported from my first view at the water's edge to her decks is clouded by forgetfulness. There must have been a boat. Whether it was a local man earning a tael for his ferry work or one of the ship's company come to fetch her passengers, I cannot say.

She was crowded with drums and bales and capstans—all the furniture of navigation and its intents. We looked back at the shore from the rail. Much water stretched between us and land, a river wider than all the ditches in all my father's fields laid together. I tried to imagine how many rice paddies could be flooded from this sea that was kept so far from my home.

The look of the water desert was alien, strange as if the sky had been bound directly to earth. Shore was more familiar. The houses and barns seemed so small. They were built with mud walls, just like Papa's hut, except here in this place people washed their buildings over with pale colors. Some bore painted designs, flowers and wheels of lightning and lizards and things I did not have names for. The land rose behind the town, bearing with it the single road we had walked down the night before.

"You brought me far to test my strength," I said.

"Hmm." The maggot man did not lend any words to his answer.

I had walked that distance. I could walk the same distance back. I stared at the land so brown and gray above the ragged colors of the town at the edge of the sea. After a short time, he tugged gently on my shoulder. I turned to the chaos of the ship. The maggot man and I headed for a little house amid the jumble of men and equipment and cargo.

"Here," he said as we pushed within. "Here we stay." This was followed by another burst of his Petraean gabble.

My first thought was that the floors were wood, not dirt. The place was handsome enough, lit by a round window filled with glass. There were two beds, each larger than any I had seen in my life until then. A table with a chair before it clipped to the floor. A black mounting gaped in the ceiling, from which a chain depended, holding a small oil lamp with a hooded glass.

No cage waited in the middle of the room.

I had never seen such a wealth of space and privacy. Not to be shared, surely as our room the night before was, but dedicated to one man and his needs. One man and his girl.

The iron rail at the base of the bed was firm and cold to my touch. The paint was textured with generations of repetition, layers over layers of flecking and pitting. "What do we do here?"

He answered in Petraean.

I whirled on him, my voice rising as my dignity slipped away from me. "What do we do here?"

The maggot man smiled, his mouth tight and sad. He answered once more in Petraean. He then added in my words, "We journey across the Storm Sea to Copper Downs."

I seized on petulance, the last refuge of children. "Don't want to go to Copper Downs. Want to go home."

His smile shrank to nothing. "Copper Downs is your home now."

This I considered. We had not brought my silk with my thousand bells. "Papa will be there? And Endurance?"

"Your *new* home." This was followed with another burst of his alien words.

Lies. All was lies. He had lied to Papa; he lied to me. Endurance had tried to warn me, but I'd followed my father's words in coming with this man.

Had Papa lied to me as well?

I resolved I would go home and ask him. It only waited for my moment. I gathered myself on one of the beds and watched the maggot man carefully.

Soon enough he tired of watching me in return, and set to his little table. He brought papers from a box and made more of his scratches. Once in a while he glanced at me, but his heart was in his reckoning, not in being my guardian.

The floor groaned and swayed like a tree in a storm, though the window's light was bright with a clear sky. The yip-yip of the sailors seemed unexcited. The boat shifted, I realized, like Endurance settling in for the night. Below the floor, something huge chuffed and squirmed. Perhaps they had a giant ox to tow them through the sea?

It did not matter to me. I was leaving soon. Though I could no more stop my mind wondering than I could stop my lungs breathing, I did not care.

This game was over.

I waited until the time between each of my captor's glances at me was more breaths than I could count. It was easy enough to occupy myself studying the latch on the door to this little house. A great shiny lever was placed below a handle which was obviously meant to be grabbed. When we entered, the maggot man had used it to close the door.

Though I had seen few doors in my life, animal pens had gates. This was no different. I had been wrong about the lack of a cage, I realized. This cage was bigger, the bars less visible.

At his next glance and return of attention to his papers, I was ready. I leapt from the bed, grabbed the handle, and threw open the door. Head tucked down, I sprinted past the knees and thighs of the sailors toward the rail. I was faster than any of them suspected. The floor of the boat was just as crowded as before, with more ropes coiled as great cloth sheets were raised snapping into the wind.

Men shouted, but it was less than a dozen steps to the edge. No one had been waiting for me. No one had been watching for me.

How far could we be from the shore?

But when I vaulted the fence and dove for the sea, I saw there was no land nearby. Water was water. I could swim here as well as in a ditch at home. Unfortunately, this ditch had grown to the width of the world, too far to reach the other side.

Then I was in the sea. The water was colder than I had thought, and stung my mouth terribly. This was the taste of the sweat of the earth. Everything beneath was dark and gray. I could see nothing.

I found the surface easily enough and began to swim away from the boat.

Behind me they shouted. I rolled to my back and looked as I continued to swim. Angry men lined the side rail, pointing and yelling. I smiled at their discomfort even as one raised a great spear.

With a flash, a silver arrow sped toward me. I started to scream as it passed above my head. I turned again, almost slipping beneath the water.

For a long moment I could see the end of everything. I don't imagine death meant anything sensible to me at that age, but I knew people did die, and once dead they did not return.

A triple arch of jagged teeth yawned above my head. This monstrous thing was the very mouth of hunger loosed in the sea. I could see the pale curves of its maw behind its teeth, narrowing to a dark throat that could take me down whole. A chilled stench of blood and filth shivered my spine.

That dart flew into those pale geometries and embedded itself in the roof of the monster's mouth. A blue spark exploded in that darkness bright enough to sting my eyes. I heard a shriek like a woman in pain.

With an enormous splash, the mouth closed. It sank beneath the water, dragging with it a rough, gray head larger than Endurance. For a long, slow moment, somewhere between one of my heartbeats and the next, a black eye stared at me. It was ringed with flesh as pale as the maggot man's skin, and had the filmy hue of the dead. Though this glaring orb lacked the wisdom of Endurance's brown eyes, or even the simple flickering life present in the eye of the smallest birds, still I felt the sea-beast place my name among the secret hatreds graven into its frozen heart.

I kicked in place a moment, my heart chilled as cold as the surrounding water. The monster had nearly taken me. Worse, there was no land to reach, no matter how far I swam. The boat creaked and groaned behind me, men calling out as it turned to fetch me from the waves.

Water at home had held only snakes, frogs, and turtles with knife-sharp beaks. The sea held every kind of throat ready to swallow me whole. When they threw the ropes down to me, I grasped readily enough at the rescue.

The tears I cried for my home were mixed in with salt spray when they hauled me aboard. Once more I went willingly into the house of my captivity. If I did so a third time, I knew I would be lost to myself forever.

Federo handed me back the slate. "Write the letters once more, girl," he said. In Petraean.

Despite my resolve, his language was sinking into me like dye in cloth. Many of the deckhands spoke it, as did all the officers. Federo used the tongue almost exclusively with me. He gave me no name at all except "girl" which would serve to call half the world.

"I have written them a hundred times," I said. "Snake," I muttered in my own tongue.

He slapped me hard across the top of the head. The blow stung, but little more. I did not cry out. I never cried out, not where Federo or any of the sailors could hear me, which was everywhere on this ship.

"Then you will write them a hundred more." He leaned close. "Without letters, you are nothing in the world where you will be moving. People's lives and deaths are written in polite notes that must be passed among the powerful like dance cards."

These words. I had no writing to master at home with my father. I had never even heard of letters. You talked, people listened, or they did not.

Letters were a way of talking so anyone could hear you at any time. Like standing on the corner repeating yourself forever, but without the endless effort. Their shapes were strange, though, bearing no resemblance to their sounds—bent trees and stumbling drunkards and the wanderings of chickens. "Whoever made up such a thing?"

He slapped me again. "In my language."

I clenched my fist around the chalk and tried again with his words. "Who made these things up?"

"I do not know a name, girl. I do not know. Much like fire, the gods gave letters to men." His smile was crooked. "Some might say they were the same gift."

We had no gods back home, not really. Just dead people who watched over us, and the tulpas who moved among the dust and clouds and hid their faces in the ripples of the water.

If I had a god, that was Endurance. But he was as real as me, while gods were more of an idea. Like letters, really.

"What if the gods are in the letters?"

Federo opened his mouth, closed it, then opened it again without speaking. He sat heavily on his bunk. "Your mind is a jewel, child." He sighed. "Hoard it well. Others will be jealous of the way your thoughts sparkle. Mark me"— he waggled his finger—"play the dullard a bit and you will live a happier life."

I refused to be distracted. "And what are gods?"

"Gods are . . ." He paused again, gathering his thoughts. I already knew that Federo chose his words for me with care. I resolved to learn what lay in the dark spaces between the light of speech. "Gods are real. More real in some places than others. In Copper Downs we . . . Ours were put aside for us a very long time ago."

"They are dead?"

"No. But neither do they live."

"Like a tree," I said. "Cut to make this ship. It moves as if it were alive. It is not dead on the ground."

He laughed. "Except that we do not use our gods for much in Copper Downs. The Duke has found better ways to occupy the spirits of his people." Leaning forward, he tried his best glare. "Now, you owe me some letters, young lady."

I could not escape. There was nowhere to go but the ship itself. At the same time, it was clear to me that rebellious silence would serve nothing except to make a point my captor already understood quite well. He looked less like a maggot to me as the days went by, and more like a man. He spoke; I listened. I asked; he answered.

His words sank further and further into me every day. Now that I had some decent Petraean, Federo refused to acknowledge me if I spoke in my own tongue. His was a language of ideas, thoughts bigger than a barnyard or a rice paddy or a frog-filled ditch. I felt guilty at finding any pleasure in my captivity.

Just as true was the fact that I now ate better than I ever had before. I slept on sheets, a thing unheard of at home. Simple dresses covered me from shoulder to knees, the first time in my life I had not mostly been clad in sunlight. I had *soap*. Whatever god had given these maggot people that boon had indeed granted a blessing. I had never imagined what it was like to be utterly clean. At home, we were washed so thoroughly only at birth and at death. The rest of life was for living amid the dust of the world.

When he was not at his figuring and scribbling, or mastering me at lessons, Federo would read to me. He skipped past the little box of simple books for children, instead picking from his personal collection of texts on trade, geography, the engineering of steam power, the working of metals. Most of it meant little to me, but there was always a harvest of new words, and questions piled on questions, which he would answer as best he could.

Maps were my favorite. At first, making my mind understand that a picture on a sheet of vellum could be one and the same as the land and sea around me was like forcing myself through a small box. Once understanding dawned, I saw how I could travel without ever getting up from my seat on the bed.

Federo showed me distant places—the channel connecting our Storm Sea to the Sunward Sea, which ran below the ironbound overwatch of the Saffron Tower, far to the east; the Rimerock Range and its endless northern majesty; the extents of empires so long vanished that their cities were remembered only as rock quarries. The entire plate of the world could be scribed rock by stream on papers. We looked at everything he had to show me, except my homes old and new.

"Why will you not show me Copper Downs?"

Federo set his lips. "I am forbidden."

"By who?"

"By *whom*."

"By whom?" I muttered in my own tongue: "Stupid words," then continued. "Why can I not see the pictures of my home?"

"You are to be unspoiled."

"You have said you take me to Copper Downs, but you have never said why." My chest shuddered at a memory of Endurance's placid gaze. There would be no bells for me in Copper Downs, neither my silk nor the ox's.

"You are to be raised up as a great lady. Every moment will be a lesson. Hush now, and let me show you what I can."

A few days into the voyage, as Federo and I settled in to our routine of living, I begged a length of cloth from the sailmaker. He gave me a stretch of poplin torn from a wrap for sails, and two old needles nearly blunted. These I hid beneath my bunk while I considered the problem of bells. I picked threads out of my sheets, and sewed a knot for each day of my captivity, vowing to add the bells when I could, and to make up once more the thousand bells sewn at the start of my life by my mother, then my grandmother, then me.

Pleasant as he might pretend to be, I would not allow Federo to steal this from me.

Once the bosun conceded that I wasn't likely to jump the rail again, I was permitted to be on the open deck. There were at least a few hours each day where I was doing little enough, so I wandered about *Fortune's Flight* in small stages to watch the crew at their business and look for something that might serve me for the tiny bells I required.

The sailors mostly found me amusing. Some growled, others gave me long, cold looks, but many merely smiled and showed me their work. We had an easy voyage, unusually free of storms, as I later came to know. The great steam kettle at the heart of the ship did most of the work of our passage. The master set the sails to gain the extra push the winds might lend her progress.

I watched ducks being herded from their pens to the fantail to take the morning air. I watched the ropemaker splicing and braiding his hemp. I watched the deck idlers shift cargo as the quartermasters sought better trim, or just for the practice. I watched the gun crews work their pieces, though they never actually fired. In time I wondered if the guns functioned or were just for show. I watched men fish off the stern and cast harpoons from the waist of the ship. I watched the carpenter rebuild braces. I watched the smith hammer out hinges.

From him I found something to serve as a bell. Clearly I did not want any actual ringing in my cloth, for Federo would know in a moment I had some small treason afoot. But the smith had nails and scraps, and a dozen kinds of iron slivers and shims.

"I am playing at soldiers," I told him the third day he'd tolerated my presence at his forge.

He was a huge man, in the manner of smiths everywhere. His hair was pale, though always slicked dark with sweat, and his eyes the cutting blue of a gemstone. "Aye, and is yer winning, missy?"

"No one wins at war," I told him primly. "Some lose less than others, if they are lucky."

The smith chuckled. "And I am seeing why the dandy man has taken such a liking to yer."

Dandy was a new word to me. I set it aside for later consideration. I understood even then that I should not ask Federo why the smith had called him so.

"He is good to me," I lied. "But he will not play at soldiers."

Another chuckle, then a storm of metal noise as the smith hammered at an iron collar meant for some cross-tree high above us.

"Can you give me a few soldiers, sir?" I finally asked. I looked him in the eye as I spoke—that directness seemed to work best with these pale men from across the sea.

He paused his work, wiping sweat from his brow with his right wrist while still holding the hammer in that hand. "I do not have the casting of lead for toy men, missy. T'ain't no one on board for that, 'less one of the gentlemen of the stern plays with little men in his bunk at night." The smith snorted with laughter. At the time, I did not take any of his meanings.

"Just shavings or scraps or nails, sir," I said quickly. "That I might march them in martial array." That was a phrase from Federo's reading the evening before, an epic poem concerning a battle that seemed to consist largely of a competition of colorful uniforms.

"A bag of sharp, pointed oddments the missy wants." He gave me a long stare, a spark of inner shrewdness rising from the well of his usual bluff density. "Well, yer not loading a cannon, nor running from foot nor horse."

"No, sir," I said quietly.

He leaned close, hammer still clutched in his hand. "Don't call me sir, missy. Iron you wants, iron you shall have."

Later I stole some pliers from the carpenter's mate, to bend the nails and scraps with. So it was that I began to affix bits of metal to my poplin, to stand in for the bells and silk of my home. I would sew quickly when I knew Federo to be at the captain's table, or late at night when his breath was slow and even. I pretended the clanging bells that marked the hours of the watches were Endurance watching over me, that the rumbling of the steam belowdecks was the bellows of the ox's great lungs.

So I marked the days of my passage across the calm sun-drenched waters of the Storm Sea in learning everything that my captor could put before me. My nights I observed by pricking my fingers in remembrance of a home that already seemed infinitely dim and distant in my recall.

———

We packed away our belongings as *Fortune's Flight* made her approach to the Stone Coast. Which was to say Federo packed away his belongings with some small assistance from me. I had nothing except the cotton shifts he had given me to wear, and my length of poplin folded away beneath my bunk with my stolen supplies.

The problem of how to get that ashore loomed large. The only answer I could imagine was to fold it into Federo's baggage somehow and hope to sneak it away from him later. He was keeping a close eye on me that day. I suppose he was afraid I'd dive over the rail again. I knew better—how would I walk home from Copper Downs?—but he had no sure way to trust.

I finally tried slipping the cloth beneath my shift as he was distracted, but my waist bulged in such a strange manner that it was impossible to keep it hidden. I dropped my burden beneath the bunk as he turned. The clatter caught at his ear.

"What have you there?" he asked me in that slow, gentle voice that meant he knew I was about something he would not approve of.

"Just trinkets." *That lie which stands closest to the truth stands tall as well,* one of his books had told me. "I have wrapped some little metal soldiers in cloth, for my playthings."

A strange expression flickered across his face. "I have never yet seen you at play, girl."

"It is only when you are away," I said modestly.

He bent to look beneath my bunk. I itched to kick him in the neck, or at the fork of his legs, but did not. To what purpose? I could not escape on my own. Not unless I could swim the ocean.

"Let me see." He tugged the wrapped bolt of cloth out. It fell open, spilling pliers and needles and thread and iron bits upon the deck. Federo gave the fabric a shake. Nothing jingled, for there were no proper bells at all, but the sewn-on bits of metal clicked. "Ah."

I withstood his long, slow look.

"I should beat you purple for this," he finally said. "And make you eat some of these filings. But you are no silly thing to be cowed by force or fear." He bundled it up again, and my tools within. "Listen to me, girl. Mark me well. Forget the bells of your silk. Where you are going next, any effort to reclaim the land and standing of your birth will be almost the worst offense you could hope to commit. Your journey is forward, not back."

Stubborn resistance rose within me like flowers under a spring rain. "My feet have not chosen this path."

"No." His voice was sad. "But still it is your path. You cannot unchoose what has been done. You can fight the journey, gather bruises and scars until you fail and are cast aside as too broken to complete. Or you can run ahead, beat the racers at their own game, and claim your prizes."

"What prizes?" I hissed.

"Life, health, safety." He grabbed my chin, not too hard, and tried to send me some secret message with the narrowing of his eyes. "The right to make your own choices once more."

Releasing me, Federo tucked the roll under one arm. "We have never spoken of this. I will not recall our conversation again. Best you do not either. Set it aside, along with the entire matter of the bells."

He stalked out of our hatch, across the busy deck, and without a glance back at me idling in the doorway, he threw my poor attempt at reclamation into the bay.

I knew I had been told too much, but I did not then know too much of *what*. Adults almost always speak above or beneath children. It is an error I remain mindful of even now. That day all I saw was another betrayal in a line of betrayals.

I will not willingly take his binding a third time, I promised myself.

"Come," he called from the rail. "See the city that is your new home."

Slowly I dragged my feet across the deck.

My bells were lost to me, but *Fortune's Flight* had her own. They rang brazen-bold as she moved into harbor, along with scores of streaming pennants like prayer flags. Bells floating on little platforms in the harbor answered in time to the swell of the waters. More bells ashore and aship responded in their own manner.

Copper Downs mocked me, displaying endless ringing rounds in a reminder of what had been stripped from me. I resolved anew to hate the god-raddled city and her pale, dead-skinned people.

This place was greater than a thousand of my villages. There were more people before me than I had thought to exist in the entire world. Buildings stood far taller than even the burial platforms of my home—those pillars are the highest things we make, in order to carry souls closer to the freedom of the sky. The city spread along the shore at least an hour's walk east and west of the jetties toward which the harbor pilot even now steered *Fortune's Flight*. An old wall rose ragged amid neighborhoods along a hill just to the west. East of the docks, I could see great rooftops clad in the shining metal that had given the place its name.

Despite my anger, the city fascinated me.

"The Temple District," Federo said as he followed my gaze. "Houses abandoned by the gods, though their doorsteps are yet swept by priests."

"Those are warehouses by the shore." I pointed to the huge buildings by the docks. "Where the wharfingers and freight brokers ply their trades."

"Indeed." I could hear a smile in his voice. I had learned so much already on the voyage.

With much shouting and the whistling of pipes, *Fortune's Flight* was brought to a pier in the middle of the bustling dockside madness. I had thought her a great vessel when I'd seen her anchored off the shores of my home country, but here, she was just another ship. Few had her steam-kettle guts, though I didn't know enough at the time to see it, for all the vessels sprouted the trees of masts with their webbing of lines.

Idlers and brokers and customs agents waited in a throng along the dock as the thick mooring lines were thrown down and the ship warped into place for her cargo to be taken off. Even this one crowd was more people than I'd ever seen. Compared with the masonry and copper immensity of the city, their numbers were far more personal as they stood shoulder to shoulder, shouting and waving colored ribbons or slips of paper. *Each must signify something*, I thought. A job or an offer of service.

Easier to focus on what they did than on who they were. I found scorn for my younger self who had asked Federo whether Papa and Endurance might be waiting here. The ox would be dinner for fourscore men, and Papa lost in the crowd as surely as a weed among the rice shoots.

Guilt flooded me at that dismissal. I know now that Federo had continued to take from me without my consent or even awareness, remaking me in the process of the voyage. His plan was steady, sure, and certain. All that I knew then was that he had caused me to wrong myself in some manner I could not define.

Federo grasped me tightly, more for safety than fear of flight, as the deck began to pour onto the dock and vice versa. The din was immense. Ship's officers wielded stick and blade to keep order, or *Fortune's Flight* would have been overrun. Still, it all had the flavor more of playacting than a brawl, as if the docksiders were expected to push and the ship's company were expected to resist. A dance in five hundred parts, for men and cranes and plunging mules.

Federo leaned close and yelled something in my ear that I could not make out over the racket. I nodded as if I understood. The grip on my shoulder relaxed a trifle.

Soon enough the chaos sorted itself into a systematic ebb and flow. All the shouters had an intended audience. Everyone on deck knew who they were looking for. Gear was broken down and packed off quickly, hatches to the cargo holds thrown open, sailors told off for liberty with pay in their hands all in one swirling rush. Federo soon spotted his contact deep within the churn.

"Come!" he shouted.

Sailors carrying Federo's gear surrounded us. With the aid of their muscles and fists, we pushed through the mob to a high-sided cart that waited on the cobbles at the head of the docks. Its surfaces were a deep, glossy red traced with gold striping and a small black design upon the door. The huge wheels were finished to match the body, with iron straps around their rims. A pair of large black animals, mad-eyed with trailing tails and flowing hair along their graceful necks, stamped in their traces under the watchful gaze of a man on a high bench at the front.

Federo opened the door and pushed me inside. He then slammed it shut to shout orders concerning the stowage of his gear. Several small windows admitted light, but the carriage was so tall, all I saw were rooftops, sky, and circling birds. I sat on a leather bench which was the softest thing I'd ever encountered in my life. Useless little buttons were set deep in the seat in a mockery of how I'd sewn my twice-lost bells. I picked at them and smelled the oils someone had used to polish the interior—lemon, and the pressings of some vegetable I didn't know—until Federo returned.

He climbed in and took my hand with a firm squeeze. "We are almost there, girl."

"I have a name," I said sullenly. I must have still known it then.

His voice grew hard. "No, you do not. Not in this place. It is gone with your bells. Forward, always forward."

As if responding to his words, the carriage lurched into motion. I could hear the coachman's whip crack, the whistles and *hup-hup-hups* as he signaled his team, the curses as he shouted at the traffic. Soft as the seat was, the ride ran rougher than *Fortune's Flight* even on stiff swells. Though Federo had told me of cobbles, I had never seen a stone road before that hour. The ride was miserable.

I stared at the passing rooftops and wondered if I should have thrown myself into the harbor after all.

We bounced past bright painted columns and burnished roofs and, once, a tree of copper and brass that overhung the road. I knew that if I climbed on my knees to stare outside, a parade of marvels would pass before my eyes. Later, I would wish very much that I had done so. In that moment, I merely wanted to go home.

The carriage passed through a large gate, then a smaller one, before finally creaking to a halt. Looking up through the windows, I could see walls all around us. The bulk of a large building loomed on one side, anchoring them. Walls and structure alike were made of a pale blue stone of a sort I had never seen. My entire village could have fit within this place.

Federo banged on the door. Someone opened it from the outside.

Our carriage could not be exited from inside, I realized. Caged again.

He stepped out and ushered me down. I saw the coachman climbing cautiously back onto his box. His eyes were now covered with a length of silk. That had not been true down at the docks.

This was a great puzzle.

Opposite the tall building was a low, wide structure of two storeys. The upper balcony provided deep shade for the lower floor. Its posts were carved with detailed scenes now overgrown with flowering vines. The second storey was roofed by more of the bright copper, backing up to the rise of the bluestone wall. A pomegranate tree grew out of a little circle of raised stone in the middle of the cobbled court. Somehow that lone, lonely tree reminded me of home.

Federo crouched to meet my eye level. "From here, you are among women. You have left the world to be in this place. I am the only man you will speak with, expect for the Factor himself, whenever he comes to see you. Use your head, little one."

"I have a name," I whispered once more in my words, thinking of Endurance's bell.

He ruffled my hair. "Not until the Factor gives you one."

My maggot man stepped back into the carriage and slammed the door behind him. The coachman cocked his head if listening, then drove his team very slowly around the pomegranate and through a narrow gate that shut behind him, pushed by unseen hands. The doors were some age-blackened wood, bound with iron and copper. They seemed as stout and unforgiving as the surrounding walls.

Though I saw no one, I heard throaty laughter.

"I am here," I called out in my own words. Then I said it again in Federo's words.

After a while, a woman not very much taller than I, but fat as any house duck, with protruding lips curved to match, waddled out from the shadowed porch. She was swathed in coarse black cloth that covered even her head. "So you're the new one." She used Federo's words, of course. "I'll have no more of that . . ."

The rest I did not understand. When I tried to ask what she meant, she slapped me hard upon the ear. I knew then that she intended me never to speak my own words. Just as Federo had warned me.

I resolved to learn her words so well that eventually this duck woman could never order me about again. *I will clothe myself in bells,* I thought proudly, *and leave this place with my life in my own hands.*

"I am Mistress Tirelle." She didn't look any less like a duck up close. Her lips stuck forward, and her two small eyes were so far apart, they threatened to sidle outward to her temples. She wore her black dowd like a badge of honor. I was never to see her clad in colors of any sort. Her thin hair was pulled back hard and thickened with some fiber, then painted black as a bosun's boot.

She was a woman pretending to be a shadow pretending to be a woman.

Mistress Tirelle walked around me, stepping back and forth as she inspected. When I turned my gaze to watch, she grasped my chin hard and pulled it straight forward. "You never move without purpose, girl."

I already knew there was no point in having that argument with this aging troll of a woman.

She leaned in close behind me. "You do not have purpose, girl, except what the Factor lends you. Or I in his place." Her breath reeked of the northern herbs that had found their way into the stockpot aboard *Fortune's Flight*— astringent without any decent heat to them, and strangely crisp, the smell gone half-sour from its journey through her mouth.

The woman continued to circle me. I remember this, like so much else in those days, through the lens of later understanding. In that first season, I was little taller than her waist, though by the time the end came between us, I could see the part in her hair without craning my neck. Somehow in memory I am both sizes at once: the small frightened girl whom Federo had spirited away from the fields of her home, and the angry gawk who fled those bluestone walls with cooling scrapings of a dead woman's skin beneath her fingernails.

She was to be my first killing, at a time when I should already have known far better. I would have slain her that initial day, out of simple spiteful anger. It was the work of years to lacquer the nuances of a worthy, well-earned hatred over the fearful rage of the child I was.

Memory or no, I did not have any cutting answers for her. Federo had been too frank with me to awaken any sense of how words duel, and I suppose I was too young for a bladed tongue then. I stood while she circled me again and again. Her breath heaved like the steam kettle deep within the decks of *Fortune's Flight*. Sweat sheened on her brow like rain on a millstone.

We had not moved from the spot in the courtyard where Federo had deposited me. No one was about—the possibility of hidden watchers would not occur to me for quite some time, and in the event proved false within the Factor's cold, towering walls. I only had eyes for the withering pomegranate tree, occluded from moment to moment as she passed round me.

I startled when Mistress Tirelle slipped a gleaming blade from some recess in her wrappings. She was ready for that, and slapped me again. "Soon I shall not be able to leave marks on you, girl, but for today discipline is my own. Even later there will be ways. You. Do. *Not. Move.*"

The duck woman stopped behind me. I shivered, wondering what she intended with that blade. Surely Federo had not brought me over an ocean just to be cut open like a sacrificial goat. The left shoulder of my shift fell away with a snick. Another snick, and the right was gone, the simple dress with it.

That was my first encounter with scissors, and they startled me. Being bareskinned in this place with such a shy sun and chilly air was strange to me as well. Much as Federo had done, Mistress Tirelle began to prod my back, my shoulders, my hips. As she pushed and poked at me, she issued terse commands.

"Hold your right arm out straight, and do not drop it again.

"Let me see your teeth. All of them, girl.

"Bend. Now touch the courtyard. With your palms laid flat."

The examination was not painful, but it was thorough. Finally she was in front of me again. "I don't suppose that young fop bothered to read your bowels."

"He di—," I began, but was stopped with another slap.

"When I want you to answer me, I will address you as Girl, girl."

Even then I could hear the word becoming a name. My own words spilled out of me. "I have a—"

This time the blow caused my ears to ring. "You will take ten minutes of standing with warm ashes in your mouth every time I hear a single word of that filthy dog's tongue out of you, Girl."

I nodded, tears pooling hard and bitter in my eyes.

Words, it all came down to words. Federo had bent my father's will with words long before that little sack had passed between them to buy me away. These northern people were continuing to remake me with words.

Someday I would own their words.

Mistress Tirelle dragged me to the shaded porch and bade me stand by a post. A moment later she was back with a ladle filled with ashes. I choked spooning them into my mouth, but I resolved not to give her reason to beat me further. She seemed to take much joy in raising her hand against me. In this I would not please her.

So I stood weeping, my chest spasming with coughs I was desperate to swallow. I kept my eyes tight set against her, and my heart closed.

After a time, the duck woman put an empty bucket before me. "Spit," she said. "And do not trail your peasant slime upon my floor." Once that was done, to much gagging and heaving, she gave me a little mug of tepid water to wash my mouth out.

I wondered if *she* had ever been schooled to hold ashes in her mouth and take beatings at the slightest word.

"I believe we understand each other now," Mistress Tirelle announced. "This is the Pomegranate Court, in the House of the Factor." Those names were just strange words to me at the time, though I came to understand them soon enough. "You are the sole candidate in residence within this court. This is as it should be. These walls around us are your world. You will see no one that I do not bring you, speak to no one that I do not introduce first. You belong to me and your instructresses, until the Factor says otherwise." Her face closed in a scowl. "Filthy little foreign chit that you are, I should not think you will ever be so lucky."

She pointed to the bucket and the mug. "I will show you where to clean these. Then you will learn the rooms of your world. Do you understand me, Girl?"

"Yes, Mistress Tirelle." My tone gave no ground, but it made no assault on her dignity either.

We went first to the kitchen of the Pomegranate Court.

Much later I came to understand that all the courts in the Factor's house are named for their tree. In a few cases, the tree-that-was. Whether Pomegranate, Peach, or Northern Maple, each court was substantially the same. I lived in a factory, after all, dedicated to the very slow and delicate process of manufacturing a certain kind of woman, run by ruthless termagants only too willing to find fault and cast a candidate aside like a badly thrown pot.

The ground floor of the building that housed the rooms of my little court was laid out simply enough. A kitchen stood at the eastmost end. Several huts the size of Papa's could have fit within. It held ovens of three different types, two hearths, and an assortment of smaller fire vessels. Great blocks of cured wood, smooth-sanded stone, and a strangely porous ceramic stood awaiting use. Pans, pots, and cooking tools in a bewildering array of shapes and sizes hung from the high ceilings or along the walls next to bins for grains, roots, and produce. Basins waited for rinsing and washing. There was even a great box half-filled with ice.

The only thing missing was knives. I'd learned aboard ship that no cook is ever without a good blade, but whoever cooked here did their work with unaccustomed bluntness, or took their tools with them.

Though Mistress Tirelle gave me time to fill my eyes, I did not ask questions. She had not spoken to me, after all.

Some lessons are not so hard to learn.

Next to the kitchen was a dining room. A long table polished to the same sheen as Federo's carriage was surrounded by spindly chairs that did not look strong enough to hold me, let alone adults. Where the kitchen's walls had been brick and tile against the danger of sparks, here they were covered with a bellied cloth of pale amber shot through with gold thread. This room had been painted by someone with a very delicate hand. Birds were rendered in full detail smaller than the nail of my thumb by the application of two or three strokes. Where their eyes could be seen in their pose, some green stone had been affixed to the cloth in fragments smaller than a sesame seed.

These birds swarmed in a flock of hundreds around a stand of trees that I took to be willows. Each leaf and twig on the willows had been painted as well. A stream wound among them just above the low cabinets that lined the room. Bright fish and reeds and little flowers spun on its current.

I know now that those walls had been a lifetime's work for some artist bound to the Factor's will. All I knew then was that they looked so real that I might step within them.

For a moment, I longed to do so. The flight of the painted birds seemed beautiful and free. But I knew even at that first part of my life in Copper Downs that someday I would leave this room. Those birds were trapped forever in their moment of time, rendered immortal but static against the cloth of the walls.

Already Mistress Tirelle pushed me onward. My leaving was not someday, but in that moment.

The central room of the ground floor opened to the courtyard beyond. Hidden folded panels could be fitted in place at need depending on the weather, but otherwise the room's low seats and padded benches were subject to whatever noise and wind stirred without. A hearth backed this room as well, while the walls were lined with frames and stands representing the tools of various arts. A rack of scrolls and books and bound sheaves of vellum and parchment stood on the west end, a door open in the midst of the shelving.

Still without words, Mistress Tirelle forced me on through.

The last room on the ground level was windowless just as the dining room had been. These walls were padded with a much coarser cloth. The floors were covered with tight-woven straw. No furniture was present except for a low wooden bench that seemed to have been abandoned on a whim. It did not fit the sense of purpose that coiled invisible but strong in the rest of this place.

"Outside, Girl," Mistress Tirelle growled. I marched a quick step ahead of her fist, until she caught me across my still-bare shoulders. "Do not walk so— it is undignified."

I bit back a reply. We were on the porch now, in the deep shadows beneath the columned ceiling that was the balcony above.

Mistress Tirelle turned me to face her with a bruising grip on my shoulder. "You will never be in these rooms I have shown you except as part of a lesson. Some Mistress will be with you at all times down the stairs. Do not descend to practice, or seek a lost scarf, or any other excuse which ever enters your foolish head." She pointed to the end of the porch just outside the empty room. "We go up now. That is where you will sleep, and bathe, and take meals unless you have been brought down here."

I stared at her, round-eyed and silent.

"You have leave to ask a question, Girl."

"No, thank you," I said. Not a question, and so I had pushed past the letter of her word.

She did not strike me for that. *So there are limits to her limits.* I made careful note of this discovery on the secret list that was already forming deep within me.

Upstairs the rooms were far plainer, though still pleasant and well-appointed beyond anything I might ever have imagined back in Papa's hut. Neither Federo's room at the wayhouse nor our cabin on *Fortune's Flight* had approached this simple comfort and well-wrought craft.

The deep porch formed a wide balcony, with a few chairs and a table of woven cane and whip-thin wood. All these second-storey rooms opened outward rather than connecting within as below.

A smaller kitchen above the great one would still have served to feed our entire village at home. Walls and floor alike were tiled with ceramic squares painted in the pattern of a lion devouring a snake, which in turn devoured the next lion beyond, and so forth.

The eating room was dominated by a large but simple table polished smooth as the mirrored gloss of the great table downstairs. Instead of the unnaturally detailed silk, these walls were wood that had been washed over with a pale color.

Beside that was a sitting room with a few wooden chairs and small tables, and a smaller hearth than the receiving room downstairs. The two rooms past were sleeping rooms, the one for Mistress Tirelle next to the stairs. I had no doubt she slept with the ears of a bat.

The high-walled courtyard, the baths in a cellar below the great kitchen, a double handful of rooms, and the struggling pomegranate tree were the entirety of my world for a very long time to come. All of it ruled by Mistress Tirelle.

I was clad in simple shifts much the same as what Federo had given me during our travels. There were three of them, and it was my responsibility to keep them exceptionally clean. A speck of dust on the hem, a spot of food on the front, and my ears were boxed or my head slapped.

At the first, we lived only upstairs. Mistress Tirelle was taking my measure in subtler ways than her ungentle prodding in the courtyard that first day. She had me cook, or at least try to. After my grandmother died, Papa had always prepared our rice mush for dinner. Besides which, I been too young to tend the fire.

She had me sew, and was surprised at my skill. The bells that had been between my fingers since before I could remember had taught their lessons well. I did not explain. Mistress Tirelle did not ask.

The duck woman also made a cursory review of the arts of the mind which Federo had begun to teach me, testing my comprehension of letters and simple arithmetic. I was careful not to show more wit than the questions were intended to discover.

Though she carped and grumbled at every little thing, and was quick with a hard hand, I took quiet satisfaction in seeing how little Mistress Tirelle had to complain about. Other than my attitude, of course, which she tried alternately to beat out of me or lecture to death.

I never did bow my head quite deeply enough, or answer quickly enough, or remain quiet enough for her. Mistress Tirelle had spent her life with candidates. She knew how to read the set of a girl's back. Bidden to silence, in those early days my only weapon was complete obedience combined with a sullen insolence. We both knew it well, and hated each other for it.

So began the years of my education.

"First we shall learn to boil," she told me one day. I had been there less than two weeks and was already keeping a secret tally against the day I found a way to reclaim my silk and bells.

I nodded. There had been no question addressed to me, no permission granted to speak.

"All life came from water," Mistress Tirelle continued. "Water lies within us all. You spit water from your mouth and pass water from your vagina. So first we cook with water, to honor who we are and make our food separate from the browsing of beasts." She gave me a shrewd look. "Do you understand?"

I did. Papa had boiled rice after all, though I couldn't recall having the word *boil* before beginning to learn Petraean. "Yes, Mistress Tirelle."

"What is it that we do to boil water?"

"We make a fire beneath a pot, ma'am." I hastily added, "A pot filled with water."

"Hmm."

She wanted some deeper answer, but what I had said was true enough. After a moment, Mistress Tirelle went on: "Later we will discuss the size and shape of vessels, and why you boil some things thus and others so."

I nodded again. Cooking seemed a strange place to begin whatever journey Federo had set me on, but here we cooked.

She built a fire in a little metal stove. After it was burning well, she drew a knife from within her black wrappings and proceeded to slice a bundle of dark green leaves shot through with pale gray veins. They smelled sharply of a strange yellowy scent on the edge of unpleasantness. "We cut these spinach leaves in order for them to cook evenly." Something close to a smile quirked across Mistress Tirelle's face. "Not all is ritual, Girl. Some purposes are as simple as everyday hunger."

I forgot myself and answered her. "Hunger isn't simple, ma'am."

When she struck me with the knife handle, it left a mark on my forehead that was many days in fading.

"Obedience is simple," the duck woman said, standing over me as I crouched on the floor, swallowing my sobs. "It is also the greatest everyday virtue any woman can possess. Most of all you."

We cooked. We washed. We swept. We sewed. For a long time, there was no one but me and Mistress Tirelle. Food was brought to the gate and accepted there by her from persons unseen. I then carried it to the upstairs kitchen under her supervision. The slops and night jars went down a drain on the far side of the court, adjacent to the high blank wall of whatever central building lay beyond.

I came to realize there were more courts besides mine. If I stood at the deepest part of the porch, I could see two other treetops. Occasionally a voice would be raised, then break off. I knew there must have been an array of guards and servants elsewhere in this place, but Federo had spoken truly when he told me I was leaving the world to be here. I knew only the company of women, and of women only Mistress Tirelle.

The sun moved, too, growing a bit more southerly in its track across the patch of sky that had been given me. At home, if I climbed a tree, I could see for furlongs on furlongs, across rice paddies to the village and far beyond. Here, there was only a bit of the heavens, cold stone, and air that never tasted right.

The days also became shorter as the sun slid ever southward. The pomegranate came into fruit with the cooler weather. So began my first instruction beyond the basics of obedience and housekeeping.

"One mark of distinction is the ability to choose without seeming, and always be correct in one's choice." Mistress Tirelle held a small knife in one hand—I was still not allowed blades at that time. A dozen pomegranates were set before us on the wooden block in the large kitchen downstairs. This was the first time we'd used that kitchen for anything since I'd arrived here, and I was fascinated by all the half-remembered shapes and surfaces.

The fruits were several shades of pale melon red, ranging from unripe to ready to overripe. Some were irregular, their ends lumpy and misshapen. Others were closer to the most ordinary form of the pomegranate.

"Which one, Girl?"

I pointed toward one at the near end of the table. The fruit had even coloring and a pleasing shape. "That one, Mistress."

She handed me the knife, reversing the blade as she did so. For a moment as the wooden handle slipped into my grasp, I imagined lifting it against her. It would be nothing, the work of a moment. Then she would have my feet out from under me and I would earn the beating of my life.

Instead I sliced open the pomegranate.

The white webbing within spilled out, reddish-purple seeds in their soft cases clinging to it. I touched a few of them, pulling the seeds away from their sticky entanglement.

"A fair choice. You looked well. Now put down the knife and pick a fruit from that basket behind you. You may look for only the count of three."

I looked over my shoulder to see a basket tucked behind the small block. It was filled with pomegranates. All the fruits on top were unripe, several dusted with some molder.

Quickly I reached in and grabbed a firm one, then rushed to place it on the table.

The fruit was of good color, but the shape was distended, with lumpy ends. "A woman might eat of that," said Mistress Tirelle. "But you could have done better."

I wanted to ask how, but I had not been given permission to speak.

"Let us go outside."

I followed her into the courtyard. The breeze was up a little, with a faint coolness on it I had never felt before. The tree was heavy with fruit. A few more lay on the cobbles around it. Most of the windfall was in the basket in the lower kitchen, of course, picked up by someone other than me.

"You have until the count of three to select one from the tree."

I looked. There were a hundred in my vision if there was a one. I pointed at a flash of melon-colored flesh halfway up.

"Hold your hand steady," she said, then fetched a long pole with a little metal basket at the end. I had never seen that tool before. The night sometimes brought so much to our little court.

Mistress Tirelle used the picker to bring down my pomegranate. I could not say how she knew which one, but so far as I could tell, she pulled down mine.

"The skin is split," she said. "See? There are blackflies within. You will learn to pick well, the first time."

We went back inside, where she made me eat the spoiled fruit I had chosen. The mealy flesh was bitter enough to bring tears to my eyes while the blackflies stung the inside of my mouth. I had the better of her, though, in that I sucked the flesh off some of the seeds and spat them into my hand, so I could keep them in place of my lost bells.

The following week Mistress Tirelle and I were in the courtyard beneath the shadow of our tree. The air was strangely chilled, the sun a wan and sullen disc in the sky. We were exercising my fruit-choosing skills. She would whip a blind off my face, and I would select a pomegranate with only a moment's glance. Down it would come, and we examined its defects together.

"See now," she said, "how much your eyes can know before your mind does. Let that first choice be true, and all else will follow from it. Let that first choice be false, and trouble will out every time." The duck woman leaned close. "Never allow yourself to be seen to make the effort. It must come from within, on the moment."

We were interrupted by an iron clangor which took me by surprise. I had not heard that sound once in the whole time since being brought here by Federo. Mistress Tirelle looked up and passed a quirk of her lips.

"Your next Mistress is here," she said.

For a moment, I thought I might be free of Mistress Tirelle. That flash of elation must have shown upon my face, for her eyes narrowed and the smile that hadn't truly been there vanished with the finality of a tight-closed door. She drew back her hand to strike a blow, then stayed herself, instead saying, "Come with me."

We walked to the dark gate through which I had come. The archway was large enough to admit a carriage, but a postern was let within. A bell hung there, which Mistress Tirelle rang once. The door creaked open, and a slender woman of sour aspect stepped through. She was as pale and sharp-eyed as all the other maggot folk of this city, wearing a long apron of dark blue over gray skirts and a gray blouse.

"Girl," said Mistress Tirelle. "This is Mistress Leonie. She will work with you on your sewing."

Thus we moved on to the next phase of my education. I was broken to the harness. Now it was time for me to learn my tricks.

I received my first real beating shortly thereafter, upon being cross with Mistress Leonie. She was quieter and of gentler voice than Mistress Tirelle, and so I was lulled into a sense of trust. I'd thought anyone would be better company than the duck woman with her casual cruelties and calculated rages.

My basic needlework having already been established, Mistress Leonie had moved me into different kinds of stitches. We worked with an assortment of needles and types of thread. Some were difficult for me to manipulate. I hissed in frustration during our morning hours one day.

"What is it, Girl?"

"This silly needle slips in my hand," I complained. "I hate the silk thread."

"You will do as you're told."

"It's stupid. We can use an easier thread."

She looked me up and down, then stepped to the doorway and called for Mistress Tirelle. They whispered together a short while. Mistress Leonie came back and resumed her seat with a smirk.

Mistress Tirelle reappeared a moment later with a cloth tube in one hand.

It was fat as a sausage and slightly more than a foot in length. "Remove your shift," she ordered.

I glanced at Mistress Leonie in a rush of embarrassment. I still did not realize what was about to come, and thought only for my modesty. Even that idea was new to me, brought by the language of my captivity and the chilly necessities of life in the Factor's house here so far north of the country of my birth.

Shrugging out of my shift, I faced her.

"Turn and bend to grasp your knees."

Mistress Tirelle began to beat me across the buttocks and thighs with the silk tube. It had been filled with sand, then wetted, so it was heavy and struck me with a harder, deeper blow than the flat of her hand could do. I cried out at the first, which earned me a growl to silence and another, sharper blow. She laid into me for the count of twenty. Then: "Don your shift, and continue with Mistress Leonie's instruction."

Sitting was agony, but I did not dare show it. As I brought my shaking hands to the needle and thread, I saw the flush on Mistress Leonie's cheeks. She looked *happy*.

Thus we went on. Now that the silk tube was out, punishments became far more frequent and for less cause. I was beaten if I used one of my own words. I was beaten if I came late to instruction or the table. I was beaten if I was thought to be disrespectful, something Mistress Leonie found to be the case at least two or three times each week. If I merely forgot something, Mistress Tirelle beat me for that as well.

Though Endurance had first taught me patience, Mistress Tirelle made that lesson my way of life. The slap of her sandals on the wooden floors took the place of the bell of Papa's white ox. Her coarse, labored breathing was Endurance's snorting to call me back, though now the danger was greatest at the center of my life.

The courtyard outside grew ever colder as my first northern winter arrived. Grim rains would set in that lasted for days. I was miserable with the chill. Mistress Tirelle swaddled herself in more wool than ever, but did not bother to offer me anything to put over my shift. I cured my pomegranate seeds in the small warming pot allowed me for the nights, and stole wisps of thread for my silk.

Soon, I would steal the whole cloth. I had only to find a way to distract Mistress Leonie.

She had brought a flat chest that opened from the top into a series of draw-ers like wooden wings spread ever wider. Cloth lay folded within—muslins, cottons, poplins, silks, woolens, and other fabrics—all of it heavy with the smell of camphor and the scent of the cedar wood from which the chest had been made. Some lengths were in colors that might have shamed a butterfly. Others were simple and somber.

"Each of these is as fine as you will discover in any market," Mistress Leonie said.

I had never been in any market, but she was not interested in the tale of my short years.

"I have shown you how to tell the thread count. With practice, your eye will gauge the quality even from a distance. That is not everything there is to cloth, but it stands for much." She turned a yard-long run of fine wool over in her hands. "I will bring a loom, for you should see how this is made." That dangerous leer crept across her face, which spoke of a beating soon to come. "Tell me, Girl, what is the wool I hold?"

That question was a trick, for we had not yet discussed the kinds of wool. But I had overheard her talking to Mistress Tirelle of the materials, and so took a guess from the words I'd heard. "It is cashmere, Mistress."

Her face fell. "You are clever. Mind how you use that knife between your ears." Her pique already passed, Mistress Leonie called me close to feel the tight weave of the wool and discourse a short time on the husbanding of cer-tain goats to be found in the Blue Mountains, whose very fur was as fine as all but the most costly thread.

With one hand behind me and out of her sight, I eased a length of silk from the box and let it fall to the floor. Mistress Leonie was with her goats in that moment, running her fingers up and down the length of cashmere, and she did not see.

I was content with that. She would surely see it, but without me trying to push the cloth beneath a chair or hide it somehow, its fall would be an acci-dent of the cloth case and nothing more.

Her eyes were better than I had credited, though. When Mistress Leonie folded up the cashmere, she bade me stand beside the chest and went to call for Mistress Tirelle and the sand-filled tube.

An hour later, I was in the courtyard, shivering away the last of the day's gray light beneath the pomegranate tree. The cold let me pretend I was not still shaking from the sobs. These people were wicked monsters. I would slay them all like a god before demons, then march home across the waters.

I knew better, though. Federo had taken me from my father with words, not a dandy's dueling blade. I would take myself from these maggot women with words, not weapons.

The gate banged open, startling me. A mounted man swept in to ride at a trot across the Pomegranate Court. Federo, of course, appearing as if summoned by my thought of him.

He caught sight of me before reaching the building, and slid from his horse in a single motion.

"Girl." A genuine warmth filled Federo's voice, the first warmth I had found since coming to this place of stone and suffering. "How do you like it here?"

"Oh . . ." I was ready to spill my woe and fear. Then I glanced at the house. Mistress Tirelle stood in the shadows of the balcony. "The rain is cold, and the sun is too small in the sky." That also was too much of a complaint, most likely.

"Silly thing." He bent down and stroked my hair away from my cheek. "Wear a wrap, and you will be warm. This city is not so blessed by the sun."

I had not been given a wrap, but I knew I could not say this where Mistress Tirelle might overhear.

He took my chin in his hands, tilted my head back and forth. He then looked at my bare arms and shoulder. My skin was still flushed and stinging from the beating, but there were no bruises. I realized in that moment the purpose of the sand-filled tube was precisely that: to discipline me without marring me.

"What have you learned?" he asked.

"I can cook spinach. And sew eleven different stitches." I smiled; I could not help myself. "I know when to use the juice of lemons and when to use palm oil on a scratched table."

"We will make a lady of you yet." His grin was large, as if this imprisonment of mine were the best thing for everyone.

"What do you mean by 'make a lady'?" I asked him. No one had yet told me my purpose here.

"In time, Girl, in time." He ruffled my hair again. "I would speak to Mistress Tirelle once more. Mind my horse, if you please."

I knew nothing of horses except that they were as tall as Endurance but with the mad eyes of birds in their long, slack faces. I decided to mind his horse from behind the pomegranate tree, in case the beast took a fit. A chill rain began to fall as I waited.

After a while Federo came back out with a troubled look. "You are more difficult than you should be, Girl," he told me. "Your intelligence and your pride perhaps serve you too well. This is a game for the patient."

"You are wrong, sir. This is no game."

"No," he said. "Perhaps it is not. Nonetheless we play." He leaned close. "I will be back to check. You will tell me if things go awry."

Things were all awry, had been since the day this man had dragged me away from Papa's ox and my belled silk. That was not what he intended, and not what he wished to hear. *"Yes,"* I told him in the words of my birth.

He smiled and climbed back into his saddle. Mistress Tirelle waddled out and with very poor grace offered me a shabby wool cloak. "Here, Girl," she said. "You might be cold."

I stood in the growing icy rain and watched her march back into the shadows of the house. I wondered what words I might ever summon to break her down.

Mistress Leonie and I continued to sew clothes, but they did not seem to be for me to wear. Or for anyone else.

"You will never in your life lift a needle once you leave this place, Girl," she told me as we pieced together the shoulder yoke of a blouson.

I nodded. That was sometimes safe. Of course, I was forbidden to answer, or question further. They were training me in all the arts of a lady, but I would be permitted to practice none of them.

There was little point to this that I could see. I had already resolved to be the best of them at everything they did. In service of that determination, I pushed my anger down.

Her next remark echoed my thoughts. "Do you know why this would be so?"

"Am . . . am I to answer that, Mistress Leonie?" My back itched in anticipation of the blows of the sand-filled tube.

"Yes. You may speak."

"I am to understand these arts, without practicing them."

"You are a little snip." Despite her words, her voice was without rancor. "You will be called upon time and again to judge the worth of a thing, a deed, a place, or a person. Is this woman's dress what a great lady of Copper Downs would wear, or an imitation crafted by mountebanks in pursuit of a daring theft? Is that room cleaned so well that a god might be received within and accorded due honors, or have the maids been lazy? What of that soup whose bay leaves were picked too green—will it poison your noble guests?"

"So I am to understand the arts in order to assess the work of others."

"Precisely." She smiled, her delight in me as her pupil overcoming the power she preferred to hold above me. "If you know a Ramsport stitch from a pennythreaded seam at a glance, you can tell much about the person who stands before you."

"I might know if they had a good tailor, or only a swiftly made copy."

"Again, you have the right of it. Now turn this sleeve over and show me what we have missewn. There is an error, I assure you."

In the course of that work, which was one of the most pleasant days I had passed with Mistress Leonie, I was able to free some silk for my purposes.

It took me many nights of effort to find the best way to thread a pomegranate seed. Little meshes such as I had used aboard *Fortune's Flight* with the metal scraps were no good. Instead I employed a stolen needle for a drill and cut my way through each pip. I then sewed it to my silk.

The cloth was nothing like a proper swath of bells from home. It made no noise except when I folded it on itself. Then the beads clattered with a wooden whisper. Still, they were there, nubbins beneath my fingers that resumed the twice-broken count of my days.

I found a place in the ceiling of my sleeping room where beams met the wall. There I stored my silk, my seeds, and my little sewing kit. Nothing else here at the Pomegranate Court belonged to me, not even my own body. This was mine.

While I was plotting at my past, winter settled in outside with a blanket of frozen misery covering the stones and the ghostly branches of the pomegranate tree. I spent the cold nights abed as I clutched my silk close and ran my fingers over the pomegranate seeds. I hoarded enough of them to account for every day of my life, or as close as I could reckon. They were not bells, but their shapes beneath my fingertips reminded me of who I truly was, beyond the arts required of a lady of Copper Downs.

Would these count? Did they serve to mark my days and give my soul a path when it was needed? What would my grandmother have said? Endurance would never have minded. My father would not have known what to say—I am not sure the affairs of women had ever made much sense to him.

Which is why he sold you, a traitor thought whispered in my head. *A boy he would have loved enough to keep.*

I cried then, open tears for the first time in months here in this cold place. I did not think I was sobbing aloud, but in time Mistress Tirelle came to find me curled on the floor wrapped in misery.

"Girl," she said, her voice soft with the huskiness of sleep. "What is that cloth clutched in your hand?"

She drove me out into the snowy courtyard with a wooden spindle. Mistress Tirelle seemed to have no regard for the marks of the beating this time. She almost shrieked her fury with each blow.

"You *will* let go of this obsession, you idiot trollop!"

"I'll never let go!" I shouted in my words. My old words.

Her fist caught me on my chin to send me sprawling. My shift was already soaked with sweat and blood. The snow traded its cold through the damp, clinging fabric to chill my spine and ribs.

"So help me, if you speak that heathen trash one more time, I shall fork your tongue. The Factor will have you sold for a tavern wench, and you'll be dead of men before you're twenty."

I tried to get away from her, but she swung the spindle again and caught me across the knees. The pain was stunning.

"You will burn that silk now, out here under the stars."

"There is snow—" I began to answer, but Mistress Tirelle slapped me.

"You were not given leave to speak. Remain here."

She waddled back to the porch and up the stairs. I sat shivering in the snow, swallowing my own blood and wishing I had a way to die.

The duck woman was back a minute or two later with one of the copper coal urns used to keep our sleeping rooms warm during a winter night. "Here," she said. "Tear the silk in pieces and lay it within."

Crying, I did so, or tried to. The silk was strong, as its kind of cloth always is. Mistress Tirelle found a knife within her swaddles and nicked the swath for me.

My tears stood near frozen on my face as I fed the strips to the glowing pit. She handed me a vial of oil. "Pour it over."

I poured. The days of my life burned away as if they'd never been. The pomegranate seeds crackled in the heat, popping in little groups, taking the ghosts of what had been mine away with them.

May this burning reach my grandmother, I thought.

When the fire had died, Mistress Tirelle forced me to carry the urn to the upstairs kitchen. Even through a heavy pad, the metal reddened my hands and wrists. When we arrived, she rubbed oil of the palm on my burns with a rough, careless grip, then found a wide, low pot of the sort used for cooking small fowl atop the fire rather than within it.

She scooped the ashes of my silk and the burnt husks of pomegranate seeds from the warming urn to the stewpot. Some wine and some water followed, and a generous handful of salt. Mistress Tirelle mixed this awhile, watching it bubble until the mixture steamed.

The smell was awful.

Everything fit into a large serving bowl, which she set before me, saying, "Eat."

The stew was a mass of grayish brown.

"Eat it," she said, "and we are done. Do not eat it, and you are finished."

I choked through the bitter stew of ashes and salt. I was eating my past. But I vowed that I would still have a future.

Later in my rooms, I sat in the bed and looked outside the door, which Mistress Tirelle had left standing open. In the shadows of the snow-heavy pomegranate, for a moment, I thought I saw a sleeping ox. I knew it could not possibly be so, but still the sight comforted me.

After my first year in the Pomegranate Court, new Mistresses entered as well, for other arts. Mistress Tirelle still worked with me in the kitchen. Mistress Leonie continued with the sewing and fabrics. Mistress Marga, who was much younger than the other two, came to show me the ways of a true and thorough cleaning of the building, northern style. Mistress Danae brought sheaves of paper and the wandering letters of Stone Coast writing to me, renewing what Federo had begun aboard *Fortune's Flight*.

Each in their way demonstrated the mysteries of their art. Mistress Marga showed me how different oils were selected for varying woods, depending not only on the nature of the material itself, but also on how heavy the use and whether it met with direct sunlight. She spoke hours on starch, and why the proper stiffening of a cuff or collar could speak so thoroughly of a gentleman's worth and station in the life of the city.

Mistress Sualix came to show me the secret magics of numbers, how they danced in lines and columns and arrays to give birth to new numbers. Her voice was close and quiet, and seemed careless of the discipline in which the others held me. To her, all the world was numbers. They moved ships and coin and the booted feet of swordsmen. She soon had me believing this, too, so that I thought I heard the measured breathing of the entire city in a small stack of coin.

Mistress Balnea came to instruct me on horses, dogs, and the rarer pets of which some women made their playpretties. She displayed tinted pictures rendered on stretched hides, and spoke of shoulders and stance and colors, and promised me a ride of my own in the spring. I did not see much point in mounting a pony only to circle the courtyard outside, but I did not tell the horsemistress this.

Music came, too, in the form of Mistress Maglia, a thin, vengeful woman who made Mistress Leonie's malices seem like caresses. Her feelings were not personal, quite the opposite, but she made it most clear that I was nothing to her but another instrument. Her purpose was to fit my voice to the singing best regarded among these northern folk, and ensure that I knew a spinet from a harpsichord. I was still quite small when Mistress Maglia first began my training, and my voice had that angelic sweetness that very young children may possess. She warned me of the wreck I would become before I finished growing, then threatened to break me before my time if I did not mind every note and work exactly as she bade.

"I'm not afraid of the Factor like these other biddies," she snapped. "You will be perfect, or you will be nothing, by my own hand."

Two good things came from this new flood of Mistresses. One, my days were more varied and busy than when I had first arrived. This meant less time with Mistress Tirelle, and more distractions to occupy me. The world was already unfolding in a way I would never have imagined finding within a cage such as the Pomegranate Court. I felt guilty for comparing this favorably to spending my days swimming in ditches beneath the brassy sun.

Still, I was never beaten at home.

Two, with more Mistresses coming and going, I had an increasing sense that there was a world beyond these bluestone walls. Sounds rarely reached within the courts, and when they did, such noises were indistinct and meant little. The women who taught me came and went to other errands that implied they had responsibilities, schedules, things required of them. They often stopped to chatter. Care was taken to keep the words from my ears, but not always and not enough. Their bits of gossip told me of other girls being raised in other courts of the Factor's house. These girls were all rivals to one another and to me—this sweetling was a genius of spice and flame in the kitchen, while that little flower inked calligraphy to match the very angels.

I was but a small child when such words first crossed my ears. They only strengthened my resolve to master everything before me. Someday I would walk free.

My bed was a great square so soft that I sometimes slept on the floor beside it. At night, when Mistress Tirelle had retired huffing and grumbling to her sleeping room, I would lie awake and tell myself stories in the language of my birth. I quickly came to realize how little I knew of my own tongue, compared with my increasing mastery of the rough, burred Petraean of these Stone Coast people. I could speak of fruits and spices and tailoring and the finer points of dogs only in the language of my captivity.

In my own language, I did not even have a word for *dog*. Endurance had been our only animal, besides a few scrawny jungle fowl scratching about Papa's hut. I could chatter of turtles and snakes and biting flies, but still the world those words encompassed was small enough to crack my heart.

One day I had pieced together another few lines of *Seventeen Lives of the Megatherians*. Mistress Danae believed that a lady should always reach beyond herself. The words were gigantic, speaking of ideas I did not understand at that time. What does a small child know of transmigration and condonation? Still, the sounds were present in their tricksy, shifting letters. She guided me through them one slow, patient step at a time.

I rose from my lesson. My bladder was full, and it was not quite the hour for me to assist Mistress Tirelle in the upper kitchen. With her keen sense of cruelty in full flower, she had decreed we would work with soups for a while.

To my surprise, she waited just outside the door of the common room. Mistress Tirelle was not in the habit of standing about in the cold. Not without great need.

"Girl," she said, then paused a moment. Such a lack of assurance was also unlike the duck woman. "A new Mistress is here for you to meet. She is . . . is not on my schedule, but Federo has sent her." Eyes narrowing, Mistress Tirelle went on. "Be warned. This is not someone you should warm to as you have your other Mistresses."

It was all I could do not to burst out laughing. Who had Mistress Tirelle thought I might have warmed to? That she should imagine such an idiotic thing was beyond credibility. I nodded instead, then looked down at my feet to hide the light undoubtedly dancing in my eyes.

"You believe that I jest." She grabbed my ear, then thought the better of it even as I braced for the shock of pain. "This is something else, Girl. None of your little rebellions—no foreign talk, no thieving, no nothing. You get the urge to earn a beating, you just come tell me and I'll knock the pores right off your skin. But do not play the monkey with this new Mistress."

I nodded, still not meeting her eyes. Was this new Mistress a fearsome queen of arms? Or some mighty priestess with a hex in her milky eyes? Mistress

Danae's stories were full of such women, strange beyond measure and powerful in quiet ways that escaped the notice of most men.

Mistress Tirelle led me downstairs, through the receiving room and to the practice room. I followed with my head still bowed, my face hidden, until I was looking at my feet, streaked with dirt, standing on the straw padding of that place.

"Girl," the duck woman said in a voice overloud with the pitch of fear, "this is the Dancing Mistress. Mistress—ma'am. This here's our Girl. The candidate of the Pomegranate Court."

"Thank you, Mistress Tirelle." The Dancing Mistress' voice was deeper and rougher than I had heard before among women. I raised my eyes and looked up at someone too tall, too thin, covered with fine fur, a tail whicking behind her. The tips of claws peeked through her oddly blunt, wide fingers.

Dangerous, monstrous even.

A shriek rose up within me. The Dancing Mistress touched her mouth with her finger in the simplest of shushing motions. Her gesture was so unexpected that it distracted my panic, as she must have known it would.

Not a monster, I realized, but someone who was far more different from me than these pale maggot people of the Stone Coast. Her ears were high on her skull, set back with small round flaps above them almost like a mouse. Her forehead was high, over water-pale violet eyes in a pointed face descending with a mouth split wide as mine or anyone else's, rather than the fanged triangle of a beast. Her nose was flat, but also human rather than animal.

What had startled me most was the silver fur that covered all of her that I could see. People could look like anything, be many colors and sizes, but no person I had ever seen or heard of was covered with such fine and beautiful fur. Nor did people have tails that swept to the floor, as the Dancing Mistress most certainly did. At the same time she was clearly a person, clad in a wrap of blue cotton printed with a subtle flowered pattern. The clothing covered her bodice and hips, just as any lady would take care to do.

"I am a woman of my people," she said quietly. "Your kind refer to us as pardines. I am come to live among the humans of Copper Downs and work for my own living. I teach girls and women, and a very few men, to dance, to walk with grace and balance. Sometimes they learn to move so fast and fall so far that they can avoid the sorts of pointed dangers that come driving out of the shadows of great houses."

I stared. No one had ever before surprised me so much that they stole all the words from my mouth.

She stepped away from me and sat on the little wooden bench of the practice room. Mistress Tirelle had departed without me taking any note of her movements. "We shall require mirrors here, I am afraid." The Dancing Mistress seemed regretful. "Now tell me of yourself, Girl."

"I am to speak?" I almost choked on the words.

"Yes," the Dancing Mistress answered. "You are to speak."

"I . . . I am a girl of my people." I took a deep breath. For the first time since being brought here, I would risk the truth. "Stolen away to live among the enslavers of Copper Downs and work toward my own freedom."

Blows did not fall. Nor shouting, slaps, shoving. Instead a deep wave of melancholy passed through the Dancing Mistress' angled violet eyes. She opened her arms, and I stepped into them—to be clasped by friendly hands for the first time in my recent memory.

I did not sob into her fur, though I mightily wished to do so. I just let her hold me a moment while my breathing steadied.

"Girl," she finally said. "Your thoughts are your own. I do not blame you for a syllable of what you said. But if you value your life, and any power you may ever hope to grasp hold of, keep those words within you and never let them out again among these walls."

Her words were a scrap of hope fed to a starving girl. "Yes, Mistress," I muttered, then pulled away from the fur and cotton of her shoulder. "What is it you are here to teach me, please?"

She looked surprised. "Why, dancing, of course."

We danced awhile.

I could not see how to make another belled silk and keep it a secret. Instead I began sewing one in my imagination. Each night before I slept, I would count the bells of my life to date. First there were the simple tin bells of my time with Papa. Then there were the scrap iron bits of my voyage with Federo. Then there were the pomegranate seeds of my months in this house.

In my mind they all rang, even the wood and iron bits. Each night after I had counted them all to the best of my recollection—some spans of days I had to guess at—I would make a game of sewing another one on. Because it was only in my head, I could use needles of bone or ivory, steel or wood; likewise the thread was as I decided it was.

The important thing was to keep the count. In the Pomegranate Court, weeks were marked by the pattern of daily lessons, and by the delivery of certain foodstuffs. We kept no calendars. The count of my bells was the count of my days, and how else would my spirit know the way home when I was done with my life?

I never breathed a word, said nothing to anyone, even the Dancing Mistress. I could not do this thing without punishment falling so hard upon my shoulders that I would bleed rivers.

Even so, she was a hidden friend to me through the darkest days of my second winter and the wet, gloomy opening of the spring that followed. The one hour of any day where I could speak even the least portion of my mind was in the practice room with her. We worked on steps, balance, how I walked, my sense of my body and the space it filled. Sometimes it was truly dance, but more often it was just movement.

"Most people think of their bodies as being flat, like a drawing of themselves," she told me. "Imagine that you made a paper poppet, and moved it about on a little stage. Except it's not at all true. You have *depth*. Your heels and elbows swing back. When you turn, there is a curve your body fills in the space around you."

While the words made sense to me, it was hard to understand the idea that lay beneath. She set me to skipping rope—a pastime of which I had never heard—first forward, then backwards. To hop as the rope came down behind me required that I know without looking where both the rope and my feet were.

This was much like Mistress Tirelle making me pick fruit with a single glance, or Mistress Leonie's endless tutelage on the niceties of seams. I had to see beyond what lay before my most casual gaze, to what was really there, as invisible to the eye as my own back was.

These lessons were strange, and quiet, but soon enough I could feel the grace they lent me. I could catch a dropped knife in the kitchen before it struck the tile, leap down the stairs from the balcony to the lower porch. I found I was strong, too. Very strong, the Dancing Mistress told me—more even than most boys. How was I to know? She helped me learn to use that advantage as well. Once the weather cleared a bit, I was able to climb the pomegranate tree speedily and without fear.

For that feat I was beaten so hard, I could not walk for two days. Mistress Tirelle and the Dancing Mistress had an argument, the only one I ever heard between them. Then the duck woman came waddling into my sleeping room. "This is your place," she said quietly. "Do not look over the walls, do not peek out the gate."

I forgot myself again and blurted out, "What is beyond, that I should fear it so?"

Mistress Tirelle pretended not to notice my infraction. "A world you will see when it is your time. Girl, you are being made ready for greatness. Let that making unfold in the way your teachers know best."

Like Federo, she believed my being here was for the good of all. How could they think such a thing?

Spring became summer, the rhythms of the seasons continuing to mark my time in the Pomegranate Court. All I remembered from my earliest days was the endless heat and the sun pouring like a golden hammer upon the land. Here the heavens were a clock, a slow march of the long now following the course of plowing, planting, harvest, and fallow.

Not that I'd seen agriculture. Only my one pomegranate tree carrying its hidden burden of seeds, now lost like my bells, but far more likely to return. Once the art of reading had settled into my head, Mistress Danae showed me ever more books. Among them was a treatise on farming, *The New Horse-Houghing Husbandry*. This was the first truly old text I'd read. The book took me weeks on end to puzzle through, and I understood perhaps only one part in five.

Still, I had been born into the practice of farming. Papa and Endurance worked the paddies, brought in the rice, trod the husks. I recognized some of what Tullius, the author of this book, was describing. My interest was born of that—an echo of the familiar, mixed with stories of princes and battles and demigods and the colors of the world.

The other thing I learned from *Husbandry* was that the very speech of people could change over time. There were seasons to language, just as there were seasons to the years or to the lives of women. I went about for a while muttering in archaic Petraean, though I never had the nerve to answer Mistress Tirelle or my other instructresses in that form.

My lessons moved downstairs as well. We began cooking in the great kitchen more often. The selection of vessels, utensils, spices, and cooking methods was much more varied than upstairs. Mistress Tirelle and I broke our fasts there almost all the time. Some days we also took quick, simple midday or evening meals there. More to the point, downstairs was where I explored what could be done with food. The lessons were simple at first, but it was already clear to me that there might be no end to them if someone had the means to spend their lives in a glorious kitchen.

One day we were washing earth pears—small wrinkled lumps with purplish skins and hair-fine roots branching off them.

"This root must be cooked over a hot fire or on a high boil for at least ten minutes," Mistress Tirelle said.

Nothing was ever written down. I was simply expected to *remember*. The array of details in the kitchen was staggering.

I clasped my hands briefly. This was how I indicated I wished to ask a question regarding whatever lesson was under way.

"You may speak, Girl."

"What will happen if it is eaten raw, or poorly cooked?"

She gave me a long look. "A person could become quite ill, or even perish."

It had never occurred to me that food could be a weapon. "So the earth pear is harmful?"

Mistress Tirelle put down her root and dried her hands. "Girl, your question runs ahead of your learning, but I will answer it nonetheless. Everything can do harm. The oils we use for frying would ruin your digestion if drunk down like wine. If I made you eat salt until you gorged, you would die of thirst soon after. Some herbs, or things that resemble herbs, can kill even as a small pinch of powder."

"Then this art is like all the others I study." I waved the earth pear in my hand to point around the great kitchen. "It is not that I should cook. It is that I should know cooking so well that I can see when someone is trying to poison me with salt or bad oils or the powder of killing herbs."

Mistress Tirelle's ghost of a smile briefly returned. "Federo chose you well, Girl."

I looked down at my earth pear and wondered how I might feed it to her. *Words,* I reminded myself. *You will triumph with words.*

The lesson was clear: Anything could harm, if used in a certain way. Food. Words. A length of silk sewn into a tube and filled with sand. Even a person.

Are they training me to live well? Or to know different ways to kill and to die?

My lessons changed as the seasons did, along with the lengthening of my legs. Mistress Balnea brought the promised horse into the courtyard one day, and we began the study of the living animal instead of the illustrated scrolls and parchments. Our example was an old brown mare with a white blaze on her head who stared at me with empty eyes and suffered herself to be touched and poked and prodded. I was given to understand that in time I would be permitted to mount and ride, as if this were some great treat. At times she brought a dog instead, different breeds on different days, and pointed up their skills and purposes, what their requirements were, and the conformation of their bodies. The dogs had more spirit than the broken old mare, but they also seemed easily cowed.

So, too, other teachings changed. A great loom was delivered and set up overnight beneath the pomegranate tree, with a dyed canvas sheet for shelter from the rain. Mistress Leonie began to teach me the more commercial aspects of weaving. A whole pig carcass arrived, which Mistress Tirelle and I spent three days butchering so I could see where on the animal's body each cut of meat came from. Some we cured; some we cooked. Much went to waste.

Whatever they truly meant to make of me, I became increasingly aware of the substantial investment of time and resources the Factor was lavishing on my education.

The best change in lessons came, as I might have hoped, from the Dancing Mistress. She arrived one evening after dinner, not her usual schedule. Mistress Tirelle's habit at that time was to have me read or practice my calligraphy in the last hours. She would then retire early. Thus I was surprised to see any of my instructresses at such an hour—especially the silver-furred woman.

"Come outside, Girl," the Dancing Mistress said to me from my doorway. Behind her, Mistress Tirelle made some grumbling huff at the bottom of her breath. Judging by the look that passed between them, this argument had already been waged and lost.

In the courtyard, the moon spilled careless light on the cobbles. The newest shoots on the twigs of the pomegranate tree were silver-dark, while the shadows seemed to breathe ink. We stood awhile under the cold stars, exchanging no words.

That, I was happy enough to do. Every moment of my life was ruled by a guided watchfulness. Sharing the airy silence with the only friend I had was a goodness.

"You climbed well," the Dancing Mistress said. "This pleases me."

I clasped my hands.

Her voice deepened with sadness. "You are free to speak while we are at this lesson."

"Mistress, I enjoyed the climb."

"Good. Would you do it again, by moonlight?"

"When the tree is dark?" How hard could it be to find my way up? I was still quite small then, and had little fear of fitting my body anywhere I was permitted to go in the first place.

"Your friend the moon will provide hints to your eyes, Girl."

I wore nothing but a shift, under a rough woolen wrap I'd woven for myself. My hands and feet were bare.

Up I went. The memory of my prior climb was strong. The tree's bark was knotted and twisted to welcome my fingers. The branches alternated, so I could reach them like the rungs of a ladder.

Climbing was a joy. This was as close as I'd come to freedom since first walking away from the sound of Endurance's bell with Federo's hand clasped firmly around my own. No wonder Mistress Tirelle had so violently disapproved of climbing. My spirit soared with the lifting of my body, and the ancient moon was my oldest friend.

If the tree were tall enough, towering over the whole city of Copper Downs, could I see all the way home to Papa's fire and the whuffling breath of the ox?

The upper branches were light and thin. They swayed even beneath my then-small weight. I could see the roof of the Pomegranate Court, the copper sheaths that kept the rain off my head, gleaming back at the moon. The bluestone walls were topped with a wide, flat walkway that I could not see from the ground. A place for soldiers to tread upon their watch, I realized, thinking back on all the battle poetry Mistress Danae had read to me. At least, if this house were in need of soldiers. Rooftops poked beyond, hinting at the city I'd seen so briefly on arriving in the harbor, and had been hidden away from ever since.

I turned and looked the other way. The taller inner wall of our courtyard was more clearly seen as a tower. Other treetops were visible in the other courts I had glimpsed before. For a long, strange moment I wondered if other Girls had been set to climb this night, if I would meet the eyes of my rival slaves over the rims of the walls set to keep us isolate and inviolate.

The Dancing Mistress had not asked me to move with speed, and so I did not return right away. Instead I looked down at the canvas that covered the loom, at the chest where the gear for the horses and dogs was kept, at the gatehouse marking the path to freedom.

Mine was a tiny, tiny world, but still far richer than the frog-filled ditches of Papa's farm. I had no word for *farm* in my own language—where we lived was where we lived. I would not have learned to read, or anything of arithmetic, or the finer arts of cooking with all the poisons of the world, if I had stayed there.

I would not have been a slave if I had not come here.

"No one will own me," I said in my own words.

The climb down was more difficult than the climb up had been. I picked my way with care and still slid twice, before falling the last ten feet and just barely missing the loom's canvas. Still, I landed upright and kept my stance.

The Dancing Mistress stared at me, her eyes hooded by shadow. "What did you see up there?"

I opened my mouth, then stopped. She did not want a report on the copper roof of my house. *What* had *I seen?* I wondered. I blurted the deeper answer as it came to me, without further thought. "The path to freedom."

"Hold that in your heart. I cannot release you from this place, but together we can visit freedom."

I longed to ask her how, but the patience that had been beaten into me was a lesson well-learned.

"Now you will run about the courtyard as fast as you can go," she said.

"For how long?"

"Until I tell you to stop, or your legs slip from beneath you."

Eventually I went back inside with my shoulders aching and my mind racing.

I had trouble walking again the day after that first run, though I was pleased this time rather than humiliated. The pain had been earned. There was no cruelty. Just honest effort. The Dancing Mistress told Mistress Tirelle that I had bruised myself practicing cross-steps.

Federo came again that day. He was afoot instead of ahorse this time, and appeared wrung out. The sea had stained his clothes so that his velvet finery was ragged, while the sun had colored his skin so he less resembled a maggot and more a ripening berry.

He found me in the courtyard with Mistress Leonie and the loom. She excused herself as soon as she noticed Federo and went in search of Mistress Tirelle, or so I presumed. He sat on her little padded bench and stared at me awhile.

I offered him the small smile that was all I ever let out.

"How is it with you, Girl?" he finally asked.

"I learn."

"Good." Federo reached out and took up my hand. He turned it back and forth, looking first at my wrist then my fingers, at my palm then the back. "Do you learn well?"

"Some lessons are harder than others."

"Which of the Mistresses do you favor most?"

A real smile escaped for a moment. "The Dancing Mistress."

His smile answered. "Good."

"I have a question." I had not yet found the nerve to broach this one to her.

"You may ask it," Federo said formally.

"Why do all my Mistresses have names save her? She has only a title." *And not a squarely accurate one*, I thought.

"A fair question." He tilted his head slightly. I could see a bloom of blood marring one eye, as if his face had recently been struck. "Her people are a race of few numbers, scattered far. The pardines do not give their names away even to each other. It is their way, what they call the paths of their souls, to keep their true selves hidden. It is said those selves are so deep that they survive braided among the soulpaths of other pardines long after the death of the body." He shrugged. "In any event, whatever the state of their souls, some have titles. Others might be called by the color of their eyes or their favored food."

"I do not have a name." *Though I did once.* "Yet my true self is not hidden at all. These Mistresses stare at every aspect of me all the time. They are remaking me by inches and days."

The last of his pleasure fled as a bird before a storm. "It is not a lesson to be taken. Your circumstances and hers are as different as the stars are from the lamps of your house."

"Both light the night."

He touched my hair a moment. "Never forget who you are."

"I am not yours," I said in the language of my birth.

"Silence is your friend," he answered in the same words.

I watched him walk slowly into the court to speak with Mistress Tirelle. After a short time, Mistress Leonie came out to resume my instruction in the textile arts.

There were stranger lessons to be learned as well. In my readings I came across the same story in two very different forms amidst Mistress Danae's books. That tales of the gods could be told and retold was itself a sort of revelation, given how much priestly writing seemed concerned with assurance and certainty.

The first I found was a man's story about the goddesses who made it their business to care for women. Much later in life, this tale would give me long pause for other reasons, but then it was simply the view of the world that caught my attention.

THE FATHERS' TALE

Long ago, the world was a garden and each race of being and kind of creature grew in neat little rows tended by the titanic gods. Father Sunbones, first among them, walked each day among the rows and remarked upon the health of the crop. Mother Mooneyes came by night to prune the shoots and claim the harvest.

Desire, their third daughter, was allowed to play among the fish-trees and the bird-vines, but forbidden the rows of anything that had fur or hair. "Your nature will wake them out of time," Mother

Mooneyes said as they feasted in the Blue Hall of the Sky. "Stay rather with the cold waterbreathers and the thoughtless fliers who will not feel your pull."

"It is not fair," Desire complained in the manner of children everywhere.

"Nothing is fair," rumbled Father Sunbones. "We are lucky if we merely find order in this world, let alone fairness. Your brother Time complains of being denied the fish-trees for himself. He whines constantly of fairness as he walks among the trellises where the souled ones grow."

It was the souled ones Desire wished to sport among, those with two arms and two legs and thatches of forbidden, lovely, unruly hair. Though their eyes were not yet open and their souls had not yet flowered, she imagined embracing one then another, pressing her lips to theirs, touching their bodies with hers, until she hung like they from their trellises to voice her lust to her cousins the stars.

"I know your thoughts," whispered her brother Time. "Later, I will help you."

"It is always 'later' with you," Desire hissed. "I want what I want."

"My power is in passage, not fulfillment." Her brother smiled with faint promise. "Take me for what you will."

Desire could not keep her thoughts from the men in all their colors, as well as the ogres and fey and sprites and all their close-kinned kind, so she sought Time in his observatory tower at that part of the day where Father Sunbones and Mother Mooneyes exchanged their pleasantries in the privacy of the horizon's blanket.

"What is this help you offer me?"

Time smiled again, the promise in his face a little larger. "Lie with me, for the fulfillment of my dreams, and in return I will grant you stolen hours to lie in the garden with the souled ones."

"Lie with you?" Desire laughed. "You are a stripling boy with a hollow chest and eyes as dark as Uncle Ocean's dreams." She touched her generous breasts through her shift, lifting them toward Time in mockery. "Why would I share my bounty with you?"

Time smiled yet again. The promise had become great. "Because Desire will always be subject to Time. Absent in an infant, unformed in a child, raging in a youth, unfulfilled in an elder. My grant of hours to you will return a hundredfold in the world that is to come when Father and Mother awaken the garden."

So Desire lifted her shift above her head and showed her body to her brother Time. She was the perfection of woman, hair every color, eyes flashing so bright they were no color at all, lips as full and rich as the lily between her legs, skin smooth as a new-ripened peach. And though Time was hollow-chested and pale, and his manhood not so great, he could hold himself at stiff readiness forever if he chose—the power of his Name—and so he rode his sister long into the night, until her cries of pleasure became pleas for release. For even Desire can eventually pale of her appetites.

Time finally spent the last of his seed upon her breasts. He rose, tore a strip from the nail of his least left finger and pressed it into his sister's shivering hand. "Take this into the garden with you. Keep it close to your person always, and the time you need will be yours there."

Desire was so tired and sore that she shuddered to imagine another penis coming near her body. But she burned to put Time's promise to the test. Gathering her shift over one arm, for she ached too much to reach up and draw it onto her body, Desire limped slowly into the garden.

She smelled so of sex and fulfillment that even the cold fishes in their trees stirred at her passing. Birds thrashed on their vines, hungry for her flesh or just the hard salty scents on her breath. When Desire walked among the furred animals, they strained and bellowed, disturbed within their dreams.

But when she came to the trellises where hung the fathers and mothers of all the souled races, their eyes flickered open pair by pair. Penises rose erect, nipples sprang from firm breasts, tongues crossed lips. Every being in that garden smelled her, wanted her, lusted for her.

In her soreness and fatigue, Desire took fright and fled to the Hall of the Blue Sky. She dropped her shift and Time's nail paring in the garden as she ran. Later when Father Sunbones came to check his crops, he found the souled ones awake and the animals disturbed. He also discovered the evidence of Desire's passage and Time's complicity.

"The damage is done," Father Sunbones told Mother Mooneyes. "Our children have roused the souled ones. The newcomers will go into the world with their spirits unformed." He wept golden tears that seared the soil.

Mother Mooneyes peeked out from the daylit heavens. "Perhaps that is well enough. Each can find his own path. Each can grow his own soul fit to suit who he is."

"But so many will be lost. Heartless, vicious, cruel."

"You name more of our children, Father. Not every child is Loyalty or Truth. Let the souled ones have their lives."

Father Sunbones listened to the counsel of his wife. He threw open the gates of the garden, plucked all that they had grown there, and herded his charges into the world. The fish fell into the rivers, lakes, and oceans. The birds took wing into the spring sky of a new world. Animals bellowed and fled across the land. And the souled ones took themselves to those places that suited each best and began to make towns and farms and tell each other stories of the hot dreams that invaded their long nights' sleep.

Then Father Sunbones went to Time's observatory tower and cursed his son's disloyalty. Ever more Time's strength wanes with the year so that he passes all the pains of a life between each winter solstice. This is his punishment for lying with his sister Desire.

Then Father Sunbones went to the Hall of the Blue Sky and banished Desire to her chambers for a year and day, so that she might not come out until her brother's curse had fulfilled its first round and she could learn what had been done to him.

But Desire had quickened with Time's seed. While she stayed hidden in her chambers, she gave birth to a torrent of sisters, one for each little animalcule that her brother had spent within her womb. She fed the daughters from the seed that still lay upon her breasts, so that they drank milk of both man and woman. These thousands of sisters became the goddesses of women and spread out into the world in the aid of midwives and mothers and sapphists and prostitutes and girl children everywhere.

Ever after, the gods of men made it their business to send these sisters home to Father Sunbones whenever and however they could, though it is a terrible and difficult thing to kill a goddess. The gods who were most passionate about this errand each gave a scrap of themselves to a holy order that raised the Saffron Tower in dedication to restoring the purity of souls and righting the wrongs of Desire.

I was quite taken with the contrast between this strange story and the other, which I found a month or so later, the latter a woman's view of what were obviously the same events. Mistress Danae could not tell me if these were true history or teaching stories, but as she said, did it matter? She also told me that

I should have a theology Mistress, but that was never in the Factor's plans, and so she gave me more books to read that discussed the strengths and failings of the gods.

For my part, I learned something from both these tales.

THE MOTHERS' TALE

Once when the world was new, Mother Mooneyes ruled the skies as first among the titanics. Father Sunbones had not yet woken to his place at her right hand as consort, but rather slept endlessly on a bed of burning sand beneath her ivory-walled halls. Mother Mooneyes sometimes went to him when she rested from her labors in the heavens. Even in his sleep, she could draw forth Father Sunbones' seed to make her children.

Mother Mooneyes' favored daughter was Desire. Desire was possessed of a beauty which challenged even that of her mother. Desire's hair was the gold of summer wheat and the brown of autumn leaves and the black of winter ice and the palest rose blush of spring all at once. Her skin shone with the luster of starlight and the richness of cream. Her lips were more sweet than honey with the heady fullness of wine. Every portion of Desire mirrored the perfection of the morning of the world.

Now it happened that Mother Mooneyes kept a garden in the lands around her ivory halls. This garden held all the promise of the world to come, ripening on vine and root and tree. To the east, cattle lowed and snuffled within their cradles of soil. Other beasts of the field were clustered around them, each with its own stalk and stem. To the north were the cold creatures and those on the wing, which partake of the world without fur or fang or thinking. To the south were the hot animals, those that would hunt and feast on the flesh of others once they stalked beneath the bright regard of Father Sunbones.

Mother Mooneyes knew that to harvest the garden, she would have to wake her consort. Like all men, Father Sunbones would take counsel from his loins as much as from his thoughts. She held that dread day in abeyance as long as possible.

In the west of the garden was the plot where the souled ones grew. Each lay at sleeping ease upon a bed of soft leaves. Each was watered and cleaned by a sweet spring. These were Mother Mooneyes' special care, that the world would be populous and happy. There were men there in all their colors and shapes—aelfkin and dwerrowkin; nixie, pixie, and sprite; giant and troll—all the manifold imaginings of Mother Mooneyes' busy hands in the long shadows of the morning of the world.

Just as men had their sibs, so did Mother Mooneyes' children. Desire sported with Love and Understanding, the twins Truth and Mercy, Justice, Obedience, and all her sisters. Outside their windows along the lawns of the ivory halls, their brothers wrestled and fought and hunted each other with arrows tipped with sky-iron.

Watching the boys at their play, Desire had formed a lust for her brother Time. He was a likely lad, robust with all the years of the world on his broad shoulders. One day when Mother Mooneyes was about her travels in the heavens, Desire invited Time into her chambers.

"Brother, come, I have a game to show you," she said as they met upon the western steps. Desire licked her lips so that Time might not mistake her intent.

"Is it a manly game?" he asked, for while men are ruled by their loins, those loins have two small brains each no larger than an olive and thus do not think well.

Desire touched her breast and smiled. "The manliest of all." Surely he could not misunderstand.

"Then I shall invite my brothers!" Time declared. He turned to spread the word.

Desire grasped his arm and pulled him close, as she set her other hand upon his sex. "A private game of man and woman," she whispered in his ear.

At last Time came to understand what she wanted of him. He followed Desire to her chambers, but was so eager in his lust that he pushed aside both her shift and her needs with a sweep of his hand and spent himself in moments of careless thrusting. She cast him from her chamber with hard words, chasing her brother out to the western steps. There he fled laughing.

Desire's breasts were heavy with need, and her loins were hot with the quick touch of her brother Time. She took herself into the west of the garden, where the souled ones were couched in their rest, and there she lay with them one by one, male and female alike, to slake her appetites. Each smiled in their sleep as she quickened their sex. Each murmured their thanks and slipped into the pleasant dreams of lust to which we all are heir.

Finally Desire returned to the ivory halls. Though filled with seed and the scent of all the souled ones of the garden, her loins still quivered. She went beneath the earth to her father's bed of burning sand and there took the guise of her mother. Desire rode him harder than any mortal man could bear, making her use of his godly strength, so that Father Sunbones woke fully in the midst of their coupling. Thinking he saw his wife, Father Sunbones drew Desire closer and made her body his toy in all the ways that a woman can be used.

Mother Mooneyes came home to find much moaning in the west end of the garden, and giggling among her sons. She stalked quickly into her house, where Father Sunbones' radiance already painted the walls with dawn's orange glow. She found Desire coupled with Father Sunbones and in her wrath banished her daughter to her chambers for a year and day. Then Mother Mooneyes lay with Father Sunbones herself, to see if she could coax him back to sleep.

It was too late. Desire had woken the world. Men stirred in their lust, and Father Sunbones rose from his bed aflame with heat and leapt to the skies. Much that is ill in this world comes from those early awakenings, but perhaps the good also. Desire's daughters were born to her in her chambers, some for each of the races of the souled ones. She taught them all she knew—the lists of who had grown in the garden, the names and powers of her brothers and sisters, the constancy of Mother Mooneyes in her unvarying cycles—and sent them into the world to watch over the women of the souled races, whom she had mistakenly betrayed in the innocence of her lust.

Ever after, the goddesses of women made it their business to shelter females from the predations of men and turn male urges to their advantage. The marriage bond, when wrought well, can bind a man to a woman's bed. A coin spent for an hour's fancy can at the least sap his anger away. The choice to lie only in the company of other women is another comfort and safety. Always these goddesses watch over their shoulders, for there is ever an angry man or his god at the window. And so the temples of women have thick walls and heavy doors.

Books and cooking carried me through the winter, but the following spring, the Dancing Mistress found a much better way to occupy my time. Our nighttime runs around the courtyard had long since grown sure-footed and stretched sometimes into hours. She also had me climbing the pomegranate tree for time, to see how fast I could go and how much I could better my previous records. We danced along a low wooden bar she had brought into the practice room, along lines of cobbles in the courtyard, up and down the stairs until Mistress Tirelle shouted for us to stop ruining her house.

All of that was great fun, and took energy from me almost as fast as it gave back more. But one night she came with a leather satchel over her shoulder.

"Here," she said as we stood behind the tree, away from the sight of the Pomegranate Court itself.

I opened the satchel. Inside were several bundles of dark cloth.

"Climb the tree and place these within the branches. Hide them so no one looking from the ground or the balcony will easily spy them."

"From Mistress Tirelle?" I hid nothing, not even my bowel movements, from the duck woman. Only my thoughts were my own. Sometimes I doubted even that.

"Hide them from no one at all," said the Dancing Mistress. "No one and everyone."

I climbed. I hid them, for by now I knew this tree as well as I knew my own bedclothes. I paused and thought, then climbed down. "Whatever it is you intend, it cannot be for the evening when Mistress Tirelle looks out and awaits my return."

"No." Her teeth gleamed with a small smile.

"When, then?"

"You will know."

Then we ran awhile, with me tumbling through a roll just after I took every corner of the courtyard.

We ran every night that week, pushing me hard until my feet faltered and my breath burned. I fell into bed every evening wondering how I would know when to meet the Dancing Mistress and her mysterious dark cloths. I was smart enough not to fetch her bundles down during the day, when climbing the tree would earn me a beating. Our evening work outside was watched often enough that I did not even try to bring up the sense of the thing then.

When the riddle answered itself, I wondered at how slow I had been. As I was brewing a blackbark tea for Mistress Tirelle, I realized that I knew when to meet the Dancing Mistress. I crumbled some of the passionflower leaves into the infusion, to encourage the duck woman to sleep more heavily—we had once more been discussing the difference between savor, flavor, medicine, and poison. Then I drank a great quantity of spring water, so that the needs of my bladder would force me awake an hour or two after we retired.

That evening I received neither a beating nor a lecture. I lay in my bed until I could hear Mistress Tirelle's snoring—her breathing was loudest when she slept soundly. Too much danced in my head for sleep, and as planned, my need for the chamber pot caught up with me before my elusive dreams ever did.

Getting up, I did what was needed. I then slipped out onto the balcony and padded very quietly past Mistress Tirelle's door. She had set a line of bells at the head of the stairs, but I slipped over the rail and slid down the outside with my palms upon the banister.

Once on the porch below, I walked to the pomegranate tree and climbed. The bundles were where I had left them, of course. No one here besides me possessed the will or the means to climb the tree except for the Dancing Mistress herself. I gathered the cloth and slid back down to stand on the side of the trunk away from the Pomegranate Court.

Unfolding the bundles, I found leggings, a jacket, and a small bag that after a brief time I realized was a hood. They were cotton dyed black.

I pulled on the leggings, tucked my tunic in, and tugged the jacket on. The hood felt odd, but I pulled it over my head. I half expected the Dancing Mistress to step out of the shadows, but she did not. I waited a moment, feeling foolish, then began to run the circuit of the courtyard. Silence was my goal, and I moved quietly as I could. At each cornering, I took my tumble. I ran and ran under the starlight, for the moon was a dark coin already spent, though my legs and back ached.

When I rolled out of the tumble at the third corner, between the gate and the tackle box, the Dancing Mistress fell into step next to me. Her fur was dark in the starlight, and her face was deadly serious.

"Mistress," I said, speaking within my breaths. "You were right. I knew when to meet you."

The Dancing Mistress nodded. "Let me show you something new."

I followed her as she climbed the post at the west end of the porch. We gained the copper roof, then swarmed the bluestone wall beyond to the wide, flat rampart I'd seen from the top of the pomegranate tree.

The street was open below us. Very quiet even during the daylight, at this time of night, it was empty. A row of buildings stared back at me, windows like vacant eyes beneath the irregular peaks of their roofs, though a few glowed with the light of reason within. The great structures of the city lifted beyond, some gleaming copper, some dull tiles, some with turrets and other features I could not name, for I had not yet had a Mistress who would discuss with me architecture and the life of cities.

The path to freedom lay before me.

"May I go now?" I asked.

"You are too young," she said quietly. "Though your mind is sharp as any I've ever seen, and your beauty unmarred, you cannot make your way alone. Bide here, learn at our expense, but know that someday you will have a road if you need it. There may be different choices you will come to make."

"No, I do not think so. I will never choose to be grasped within the hand of another."

"Even birds build their nests together." She gathered me close for a long time; then we went below to put away the tools of my newfound stealth.

As the spring warmed, the exercises grew more strenuous. All of them. Mistress Leonie's textile arts were showing me things of which I'd never considered the possibility, such as the weaving of secret messages into the warp and weft of a courtier's cloak. Likewise Mistress Tirelle in the kitchen. Sometime during a month spent with the making of sauces, we reached a nearly amicable truce around the rhythms of the cooking—she still raged and threatened and beat me away from the fires, but we found a calm before them.

I was permitted to mount a horse, and taught the ways ladies rode, and something of the styles of men that I might judge the quality and training of a horseman. A new woman, Mistress Roxanne, brought boxes of rocks and gems and colored cards to begin my lessons in jewelry. She was thin, sly, and chattering.

As my reading improved, the selection of my books broadened. At the time, it seemed to me that the whole subject of books was haphazard, though later I understood the pattern Mistress Danae was applying to my reading. No recent history, nothing of the city of Copper Downs, and nothing whatsoever concerning the Duke, of whose name and very existence I had then heard only bare rumor.

The greatest effort was expended with the Dancing Mistress. She did not slack with me during the day—we walked through movements, poise, and balance. She brought a clockwork box on a little stand that marked the measures of a rhythm and trained me to its timing. Padded benches and hanging bars arrived for the practice room. We talked about the way my muscles and bones would grow over the next few years, and how making them strong now would help keep them strong later.

After that first period of evening runs, she never again came back early when Mistress Tirelle would know of her visit. Rather, on days before we were to make a late-night run, the Dancing Mistress would leave a scrap of dark cloth on the plain bench in the practice hall. Once Mistress Tirelle was sleeping soundly, I would slip outside in my gray wool wrap and climb the pomegranate tree to dress in my blacks. Without fail, when I descended she awaited me at the bottom. I handed the Dancing Mistress the scrap of cloth, and we would begin our work against the stones.

There was a great deal of running. I climbed, tumbled, fell, spun, leapt. We used the walkway capping the outer wall, measuring distances for me to cross without touching the stone. Before long, I became accustomed to my view of the city beyond, and wondered when and how I would see more.

"Why do we run atop the wall?" I asked her one night in the late spring, as the northern summer was beginning to unfold. The air even at that hour still remembered the warm hand of the sun. "Does the Factor not have guards?"

We spoke as we climbed, practicing finding the cracks in the sheathing stone of the courtyard walls.

"No one would dare breach the Factor's walls. Not even the most desperate, drunken petty thief."

"Still, we are visible from the street."

"No one without looks within. Even if they see us there, who are we? Who would they tell?"

"The Mistresses come and go."

"Have you ever seen a Mistress come or go at night? Besides me?"

I thought about that. "No—no, I have not."

"Consider that there might be great and terrible wards on these gates."

"So they cannot be passed, even by the Factor's friends?"

The Dancing Mistress laughed. "To be sure. Such a thing makes the guards lazy. As they are not permitted to gaze within the courts on pain of blindness followed by death, they do not watch what we do."

As Federo had said, except for him, I would know only women.

One night our run was different.

I dropped out of the tree freshly clad. My thighs ached from time spent on a strange horse that day. I was still too small to sit properly astride with any comfort. The Dancing Mistress stood there, her tail twitching as it emerged from a slit in her own blacks.

"Mistress," I said, bowing my head as I clasped my hands for permission to speak.

"You have the count of twenty to gain the walkway of the outer wall."

I ran, swift and light as she had trained me. There had been no fog or rainslick tonight, so I could move in safety. I did not bother with the stairs, both for pride and to avoid risk of waking Mistress Tirelle. Instead I scrambled up the wall where the east end of the Pomegranate Court house met the bluestone, then gained the copper roof, then made the last climb to the top.

My count was sixteen.

A moment later, the Dancing Mistress was with me. "Next time you will have the count of fifteen."

"Yes, Mistress."

She guided me to the outer wall and pointed that I should look over the edge. The street below was a drop of about forty feet.

"How would you make your way down?"

I thought a moment. "I might descend the outer wall, but I do not know if it is slick or rough, nor how well spaced the mortar joints are. Or I could fall, and try to slide along the stones as I descended. I do not think that would serve me well, as it is too far to let my body land in safety."

"Hmm."

I looked around. As I'd seen many times before, the walkway extended around the outer edge of the Factor's house. We had never left the borders of my own court before, even though nothing on the walkway barred me except the distance between one step and the next. "If I pass beyond the boundary of the Pomegranate Court, there may be another way."

Her voice dropped even lower, not so much a whisper as the shadow of one. "What will happen if you are found beyond the Pomegranate Court?"

"Mistress Tirelle would cut me, then turn me out for a tavern slave. The Factor has gone to a great deal of trouble to keep me bound here in quiet secrecy."

She did not answer. I stood awhile, feeling a sudden chill that was not of the night air. What were they making of me here? Except for Federo mentioning that I should be a lady, no one had said. What would the Dancing Mistress make of me? Something Mistress Tirelle, and therefore presumably both Federo and the Factor, did not want of me.

"I am not your tool," I whispered harshly, then sprinted east along the wall past the boundary of my life.

Federo returned to marvel at my height. "You have been growing while I was away," he said with an easy laugh.

By then I thought myself sophisticated. Some of the lessons about jewels and clothes had sunk deep within my thoughts. This man was my last connection to my father and Endurance, and the only person alive who could tell me exactly where I was born. He did not dress the part, though. Instead this day he was windblown and carefree, clad in strange belled pantaloons and a muslin shirt that fastened across the shoulder.

Not at all the respect my station was due.

"I grow," I told him. "And learn." *And count my bells, secret though they are.*

"Good." He bent his head, examining my face from an angle rather than turning my chin as he might once have done. "How much does she beat you?"

"Less so these days," I admitted. "I have found the lock to my tongue, and fight only when I must."

"Good. I was afraid your stubborn independence would lead you too deeply into trouble."

With those words, I remembered once again that Federo was not my friend. A friend would have cared for my fate, not whether my words caught too much trouble.

"How is your hunting and trapping, then?" I let my voice grow nasty, much the way Mistress Leonie did when her talk slipped from gowns to gossip.

Federo looked pained, and turned away. "It is more than you know, Girl."

I watched him walk away and did not feel sorry for a moment. This man had stolen me away from my life and family. What guilt was it on me that I hurt his heart for a moment? He would ride free, and I would remain here under the watchful eye and the hard hand of Mistress Tirelle.

Instead I closed my eyes and thought of the smell of rice paddies under the morning mist until the duck woman came to punish me for my insolence.

The next time the Dancing Mistress handed me the dark scrap during our daily exercises, I was ready for a night run. I wanted to show everyone how wrong they were, how shallow and evil they had been. Words were still my way out of this place, but if I could strike a few hard blows before I left the Pomegranate Court, my heart would be gladdened.

Dropping from the tree to the cobbles, I saw she was not there. I froze a moment on the fulcrum between panic and fear. Then I spotted her waiting for me at the top of the wall. I scrambled across the courtyard and up so quickly that the count would have been reset for me.

She watched me come, then caught me as I rushed toward her, spinning to throw me down. I rolled and fell, landing well enough, thanks to the training she had been giving me the past two years.

"What is it?" I hissed, regaining my feet.

"Are you too good for your friends?"

For the first time I realized how freely she and Federo must discuss me.

"No." My breathing was hard, and my rib twinged.

"Much is risked on you. I cannot imagine you should be grateful. I would not be, not in your place. But you could at the least be respectful."

"Of what? The risks taken by people who walk free each day?" I spat on the stones. "This slave girl does not sorrow for displeasing her owners."

The Dancing Mistress gave me a long silence in which to consider my own words. They were prideful, but pride was all I had. Everything else had been taken from me, stolen away over and over.

Finally she spoke: "I do not own you. Nor does Federo, or even Mistress Tirelle."

Taking a deep breath, I tried to find a voice that did not lash out with the sting I harbored in my heart. "No, the Factor owns me. You support his claim."

"You do not know, Girl."

"No, I do not." I glanced at the street below. Surely we had meant to finally climb down the wall tonight? Dreading that I might be giving up my only escape with my next words, I said, "I will not be yours, any more than I will be his."

The Dancing Mistress folded my hand around the scrap, which I still clutched. "Your choices are your own. When you are ready for me to come again, return this to me."

"When I am ready?" I repeated stupidly.

"When you are ready." Her face was lopsided with a mix of loss and anger. "Perhaps I will even come back then. As for now, fold away your blacks and climb into your bed. I will have no more of you for a time."

I climbed back down, slipping twice, and forgot myself to the extent that I went back to my sleeping room still wearing the Dancing Mistress' blacks, along with the soft leather shoes and gloves I always stored with them. When I tugged my gear off, I balled everything up, snuck to steal needles from the sitting room, then sewed it all into a little pillowcase I had been stitching with the design of pale flowers growing through a broken crown.

My heart was hard for the next weeks. I still had my daily lessons with the Dancing Mistress, but there was no warmth between us. She did not push me away or cause me to be punished, but neither did she embrace me nor spare me good words. A few times I thought I caught her studying me when she believed me too busy to notice, but that was her concern.

At the time, I thought we were done. Pride, like patience, can be taught. But as patience may be unlearned all at once in a hard moment, tenacious pride can be acquired in that same hot rush.

I had not lost my ability to stalk the future, and the villains who ruled my life. I had lost my ability to tell friend from foe.

Mistress Tirelle must have sensed that some break had occurred between me and my favorite teacher. She interrupted a long course of instruction on the mechanics of baking—leavening, flours, inclusions and exclusions to dough—to show me how we might make sweets. These were little crushed preparations of bitter almonds, oil-packed dates, and diced apples, which we rolled in sheets made of pastry and grape leaves. When they were fresh baked, I ladled pine honey over them to set up with the heat and a mixture of scents that made my mouth water unreasonably. We then experimented with sugar reductions, and how fanciful designs could be scribed on the sweetmeats with the appropriate flick of a spoon.

"You must know how someone is honored with the preparation of the final course," the duck woman told me. "A person can be insulted as well, in the subtleties of preparation. Food is a language."

I clasped my hands. She nodded.

"What of foreigners?" I asked. "Is their language of food known to us?"

My question earned me a suspicious glare. Mistress Tirelle had always been troubled that I had come from across the Storm Sea, as if the circumstances of my birth were somehow my doing. After a moment, she seemed to decide I was not making a subtle slight against her charter here in the Factor's house. "Sometimes a cook will trouble to learn a foreign way of eating, to show a bit of respect to a powerful merchant or prince." Her tiny smile ghost-danced across her face. "Remember, those from far away will never measure up to our standards. At need, we make allowances for them, but it is always a charity they should know enough to refuse."

My unintended criticism is returned fivefold. I never seemed to be in good standing with any of my Mistresses, for all that some were civil enough. Only the Dancing Mistress had treated me fairly. *Then she cast me off as well,* I thought.

I stepped away a moment to tend the sugar kettle, which served to hide the tears in my eyes.

"Girl."

Turning around, I looked at Mistress Tirelle, not even trying to swallow the misery that must have been naked on my face. To my good fortune, she seemed to believe her slight had cut me to the quick.

"We will be sending a fine bread out tomorrow." Her voice dropped. "To be *judged*." A strange, false smile drew her lips upward like dead men plucked reluctantly from the soil. "Think on what you will make that will reflect best on the Pomegranate Court."

I clasped my hands again. She frowned, but tipped her chin that I might speak.

"Judged by whom, Mistress?" I asked. "Against what?"

"What happens outside the walls of the Pomegranate Court is no concern of yours, Girl. We'll send your work out, and it will be judged."

The answer seemed clear enough to me. There was to be a competition among the courts of the Factor's house!

I swallowed my own answering smile. Several years in this place, and finally I could show my worth. I could only thank the sun there was not to be a riding competition. It might have been better for me if we were playing at tree climbing, those invisible girls and I, but this would do. This would do.

Early the next morning, I sifted through grades of flour and sugar in my thoughts. Duck eggs, for their richness, or quail's, for their delicacy? I was still considering inclusions in the bread, but a wash for the top seemed apropos. Coarse sugar and cardamom could be sprinkled to accent the loaf.

My washing went quickly, and my cotton shifts were ever my cotton shifts. We were approaching autumn, but I did not need a wrap yet, not even early in the morning. Heat and cold were almost the same to me now, except when my breath stung or I was required to protect my feet.

Out on the balcony I saw a mist swaddling our little courtyard. The pomegranate tree bulked strange in the poor light, its branches splayed like broken fingers. The air smelled of cold stone and the not-so-distant sea. My eyes strayed to the branches where my night running blacks should be. They were stored away now, and the Dancing Mistress' little scrap with them.

Baking was so much . . . less . . . than pushing myself in darkness. Would I rather be a girl who could make a pretty loaf to please a lord, or a girl who could gain a rooftop on a fifteen count unseen by those within the house?

Neither choice held a purpose, I realized. Mistress Tirelle had told me time and again I would not be expected to ply my arts. Only to know them very, very well.

A frightening question occurred to me: Were the Mistresses failed candidates? Perhaps Mistress Danae's knowledge of letters or Mistress Leonie's mastery of sewing and weaving were the result of a dozen years behind these bluestone walls before some defect or small rebellion had cast them out.

I wanted to go home. More than anything, I wanted my life back. But if somehow that never happened, I did *not* want to spend my years here teaching other girls lessons I'd learned under the blows of the sand-filled tube.

That brought to mind what I missed most about my night runs with the Dancing Mistress. Not the work, but having someone who would allow me to speak, and without reservation heed the words I spoke.

Then it's too bad for her that she used me ill!

The anger buoyed me. That emotion I put away to sustain me through the day, and headed downstairs to the great kitchen. I would not break my fast until Mistress Tirelle gave me permission to prepare the morning meal, but I could look over my spices and flours and bring my earlier thoughts closer to the oven.

This was the best day yet with Mistress Tirelle. We had a project, and my skills had grown strong enough to lead.

The Pomegranate Court had recently taken a delivery of a batch of exotic fruits, which I was told had been grown in a glass house that brought a little sliver of the southern sun to the Stone Coast. I chilled plantains on ice, then sliced the fruits thin and fried them with sesame seeds. The smell of that cooking was heavenly, for sesame improves almost everything. At the same time, I reduced guavas to a jelled paste into which I folded crushed almonds. That sweet-and-bitter combination made my mouth water as well.

For the crust, Mistress Tirelle and I made a very buttery dough, which I stretched and folded and stretched and folded, layering coarse sugar and thin-sliced almonds in at the last. The dough I cut into a dozen squares. I spread the guava paste within these, arranged the crisped plantains, then folded the dough over again. I topped each with a wash of quail's egg, more coarse sugar, a few grains of rock salt, and a scattering of sesame seeds. I placed a whole nut in the top of each so that they would bake up with a dent, into which I planned to place a slice of chilled plantain when the pastries were out and cool.

When completed, these little creations looked each as beautiful as anything Mistress Tirelle had ever made as a demonstration for me. She studied my work, sniffing and touching the pastries very lightly with a long spoon made of wood.

"Girl," she finally said. One of those elusive smiles crossed her face. "These might do. You reflect well on the Pomegranate Court."

I am the Pomegranate Court. I knew better than to speak, especially in the face of the only real praise she had ever offered me. Instead I nodded and answered with a smile of my own.

The day drove on in hard work with a brace of hounds, careful threading of a rug loom, exercises in the lettering and usages of the writ of the Saffron Tower far to the east, and all the sorts of things that fell to my lot. I did not have an hour with the Dancing Mistress, which I found odd. Much later, I realized she was never present when the Factor was in the house, but I missed her, then was irritated with myself for the missing.

We heard nothing that day. We heard nothing the next, either, though the Dancing Mistress was back. She had a new form to show me, a kicking dance from some islands in the Sunward Sea that involved two partners leaping past each other in a flowing lunge that crossed through the line where their eyes had met. I, of course, fell to the straw-padded floor a dozen times, bruising myself worse than I had on any night run. Just another round of small injuries for Mistress Tirelle to ignore, as if she had inflicted them herself.

Vengeance? A message? I wondered what it was she intended to tell me, then dismissed it. She would not get satisfaction from me. There were other proofs of my independence. Challenging the girls of the various courts at their games would be my triumph.

The day after, I stepped out of the sleeping room to a hard blow from the flat of Mistress Tirelle's hand. "Strip your shift," she demanded, slapping the sand-filled silk tube against her forearm.

Whatever had passed between us in the kitchen two days before was long gone, vanished within the bullying hatred that always intruded. She finally stopped the beating, breathing so heavily, it might have been a sob. "Your little baking experiment nearly got your tongue slit and you sold away," Mistress Tirelle growled in my ear. I smelled wine on her breath, and the stink of fear. "Only that idiot fop Federo spoke for you, and saved you."

I understood then that in saving me, Federo had saved her.

There was nothing to say, nothing to ask. I gripped the rail tight and let my legs shiver. Silence was my only armor as she resumed.

When she was finished, she slumped away, before leaning close again. Her hand gripped my shoulder so tightly that I knew I would have fingertip bruises there later. "One of the Factor's household became very sick from your almonds. Her lips burned and she could not breathe. They called it poisoning at first, until a maid spoke up that the woman had always taken ill from certain

nuts. Federo said you could not have known, and calmed the Factor's anger.
You are a very lucky girl, Girl."

After Mistress Tirelle left, I gathered my shift and slowly pulled it back over
my head. The greatest, strangest marvel of these people in the Factor's employ
was how they seemed to believe it was my luck to be beaten and abased by
them. As if they had longed to be stolen away and treated without mercy all the
days of their childhood.

Later that day, enduring my silent passes with the Dancing Mistress, I gave
her back her dark strip of cloth. She said nothing, made no sign she took my
meaning, but I knew. My muscles ached, and my legs shook. Still, I resolved
to stand firm.

That night I waited for Mistress Tirelle to go to sleep, thinking on how I
might strangle her in her bed, or smother her with a bolt of belled silk so that
her death cries chipped her teeth against the metal. A good thought, but the
Dancing Mistress had held the right of it when she told me to abide and
gather what power might come to me.

Eventually I rose and plucked the seams from my pillow. The blacks were
as I had left them, smelling of tree bark and my old sweat. I shook them out
and slid into them there in my sleeping room, heedless of whether I might be
caught. As I stepped onto the balcony, Mistress Tirelle groaned and stirred.

Freezing a moment, I stood silent as the mist that had once more risen outside. I heard a creaking, then the unmistakable ring of water being passed into
the night pot. Even my breath was noiseless, held close and shallow.

She groaned again, then fell heavily back into her bed. With one last, regretful thought for the blanket I could wrap around her face, I took hold of the
balcony rail and dropped to the stones below. No sense in risking the stairs.

I had miscalculated the effect of the muscle pains from the morning beating.
The fall went bad, and I wound up flat on the cobbles, breathing heavily. A moment later, the Dancing Mistress stood close above me, her small rounded ears
outlined against the sullen silver glow of the night sky.

She extended a hand. I brushed it away, still angry at her, at Mistress Tirelle,
at everyone. Most angry at myself, truly, but I did not want to examine that
thought too closely.

I found my feet and stood swaying. We eyed each other in the dark.

"First," I whispered, "you will show me how you threw me down on our last
night run. Then, when you are satisfied that I know how to see to my own
safety, we will cross the wall and you will take me out into the world."

"I do not accept orders from you." Her voice was quiet and calm, but I
could see her tail standing out almost straight.

"I, too, am done accepting orders." Even as I said the words, they surprised me. "I will stay because I choose to. I will beat these Mistresses at their own game, better them and all the girls of the other courts, and eventually best the Factor himself. When I choose to, I will walk free of this place."

Her silence answered me, though her tail flicked now instead of standing brush-straight.

"And you . . ." Even in the dark, I could feel myself blush. Surely my face was a beacon. "Will you teach me what I need to know to choose my path?" I stared down a moment. "P-please?"

"Hmm." Her tail curled. Then she extended her hand again. I took it in mine, clasping my other across it as if I were asking permission to hold her close. "Let us talk of throws and falls." She led me across the courtyard, over by the horse box, where we began to work on my center of mass.

Things were different after that. Mistress Tirelle remained angry, but also nervous in a strange way. Some edge had shifted with the little competition of foods. It was as if I had won a point, even while passing perilously close to a forfeit of the entire game.

I did not become reckless, but I became bolder. I was quicker to ask permission to speak. My questions were pointed, challenged my instructresses more. I tried to think several steps beyond what was being shown. Food was for eating, but it was also a weapon, a display, a competition, a threat, and a challenge. Dogs were servants and also in their strange way masters—their shallow, sharp-edged minds seeing the world through the brittle lens of scent and pack loyalty to bring news of old happenings to the ears of their handlers. The language of cloth and fold and pattern was focused tight as any logical discourse of Mennoes the Great or the Saffron Masters.

So I asked, and challenged, and turned, and was turned on in my time. My mind unfolded at this. Strangely, the beatings became more infrequent. I had found my stride and was running the course. As Mistress Balnea would say, the rider had laid free of the whip.

The Dancing Mistress showed me steps and falls a night each week for the entire turn of the moon. "This is the most basic of the work," she said. "To keep your center and find your feet and not be broken by the throw." I learned to see and step around the blows she launched, though she demurred from teaching me the strikes. "Another time. Later. We have years yet."

I had asked to be made safe for the streets. She was making me safe for the streets, no more than that. They would have nothing to fear from me.

Finally, on the turning of the next moon, we met again at the base of the pomegranate tree. Mist was in the air to bring the chill that would banish summer once again. I slid down in my blacks to find the Dancing Mistress waiting as always. We had not regained the comfort of our prior friendship, but reason and compassion had been restored between us. Though I hungered for more, that was enough for now.

She set a hand loosely on my shoulders. "Are you ready?"

"Yes." I grinned.

"No," she said with a much smaller smile. "You are not. But you are never ready—you merely go forward when the time comes."

"Then we should go forward."

"You have a ten count to top the wall."

I raced as though my legs were afire.

Later that night, I took out my imaginary silk and set another bell in place. Then I spent a long time telling myself a story in the words of my birth, of a girl who swam in ditches and was watched over by an ox named Endurance. Only he, with his great brown eyes and his endless patience, had not betrayed me by dying or sending me away. That my words were few and difficult pained me. I knew that the poverty of my own language was more to do with my age when Federo took me away than with any lack of the tongue itself, but still this was distressing.

I cried at that. The pillow swallowed my tears and eventually the racing of my mind as well.

A few days later, I was out in the courtyard with Mistress Tirelle, whipping off a blindfold to spot fruits on the moment. What had begun as a simple cruelty was almost a game between us now. As I moved to replace the blind after a good pick, the little man-gate inside our greater gate was opened from the other side.

We both looked to see Federo stepping through.

This day he was dressed as a gentleman-merchant of the city. Mistress Leonie had of late been training me to recognize the meaning of hats, feathers, scarves, and pins—how their array signified rank and station, and also how they changed over time so that no lesson remained true for long.

He had two peacock feathers sweeping crossed on the left from a violet felt snood. His suit was a matching violet cutaway in the same felt, over a cream-colored shirt buttoning on the left and a thin collar with three silver clasps. His trousers were a dark herringbone tweed seamed in the Altamian style with the tapered cuffs over dark purple leather half boots. A scarf so deeply blue that it was almost black had been thrown across his shoulder.

I thought he looked rather silly, for all that his attire spoke of his elevated station in the ranks of society.

"Hello, Girl." Federo then nodded briskly to Mistress Tirelle. "How fares the candidate?"

"My report will be made when time comes, sir." She shot me a glare for having the temerity to be present during this conversation.

Bowing my head, I waited to see what he wanted of me.

"I would speak to the girl a little while." His voice was pointed.

"You may find me in the sitting room." Mistress Tirelle waddled off with another expression that promised misfortune.

I clasped my hands as she clumped into the shadows of the porch. I had long understood that Federo and the Dancing Mistress must in some fashion be in league over me. I could not see what it came to—but then, so little of my life was clear.

He dropped to one knee. "You need to know that I will be gone awhile. Possibly a year or more."

I nodded.

"Speak, Girl. I am not one of your horrid Mistresses with a mousetrap mind and cheese for brains."

"Fare well," I said. Though I had no desire to be rude to him, facing him down, all I could think of was the day he had bought me away from Papa. Was he off to purchase more girls from their cradles?

"I hear you are learning well."

"The dancing is good."

His answering smile told me I had struck correctly. "Excellent. I can do little to help you, except to watch over your progress. Others . . . she . . . may do more."

"I regret my rudeness before."

His face grew long a moment, shadowed by memory. "Truth may be hard, but I do not call it rude." His hand touched my chin, as if he wished to tilt it back and examine me once more. "We each pace against the bars that cage us."

"Your cage is the world," I said in frustration, though I did not mean to strike for his heart.

"Everyone's cage is the world. Some worlds are smaller than others."

With that, he went to speak to Mistress Tirelle. I was left with the fruit picker and the last pomegranates of the season.

———

My next run with the Dancing Mistress set the tone for the work we did through the winter. That night she took me over the wall for the first time, to venture inside one of the Factor's empty houses. We slowly climbed dusty stairs, pausing every two or three to sweep behind us and spread the dust again. That was something of a revelation for me—under Mistress Tirelle, I had learned at great pain that dust was an enemy. Yet here it was a friend to conceal our trail.

Even at that pace, we gained the roof in less than ten minutes. Spread before me was a landscape of sloping tiles, chimney pots, small peaks with inset windows, pipes topped by little rain caps and vents. In short, terrain. Like the groves of home, except these trees were metal, wood, and brick.

"This is a rooftop," the Dancing Mistress said. "When we run here, there are many ways to be unlucky."

"Yes, Mistress."

"Even on the ramparts of the Factor's house, you are largely safe except from some accident of discovery. Here, a loose tile or a slick stone could easily send you to your death."

"Yes, Mistress."

She sighed. "At some point, when I judge you ready, we will begin jumping."

"Thank you." She seemed to be waiting for something, so I asked the question that hung in my mind. "If the danger is so great, why do we pursue this course?"

"So that you will be everything you can someday."

"You do not dance so with your other students."

"No, Girl. Almost never."

Her smile was sad. I could see it even in the darkness.

We began to walk the roofs of that block with whispered warnings and brief lectures through the moonlit dark. How to stand or slide on a slope, the virtues of ridgepoles, which chimneys to avoid and what were the tells that warned one off. The street had been complex with faces and odors and dangers of a certain kind. This place higher up was complex with angles and textures and dangers of a different kind.

When the ice came, the rooftops were a whole new variety of danger. Even the street was hard to cross with snow betraying our steps. We worked the quiet darkness of the blocks around the Factor's house all the winter, except for those weeks when the weather was too much to be out without catching some grippe that would betray me to Mistress Tirelle.

The duck woman noted the improvement in my spirits that season, though her response was to question me closely about whether one of the other Mistresses had been bringing in some forbidden material to my lessons. I would never tell the Dancing Mistress' secret, so I led her to watch Mistress Leonie, Mistress Danae, and all the others with increasing suspicion. It amused me to see these mean and bitter women snipe at each other all the more. They sniped at me as well, but at least they were not conspiring at my humiliation.

True to his word, Federo did not come back for over a year. I continued to grow, unfolding into a coltishness that I was repeatedly told I would not lose until my womanhood came upon me. I became clumsy, which distressed both the Dancing Mistress and me at our daily lessons in the practice room, and far more so on those nights when we sought to climb and run the high air.

Mistress Ellera arrived to teach me the arts of paint and charcoal, and together we discovered a gift that none had suspected in me. Quite soon I was fit to draw a most pleasing portrait in blacks and grays on a pinned-up sheet of foolscap. I amused myself sketching each of my Mistresses, until Mistress Tirelle forced me to stop. She seemed to fear a descent into cartoonish mockery. Still, Mistress Ellera's palette of colors and shades and brushes showed me a window into the world that I had never expected.

I nearly lost my privileges the week that all unthinking I produced a portrait of Endurance standing to his knees in a rice paddy. Mistress Tirelle somehow suspected the picture for what it was, but I lied convincingly enough to persuade her it was Prince Zahar's divine cow from one of Mistress Danae's storybooks.

Otherwise I endured the occasional beatings for forgotten lessons or talking out of turn. Life was as always.

Clumsy or not, the Dancing Mistress and I ran ever farther on the rooftops. We followed streets farther away from the Factor's house before climbing a shadowed drainpipe or a vine-wrapped trellis. The presence of people no longer gave me such worry and distraction, but I still preferred the high silences.

We met a few others up there. They were fellow skulkers and travelers for whom silence seemed the best greeting and fondest farewell. All of us shared a secret under the stars, and I loved those nights in the open air.

My existence had settled into a rhythm that suited me when I did not think too hard about the terms of my confinement. I still kept my imaginary belled silk close every night, but my burning sense of injustice had faded beneath the combination of almost-comfortable habit and the continuing discovery my lessons had become.

That summer, as I began to look time and again toward the gate to see if Federo would return, the Dancing Mistress made another change in my training. Instead of running the roofs, she brought me two blocks from the Factor's house and into a narrow court crowded with garbage and glint-eyed rats. Only a sliver of sky showed above. The odor was foul, and the refuse rustled strangely.

"We travel a different route tonight," she announced. "Can you tell me where?"

"Not above, and not within." I looked around, then at the metal grate beneath our feet. "Is there a below?"

"Below is the life of a city." Her smile flexed toward the feral. "Now you will learn the truth that lies beneath." She took up my hand. "Never stray away from me down there. Not for a step or a corner. You can always climb down off a roof if you become lost, and find the pavement and from there your way back. Below, there are no landmarks as you know them. Exits are rare and tend to be located in odd places."

Going from a rooftop block to another rooftop block involved much climbing up and down, which in turn required a great deal of waiting for a quiet moment and good shadow. I could immediately see the value of traveling Below, if there was a place in which we could make the run. "How far does it go?"

"Not everywhere," she admitted, "but more places than you might think. There are layers beneath this city."

"The water flows deeper?"

"The sewers are channeled to the harbor, for the most part. But mine galleries run beneath them, and warrens from some other age of history when people here felt a need to build below the surface."

I was fascinated.

We pried open the grate and looked down a mossy hole that smelled of mold. Rungs were set in the wall, just as slimed over as the bricks around them. "I will always go first," she told me. "Unless I instruct you different in the moment."

She slipped down the rungs. I followed. Having no way to pull the grate after me, I left it standing open.

At the bottom of the climb, there was a drop of eight or nine feet. The Dancing Mistress helped me land. I looked back up to see a circle of stars, as if the new moon had inverted itself to cover the entire night sky and left only a single disc of stars behind.

Water trickled. The mold smell had given way to damp stone and old rot. I could see nothing at all when I looked around me.

"You can step into a pit and never know it." Her voice was not where I had expected it to be, and I jumped in startlement.

"There are things that live down here. Most of them are nasty." The Dancing Mistress had moved again, again without my knowing. She walked in absolute silence. Her unpleasant little game made me realize how much I depended on my eyes.

"There is no light except that which you bring." This time I thought I heard her feet pad on stone.

"Close your eyes and spin round." Her hands touched my shoulders and moved me. I spun. Strangely, closing my eyes made it worse, as if my balance were partly anchored in what I saw even within the impenetrable dark.

She spun me around time and again, then eventually slipped me to a halt. "Take a step."

I tried, and collapsed. I bit back a cry of surprise and pain. The stone was slimed beneath my touch, and my knee felt as if I had wrenched it.

Something writhed beneath my hand. The squeak that left me was no more in my control than was my heartbeat.

"Do you want to be here?" the Dancing Mistress asked from close above me. Her breath was hot, and I thought I could see the faintest spots of gleam where her eyes were.

"Y-yes." I held on to my fear, clutching it close as I clutched my anger and sadness when I stood inside the Pomegranate Court. This was freedom, too— free as the starry skies over the roofs, and more so, for I could find direction and distance here. Mistress Tirelle would cut me and cast me out, if she did not kill me in the moment, for being down in this place.

Going underground was the greatest rebellion I knew. I needed the Dancing Mistress' hand in mine to pursue this. There were no walls Below except the bounds of tunnels. A cage the size of the city lay beneath the feet of my captors.

"Yes," I repeated. "I want to be here."

"Good," she said. "Never forget the fear, though. It will keep you alive down Below."

Fear doesn't keep me alive, I thought. *The account that I must repay keeps me alive.*

"Take this." The Dancing Mistress handed me a length of dark cloth.

We were out in the courtyard on a chilly night nine days after she'd taken me down beneath the grating. I was eager to run in the underworld again.

"What is this for?"

"Draw it over your eyes."

That was an old game. I had done the same with Mistress Tirelle often enough, when we worked on my seeing. I triple-folded the blind, then tied it around my head so that my eyes were fully obscured. Though I did not realize it, one of my most valuable lessons was about to begin.

"Now slowly walk from here to the horse box." Her grip tightened on my arm, until the claws caught at my skin. *"Slowly."*

She turned me toward the far wall of the courtyard and released me. I took a confident step and slammed my shin into the low wall around the pomegranate tree. I stumbled at that, and fell hands-first into the bark. Pain erupted in my forearms to match the throbbing ache in my shin. I swallowed back a shout, then stammered, "Y-you t-turned me!"

I could not keep the sense of betrayal from my voice.

"No," she said. "You turned yourself. All I did was point you wrong."

"That's not fair."

Her voice hissed close to my ear, just as it had down Below. "Is the world fair?"

"N-no."

"Then why should I be fair? You've lived here more than three years. You know every cobble of this court. How is it that you need my help here?"

I shook her off and stood still.

Her breathing dropped to near silence, just the faint passage of air. I extended my arms without moving, and looked with my ears.

It was silent, as always in the Factor's house. But the silence of a city is not an absence of noise, any more than there is silence wherever people live.

At home, when I was very small, the fire had crackled, even well after it died to coals and the eye-watering odor of ash. Endurance whuffled in his pen, his gut rumbling all night long. Animals yipped in the stands of trees. Night-hunting birds sang their prey songs.

Aboard *Fortune's Flight,* the sea had constantly slapped the hull. The boiler's kettle burbled below the deck, while someone always must run to orders or coil a line or call out a log reading, even in the deepest hours of the night.

Here the silence was eased by the faint snap of a fire within the house. The streets away from our walls echoed their noises. The wind eddied differently around the high, blank inner wall than it did rattling through the pomegranate branches or sliding along the copper-clad roof.

Now, concentrating, even the Dancing Mistress' breathing seemed loud.

I listened to the tree a moment, let its damp bark smell tell me where it was. I turned from there toward the faint echo of the breeze worrying at the inner wall. One slow step, to find the slight slope of the cobbles away from the pomegranate tree's little circle of stone-bounded soil. Another slow step to the flattening out. Vague echo of street noise behind me. Wall before me. I began to walk with deliberation, keeping my hands loose and ready for a fall should there be an unstable cobble or some trap left by my Mistress to teach me further wariness.

After twenty-two of my paces, I reached up to touch the inner wall. I'd *known* it was there. The horse box should be a few steps to my left. I listened for a while. The box made no noises, for it was fairly compact and had sat there through many seasons. It was too small to trap the slight breeze that blew. Memory would be my guide.

I turned, took a step, and slammed into it. The stones caught me hard as I fell flat.

She was above me a moment later. I heard the last of her footfalls, while her breath huffed close. "You know this place as well as you know the fingers of your own hand. Yet mark where you are right now. How will you fare below ground?"

"By following you, Mistress."

"By following me." She knelt—I could tell by the faint creak of her joints, the rustle of her tunic, and the change in the sense of warmth as the Dancing Mistress came closer to where I lay flat. "I see differently from you, Girl. Heat is almost a color to me. Underground tends to be very wet, and the water is not at all like dry stone in that view."

"I do not see heat, Mistress."

"No, you do not." She touched my shoulder. "There are other ways. It is always dangerous to show a light down there. Fire mixes poorly with bad airs in some tunnels. Other people and . . . things . . . will see you from an unfortunate distance. But there are small lights, coldfire scraped from a certain mold on the walls, that can aid you without substantial risk of betrayal."

"I understand the danger," I said.

"Good. Now run the courtyard with your blind."

I fell six or seven more times, but I ran the courtyard around the outer edge. I feared she would make me climb the wall, but she did not.

The next day, I wore an ankle-length skirt to hide the bruises. Mistress Tirelle said nothing, but I feared stripping it off for a beating, so I took care to be especially pleasant and tractable.

———

Federo came again shortly thereafter, somewhat beyond the conclusion of his promised year. Snow had not yet reached us, but frost was on the cobbles in the mornings. The pomegranate tree had shed the last of its leaves, while the wispy clouds that painted the highest part of the sky in winter had begun to make their appearance. I detested the cold, but the smell of the season always lent me energy.

When my captor appeared at the entrance to the upstairs sitting room, I threw myself into an embrace.

He caught me, staggered back, then pushed me to arm's length so that he might give me a good look. I was able to do the same for him.

I knew he saw a girl longer in leg and arm, but still far from a woman. They had never cut my hair here, except to trim the ends, so it reached below my waist. My clothes were better—I had made them myself, of course.

As for him, Federo looked worn. The year of his travel had added five to his face. I did not remember him with lines in his skin before. The bones of his cheeks were visible.

"Have you been ill?" I asked.

Behind me, Mistress Tirelle cleared her throat with a hard-edged rattle. I had spoken out of turn, though I knew she lacked the nerve to discipline me in front of Federo.

"A bit." He smiled, and I saw his teeth were yellow. "Sometimes foreign food does not agree with my digestion. I have heard good reports of you, Girl."

It took great restraint for me not to look at Mistress Tirelle. Her eyes bored into my back fiercely enough, I was certain.

"I shouldn't know, sir. I follow my lessons diligently and always mind the Mistresses." He saw my face, and knew that I meant more than Mistress Tirelle heard. I added, "I may never use these arts again."

"You are meant to be exquisite, not bent to labor. Even the labor of great ladies."

Mistress Tirelle cleared her throat once more. Federo had said too much.

"I will speak to your Mistress now," he said. "Go and play some instrument, should you have one."

My bone flute sat on a stand downstairs, though both Mistress Maglia and I despaired of me ever wringing more than the most vapid melody from it. "Yes, sir." Curtsying as I was being taught lately, I raced away.

The years unfolded. Federo passed in and out of my life on a schedule only he understood. Mistresses came and went, teaching me etiquette, lapidary, manners, fencing—that with the man's blade so I would know what I saw before me—as well as architecture, joinery, the management of funds, and the true secrets of how goods were made and sold into markets and great houses.

At the same time, the Dancing Mistress worked me on jumping and tumbling and stranger things—running in place on the back of a teetering chair, or swinging from a curtain rod, for example. We danced as well, for the benefit of Mistress Tirelle and any other listeners: the bright pavane and the lesser pavane, the women's sarabande and the season-wheel, the prince's step and the Graustown bend.

One night every week or two, we ran the rooftops, the underground, and occasionally the streets. As I grew taller, she coached me in changing my climbing technique, forcing me to continually relearn my falls. In the darkness Below, we practiced some of the throws and blocks she had used on me the night I had tried in earnest to fight her.

That was an education all over again. Meeting a sparring partner in the deepest dark, moving only by sound and breath and marking the placement of her feet. The bruises on my face we explained as we always had to Mistress Tirelle—from hard work in the practice room. The lie had become notably threadbare, but whatever fear the Dancing Mistress held for Mistress Tirelle had not lessened over the years.

That all flowed through Federo, of course. Over time, it had become very clear to me that they were training me for some vigorous task. Not to bring about violence, I thought, for all the lessons in the night were about movement and defense and survival, but some other purpose, which entailed the risk of being a target. This was layered within the work of making me a great lady of the Stone Coast.

Those lies were threadbare as well, though it might be fairer to call them avoidances. The Factor's women could hardly spend every waking hour sharpening my mind, then expect me not to use all the logic and experience being poured into me.

When things went well, I almost enjoyed myself. There is pleasure in painting, or reading a history, or making the numbers move to your command. Even today, I have not lost appreciation of those gifts.

Still, the hard hand was close behind. Except in the matter of the Dancing Mistress, I was watched as carefully as any virgin princess in a children's tale.

None of these women owed me love, or even respect. None of them thought of me as anything but a difficult task representing a risk of terrible failure.

Only the Dancing Mistress took me for who and what I was. Not what I had been—that was hidden to all but Federo, and he would never speak of it—but who the Girl was inside the forging they made of me.

To be fair, Mistress Tirelle in her strange way saw the reality of who I was. Somehow the fact that she could know something of my inner self, and still treat me with cruel caprice, was all the more hurtful.

I kept my imaginary belled silk under the invisible needle. My stories of the first days of life faded over time to mere images, though still sorted over in my mind as carefully as any box of prints brought to me by Mistress Danae or Mistress Ellera. The old words were there, but they seemed fewer and fewer with each passing season, slipping away in favor of the Petraean speech and all the knowledge that tongue brought flowing like a river through the days of my life.

One day I could not remember my name. I had been "Girl" for so long, and I had not heard my name since the first seasons of my life. This may seem incredible, but by then I had been in the Pomegranate Court for more than six years. No one had ever addressed me as anything but Girl. My true name, the secret name of my birth, I had not even whispered to myself in the quiet hours when I remembered my oldest stories.

Only the ox Endurance remained, his name as strong as he was. The other images from those first days—my grandmother and the bells of her funeral, the frogs in the ditches—they were strong, too. But both the words and names slipped away like sand beneath a tide.

I cried that night, so hard, the sound slipped from my mouth until I overheard Mistress Tirelle stirring. She made such noise that I found a way to stop. After a while, I realized her groaning had been purposeful. She had spared me another beating to leave me to my tears.

Was that a form of love?

The question made me cry all over again, this time in shuddering silence.

Over time, we began to meet people on the underground runs. Where the rooftop wanderers remained silent and separate as the distant stars, a different etiquette prevailed beneath the stones. When you crossed a path down Below, you paused a moment to let the other examine you.

"This is how we mark foes," the Dancing Mistress explained after one such passage. "Someone who does not pause is as good as raising a blade to you. The beasts and those lost to reason will not stop, and so you know them dangerous."

"What of friends?"

"There are no friends beneath the stones."

"Not even us?"

"That is for you to decide, Girl. I am who I am to you."

That remark I turned over in my head a long while.

Some months thereafter, the Dancing Mistress began to speak at certain of these meetings. "Mother Iron," she whispered one night.

The other nodded. She was a short woman, only a silhouette to my view, though her eyes gleamed with the faintest reflection of the coldfire in my hand. She had a misshaping about her, though I could not say if it was clothing, armor, or a strangeness of her body.

"This is my student," the Dancing Mistress said.

Mother Iron answered in words I did not understand. Her voice came from a deep place, as if she were much taller than she looked, with a chest the size of a horse—I had just then been studying more of the science of sounds and had acquired some sense of how they were made.

The Dancing Mistress answered in the same words. They both nodded, and Mother Iron stepped around us. She did not smell right at all, more like the bottom of the horse box beneath the leather and metal of the bits than any person I had met.

I knew better than to question there, but later I asked, "Who was that?"

"Mother Iron."

We were crouched behind the pomegranate tree as I took off my blacks.

"But what manner of person is she? What does she do there?"

"She is her own, and pursues her own affairs."

A spirit then, or some small god perhaps. "You will not answer me in this."

"No, Girl." The Dancing Mistress smiled in the moonlight. "But I will tell you this: Anyone you meet Below whose name I give you is not an enemy."

"No one is my friend."

"Yes. But should you find trouble, Mother Iron might attend. If it suits her. She is unlikely to further your woes with purpose."

"Thank you. I think."

"You are welcome," she said gravely.

There was one Below who was far more than a name heard once or twice a season. We first encountered him under the warmest night of the year, in the middle of the passage of the weak northern summer.

The Dancing Mistress had me doing falls in the dark those months. She would bid me stand in someplace fairly safe, then slip away with my coldfire in her hand. A minute or two later, I would hear her click her tongue, one click for each yard-length of the drop. I needed to summon the courage to step forward, find the edge, and jump blind.

The first time we tried that, with a fall of less than three feet, I was terrified. With practice, though it never became easy, the discipline grew reasonable. I learned how to trust a partner, and I learned how to fall in the dark.

"You can already find walls by listening for echoes," she told me. "We will work on you judging the depths the same way, once you know how to drop in safety."

A strange exercise, but I'd long since realized her greatest purpose lay in pushing me past my own limits, time after time.

I stood on a balcony, a low rail a foot before me, though I knew that only from experience. The Dancing Mistress clicked four times. A fall of about twelve feet. That would require a forward tuck with a full roll, before I landed four points down. No need for the bone shock of striking on two feet when hands could ease the blow. The shoes and gloves spared my skin on these exercises, but I could twist a joint or jam a forearm or leg easily enough. My size would help avoid this, while I was still young.

As I was bending for my leap, someone touched my shoulder. I yelped and dropped. The stone balustrade trapped me immediately. My attacker bent close.

I caught him in a wide-handed slap. He backed away with a sharply indrawn breath. I could hear the soft noises of the Dancing Mistress hurrying to my aid. A moment later, the gleam of coldfire appeared.

"Ho," she said softly.

"Unnh . . ." The stranger's voice was muffled. I realized he had a hand on his face, and that he was in fact male. "You boke my node!"

"This is the girl, Septio. Girl, this is Septio."

"Sir," I said cautiously. My tongue was tied with a strange fear. I found my feet, but kept the drop behind me close in mind. If they came to blows, or even sharp argument, I'd go over into the twelve feet of darkness to be out of his reach and away from whatever violence this newcomer and my Dancing Mistress might commit together.

"I didn't bead to scare you." His voice was still strange. I scented a new metal-salty tang. *So that's how it sounds when a man's nose fills with blood,* I thought.

The Dancing Mistress chuckled. "Septio is a Keeper of the Ways."

I heard it as a title. Titles had been much discussed lately in the Pomegranate Court. I wanted to ask for whom, and of what ways, but I chose silence. In my experience, others often would fill it.

"Do you know of the Ways, girl?" Septio asked, his voice clearing. I realized then from his tone that he was little older than I. A boy, down here in the dark alone.

The Dancing Mistress touched my shoulder. "She is from across the Storm Sea. What she has been taught is extensive, but very . . . focused. The Ways are distant from the agenda of her keepers."

I had never heard so much said directly about the purpose of my time at the Pomegranate Court

She squeezed my shoulder harder. "You may answer for yourself."

To speak to a stranger! "The sun is just as hot for every man," I told him in my own words, my old words. By then that was one of the few things I could remember Papa saying. Then in Petraean: "I do not know, sir. The Ways are hidden from me."

"The Ways are hidden from most people." He took his hand from his face and drew a deep, snuffling breath. "You have good reflexes."

He and the Dancing Mistress exchanged pleasantries; then Septio moved on into the quiet depths.

"That was a priest," I finally said.

"They are not generally so young."

I awoke one day to the sound of voices. A crowd of women had gathered in the courtyard. They were placing chairs and sorting themselves into positions in the dawn light. I had never seen so many people at once in the Pomegranate Court—four at the most before this morning. If not for the Dancing Mistress' night runs, I would not have seen more than four people at once in the years since Federo drove me here from *Fortune's Flight*.

Each one of the women wore a straight-backed gown in black satin, with ribbon cross-lacing bodices that were slashed to show gray silk beneath. A uniform of sorts, shared by the two dozen of them.

I dressed myself as well as my unprepared wardrobe allowed, then stepped outside to find Mistress Tirelle and Mistress Maglia awaiting me. Mistress Maglia was clothed to match the women below, while Mistress Tirelle was swathed as always.

"Come, Girl," Mistress Maglia said. That was unnecessary. I could see what was wanted. Besides, it had been years since I'd let my rebellious nature overcome my curiosity.

I followed the Mistress until she set me in a chair upon a small riser. That placed me high up overlooking the uniformed women. Instruments emerged from cases, carriers, and sacks. Polished brass gleamed in the morning sun. Mellow brown woods shone in the shape of a woman's curves. Narrow silver pipes trilled as their warming-up began.

What I had studied as harp and spinet and flute, one instrument at a time, was about to unfold before me in the array of a performance. I was entranced. My own skill with anything but voice was marginal at best. Mistress Maglia had given me only scraps and foretastes of this.

Mistress Tirelle stood close, stretching to speak with me. "You know the tests of the fruit. This is the same, with music."

Mistress Maglia came to my other ear. "They will play pieces of music known to you. The first is the overture to Grandieve's *Trollhattan Moods*. You will listen through. Then they will play again, but certain musicians will play flat or off-key or out of tempo from time to time. When you hear an error, you will point to the offender."

I clasped my hands. She nodded, a sharp smile on her dark-browed features. "When I am wrong, what will happen?"

"Mistress Tirelle will record your marks as given by me, and show you punishment later."

I had not taken a beating in almost two weeks. It seemed improbable that I would finish the day without a score of blows due to me.

When they played, the women made a beautiful sound, which twined around me. It must have been audible in the other courts as well. The Grandieve piece is a study of moods, a series of tone poems about an icy island in a high-walled northern bay. Mistress Ellera had once shown me a painting of Trollhattan. I could see the sound pictures even when I had first practiced it on my little flute.

The orchestra made it as big as the sky.

They played through perfectly, then fell silent. At direction from Mistress Maglia, they resumed. This time one of the horns was flat in the very first measure. I pointed, the woman nodded and set aside her instrument. Two bars later, a viol slipped out of key. I pointed again. Another nod, another instrument fell away.

By the end, I had missed but three. Only four players still carried the composition.

If not for the promised punishment, this would have been a fascinating exercise.

So began my training with others. All women, still, but more and more came to the Pomegranate Court in the months that followed. We staged dinner parties where some women wore black sashes to indicate they would be served and eat as men. Women in leather trousers marched in review as if they were a squad of guards. Women in pairs danced alongside me in the practice room or out in the court while a small orchestra played.

I was learning to be in the world. Somehow this was stranger and more frightening than being below the stones, because this was the truth of what they pushed me toward.

Every night I took my belled silk from its imaginary hiding place and added to it. These days, the bells were a cascade of tones and keys, different sounds that would have been a waterfall of music had such a thing ever existed in truth.

I loved it, for all that it was pure figment.

We found Septio again and again underground. Our paths crossed often enough that I soon realized it was not coincidence. He, like Federo, played a role in the silent conspiracy that wrapped my life with an invisible thread.

I did not strike him again, and Septio did not remind me of my first attack. Instead we took time to talk on occasion.

"The gods of Copper Downs are silent," he told me. "They are real as the gods of any other country. I could show you their beds and bodies, except that their power would strike you blind."

"It's not merely silence if one has been reduced to bones."

"Gods are different."

Later, the Dancing Mistress and I spoke quietly while taking turns climbing an ornate wall and dropping free.

"His god's name is Blackblood," she told me.

"Not someone you should want to invoke, I think."

"I do not know. Septio has common cause with others who disagree with the Duke of Copper Downs. Common cause does not mean common interests. My folk are not usually of significance to the gods of men, nor they to us."

There was small purpose in asking the Dancing Mistress of her gods. She said so little of her people that I did not even know their name for themselves. Any more than I knew hers. I understood, though, that they were quite concerned with paths and souls and some connection that ran between them one and all.

"I am human," I said quietly.

"You are not of this place. Your home has its own gods and spirits. They should be of importance to you."

"Tulpas," I said, the word leaping to memory. "Like the soul of a place, or of an action. An idea, I suppose."

"The tulpas concern you. This city belongs to Blackblood and his fellow sleepers."

"I am of this city now." That was a hateful thought, but true. "I can scarcely converse in the tongue of my birth, while in Petraean, I can speak learnedly on dozens of topics. The music of my people is unfamiliar to me, but I know what instruments they play here. Likewise the food, the clothing, the animals, the weapons. My roots may be in the fire-hot south, but Copper Downs has been grafted over me."

"Perhaps," she said after a little thought. "They have dozens of gods here in this city. Blackblood is only one. Each has their concerns, their purposes, their temples and priests."

"It is like a market, then. Each stallholder calls his wares, and people pray where the fruit is freshest."

There was something sad in the Dancing Mistress' voice as her slow reply came. "You may have the right of it, but you miss the deeper truth. Gods are real, just like people. Petty, noble; vicious, kind; strong, weak. But you do not buy one for an afternoon and then throw her away. Each god means something to this city. They are always *of* something, called at need, staying until after all have forgotten them." She sighed heavily. "So long as it is not I who calls them."

Federo came time and again. He would sample my cooking, examine my needlework, or watch me dance. We would talk, but I always held my tongue from the words that counted. Mistress Tirelle lurked in doorways to overhear what we spoke of. If I expressed myself too frankly, or was too bitter, there would be a beating later.

Where I wish now that I had found a different way in those years was that Federo and I never spoke in my words. We never used that language for which I then had no name. He knew some of the words, to be sure, for we had spoken thus when he first bought me away from Papa.

Mistress Tirelle treated the words as if they were an infection. Federo was no different.

My stories had slipped further and further away in the nights when I lay abed and thought on my earliest memories. What always lay close to mind was Endurance, and the sound of bells.

———

I never did see the other candidates, but just as Mistress Tirelle had me working amid larger groups of people and showing more of my accomplishments, so the competitions increased. Hardly a month went by that the Factor did not send for something of skill and purpose from his girls. Calligraphy, in the classic style brought from the lands of the Sunward Sea. A dance designed by me and taught to a servant who would deliver it to him, set to the same piece of music used by others. A hound to be trained at a certain trick in two weeks' time.

The outcomes of the competitions were not reported back to me. I could on occasion gauge by Mistress Tirelle's mood when news had come, but precisely what news, I had to guess.

The truth of the whole exercise had become plain to me. The Factor manufactured women in his house, great ladies for the nobles and high merchants of Copper Downs and perhaps the smaller courts along the Stone Coast. There was pride to be taken in what I learned and mastered, but it was still slavery.

When Mistress Cherlise came, I knew this all over again.

She interrupted my nights as no one but the Dancing Mistress had done. We sat and spoke of how my breasts were beginning to bud, how my blood would soon flow. She had little books in dark leather covers filled with pictures of men and women in the throes of passion. Mistress Cherlise showed me those as well, before explaining how I would more likely be used—hard, with no thought to any pleasure but my lord's, and required at all times to smile and beg and plead and always play the soft, warm hand.

The first time she put this forward, I grew angry. I held my emotion in check, but the Mistress must have seen it in my face.

"What do you think the lot of women is in this world, Girl?"

I spoke without thinking. "T-to choose, if nothing else."

"You were not born here. You came from somewhere, yes?"

I nodded.

"A small village, or a farm?"

"Yes."

"When you grew, what would your choices have been? A farmer, no doubt. A boy from some neighbor's land who would know nothing more of love than what he'd learned from his father's bullock. Here, at least, you know what can be, and how to achieve it if you get the chance. There, your choices would have been narrow as a thread, and brought you little joy at all."

They still would have been my *choices,* I thought. That was my oldest argument with myself, and one I somehow always seemed to lose.

She showed me much, undressing her own body with casualness so I could see how a nipple perked with chill or damp or a gentle touch, how the curve of a breast felt beneath the fingers. Likewise her sweetpocket below. We discussed shaving and hair, how the blood coursed in the monthly rhythm, and the different fluids that came with sex. Mistress Cherlise gave me certain exercises to perform deep within my body.

"These will not defend you from a beating, nor save you from a fall, but they will help you manage your choices and keep your body safe," she said.

We both lay naked on the bed in my sleeping chamber. "When will I need the exercises?"

"Soon. Always be ready."

She sat up, and I helped her into her smallclothes.

Soon? I was not quite twelve years of age. How soon could it be?

When I had first come here, I had barely been as tall as Mistress Tirelle's waist. Now I could see the wart at the top of her head. Almost nine years I had spent in the Pomegranate Court. Growing, learning, being remade time and time again. If not for the stolen freedom of the night lessons by the Dancing Mistress, I would have had nothing but the company of women within these bluestone walls that whole time.

My education was frighteningly detailed, but it was also incomplete. I could prepare ducklings Smagadine over cream and rice, and find a flaw in a polished silver service for forty-eight at a glance, but I had no idea how to buy a cabbage in the market, or where one might hire a cart. A great lady did not need to know everything. She needed to know only those things worthy of her attention.

There were other holes, as well. None of Mistress Danae's books had discussed anything of the recent history of Copper Downs. If not for meeting Septio in the underground, I would have had no idea of the city's gods, let alone that they had fallen silent for centuries. No one ever discussed the Duke within the walls of the Pomegranate Court, either. He was another thing I learned of only in my stolen moments outside.

Government, trade, the true state of affairs in the city: Why would these be hidden from a great lady in training? The Factor's house was wrapped in mysteries enclosed in a circle of questions spiraling in on itself until the truth was swallowed like a shadow under the noonday sun.

I had added more than three thousand bells to the silk I carried in my mind. The tally of the wrongs done to me had grown so lengthy that I'd long since set it aside in favor of my original resolve to rule these people through their words. My own words I kept more carefully since I'd realized how many of them I had lost.

I lay in my bed very early in a morning of my ninth autumn in the Pomegranate Court and wished perversely that my arms were long enough to massage my ankles while leaving my legs straight. Mistress Tirelle swept into my room in a flurry of huffing breath. Her rounded face was flushed dark and miserable, like one of our tree's fruits gone to rot, and she was sheened with sweat.

My first thought was for what I might have done to wrong her. My second was a nasty pleasure in her discomfort.

"Up, up, you lazy girl!" The duck woman slapped the covers away from me.

"I am—"

Her murderous glare cut my words short. "The Factor will be here within minutes. You must present yourself."

It was not even daylight outside. He could not be so early. No one of importance rose before the dawn. Not in any book or story or hallway gossip that I had ever heard.

I remained calm in the face of her fear. Sitting up, I stretched. "Then I will wear the green silk shift. And take the time to brush my hair with a few drops of oil."

The dress was the color of Federo's eyes. It also set off my dark brown skin to great advantage. As for my hair, though I kept it coiled and pinned most often, when it was down, it flowed to my thighs and drew admiring glances from many of the women who came to work with me. Mistress Cherlise was especially taken with it. She'd advised me not to let my hair grow ragged with neglect, and never forget the effect it would have on men.

"I'll not have you play the slut with him," Mistress Tirelle breathed, her fat face close to mine, though she now had to tilt her head back to meet my eye at such range.

"This will not be so different from Federo's visits." My voice held more confidence than my heart did. The Factor was no friend nor ally. Rather, he was the man who owned me in every part and piece. I was his more abjectly than any horse in his stables.

Old rage stirred.

Mistress Tirelle pinched my cheek hard. "You listen, Girl. The Factor is very different from that idiotic fop. We would none of us have food on our tables or beds at night if not for him. His word is your life. Federo . . ." She snorted, close as she ever came to laughing. "That man is a wastrel peacock who flies the world bargaining for future beauty."

He'd bargained for *my* beauty once. Every scrap I'd eaten since then had come from the Factor by courtesy of that idiotic fop. Once again, as she always did, Mistress Tirelle saw me as receiving great favor in this house. Such charity, to raise the little farmer girl to high estate.

The small rebellions of my thoughts were no matter. We launched into a flurry of activity. First I must be washed clean, though I always kept myself fair. Especially after the Dancing Mistress' night runs, though it had been nine days since my last such. Mistress Tirelle used cotton cloths pressed into a bowl of rose water to lave my back, then set me to wiping my arms and chest and lower body while she piled my hair.

"You do not know," she whispered fiercely. "I have tried every minute of these years to make you ready. You do not know, Girl."

You could have told me what I do not know, I thought, but I said nothing. She would not beat me immediately before the Factor arrived, but there were always later days. Mistress Tirelle never forgot an infraction. She also cultivated a perfect recall of any perceived slight to her dignity.

So we worked quickly at the efforts of beauty. My hair was let loose, oiled, and brushed as swiftly as we could. I had not yet been judged ready for the scented waters and alcohols used by women full grown, but Mistress Tirelle outlined my eyes in dark kohl and touched my face very lightly with brushes from the paint pots. She traced my lips with dyes, and checked my teeth for untoward stains or flecks of last night's dinner. Then we folded me into the shift I'd tailored from a bolt of green lawn cloth. Under the instruction of Mistress Leonie, I had sewn it with a hint of bodice to signal the change that was already on its way. My painted face and the cut of my clothing would lead where my body had yet to go.

Mistress Tirelle muttered and cursed as she worked to ready me for the Factor's inspection. I submitted to her attentions. The soft touches and momentary efforts at arranging this and that were as close as she ever came to treating me with tenderness. In some strange way, we were family to one another. She had been as much a prisoner of the Pomegranate Court as I, locked within these stone walls just as I had been all these years. I'd never asked if she'd loved a man or borne a child or found a life somewhere else. I'd just accepted all the days she had given me, along with the lectures, the punishments, and the odd bits of joy.

What else was there to do?

I tried to imagine Mistress Tirelle wrapped in bells, atop Endurance's back for the slow, hot trip to the temple platforms and the union of her soul with the wide world. I could not envision this terrible old woman following the ways of my grandmother.

Here in this city of silent gods with a stranger on the throne, who was there for her to follow? The Factor, perhaps. He was certainly the focus of her fear. Perhaps he was the focus of Mistress Tirelle's faith as well.

Seeing her under the brassy sun of my birth was too much to contemplate. I could not bring the image full-formed to mind, but a smile slipped unbidden upon my lips.

"Do not smirk at the Factor," Mistress Tirelle said with a growl. She stood me and turned me, checking me in the light of my candles and lanterns. "You will not shame us," she added. "Your life has no greater moment than this."

I could make no answer that would not provoke far greater conflict, so I held my tongue yet again. She propelled me out the door of my sleeping chamber to the porch. I walked ahead of Mistress Tirelle down the stairs. She followed, and retreated to the deeper shadows of the downstairs sitting room. "You will await him by the tree," she whispered from her hiding place.

The pomegranate sheltered me in the dawn's pallid light. The sky above glowed pearlescent, some combination of mist and cloud leaching the heavens of their color in favor of a generic, glossy beauty. It had not dawned cold, but still the air had enough of a chill to raise bumps along my arm. The tree was heavy with fruit. I had already spotted enough to fill both a good basket and a beggar's basket from the pickings on the branch.

A solitary fruit lay windfall on the cobbles, out of Mistress Tirelle's view, about where the Dancing Mistress would usually stand to meet me for our night runs. I looked at the sad deflation of its curve, deformed in striking the ground.

That was me, fallen away from my roots. Except I hadn't been left to lie on the cobbles. I'd come across the sea as smartly as any fruit carried to the kitchen, and been dressed here for the pleasure of a great man.

Here I had come nearly the full circle round. Perhaps the Factor would take me to the harbor and we would board *Fortune's Flight* for a trip across the sea to the hot land of my birth. Clad in white, picking up bells as I walked along the road that ran over the highlands from that small fishing port, I would return to my father on the arm of the Factor as he smiled and reported my great progress.

Even in the momentary fantasy, though I could remember the brown eyes of the ox as clearly as if Endurance stood before me even now, the only image I could bring to mind of my father was a dark-haired man with skin the color of my own hurrying away through the rice paddies as Federo tugged at my hand.

He had never looked back at me. I had never stopped looking back at him.

The past yawned behind me like one of the pits underground, threatening

to swallow my sense of myself, my purpose so carefully crafted in this imprisoned life.

Then my thoughts were torn away by the screeching of the gate. Both great
doors were thrown open, as was done only for delivery wagons or the very rare
carriage. Horses stamped and snorted as they raced into the courtyard in a
jingle of harness under the small-voiced yips and calls of their riders: soldiers in
tall leather boots that gleamed like roach's wings, their uniforms rough with
wear but still elegant and carefully straight. Each rider was blindfolded that he
not see me, but they carried swords and spears aplenty despite that handicap.

A coach followed the soldiers, rattling toward me to creak to a stop beneath
the pomegranate tree. Its glossy black body swayed slightly on the leather and
iron straps of its suspension. No sigil or heraldry was blazoned upon the door.
The coachmen were blindfolded, too, and seemed less at ease than their escort.

Nothing happened for a time. No motion, no voice or sound from the
darkened windows of the carriage. The door did not open.

The man within owned me, owned my life. By his will, Federo had first
taken me from the hot lands of the sun and brought me here to the miserable
precincts of the Stone Coast. My hands tensed in patterns the Dancing Mistress had taught me, but I forced them to loosen.

Patience was always the greatest lesson of the Pomegranate Court, the same
patience that the sky taught to the very stones of the soil. I waited, wondering.

Surely I deserved a word from this man. The entire flow of my life had
been directed toward this moment, toward his hands.

Then the door handle of the carriage turned. It creaked. For a long second,
I would have given everything that was mine to give to be anywhere else.

The door swung open.

When the Factor stepped from his coach, my first thought was surprise that
he appeared so ordinary. He was a man of middling height dressed in a dark
morning suit of a classic cut, velvet lapels over a coarser cloth, with low quarter boots folded over at the ankle. His hair was brown, his skin had the sun-
seared summer ruddiness of so many of his Stone Coast countrymen, his eyes
were a strange gray flecked with gold. He'd run to fat in the middle and on his
cheeks. Pipeleaf spilled down his ruffled silk shirt. He came so close to me, I
could smell the oils in his hair, the ambergris-and-attar of his perfume. There
was no scent of sweat at all.

He possessed a presence such as I had never really believed a person could
have. Like a dark prince in the stories I'd read, the Factor filled all the space in

front of me and around me as if he owned the world and I were some small intrusion. The breeze stilled at his appearance. The grackles and jays at their morning chatter on the rooftops stilled and froze, until one fled. The rest followed in a panicked rush of wings.

For a moment, the sun seemed to stutter in its passage through the sky.

He studied me. His face was impassive. I wondered if I should have curtsied, or otherwise presented myself.

The calculation in his eyes told me that I was no more of a person to him than the carriage behind his back.

This man is reviewing his investment. He is not meeting a woman. But he will someday.

Here was the true architect of all my troubles in this life. This man's hand had tugged Federo's strings and pushed at the invisible stick that penetrated Mistress Tirelle from arse to scalp.

Then he took my chin in his hand and tilted my head back and forth. He viewed the angles and planes of my face a moment. Releasing me without pain, he swept my hair away from my ears and inspected them. Taking first one hand then the other, he spread my fingers, checked their length, then examined each nail in turn. He walked around me twice before stopping behind me.

A horse nickered. Two dozen men breathed loud, though I looked at none of them. Never had our eyes met. I continued to be nothing to him. I began to wonder what the Factor was about back there when he tore my green shift away.

Cold plucked at my skin, raising pimples all along my back. Shivering, my joints ached in the chill, and tears rose sudden and unexpected in my eyes. To the Factor I wasn't even an investment. I was *livestock*.

After a miserable time naked in the wind, I felt his fingers test the softness of my waist, then the firmness of my buttocks. He walked around me once more to gaze at the buds of my breasts and down to where my legs met my body.

The Factor nodded to Mistress Tirelle in the shadows behind me. He stepped to his coach, then turned back to finally meet my eyes.

My tears had been whisked away by the wind. In their place, a stinging tremble remained, which I knew would show as a redness should he choose to reach toward me and spread my eyelids back for inspection. Within, I was torn between anger and deep embarrassment. I had been masterfully trained to conceal both emotions, and so I did. I pretended the shivering in my body was the wind's chill.

As he looked at me, I returned the stare. Something in his gaze made me think of the lifeless gray eye of the ocean leviathan that had nearly taken my life off the shores of my home.

Here was the root of his power, or at least a lens to peer within it. The Factor's soulless eyes were no more alive than the sea monster's had been—filmy, quiescent. Dead.

My teeth ached as my breath shuddered in my chest. The Factor didn't seem to breathe at all, something I realized only when I saw him inhale.

"Emerald," he said, clearly and distinctly.

Then he was gone in a swirl of horses and men and clattering weapons. Even blindfolded, the guards circled with a strange precision, yipping and whistling to mark their places and guide their mounts. They moved like water gyring down a drain. Some men went through the gate first with weapons high. The carriage followed, then the rest of the men.

In a moment, they were gone as if they'd never been present. Only a few mounds of steaming dung marked the passage of the soldiers and their horses. That and the turmoil within my heart.

After a while, Mistress Tirelle waddled out to me. I heard her steps stumping on the cobbles of the courtyard before she rounded the pomegranate tree to look me over. Her face was bent into her almost-smile. She appeared nearly pleased.

"Well, Emerald, you passed."

"Emerald." I tried the word in my mouth as if it were a name. Girl had been a name that meant nothing, a description only. He had named me Emerald to mark me as a precious possession, no more.

In the language of my birth, I did not know the word for *emerald.* I determined that I would use that tongue to call myself Green. That was as close as I could come, and it was a word that belonged to me rather than to these maggot people. The Factor's precious belongings I would mock with the profane infection of my own tongue.

This was also the greatest change that had come upon me since Federo had met my father at the edge of the rice paddies. I looked into Mistress Tirelle's eyes and found all unexpected a strange species of sympathy there. "What becomes of me now?"

Her face wrinkled in thought a moment. Surely she knew the answer, and was just picking through the secrets she thought might be fit to tell me now that I had a name and standing in the Factor's dead, dead eyes.

"That depends on whether the Duke fancies a new consort within the next two years or so." She poked me in the chest. Her rough nail snagged at my bare skin. "Otherwise you'll fetch a spice trader's ransom anywhere along the Stone Coast."

Those words chilled my already heavy heart so much, I could not hide the shiver that crawled along my spine. Somehow I had thought myself in waiting for the Factor, or a great house here in Copper Downs. I had long known that this blue-walled house manufactured women fit for thrones, but I'd never fully considered what it meant to me, for who I was. For what the Dancing Mistress had once described as the power I might someday hope to grasp hold of.

Federo had not bought me for the Factor. Not for the man, at any rate. Federo had bought me for a market. Meat with two legs and deep eyes and a face and body on which he'd wagered years and untold wealth in hopes I would grow to beauty. Salable, brokerable beauty.

Federo had bought me for meat, and my father had sold me for a whore.

Words, I told myself. These were all words. The maggot people of the Stone Coast lived and died by their words. I'd known this from the first. "Emerald" marked me as a jewel in the Factor's case. Nothing more, nothing less.

I blinked away the sting of some new emotion I could not yet put a name to, and followed Mistress Tirelle back to the rooms that boxed my life.

There were no lessons that day. No Mistresses, no practicing, no drills or dances or calligraphy or punishment or anything. This was the first idle time I'd experienced in all the years since I'd come to the Pomegranate Court.

I sat before the hearth in the downstairs sitting room and wandered through my memories. Endurance, the frogs in their ditches, my grandmother's face, her bells still jingling with every step of the ox. I turned the imaginary silk over in my mind, counting the days.

Nothing helped. I was overwhelmed by the bitterness in finally reaching a true understanding of what I'd known all along: I was nothing. No person lived behind Girl, Emerald, Green—whoever I might pretend to be.

I found myself wishing my instructresses had come. The snappish ill will of Mistress Leonie would have given me some focus for the rising of my discontent. Mistress Danae would have distracted me. The Dancing Mistress would have set me through paces to draw the energy forth.

Of course, I could step to the practice room or pick up a book or sit myself before the spinet. I did not need a Mistress to tell me to do those things. It was just that nothing mattered.

In time, I noticed the shadows had moved across the floor. A plate was laid next to me, with slices of bread and cheese upon it. Mistress Tirelle had come, then. Did we speak? I wondered.

I could not see how that mattered.

Darkness eventually stole into the room. No one had eaten the bread or cheese. Both had gone stale. My bladder finally moved me from the chair. I stumbled out to find a chamber pot.

Mistress Tirelle sat before the door. She was almost lost within the shadows.

"Emerald." Her voice was soft. "Tomorrow your days begin again as always."

"I think not." I did not bother to ask permission to speak. If she wished to take after me with her stupid tube, I would feed her the sand, and follow it with the silk.

"Nothing has changed."

"Everything has changed." I pushed past her to spend a little time alone in the privy.

I emerged with my hunger reawakened to find Mistress Tirelle awaiting me. She seemed almost sad in the darkening shadows of evening.

"When a candidate is given a name by the Factor, that is the signal honor which declares he has found her fit."

"Who is *he* to find *me* fit?" Rage crept into my voice.

"He is master to us all, and answers only to the Duke." Her own voice hardened. "Sit down and listen."

Almost a decade's worth of habit sat me down quickly enough.

"The Duke is all in this city. We are not permitted to instruct the candidates in the recent history of our times, but you will learn." She glanced around, then back at me. "His eyes and ears are everywhere. He was on the throne long before my grandmother was born, and he will be on the throne long after my grandchildren grow old."

I was briefly distracted by the thought of Mistress Tirelle having children and grandchildren. The flare of interest died within the gloom of my thoughts as quickly as it had risen.

"He is everything to us, forever," she went on. "To be raised up as his consort is an honor beyond measure. The daughters of the greatest houses would cheerfully slay their lovers and their chambermaids alike to stand where you do today."

I will trade them freely without the need for murder, I thought.

"So you listen, little Emerald. We have a year or two left with you at most. If that. Once your flow begins, you will be beddable. At the price you command, you will be bedded. Spread wide and smile sweetly, and your life will be very good for decades to come. Turn your shoulder and raise that pride I've never been able to erase from your spirit, and you can still be cut and turned out like any servant girl who fails to give satisfaction."

She patted me on the shoulder and walked out to leave me alone in the darkness, contemplating the price and purpose of my beauty.

The next months went by in an uneasy peace. My lessons continued, but they were more for practice than for further education. The Factor did not return, which suited me just fine. Neither did Federo visit in that period. My feelings about his absence were more ambiguous.

He'd taken me away once. In quiet moments, I found myself daydreaming that he might take me away again. Given that Federo was the Factor's man through and through, I knew those for hollow, girlish hopes.

It was the name Emerald that stuck in my ears like a needle in my finger. Every time Mistress Tirelle uttered that word, my blood ran hot. By then, I was old enough to have a care for how well I could conceal my feelings, at least most of the time, but she must have seen the anger.

What was different now was that my tormentor turned away more often than not.

It finally dawned on me that she was finished with me. We awaited only the onset of my flow, or the whim of the Factor and his master the Duke, for me to leave the Pomegranate Court and some other girl-child to arrive through that barred gate.

That thought brought a special terror of its own. A part of me wanted to stay here in the hated center of my universe.

Was I safer within these walls or without?

The answer, of course, was that I was safe nowhere at all.

Even the Dancing Mistress seemed to be marking time with me. We ran familiar routes, worked on the same flips and falls and kick-steps as always. She was no better than Mistress Tirelle in her waiting.

"I don't want my name," I told her one night as we ran the Eggcorn Gallery, well west of the Factor's house. I hated the truculence in my voice, but somehow couldn't change the tone.

"Girl." Her voice carried a tired weight. "A name is like a mask. You can wear it for a day, a season, or a lifetime, then put it aside at need."

In truth, she had not once referred to me as Emerald since the day the Factor had dubbed me so. Somehow that didn't make me feel better.

"What do you know of names?" I demanded angrily. "You don't even *have* one."

The Dancing Mistress broke her stride. Her eyes were black-shadowed from the faint glow of the coldfire in my hand as she stared at me. In that moment, I knew I had pushed her too hard, as I had done a few years ago over the matter of Federo. I was suddenly desperate that she not leave me now as she had then.

"I am not your enemy, Girl." I could almost hear her claws flexing. "You might do me the courtesy of recalling that."

Bowing my head in the dark, I forced an apology between my teeth. "I am sorry, Mistress. Everything since the Factor's visit has been too out of sorts."

She turned and resumed her run. I sprinted after, stumbling in my first steps at a strange twinge in my groin. I was not in the habit of faltering, but pride kept me from saying anything. I supposed anger kept her from answering.

That, and she knew well enough what was happening to me. Teaching girls was her business, after all, and every girl becomes a woman in her time.

Far too soon, my monthlies came upon me. The twinges in my back had been a warning, recurring at irregular intervals for a number of weeks. One day cooking with Mistress Tirelle in the great kitchen—we were working over a brawn terrine—my stomach seemed to flip over on me. Without any warning, I bent double and spewed my breakfast on the tiled floor.

Instead of raising her hand to me, Mistress Tirelle smiled and sent me to clean myself. When I lay down afterwards, my nausea returned. I had to work to hold my stomach behind my teeth.

In time, I was forced to roll to my knees on the cold floor, spewing. My mouth stung; I loosed a bit of my bladder. This disgusted me until at a furtive touch I realized there was blood trickling down there.

Mistress Cherlise will be proud of me now, I thought. *I am beddable at last.* I tried to ignore what this would mean for me in the Duke's eyes.

Soon enough, Mistress Tirelle brought me cool water and cloths.

I had never seen her beam so.

That night I stared out my door at the moonlight. The yard of the Pomegranate Court was silvered like a jewelsmith's dream. I was to be Emerald, a jewel in the Duke's box, placed in a glorious setting to be admired for twoscore seasons before being allowed to fade to some tower apartment with a few aging servants.

The histories Mistress Danae had given me to read were clear enough concerning the fate of unwanted wives and lemans, especially those of low birth.

All that time between now and that end would be only a blink of an eye, once it had passed. There would be nothing for me. Nothing.

The moonlight was beautiful, but I resolved that I would not be a jewel. No Emerald, I, to be sold in the market of women at the Duke's command.

I wondered what it was that Endurance would have done. The question was beyond pointless. The ox was property. Papa could drive him or slit his throat and have him dressed for meat.

They could slit my throat, too. Mistress Tirelle had made that threat to me often enough, though I suppose she meant more to notch my ears or fork my tongue when she said I could be cut and turned out.

What market is there for great ladies of ruined beauty and broken spirit?

I did not care. They would never render me into such a beautiful array of meat. I was more than these people, better than them. Even the kind ones, such as Mistress Cherlise, were molding me to the Factor's will. I was merely a thing to any of them, a means to advance a purpose. My allies, the Dancing Mistress and Federo, wanted me for their own purposes only instead of the Factor's. Whatever petty plot occupied their hours was no concern of mine.

There was no way I would be a toy for the ageless Duke, used for a few decades then tossed aside. The daughters of the great houses could have him.

I slipped from my bed and down to the great kitchen. There I had learned to cook with saffron and vanilla and other spices worth far more than their weight in gold. What would we have had at home, Papa and I? A little salt, and some dried peppers from bushes that grew at the edge of the trees. Salt we had here as well, along with parsley and other common pot herbs.

We also had a drawer full of knives.

Much of what had been kept from me early on had been added in the growth of trust. The strange trust between master and slave, jailor and prisoner; but still it was a species of trust that had stood between me and Mistress Tirelle.

I found the small, sharp cutter I normally used to separate meat from bone. The blade was already well honed. No need to risk a noise to set an edge now. Instead I went outside to sit beneath the pomegranate tree in the failing moonlight and stare at the blade I had taken up in my hand.

The Factor had named me Emerald. Marked by beauty, trained to grace. Certainly this blue-walled prison was far more comfortable than the hut of my youth. "I miss my belled silk and my father's white ox," I whispered to the blade. There was so much that I longed for—the water snakes and the hot winds and the silly lizards pushing themselves always closer to the brassy sun with their forelegs, as if they could ever reach its heavy fire.

Miss those though I might, I could no more throw away my years of training here in the Factor's house than I could throw away time itself. Federo had taken me away from what was mine, while the Factor had made me into a creature of the Duke of Copper Downs.

I was no ox, nor carriage, nor cart horse. I was no animal nor thing. I could escape this place easily enough by climbing the walls as the Dancing Mistress had shown me, but I was valuable. My grace and beauty and training were the work of years by dozens of women in the Factor's employ. They would hunt for me, and they would find me. Doubtless his blindfolded guards could ride across the leagues to wherever I hid. Doubtless the Duke would ask after his new-grown playpretty, and the entire city of Copper Downs would try to make an answer.

As I was, I was worth far too much for the Factor ever to let slip through his grasp. I could not throw away those years or the knowledge they had brought me. With this blade in my hand, however, I could throw away my beauty.

I will show them whose spirit will break first.

Endurance's brown eyes glinted in the dark as I reached to slash my right cheek. The pain was sharp and terrible, but I had stood through a lifetime of beatings without crying out. Then my left, echoing and balancing the first hurt I had done myself. I reached back and cut a single deep notch in the curve of each of my ears.

"*I am Green,*" I shouted at the moon in the language of my birth. Blood coursed warm and sharp-scented down my neck to tickle at my shoulders. "*Green!*" I screamed again, then began sobbing into the night.

Mistress Tirelle came following the racket I had made and found me bleeding down the white cotton of my sleeping shift.

When she realized what I had done, she shrieked. I broke her neck with a kick the Dancing Mistress had taught me, a flowing spin that sent the duck woman's chin hard to the right with a snap that I felt down in my bones. She gurgled once, then slumped to the ground.

That was my first killing, amid rage and grief and confusion.

In some ways, Mistress Tirelle is the death I will always remember best. Her constant presence was as close as I'd known to love in all my days since being taken from Papa. She had held me at the center of her life. I repaid her with murder. Not even a shred of dignity, either, though death is rarely dignified. The dying generally do let go of whatever is within their bodies. I sometimes think the gods mean us to leave the world in a filthy state to remind us that we are made of dust and water.

I told myself then that though I hated Mistress Tirelle, I had not meant to kill her. That was not true, of course. My Dancing Mistress had taught me to kick. I had accepted her lessons. The responsibility was mine.

Mistress Tirelle's blank eyes were already fogged. I scrambled up the pomegranate tree to fetch my running blacks. I missed my footing twice, but found them where they should have been. Back down on the ground, I stripped out of my bloody shift and dropped it over the duck woman's face. Swiftly I tugged on the dark clothes.

No time now, I told myself, except to keep moving. Cut or uncut, they would hunt me, but I was my own possession now. No one else's. Rage sent me swarming up the posts of the balcony to the copper roof of my house. From there, I gained the walkway atop the bluestone walls. I could already hear shouting within the core of the Factor's house.

Sprinting for the corner where I could make the climb down, I stumbled again—I had not eaten all day, and was ill in my stomach with shock and fear and all my bleeding. As I swung over the wall, I missed my grasp and fell hard to the cobbled streets below.

The landing was poor, but not fatally so. I collapsed onto my back, breath heaving in deep sobs as gongs sounded within the Factor's house.

A silver-furred face leaned close. "Come with me now," my Dancing Mistress said. "That way you might live to see the dawn."

"No," I said in my own words. "I will have no more of you."

She grabbed my arm. "Don't be a fool. You'll throw away whatever you think you've gained, and your life besides."

Still shocked from the murder I had just wrought, I rose and stumbled after her. I muttered maledictions in my own language as we walked quickly through the nighttime streets of Copper Downs. Both Endurance and my grandmother's ghost would be ashamed of me.

I shivered as we climbed down a culvert to an entrance to Below. This was one we hadn't used before. The night wasn't so cold now, but I was.

The crack of Mistress Tirelle's neck echoed repeatedly in my mind. I had kicked high. That wasn't defense—I had not meant merely to knock her down or disable her.

Words, my victory was supposed to be in words. Yet I'd ended her *life*.

That was a theft that could never be restored. In taking her life, I'd taken my own, too. I had cast away everything I'd known in Copper Downs, almost everything I could ever remember.

I'd meant only to take myself away. That was why my cheeks and ears still stung like hot coals, their wounds a horrid itch that intruded on my thoughts. In spoiling myself for the Factor and his patron Duke, I had ruined their plans.

But a *life*.

It made no difference that she had been awful to me. I was slave and animal and work to her. Never a real girl. Never a person.

Then I'd killed her. That had made me real, at least for the span of her last moments.

We moved quickly for being Below. The passages were close-walled and low-ceilinged, slimed over as happened mostly near the surface. The Dancing Mistress held a snatch of coldfire in her hands, which was enough for me to follow. Beyond that, I paid no heed to anything but my own misery.

She stepped through a doorway into some larger gallery. I followed, only to have someone clutch at my arm. I shrieked as I was startled out of my reverie.

The Dancing Mistress whirled. Whatever had been on her lips died there.

Mother Iron held me pinched in a grip that seemed tight enough to shear pipes. I looked into her eyes. They gleamed with the orange white of the hottest coals.

"So it begins." Mother Iron's voice was rusty as a grate. Her breath gusted like a wind from a great distance, and reeked of stale air.

"We move swiftly," the Dancing Mistress answered softly. "To stay ahead of the hunt that is even now being summoned."

The old woman-thing—I was mindful of Septio's sleeping gods—squeezed my arm again. "Be true and hold your edge," she told me. Then Mother Iron was gone, vanished like mist before breaking sunlight.

The Dancing Mistress took my hand. "I had not expected that. Are you well?"

I tried to answer, but could only laugh.

Her eyes narrowed to gleaming slits as she shook me slightly. "Stay away from that clouded place in your mind, Girl."

That sobered me quickly. "My name is Green," I snapped. Hot, hard anger filled my voice.

"Green, then. I see that you are back."

Our flight ended with a climb of a wooden ladder screwed to a brick well. The Dancing Mistress led. I followed, stewing in anger rather than lost in despair.

How dare *they snatch everything away from me?* I knew my thoughts held no logic at all, but I cherished the burning spark. Guilt and fear lay not far behind it. I would much rather have my path lit by fire than wrapped in gloom.

We emerged in a large half-empty building. A bit of moonlight leached in through wide windows set high on the walls to make solid, silvery shadows of stacks of crates. I glanced around the room, seeing as I had been trained to do.

Eight of those windows on each side, some accessible by climbing the stacks before them. One end was swallowed in deep shadow where a dozen horsemen could have waited invisible. The other end gleamed with the cracks of a large doorway lit by gas lamps outside.

A warehouse, of course.

"What is in the shadows?" I asked, mindful of the Dancing Mistress' earlier words about the hunt being called.

"What do your nose and ears tell you?"

I closed my eyes and sniffed. Dust, wood, oil, mold. The scent of the two of us. No horses. No sweat-stink of soldiers. Likewise the noises. A cart rumbled past the other side of the doorway, paced by the clip of hooves on cobbles. Within were only the sounds of an old building, wood settling and the whistling scurry of rats.

There might be a lone, quiet person in the darkness, but no more. I said as much.

"There might be anyone, anywhere," she agreed. "Here in this moment, we are probably safe. Now we hide some more."

The Dancing Mistress began climbing an array of boxes toward one of the grease-smeared windows. I followed her. I wondered where we were going, but did not ask. She reached the window, then stretched tall to touch the ceiling above it. A section of slats slid away to the noisy squeal of wood on wood. I winced at the sound and looked back down for our mythical assassin.

No one was there. Above me, the Dancing Mistress hauled herself into the ceiling. I followed to find us in a much darker space with another ceiling so low that I nearly struck my head.

The roof of the warehouse, I realized: a very low-angled attic. The texture of the shadows suggested that this space was used for storage. Objects bulked dark within deeper darkness. A single window gleamed at the far end, barely brighter than the shadows, as it was so obscured with dust and grime.

"The stairs were torn out fifteen or twenty years ago," the Dancing Mistress said. "They widened the doors to admit heavier cart traffic with a turnaround, and were forced to give up this space in the process."

"A waste." I was focusing on the trivia of where we were.

"Everything has a reason. Right now we are in a hidden location above a building that no one has ever seen us enter. We are safe while we consider what should happen next."

"Safe?" The panicked laughter began bubbling up within me once more. "I will never be safe again. I will always be trapped by what I have done. I—"

She smacked the top of my head as my voice rose. "Whisper. Even better, think before you speak at all."

Anger rushed back fast as flame on oil. Mistress Tirelle hit me constantly. Now the Dancing Mistress did the same. Who was *she* to raise a hand to me?

"You must eat, then sleep," she continued. "Your fears and regrets are carrying you away."

"I am afraid of nothing!" I shouted.

Her voice was so soft, I had to strain to hear it. "Right now you are afraid of everything. Or at least you should be."

I flopped to the floor. Finally still, I realized how badly my body ached. The slip coming off the wall of the Factor's house had bruised my hips and jarred my back. The run had stretched and warmed my muscles, but here we were quiet and I could feel myself cooling down already. My foot stung where it had clipped Mistress Tirelle's chin.

"Everything hurts," I told her quietly.

"Then sleep." She offered me a piece of crumbling cheese and a wad of leaves.

I took them. The cheese had a deep ammoniac scent, overlaid with salt and the veining mold of a blue. The leaves were dry-cured kale with lard smeared amid the rolled layers.

It all smelled like paradise to my rumbling gut. I ate quickly, then just as quickly was starved with thirst.

"There are water barrels near the window," the Dancing Mistress said. "They are filled with rainwater collection, and might taste of the roof." She bent close again. "I must go out and be seen. There can be no suspicion that I am part of what is still happening in the Factor's house. Will you remain here and keep absolutely quiet?"

"Yes," I said around a mouthful of kale.

"No matter how angry or despairing you may feel, do not stamp your feet or throw things. Men will be working downstairs on the morrow, and they may hear you."

I looked at my hands, full of half-eaten food. *Mistress Tirelle would never eat again.* "No, Mistress."

"When I can safely do so, I shall return. Probably tomorrow night. Federo may be here as well."

My heart leapt at that; then I wondered why. Even my friends were trouble for me. "I will remain silent."

"As best as can be hoped for." She ran a hand through my hair. "We will do what we can to see that you are well-served. I am not sure how much is left to us, though."

"Good night," I said, and then she was gone.

Sleep brought only the memory of death. My relationship with my dreams continues uneasy to this day, but that night was the worst I have ever known. I don't recall my dreams when Federo first stole me away from Papa. The dreams of small children are said to be as unformed as their thoughts, but that cannot be true. My thoughts were well-formed even then. I knew what I wanted and did not want.

Later I dreamed of the past, Endurance and my grandmother and my little life among the ditches and fields of Papa's rice. Those were about loss and regret. As I grew older and my training became more complex, I often dreamed of the sorts of things one does then—endless loaves of bread spilling from the oven, or reading a book that bred new pages for itself faster than I could turn them.

That night, though, all I could dream of was death. Perhaps I had once killed my grandmother. How had my mother died? Mistress Tirelle's head spun away from my kick over and over as her neck snapped. The scent of her voiding her bowels as she died. The way her body collapsed, as if she had already stopped trying to protect herself the way any living person does, with or without training.

How many ways were there to kill? How many ways were there to die? Those questions chased me through the sick regrets of that night, until finally I awoke with the answers ringing in my head.

There are as many ways to die as there are to live.
There are as many ways to kill as there are killers to try them.

My body ached as if I'd been trampled by one of the Factor's horses. The pallet on which I'd slept was kicked aside, and I was lying on the old wooden floor. I didn't feel much like a killer, but I knew I was. I also knew that someday I would die. Possibly very soon, depending on whether and how the Factor's justice caught up with me.

I climbed to my feet, swaying with fatigue and an overwhelming sense of weakness. Last night's fear and rush had taken their toll.

Morning arrived amid a vague silvery light that struggled through the round window at the end of the attic. The filth on the glass looked to be at least a generation of neglect. I knew exactly what a maid would do to cut it down.

This room was huge, though a tall man could stand only in the center, where the peak of the roof ran. The low edges were filled with odd equipment—the frames from old looms, mechanical devices for which I had no name. All was covered in deep dust.

Finding the rain barrels, I drank from a little tin ladle there. The water tasted of tar and sand. Even at the edge of foulness, it was refreshing after breathing the dry air all night.

Otherwise I had nothing to relieve the itching of my cheeks and ears, and the mix of feelings in my heart. No food, no distractions, nothing.

I spent a long time simmering in my anger before Federo appeared. He surprised me in climbing through the floor in the middle of the day.

"They are at their lunch below," he explained to my unspoken question. He looked worried, and was dressed like a common laborer of the city. "I have stood the warehousemen a round of ales down the street once a week for quite some time. No one wonders at me in this neighborhood."

"You are not unusual anymore." I recalled my lessons at the art of the swift eye.

"Precisely." He pulled a paper wrapping out of his pocket. "Here is some salt beef with cold roast potatoes. It is the best I could do right now. I will be back with the Dancing Mistress tonight. We need to think on what to do with you next."

"You will do nothing with me," I told him coldly. "I will decide what to do with myself."

He looked unhappy, but retreated beneath the floor.

They would not use me. Not the Factor, not the Duke, not this little conspiracy of child-stealer and rogue Mistress. I spent the afternoon imagining ways to flee, directions to run in, but I knew nothing practical of the city or its surrounds. If I could go back to Endurance, I would, but all I remembered of the way home was that I should cross the water.

At that time, I did not even know the name of my birth country, let alone the village where Papa's farm lay. I had no money or maps or practical experience of any sort.

I realized that I had done nothing more than exchange one prison for another. This one was far less comfortable and more dangerous. My anger rose once more like a burning tide. I might be free of the Factor, but my choices continued not to be my own.

Why had Federo and the Dancing Mistress guided me toward a sense of my independence? I wondered. Would I have not been better off in ignorance? I could have grown into a lady and lived the life that had been bought for me.

They would have no satisfaction of me either, I resolved.

My rescuers came back that night with several sacks. I assumed these contained provisions. He was once more dressed like a common laborer, while she wore the same loose tunic as usual. The Dancing Mistress pushed their sacks to one side of the cleared space of floor that marked our area; then she and Federo made up a little table of two crates and three lengths of lumber. She produced a hooded lantern from one of the sacks while Federo found smaller boxes for us to sit on.

Soon we were gathered around a little table with knobby carrots, a string of sweet onions, and a handful of small brown rolls to share for our dinner. Both of them had been silent through this process. I was determined not to speak first.

"We are civilized," Federo finally said. "People at table with food before them."

"The shared feast is a tradition of my people," the Dancing Mistress added.

Both of them spoke in the tone of someone desperate to return a bad moment to normal.

I said nothing. Instead I simply glared at them both.

They looked back, Federo seemingly puzzled, the Dancing Mistress with a blank-eyed indifference that I was not sure how to read upon her nonhuman face. We all stared awhile.

My resolve broke first.

"She was a cow," I said in my language.

Federo rubbed his eyes. "Within two more years, we could have had you inside the Duke's palace." He suddenly sounded terribly exhausted.

The Dancing Mistress sighed. "We should have known."

"Known what?" I demanded.

Federo stared at me. "Stop talking like a barbarian," he snapped. "This is Copper Downs."

"Barbarian?" I bit off a shout. "You are the . . . the . . ." I didn't have a word for *barbarian* in my language. Certainly I'd no reason to know it when I was a tiny child. "Animals. You are animals."

"That could have been changed," he said. "With your help."

The Dancing Mistress gave me one of her long, slow looks. "Please, speak so I can understand you. Or we won't get far."

I begrudged her the words, but I recalled that Petraean wasn't her home language either. "Very well," I muttered, knowing my own poor grace for what it was.

"Emerald," Federo began.

"Green!" I slammed my fist into the planks of our table. "My name is not Emerald. You may call me Green."

The Dancing Mistress waved toward Federo in a shushing motion. "Well, Green," she said. "Federo had always thought you might have the heart-fire to hold your spirit true against the Factor's training. You—"

"You did," Federo interrupted. His voice had a note of pride, even now. I hated him for that. It was as if he'd made me who I was, merely by being clever enough to buy me in the market.

"Too much heart, perhaps," the Dancing Mistress went on.

"What of it?" I demanded. "Was I to be your creature instead of the Factor's? I am a person of my own, not some thing to be shaped by him or you or anyone else."

The Dancing Mistress' claws drummed on the raw wood of the table. They sent splinters flying. "We are all shaped by life."

"Indeed," said Federo. "And there is much you do not know. Am I correct in thinking you read nothing more recently published than *Lacodemus' Commentaries*?"

"Yes." What did this question signify? Lacodemus had been fascinated with men risen from the grave and people who lived on their heads, speaking by the motions of their feet. I hadn't taken him seriously. The world obeyed a certain order. Just because a tale came from far away did not mean that common sense could be cast aside in judging it.

"Then know this little bit of recent history here in Copper Downs." He leaned forward and pressed the palms of his hands flat on the rough wood. "There has not been a Ducal succession in four centuries."

"Mistress Tirelle told me as much. She did not say it so clearly." I thought of the Factor's dead eye, sullen and fatal as that of the sea creature that had tried to take me so long ago. Lacodemus had been right, in a sense. "This city is ruled by immortals."

The Dancing Mistress laughed, her voice soft and bitter. "Immortal, no. Undying? Well, yes . . . so far."

"You meant for me to kill the Duke," I breathed, barely lending sound to the words. Killing the Duke would cause the Factor to lose his power. Women . . . girls . . . would be safer. Even a new tyrant could hardly rebuild the power of this Duke's long rule with any speed.

"That was one hope, yes," Federo admitted. "There were other plans. We had played at a game of years here."

I gave voice to his unspoken conclusion. "Until I tipped over the board and set fire to the rules."

"Well, yes." I could see a smile flirting with his face despite himself. "That spirit of yours rose up, I think."

My fingers brushed at the itching scabs upon my cheek. "For all the good it has done me. What now of your plans?"

They both stared me down. Dust flecks and wood shavings floated between us. Eventually Federo's face fell back to his recent dismay. "If you can escape detection by the patrols roaming the city right now, and survive the substantial bounty that has been placed upon your head, you are free to flee Copper Downs and find a life of your own elsewhere."

The Dancing Mistress slipped a claw-tipped finger across her own furred cheek. "But you have made yourself too distinctive for safety, I fear. Easily recognized should there be a hue and cry."

I thought of Endurance's great brown eyes, and of my grandmother's bells ringing for the last time beneath the hot sun. What would my grandmother have wanted from me? Or Papa? What did he want? Endurance, I knew, wished only to call me home.

What did I want?

To go home.

But even more than that, I realized, I wanted never to see a child sold to these terrible people again. Not to the Factor and his Mistresses, not to Federo and his charming ways. This trade in thinking, talking livestock must end.

I could not say then who was more guilty, Federo for having bought me or my father for having sold me to him. It did not matter. They were but pawns on a larger board. The Duke, and his procuring agent the Factor, had first set the machinery of guilt in motion. I realized my mistake in fleeing the Factor's house, when all I had to do was stand my ground and keep my spirit inflamed in order to fight back with my beauty as my weapon.

The weapon I had thrown away in a moment of anguished passion before murdering a woman whose only real crime was to serve her masters.

A new thought dawned upon me. "There must be another way," I said. "Or we would not be speaking now. You have some proposal. One of the 'other plans' you mentioned."

Federo and the Dancing Mistress exchanged a long look. I saw fear in their faces, but I held my tongue.

He nodded slightly and began to speak in a rush, as if he did not quite believe his own words. "Allow yourself to be captured. Tell them of a plot against the Duke. Tell them of us. You will most likely be taken before him for a hearing, both for the sake of the accusation, and even more because you are his lost jewel. He will be jealous of you. Once in his presence, if you can . . ."

"If I can?" Once more laughter at these idiots bubbled up. "If I can what, kill him? I am a girl of twelve. I would be standing before him in his court. If I had been his bedmate, that might be one thing. But surrounded by men and their weapons? You are fools." In my own language, I added, "I am but a girl." My laughter slid into a snarl. "I can kick old women to death, but not a man on a throne surrounded by guards. He is beyond my reach."

The Dancing Mistress shifted her weight. Her eyes locked on mine. They did not swiftly flick away again as anyone else's would have done. I knew her well enough to see that she was measuring her words, so I kept her gaze and watched in silence.

Finally she spoke. "There is another way."

"Of course there is." I kept my voice hard as I could manage. "You taught me to kill."

"Actually, she taught you how not to die," Federo said, interrupting. "Listen to me, Green. If you wish to throw us away and walk out into the streets, that is your choice. You are no prisoner here."

"No?"

"Did you try the trapdoor?" he asked. "It has been unlocked this whole time."

"Oh." For a moment I felt foolish.

"You may go as your heart tells you. I beg this, for the sake of whatever good-will you might have borne me, listen first to the Dancing Mistress. She speaks difficult truths that may not come to pass. But before you choose, know what you are rejecting."

"*This* time," I said bitterly. His message was clear enough. Back at the Pomegranate Court, I had chosen in ignorance. Though I did not want to admit it, I saw the wisdom of his plea now.

"There is a thing about the Duke that is known to very, very few." The Dancing Mistress' words came slowly. "His, well, agelessness . . . it is bound by spells wrested from my people. There are other spells that can release those bindings—things that need to be said to him in close confidence to have their power. Not"—she raised her hand to me—"the quiet of the bedchamber. But close nonetheless. They cannot be spoken in this Petraean tongue. The Duke through his magics has bound the very words to himself, lest someone utter them in his presence."

"Can they be spoken in my tongue?" I asked.

She looked very unhappy. "I do not know if the forces will heed you. This is not my soulpath, to understand spells and how they work. Since the Duke took his throne on the strength of our magics, my people have folded away their own power like an old cloak. I can teach you certain words through the expedient of writing them in the dust here, though neither of us can speak them aloud. If you say them in your tongue . . . who knows what effect they will have? I certainly do not."

I was incredulous. "In four hundred years, no one has ever tried this?"

"It is not a common wisdom," Federo said dryly. "Suffice that we have managed to coordinate intentions now. Will you help?"

At that point, my decision was simple enough. Where else would I go? I could not swim the seas to home. If I said no and simply walked out the door, the Factor would buy more children, then Federo and the Dancing Mistress would raise another rebel in the shadows of his house. Some other child would have to make my choices anew someday.

Here I was; here I would stand.

"I will do this thing." I spoke carefully. "You may teach me the words. Federo will need to help me with my own tongue, for almost certainly I do not have enough of it to make a worthwhile saying from whatever you write before me in the dust." I turned to him. "Bring a dictionary of my people's speech, if such a thing can be found here in Copper Downs. Also, before I will try this magic for you, I want seven yards of silk, needles, spools of thread, and five thousand tiny bells like those used for dancing shoes."

"Five *thousand?* Where am I—?"

"You know what I want them for," I said, interrupting him again. "I should not want to walk toward my death without the bells of my life ringing about me. Don't pretend this is not murder of another kind. For the Duke if I am lucky, and for me almost certainly."

"No, n-no," he stammered. "You have the right of it."

"Then we are agreed."

The Dancing Mistress nodded slowly, pain written on her patient face. I gave her a small, real smile. She deserved something from me besides my anger and contempt. The girls who would have followed in my place deserved everything from me. Even my very life itself. When this was done, one way or the other, I would be home.

My grandmother would have approved. As would the ox.

———

I have never known the true number of the days of my life. The count had broken when Federo took me away from Papa. I did not understand then, but the bells of my long-lost silk would have remembered for me until I was old enough to tally the days myself. Though I had tried and tried again to return to my silk, the number had always been a guess. The count I had been keeping in my imagination these years since was more of a guess at a guess.

These were the days that were mine. I had lost almost everything from the beginning of my life except a few memories.

The attic was close and warm even in the autumn weather. Federo and the Dancing Mistress were gone once more, this time for a while. "We cannot pass in and out without drawing attention to you," he had said.

"We will return when we have gathered your needs," she told me.

I sat with salty cheese and stale bread and water that tasted like rooftop and wondered what I might have done differently. What I might do next.

When I grew bored with regrets and should-have-dones, I paid attention to the world beyond this latest prison of mine. I did not clean the window, for fear it would attract attention. The grime covering it kept me from any real sight of the street. I could hear the warehouse below without difficulty, and I discovered that if I sat just beneath the round window, I could hear what passed in the street.

Some sounds were readily understood. Teams of horses passing by, accompanied by shouting or the crack of a drover's whip. Occasionally they stopped with a squeal of iron-shoed wheels on stone. The beasts would whicker to one another as the busy noise of the warehouse took in the drover and his cargo.

People passed in conversation. No words reached me except for the occasional exclamation of surprise or excitement. I took comfort from the murmur of passing voices nonetheless.

I could hear more from the warehouse beneath me. Loads shifted in, loads shifted out, and some foreman with a high-pitched voice bawled orders I could clearly make out. Most of it was meaningless to me, the chatter of men at work: "The *other* cannery stack, damn your lazy boots!"

This was like being inside the Factor's walls and hearing the world outside. Except in this place that world was much, much closer.

In the late afternoon of the second day since I'd once more been left alone, I heard the tramp of men marching in unison. Someone shouted orders in clipped syllables I could not follow. I heard the clatter as a few were told off to my warehouse. I heard the argument that followed. Men would be told to work into the evening. There would be no pay from the city or the Duke. They would rot in hell. They would be happy to send them there. An argument without names or sides, just shouting men and, once, the meaty thump of a hard strike by someone's fist.

After a while, the boxes began to move. I heard crates shift and clatter. More cursing, of the ordinary, working kind. I lay on the floor with my aching ear pressed against dusty splinters, waiting for death to climb the walls below and find me.

Why had I insisted on my silk before I would follow their plan? I could have gone forth and had some small chance at changing the order of the world. Now I would be taken up without the words to break the Duke's spell.

If I could have stilled my breathing, I would have. Not to make myself die, but to be as silent as a piece of ceiling lumber. To be quiet is to live. I did not stir for cheese nor bread nor water nor the piss pot all that evening. They continued to move below me. An officer came occasionally, shouting for someone named Mauricio each time.

Eventually the warehousemen were released and the great door rumbled shut. I had never felt such relief as I did when quiet reigned below.

I sat up with my dry mouth and my urgent bladder only to realize that if this Mauricio were canny, he might have left a man behind to lurk silently within the warehouse. What if an ear were pressed to the underside of my floor, waiting for me to move and scrape and sigh?

That new terror kept me in place very late into the night. Finally the need in my bladder became so urgent that I could not put it off for all the fear in my heart. I crept silent as fog to do my business. The splash of the stream sounded like thunder to me, but there was nothing to be done for it except finish, then continue to hide until the danger was gone.

I realized the danger might never be past.

I was startled out of dreams of being hunted across ocean waves in a small boat. Legs kicked as I reached for something with which to defend myself. I was brandishing a small hunk of cheese before I realized that Federo had lifted the trap. A quick glance at the round window showed it was still night outside.

"I do not think that Fencepost Blue is so dangerous," he said mildly. "But I will see if I can find something a bit less stout the next time I go shopping."

Giggling, I collapsed. "I thought one of those soldiers might be hiding downstairs to catch me moving up here overnight."

"Soldiers?" Federo's face grew alarmed. "A moment, please." He reached down through the trap and brought up a pair of bulging canvas sacks. After repositioning the flooring, he sat and asked me to explain exactly what it was I had meant.

I told him what I had heard the day before, and mentioned the name Mauricio. Federo looked troubled. "They suspect you to be in one of the warehouse districts. Not that this is surprising. They searched here all evening, then departed?"

"They searched the whole area. The troop I heard marching dropped a small group of men here."

"Hmm." He took off his laborer's flattened leather cap and stroked the back of his head, thinking. "I will see what I can learn. But this is not something I can ask too many questions of. I am under suspicion already, if only for having known you. It will not take long before they realize how much contact the Dancing Mistress had with you."

"Far more than her other candidate students?" I asked.

"Of course." He reached for one of the bags. "But here, I bring news and better."

Out came a bolt of fine silk, tussah weave and forty-two inches across. Unrolled, the silk was seven yards in length. And beautiful, too. I set our hooded lamp on the floor to light the cloth. It showed a rippling sheen like water flowing down the threads. The color appeared green in the lamplight, some medium shade, though I could not say what in that illumination.

"This is most beautiful," I said quietly.

"There is so little I can ever give back to you. I thought at the least you should have a good quality measure of cloth."

He showed me the bells, a great mixture of kinds. "I could not buy so many silver bells in any one place," Federo said by way of apology. "So some are brass, or iron, and some are larger than I might have liked."

Still, they were bells. Real bells. The bells I could remember from home had been little tin cones on a pin. They tinkled, but they did not ring. Some of these were fit for a choir to sing the hymns of grace to. "I shall have music like a tulpa when I walk in this," I told him. Their multitude of tiny jingles brought me a sense of peace.

Federo produced a velvet roll with needles stuck into it. "In case some grow dull or bend." He also had several sticks with spools of thread stacked upon them.

I readied a needle and took up one of the tiniest bells. This one resembled a little silver pomegranate seed, and made a single plaintive tinking noise when I dangled it between my thumbnail and fingernail. With a silent thanks to my grandmother, I sewed the bell to one corner of the silk, which flowed like a green river from my lap.

Federo sat on his heels and watched me sew awhile. After a time, he asked, "May I help you sew, or is this something you must do for yourself?"

I considered that. The answer was not immediately obvious to me. I had always thought of the silk as something a woman made for herself. Clearly, I had not sewn my own bells as an infant, though. Just as clearly, whatever tradition demanded had long been abused and discarded in my case.

The outcome was what mattered most now.

In a sudden rush of thought, the decision was straightforward enough. "I would be pleased to have your help, but at a cost." I caught his eye in the faint light rising up from the hooded lamp. "Tell me where I came from, as you understand it. I remember the frogs and the plantains and the rice and my father's ox, but I never have known the name of the place. None of my studies ever showed me maps across the Storm Sea."

He picked up a needle and struggled awhile to thread it. I did not press him at first for words, for I could see the thoughts forming behind his eyes. Finally Federo got a bell sorted out and bent to his side of the silk. He would not meet my gaze as he began to speak. "Surely you know there was the strictest order never to mention your origins within the Pomegranate Court."

"Which is foolish. All one need do is look at my face to see I was born nowhere near the Stone Coast."

"Of course. The beauty we all prized . . . prize . . . in you was founded in part on that very thing. But to mention your birth-country would be to remind you of the past, and goad you into keeping those memories strong."

"Unlike how you and the Dancing Mistress treated me," I said dryly.

"Plans within plans, Green." He finally glanced at me, then looked back down at a fresh bell he was embarked on. "You hail from a country called Selistan. It is found a bit more than six hundred knots west of south, sailing from Copper Downs out across the Storm Sea."

Selistan!

I finally had a name for my home. Not just a place of frogs and snakes and rice paddies, but a place in the world with a name, that appeared on maps.

"Wh-where in Selistan?"

"I am not sure." He sounded uncomfortable. "Kalimpura is the great port where much of the trade from across the sea comes. I landed at a fishing town some thirty leagues east of Kalimpura, in a province called Bhopura. The town itself is called Little Bhopura, though I know of no Great Bhopura anywhere."

"We walked far from my village to Little Bhopura," I said cautiously.

Federo laughed. If his amusement had not been so obviously genuine, it would have hurt my heart. "We hiked about two leagues across a dry ridgeline separating the river valley where you were living from the coast where I landed." He smiled at me fondly. "You must recall that as a vast journey, but think how small you were then. I doubt you'd ever been more than three furlongs from your father's farm in your life. Today you could cover the distance in a few hours. You would not even notice the effort."

I recalled the sense of enormous space, walking the entire day, stopping to take a meal. He was not mocking me; he was describing my earliest childhood. Everyone begins small.

Another bell wanted threading. I focused on that a moment to gather my thoughts. Federo's silence was inviting, not angry or defensive. Below us, the warehousemen pushed their great door open and began their day.

When I spoke again, my voice was low. "Where is my father's farm?"

"I . . . I do not know. Not anymore." He sounded ashamed.

Federo was not telling me something. I picked at the thought awhile. I did not wish to push my anger at him. That well was deep and inexhaustible. Right now I was thoughtful, not angry. "Federo. What was my father's name?"

His face was so close to his sewing, he risked poking himself in the eye. "I do not know."

"What was my name?"

He would not meet my gaze at all.

My anger raced. "You bought a girl whose name you did not ask from a man whose name you did not know."

Federo looked up at me, though his face was mostly in shadow. "I have bought many things from many peo—"

"I am not a thing!"

We were both silent, staring at one another as some crate crashed to the floor below us.

"I *know* you are not a thing," he hissed after the rumble and mutter of voices below resumed. "I am sorry for how I spoke. But please, Green, you surely take my meaning."

Bending back to my own sewing, I grumbled that I understood. But how could he not *know*? How could this man buy me like fruit at a market, strip me away from my family and all my heritage, and recall nothing?

Federo resumed speaking. "I can tell you this much: A man there watches for families with children of . . . potential value." His voice dropped as he blushed with shame. "F-families where there is trouble. No money, or the death of a parent."

Which made me what? A commodity, of course. A brokered, broken child. "I suppose you have a bill of sale?" I asked in my nastiest voice.

"No." Now he sounded weary and sad. "You were a cash transaction. I have a note in my account book."

"Was I a bargain?"

He stared at me a long while. Then: "I believe I am done with this conversation."

I wanted to make a fight with him. I wanted to rage at him for stealing everything from me and then pouting at my questions. Federo had claimed the privilege of power when he bought me, and now he claimed the privilege of injured dignity in order to remain silent concerning the truths of my life.

There was no purpose in attacking him. It might satisfy my pride, but anger from me would not prompt him to tell me any more than he already had. Patience was a hard lesson. My teachers had been very thorough.

The Dancing Mistress joined us that night. She brought more food, this time strips of smoked venison along with dried braids of shallots and garlic. After our conversation failed, Federo and I had spent the day sewing in silence. Occasional comments passed between us, but the best thing I could find to do with my anger was let it retreat back down the well from which it ever bubbled.

Her arrival was a fresh breeze stirring our thickening air of mistrust. She looked at us both and must have understood what had passed. Eventually I came to understand that her kind did not judge human faces so well, but they could read human scents quite clearly. The two of us reeked of the banked fire of our argument. That evening, all I knew was that she sat down and laid out a simple meal, then quite literally interposed herself between Federo and me.

"You have made great progress."

We'd sewn over twelve hundred bells. Less than four years of my life, but a good day's work. My fingers ached with the myriad stabs of the needle. That was progress.

"Yes," I admitted.

The Dancing Mistress inclined her chin as she nodded gravely at Federo. Her voice was pitched low. "Your day was good enough, I trust."

"We spoke of things past," Federo muttered.

She turned back to me. "This upset you?"

What an astonishingly stupid question. I just stared at her.

"You are afraid," she said.

"Angry, not afraid."

"Fear and anger are opposite faces of the same blade."

I'd read versions of that statement in half a dozen texts. "Don't quote platitudes at me!"

"Just because words are often repeated does not rob an idea of its truth." Her voice remained mild. "Some might even think the opposite."

"I have a lifetime's worth of anger. What am I afraid of, then?"

The answer was simple enough. "The consequences of what lies behind you. The price of what lies before you."

"Price. Life is nothing but prices."

"To be sure." She picked up a needle and began to sew where I had left off to eat. "You are twelve years of age now, yes?"

"I believe so," I admitted.

Federo winced.

The Dancing Mistress continued. "At home, you would marry soon."

Mistress Cherlise had told me I'd be wife to some sweating farmer. True enough, I supposed, and I didn't wish for that life. But what had I become instead?

She went on as if I had answered. "Here in Copper Downs, you were almost ready to be turned out as consort for the Duke, or one of his favorites."

"Monthlies or no monthlies," muttered Federo.

"What of it?" I asked.

She was implacable. "You are afraid of that change. Both your fates have been denied you. You were born onto a path that Federo bought you away from. You were trained within the walls of the Factor's house for a different path. Even our night running work was little more than a twisting of that second way. You cut that fate away when you marred your beauty and killed Mistress Tirelle. What remains?"

"Fear," I told the silk I had once more gathered into my hands.

"Choice," she said. "Which you have exercised to join Federo and me in this latest effort."

I wasn't afraid of what would happen, I realized. That was almost beyond any control of mine. I wasn't afraid of my choices, either. She did not quite have the right of that. Even with all her cruelty, Mistress Tirelle had always prepared me for some kind of greatness. I had been spared the jaws of the ocean leviathan. Endurance had watched over me with a purpose. The prospect of extraordinary effort did not daunt me.

Everybody died. That was fearsome, but this fear was more than that. Everybody hurt. The fear I felt was somehow still more.

I thought awhile as I sewed. My grandmother had gone to the sky burial wrapped in her shroud. My silk was supposed to be the track of my life, the thing that told my days. Each bell should have had meaning, *this* one when I met my husband, *that* one when I bore the first of my children.

Finally I decided that I was afraid for my spirit.

I looked up at the Dancing Mistress once more. Her sloped eyes gleamed in the light of our little lamp. She was waiting for me to speak.

"Do your people have souls?" I asked her.

Maybe her answer would tell me more about mine.

She thought for a while, glancing at me as she worked. The hooded lamp glowed between us. Federo picked with his needle. He seemed content to wait out the conversation.

Finally the Dancing Mistress spoke. "When a child is born, we bind the soul with flowers and food. The community feasts to share the soul. That way it is not lost if there is an accident or disease, but kept alive within the hearts of many."

Curiosity competed with my fear and frustrated anger. "What about your names?"

She smiled. "Those are for our hearts alone." She gathered up a handful of the silk and shook it at me. Hundreds of bells jingled, those not swallowed in the folds of the cloth. "Here is your soul, Green. Do not fear for it. Most people never find theirs. You are making yours as real as your hands."

The sound of the bells brought me back to the memory of my grandmother's funeral procession. I was hers, through my nameless father and his nameless hut in a nameless place on some road in Selistan. I did not know his name, or the name he called me. Federo had not bothered to ask, for to him I was just a girl.

In all the years within the Factor's house, I had forgotten too much. If I lived through these days before me, I resolved, I would return to Selistan and reclaim my life.

We were done with the silk in the middle of the evening two days later. This time they'd both stayed with me. All of us sewed, talking quietly from time to time, working to be ready. The silk was flecked with droplets of blood from stabbed fingers, and my own hands were most unpleasantly stiff, but we were done.

"If you still agree with the plan," Federo said, "we will guide you out of the warehouse before dawn. You can walk the streets once it is full light and the life of the city resumes. If the Ducal guards take you then, there will be witnesses."

"Being arrested in front of witnesses tends to be healthier," the Dancing Mistress observed.

I folded my silk close, letting the bells wash over me. We did not know the true number, and so we had settled on four thousand four hundred—twelve years. They jingled like the pouring of water on a metal roof. My past held me close in that moment.

"Show me what I must know."

The Dancing Mistress drew certain words in the dust of the floor. I studied them as my bells shivered in time to my breathing. In their way, the words were simple enough. A conversation with the powers of the land. I did not know if their might stemmed from the intention of the speaker, or if there was something inherent in the arrangement of sound and meaning. In any case, these words were—or should be—the ravel that would unweave the spells binding the Duke to his life and his throne.

Federo looked at them with me, then nodded. The Dancing Mistress erased the words. "Do you have any questions?"

I looked at him. " 'Shared'?" I asked. "I do not know that word, nor the term for 'hoarded' in my tongue. Otherwise, I can say this easily enough."

"Share," he said in the Selistani language. Seliu, I had learned that it was called. "It carries the sense of something freely given, without taking."

"That will do," said the Dancing Mistress.

"As for hoarded . . ." He thought for a while, then suggested a word in Selin. "It means gathering too much. As in, well, overharvesting. More foolish than greedy, I think."

"The sense seems good to me," I said seriously.

The Dancing Mistress nodded. "You have the words in your head?"

"I do."

"Good." Federo's voice quavered. He looked nervous to the point of being ill.

I knew how he felt. My anger would carry me through, when I found it once more. Right now, I mostly felt sick myself. "I am ready," I lied.

I needed to attend to one last bit of business before we set out. My fears and worries had stalked me all through the night and into the early morning hours as we prepared ourselves. Most of them were beyond my reach. One was not.

"Federo," I said as he packed away the last of our supplies.

"Mmm?"

"I want to mark Mistress Tirelle's passing. Do you have any notion what she might have believed about her soul? Is there some prayer or sacrifice I can offer her?"

He gave me one of those long looks. In the shadows beyond him, I saw the Dancing Mistress nod almost imperceptibly. She had done the same when I had performed well in a difficult exercise but we were not free to communicate.

"I don't know, Green," Federo said after a little while. "Not many people in Copper Downs are openly observant. Especially not the locally born."

"Deaths must be marked in some manner. The passing of a soul is not simple." We did not have oxen, bells, or sky burials here; that much I knew. I was uneasy at the duck woman's fate—I had sent her from this life, after all. That fear and guilt belonged to me. My hope was to ease her passing.

"There is a common offering for the dead," he said. "Two candles are lit. One is black for their sins and sorrows. The other is white, for their hopes and dreams. Sometimes a picture of the dead is burned, if such a thing is to be had. Otherwise, a folded prayer or a banknote. That usually depends on the intentions of the person making the offering. You speak a kindness, spread the ash to the wind, and let them go."

"Then when we set out, I will have two candles, and some of that paper you just packed away."

We departed just before dawn, prior to the warehouse opening for the day. My belled silk was stuffed away in a sack along with the last of our tools and equipment from the attic. We couldn't really hide the fact that someone had been there for a while, but we could certainly take our evidence with us.

The cobbles were slick with morning dewfall. A three-quarter moon was veiled by dripping clouds. This sort of wet would burn off with the rising sun, but the east was still barely a glower. The Dancing Mistress led us to a mercantile at the end of a row of warehouses, which, judging by its stock, catered to the laboring trades. Nonetheless, among the spools of rope and chain, the racks of iron tools and heavy canvas coveralls, and all the other gear pertaining to those who build and repair the stuff of cities, we found candles.

The black was a narrow cylinder, while the white was a fat little votive barrel. I was not bothered that they were dissimilar. Mistress Tirelle and I surely had not been similar in life. Federo purchased the candles, and he bought a new packet of lucifer matches as well, before we stepped back out into the damp.

"A park will have to serve." Federo was grumpy. The risk of extra movement bothered him.

"I am sorry," I told him. "I must do this last thing. Then we can shake out

my bells and I will find the Ducal Palace and whatever follows from that."
The Dancing Mistress' words were firm enough in my head.

"Federo," she said. Her voice caught at him, and his nervous fear subsided
into a muttering calm.

A bit later, we slipped between two marble gateposts. Winding paths led
through lindens and birches beyond. Dew dripped from their branches as the
eastern sky continued to lighten. The musty scent of night was infused with
the opening of the earliest flowers, though something also rotted nearby. We
trotted along a weed-infested gravel path following direction from the Dancing Mistress, until she brought us to a little folly.

Like the gateposts, this was marble as well. Six pillars in the classical Smagadine style mounted by architraves with carvings I could not quite make out
in the early blooming light. This was topped by a pointed dome curved much
like a breast. A little statue of an armed woman stood at the tip.

That seemed fitting to me.

Within, the floor was tiled in a mosaic of birds circling a stylized sun. The
Dancing Mistress and Federo hung back. I knelt, though the cold tile hurt my
knees even through the sweep of Federo's borrowed cloak. I set the black
candle down against the sun's lidded left eye, and the white candle against his
wide-open right, which seemed to be on the verge of surprise.

I truly did not know what was needful here. What I did know was that this
part of my life had begun with a funeral—my grandmother's—and ended
with a death—Mistress Tirelle's. I sought a balance, and a show of respect.

As I'd already realized, in her strange way, this harshest of my Mistresses
had in fact loved me.

The match struck on the first try in a spitting flare of sulfur. That seemed
lucky. Lighting the black candle, I rocked back and forth as I hugged myself
against the cold.

"You treated me with a harder hand than I would raise against a cur from
the streets," I told the flame—and her soul if somehow she yet listened to me.
"Your sin was to hew too close to the word of the Factor. But who are we, if
we cannot tell wrong from right no matter what mouth it comes out of?"

I put the second match into the flame of the black candle. The flare made
me blink away bright spots. I then set it to the wick of the white candle.

"You fed me, and clothed me, and taught me more than most people ever
learn," I told her. "You gave my life a direction, whether I wished it or no."

Unfolding the paper I'd taken from Federo back in the attic, I smoothed it
flat as I could against the mosaic floor. With the burnt stubs of my two
matches, I drew an ox. Endurance, though no one but me would ever have

seen that in the picture. The image was simple enough: the tilted horns of the *aleph* glyph, humped shoulders, a sweep of the hocks, and the forelegs to balance the composition.

Rolling the paper up, I set it to the white candle's flame. *Let the offering burn in the light of hopes and dreams.* "May Endurance bear you onward as he once did my grandmother. His patience abides more deeply than mine." With a shuddering breath, I added, "I am sorry that I took from you that which was not for me to claim."

When the burning paper grew so short that my fingers began to sting, I dropped it to the tiles. It curled a moment longer, wisping to ash, before the dawn breeze hurried through the folly to snuff both my candles and carry the charred paper away.

Her shade did not answer. I had not expected anything. I had made this most unfortunate farewell.

Rising, I threw down Federo's cloak. "Where is my silk?" I asked in my own words. He and the Dancing Mistress stepped forward to array me as carefully as any squires in a courtly tale of olden tourneys.

I walked along Coronation Avenue between the two rows of peach trees gone bare in the autumn damp. My cloak of bells wrapped me close. Beneath it, I wore dark tights and a calf-length shirt, as if I were prepared to dance in some mummer's play. I carried no weapon and held my head high.

Look at me, I thought. *Here is your bounty. The Factor's emerald comes.*

People aplenty were on the street. Wagons and carriages clattered by. Even a few of the great cog-carts, balanced with flywheels and driven by strange logics patiently punched into the endless loops of goatleather rolls stored within their guts. Tradesmen and servants passed, on the business of the great houses that lined the approach to the Ducal Palace.

It was almost too much. I had not seen so many people at once since my arrival at the docks nine years earlier. Too many faces, all of them half-familiar, all of them strange as statues in the dark. I saw them through the eyes of my training. Virtually everyone could be marked out by their clothing, their stance, the tools or equipment they carried, their headgear.

In ordinary times, I might have fled to a quiet alley, but my purpose guided my steps. I was glad as the crowding thinned as the street grew wealthier.

A pair of mounted guardsmen rode by without even glancing at me. The gentlemen and ladies on their business took no notice, either. I enjoyed a strange species of invisibility, difficult to understand or describe. I wondered whether these people would have looked at me had I been naked and armed with a flaming sword.

Where was the hue and cry that Federo and the Dancing Mistress had promised? Three days ago, patrols had been going through the warehouse district building by building. Now their attention had moved to some other urgency.

Everything worn was a badge, a signal, a symbol of what role the wearer played in life and how they intended to be treated. My attire signaled that I did not belong, that I was a strange person in a stranger land. My bells told my story to anyone with the ears that knew how to hear it.

No one on Coronation Avenue had those ears, it seemed.

The Ducal Palace loomed ahead. The building's face was a vast sweep of marble in the Firthian style, with more windows than I would have imagined any structure having. I was accustomed to the blank walls of the Factor's house. It seemed as if this building stared across the city with a hundred eyes. A great copper dome towered above the center. Smaller domes of the same metal topped each wing.

I was not sure of the distance, having spent my life behind walls or on night runs, where everything was only a step or two in front of me, but it did not seem I had so far to go to just walk right through His Grace's front door. As I approached the palace, the street grew emptier. Quieter. My bells rang louder.

What might have been my wedding if my life had been different would instead be my funeral. I wished I could have ridden Endurance toward this end, much as my grandmother had.

From one moment to the next, I was surrounded by angry-faced guardsmen with swords drawn. They came upon me in a sudden swirl of rushing feet and shouting. My captors forced me to my knees, then down on the pavement. Someone kicked me twice, setting my bells to shivering all over my body. A blade's point was leaned against my neck. I bit back my cry of pain at that, just as I bit back my anger at the rough treatment.

Save your passion for the Duke, I told myself. *You will be lucky to have even a single chance. Do not spend it needlessly here.*

A runner sprinted away. His sandals slapped the street. The man with the sword knelt close behind me, though I could only see his knee and part of the ringmail of his skirt. "May's well be comfy, chit," he whispered. His hot breath was prickly on the scabbed-over notch of my ear. "You ain't got much left to live for."

"Conspiracy," I said to the cobbles. My mouth was half-pressed shut against stone that tasted mostly of shoeleather. "Against the Duke." That was my tale, meant to be told and carried to the place bearing me on its shoulders.

"Sun rose in the east, dinn't't?" He laughed. "Course there's conspiracy."

After that, they acted almost like normal people. Some told jokes about the wife of an officer. Others asked after one's sick horse, and complained of the food in their mess hall. Except for the sword pressing in my neck, I might have been nothing more than a street-corner idler listening to the chatter of men at their work.

No one was interested in me. I was just their capture. Meat, a thing, knocked down to be kept against possible future use, like a venison haunch in an ice room.

My anger began to boil again. These men were brutal and thoughtless in a way that Mistress Tirelle had never managed. Her cruelty was the calculated personal abuse of years. For the Duke's guards, I was only the trouble of a moment.

They didn't even *care*. At least she had.

It all flowed from the Duke. Everything wrong, poorly done, every hurt and hatred emanated from the way he bent the fate of Copper Downs. I kept the words in my head, waiting for my chance to use them against him.

In time, the runner returned. The men gathered in a whispered conference, speaking in awed terms of the bounty. They knew who I was now. I was dragged to my feet by a hard hand clawing into my shoulder. A man with a mild face and watery eyes threw a maroon duty cloak over my head. He laughed as he did it, then cinched a rope around my neck. I was tossed over an armored shoulder and hauled away.

We were heading to the Ducal Palace. Thus far, this was according to plan. Or so I fervently hoped.

The gait of the guardsman rocked me with a bumping irregularity that jangled my bells out of all time and tune. The men's chatter was gone, so I caught no further clues from them. We soon ascended a broad, shallow flight of stairs. I could hear other people moving, muttering, gathered around.

Whatever my humiliation was to be, it was beginning in a very public way. I decided to be encouraged by this. Their treatment of me seemed less likely to be a quick walk to a slit throat.

When they set me down, my captors were almost gentle. My feet slipped slightly on what felt like stone through my soft leather boots. Someone took my hand and led me stumbling through more hallways of stone. My training Below with the Dancing Mistress prepared me to recall my path, should that happen to matter sometime later.

As I walked, I could hear the echoes of the walls around me, and how they altered every dozen steps as we passed a recessed doorway. My bells still rang, but now they swung in time to my own movements.

The sounds were too discordant to ever be truly pleasing. It still gladdened my heart to hear them. I felt so close to my grandmother, except that *she* had not walked alive to her own funeral.

In time, my feet were on carpet. My boots crackled slightly, and slid in a new way. I smelled more now, not just dust and old stone, but also furniture oil and incense and the not-so-distant scent of baking. Doors opened and closed nearby as we walked.

No one said a word. We were among people who would not bother to question why a hoodwinked girl was being led past them. Later, I would come to understand the sadness of a city that had surrendered itself to the terror of a jealous and immortal master. Then, all I knew was that I was alone among strangers.

As always.

Finally I was stopped. A door creaked open. I smelled more incense and something musty. With a muttered "hup-hup," I was propelled through, as if I were a horse to be driven to market. Hands released me as I stepped within. After another pace, I stopped. I feared barking a shin or tripping over something on the floor.

Someone behind me loosened the rope about my neck and whipped the guard's cloak off. The door banged shut immediately thereafter.

I blinked away dust and the confusion of close confinement. There was no sign of the Duke here. Only a wide wooden table with the Factor seated behind it. My heart twisted in a cold stab of anger and regret. Two other dead-eyed men stood to his left. All three watched me blankly as my shoulders slumped and the breath left me.

Our plan was lost. The game was blown.

"Emerald." The Factor's voice was calm, quiet, as ordinary as his face except for those eyes.

"Green. You may call me Green."

A smile flickered across his mouth. "Emerald." He tapped his fingers against his thumb a moment, as if tallying. I let my eyes rove around the room. Three high, narrow windows on one wall, a ceiling far above me, shelves lined with large and heavy books behind the Factor's men and on the other walls. A door amid the shelves, a door behind me, and him in the only chair.

Nowhere to go. Nothing to use.

Whatever calculations he was making came to their end. His face was grim. "A valuable servant is dead. I now see that an extremely valuable possession has been mutilated and thus rendered worthless. I give you liberty to make a statement before I have you cast from the rim of the dome atop this building."

I was wrong. His voice wasn't ordinary. It was as dead as his eyes.

And I had nothing I could wield against him.

Yet I wasn't bound. I wasn't restrained in any way. Whichever guards had walked me through the halls to this place had vanished with the hood.

I was still *me*. I shifted my weight, testing the balls of my feet. The Duke was not here, but three of his dead-eyed servants were. More important, the Factor had ever been my enemy.

There was something I could do. Strike one of them down, any of them, and the rest might learn a little of the fear they'd beaten into me. I tensed my muscles, ready to spring and gain close purchase to pour my words in his ear. My cloak of belled silk jingled as I moved.

The Factor raised a hand, not toward me but at his two companions. "She may attempt an attack," he said. "She will not succeed."

"If you are certain, Your Grace," one of them answered.

Your Grace! How many undying, dead-eyed dukes could there be in this city? I had found the Duke of Copper Downs after all! That he went abroad on his own streets under the name of the Factor surprised me, but I realized there was no reason it should. The people who ruled this city were like those sliding boxes brought in from the Hanchu ports that folded into themselves without ever reaching an end.

I relaxed. He would not bluff me. Why did he need to? He did not know I understood anything of the words of power. The Dancing Mistress had been uncertain of them. *They* were my hidden weapon. I did not know if their strength would hold now, but there was no way to find out except to put the question to the hardest of tests.

"You were wrong," I told him.

"Wrong?" His smile flickered again. "A curious choice of exit lines. And no, I was not wrong. In what? Lifting a foreign guttersnipe from poverty? Raising you in privilege? Teaching you every skill of womanhood? Perhaps you would prefer picking rice in the tropics, bound in marriage to some laboring peasant. You were almost so much more than that."

I'd had those same thoughts, but that did not make him right. The bells of my cloak jingled again.

Words, I told myself in the language of my birth. *He tries to win once more through the power of his words.*

What would my grandmother have done? What would Endurance have me do? I could hear the snorting breath of the ox as he sought to warn me back.

The only way was forward.

Flipping the cloak of bells away from me, I flung it at the Factor's companions. I danced to my left, away from them.

He jumped to his feet and threw the table over, roaring words I did not—or could not—understand.

I leapt forward to balance on the edge of table. I had practiced this exact stance for so long. I spun into a kick from which the Factor ducked. Then I leapt to grab him around the neck.

"The life that is shared," I whispered in his ear in the language of my birth, "goes on forever. The life that is hoarded is never lived at all."

That was as close as Federo and I had been able to come to the Dancing Mistress' words. Surely, though, inasmuch as she'd given them to me in the Petraean tongue of Copper Downs, their sense had come from whatever language her people spoke amongst themselves. I hoped and prayed that sense would carry forward into my own words.

The Factor bore me down under his far greater weight. His two companions grabbed me by the wrists. I feared suddenly the rape that Mistress Cherlise had warned me about. These men would tear my body for their pleasure before they tore my life out for their protection.

"You," the Factor said. He couldn't seem to find his next thought.

His hair began to twist. It jumped like snakes disturbed from their sleep. Ripples of gray, then white, shot through it. The other two loosed their grip on me, staggering back in their own sudden, shocked decay.

"You . . ." This time he looked surprised. Finally there was some gleam of light in those cold, dead eyes.

I pushed him away from me, sitting up as he fell. The Factor struggled with something mighty that was caught in his chest. *The words worked.* I leaned close, to be sure he could hear me even as he was dying.

"You may call me Green," I said. "Green," I repeated in my own language.

He gave me a look of utter despair, which gladdened my heart. Wind and dust erupted violently. The air stank of old bandages and rotten meat, while unvoiced shrieks echoed within my skull.

I held on tight, remembering who I was and what my purpose was here. I bore these noises and the fires in my head as I'd borne the years of beatings and abuses. My patience had been schooled by the very best this man could set against me.

A moment later, I was alone in the room, amid the splintered remains of his table and the shattered wood of his chair.

The motes floating in the sunlight from the high windows engaged my attention for a while. Were these the dust of immortality? Or perhaps just the room's air stirred so much that every crack and crevice had surrendered its dirt.

Studying their texture awhile longer, I realized I was in the same shock that had possessed me after Mistress Tirelle's death. Except I did not feel guilt this time. Or pain. I was not sure it even counted as a killing. All I had done was point the weapon of the Duke's magic against him and those who served him closest. They had brewed their own poison and served it out in cups for generations. How could I regret these child-takers sipping their own bitters?

They *were* gone. The Duke and the Factor both. How was it no one in Copper Downs had noticed that the two of them had been the same man? Perhaps it had been one of those secrets that everyone understood but no one spoke of.

Everything about this Duke was difficult for me to fathom.

With them gone, I was free. The Factor was no longer in a position to pursue his complaint against me for the killing of Mistress Tirelle. The Duke was no longer in a position to offer a bounty for my head. I was free—free as any girl of twelve who stood out on these streets surely as a fire in the night.

Rarely had I thought to regret the color of my skin, for I found myself pretty enough to look at, but here and now among these maggot men, my fine brown tone made it impossible for me to hide.

What of it? I breathed deeply and searched for the courage that had driven me to face down the most powerful man on the Stone Coast, and indeed, in this quarter of the world. Resolve clutched within my throat, I stepped to the door and pressed my ear against the once-glossy panel. Now it was matted with dust and flecked with tiny pocks.

With that realization, I glanced at the backs of my hands. Dots of blood beaded them. I rubbed myself clean on my dark tights, then swiped fingers across my face. More blood, in faint smears, along with a sharp twinge of pain from the disturbed scabs.

Once more I tried to listen. No one walked or spoke immediately outside, though I heard distant shouting. I also realized there was a strange, faint roar, which I finally identified as a crowd of people giving voice outside the Ducal Palace.

I turned to gather my belled silk. It, too, had been damaged by the Duke's demise, but was still essentially whole even with a forest of snags and tears. Handfuls of bells slid to the floor when I pulled it over myself. The cloth brought the grave-dust smell of him with me. I didn't mind. That was the scent of triumph, after all. I might not live out the hour, but in this moment, I was free.

The hallway was empty. The wood of the threshold was scorched, likewise the carpet before it. The rug had abraded in a pattern of rays as if an explosion had taken place within my room. Papers were scattered loose against one wall, along with an empty slipper. People had fled in disarray. I shut the door and checked the gap at the bottom.

What *had* I survived?

We'd entered from what was now my left. The endless practice in the dark Below with the Dancing Mistress made it easy for me to find my way. Wiping my face and hands clean of bloody dust, I retraced my steps to the end of the hall, out into a wider gallery lined with bookshelves and decorated side tables.

This, too, was empty. The ceiling here was high, three or four storeys, with a long clerestory above serving to admit the light of the sky. Thin banners hung from the beams, descending about thirty feet to the height of a normal ceiling, a style I would eventually realize was typical of formal architecture in this city.

Farther from the explosion, people had also fled in panic. A dropped tray sat among a spray of shattered crystal and a pool of wine. Three leather folders were crumpled against the pedestal of a table supporting a statue of a wide-mouthed red god. Its eyes bugged like those of a frog, and seemed to follow me as I walked.

I could hear the roar much more clearly now, breaking into the separate sounds of people and horses and shattering glass. The noise of riot.

How had it happened so quickly? Unless all the Duke's henchmen had also dissolved with him. I tried to imagine the officers of the court, the leaders of the Ducal guard, even a tax inspector at his counting table before a clutch of humbled sea captains newly in harbor. If they'd all cried out in surprise, then crumbled in a whirlwind as the Duke had before me, that would send an immediate shock throughout the city.

I began to wonder what I had truly done. A man could not rule through the passage of centuries without the habits of his power becoming the habits of everyone who served him or lived within his demesne. How much had the city been overset?

How much did I care?

A servant younger than myself ran screaming from the sight of me in the next gallery. I still followed my memory of being led in, passing now from carpet to stone. Ahead of me, down a short flight of stairs, a small group of Ducal guards huddled before the great oak-and-copper doors. The entrance-way was surmounted by stained-glass windows. Everything was shut and barred; some of the windowpanes were broken out by cobbles strewn upon the floor within. The crowd just outside was very loud.

I walked toward the guards with my bells ringing. There was no point in pretense. One of their number, with a gold knot on the shoulder of his dark green woolen coat, looked up at me.

"You, there—don't go through this door!"

"Why not?" I asked, drawing myself up with dignity.

"Coz they'll kill you out there." He sounded more exasperated than afraid. "Everything's gone wrong."

All the Duke's immortals must have indeed fallen to dust. It was my great fortune these guards had no idea who I was. I thanked all the gods for the cloth that had hidden my face on the way in.

"Thank you, sir. I was visiting. Is there an exit I can use?"

"Try the Navy Gallery. Off to your left there."

One of the men spoke up. "If you're up for it, girl, just drop out of one of them windows. You'll be in the Box Elder Garden, but it lets out on Montane Street. Crowd out there hasn't yet remembered how many doors there are to this palace besides the front."

"Be off with you," the corporal added. "No use hanging here."

I took them at their word and turned into what I hoped was the Navy Gallery. No shouts corrected me.

In an instant, I knew I was right. The ceiling was painted with a smoke-wreathed battle scene showing long-hulled vessels from a much older time surrounding a burning, fat-bellied hulk. Ship's wheels and bells hung on the walls, while models stood on small tables—their detail was something I would have loved to examine at a different time.

The windows here were casements, with little cranks to turn out the glass on a hinge up the long side. I picked one in the middle and looked out at some rhododendron bushes backed by a stand of box elder trees just beyond. The noise was less here. No one seemed to be throwing cobbles at the palace.

A moment later, I was out among the bushes. Reason had crept up on pride, so I stopped there and rolled my belled silk into a bundle. I slipped out of the trees and into the stream of people approaching the front of the palace from along Montane Street. They had the rumbling urgency of a mob, complete with torches, staves, and iron tools.

A man in a pale suit with the cut of a middle-ranked trader grabbed at me. My heart chilled, and I twisted, hoping to kick his knee.

"Is it still happening in there?" he shouted. He was not even looking at me. His eyes rolled red and wild.

"I . . . I don't know." I hated how small and frightened my voice sounded.

"The Duke is dead, long live the Duke!" He glanced around, then seemed to see me for the first time. "Go home, girl. This is no place for a foreigner now."

"Green," I whispered. Nodding my thanks, I took the first side street that was reachable across the streaming flow of the forming mob.

It was done. I was free, and out of the palace, and on a path of my own choosing. I was my own person, no one's property for the first time since coming to this accursed city. And they would send no more Federos out to buy children. Not this gang that I had laid low.

Heading for the docks, I aimed to take the trader's advice. Copper Downs held nothing more for me. Perhaps I could return to what I had been—not a girl under the belly of her father's ox, certainly, but to what that girl might have become.

Since I hadn't expected to survive, I'd given no thought to what came next. I had a direction now—the trader had the right of it, so far as his advice went—but I was surprised to regret what I was leaving behind.

I had no trouble at all leaving the Factor's House behind. That was a well-upholstered slave pit, and nothing more. Some of my Mistresses had been kind. Mistress Danae, for example. And if I had friends in this life, they were Federo and the Dancing Mistress.

Once I took ship, I would never see them again. What had not even been a worry before was now a swell of regret. The Factor could be dust for all I cared, but Mistress Tirelle plucked my heart as well.

Loping toward the docks, I wiped tears from my eyes. There'd been no time to say good-bye before. Now it was too late.

I had no idea how to interpret the chaos of the waterfront when I finally arrived there. The crowding bordered on panic, everyone heedless and hurried. I needed a ship to Selistan. If I took passage aboard a vessel bound for the Sunward Sea, that would likely be a permanent error.

It all rested on how well I spoke. Certainly there had been stories aplenty in Mistress Danae's books about stowaways and travelers working their passage. Somehow none of them were dark-skinned girls.

My color hadn't mattered within the bluestone walls of the Pomegranate Court. Out here, it might hold the balance of my life. Along with my words. As I'd always known, these people lived and died by their words.

I continued to walk briskly, bound on an errand to nowhere. If I were to stand and gawk, I would mark myself as a potential victim. Instead I looked as closely as I could at each ship I passed, each wharf.

Some had signboards out to advertise their destination. Most of these were cities of the Stone Coast—Houghharrow, Dun Cranmoor, Lost Port. These I recognized from the stories and maps I'd studied. One was marked for the Saffron Tower. Much too far the wrong way for me.

A signboard loomed ahead. In shaky handwriting, it read, "South to sun countries. Calling in Kalim., Chitta and Spice Pt.s."

I trotted up to that gangplank. The ship had three tall masts, and no sign of a boiler below, unlike the smokestack I recalled from *Fortune's Flight*. A man stood there with skin as dark as mine, though he was fitted out in the duck and cotton of a sailor. He held a long board to which papers had been bound with sisal twine. He glanced at me once, then back at his board.

"Please, sir, I would have passage," I said. He didn't even glance up at me. Then, in Seliu: "I want to return home."

That got his attention. "Go back to your mother," he replied, then some words I didn't know.

"She is there," I told him. "I was stolen."

"You are a slave." He looked at me with suspicion. "Trouble rides your back." That last was in Petraean.

"Trouble rides this entire city," I answered him, also in Petraean. "If I do not go with you, I may never go at all."

"What is being your fare for passage, should I recommend to the captain that we take you?"

I took a deep breath. Here was where my plan would founder. "I have no fare, sir. Just the goodwill of my countrymen. I can cook to please the table of a lordly house, and my skills with needle and thread are worthy as well."

He snorted, and my heart fell. "Next you'll tell me you play the music of angels and can dance the Seven Steps of Sisthra."

"I sing, sir, but only in the fashion of the Stone Coast."

Something stirred in his face. "You do not know the songs of Selistan."

Switching back to our words, I said, "It has been a very long time."

Close by, a bell began ringing. Everyone on the dock looked around with frantic haste. Many ran off. An alarm, then. Riot approached the docks.

"Come." He started up the gangplank. "If we cast off with you aboard, much of this discussion will be lacking in point. Captain Shields is not likely to toss you overboard as a stowaway. Especially if you can grace his table in style."

Someone on the masts called out. Sailors pounded the deck. The ship lurched slightly, then began to drift. I realized they had a line off the stern. A boat full of men pulled hard to tow this vessel away from shore.

I tugged at the man's sleeve. "Please, sir, what is the name of this ship?"

He looked down at me and began to laugh. "Do not think me to be mocking you, little one, but this vessel is called *Southern Escape*."

"Ah." I looked quietly into his eyes. "But I am free."

"Of course you are," he answered. "At the moment." He bent close. "I am Srini, the purser. I must go see to the captain. To be sitting with those bales over there, and for the love of all that is holy, get yourself in no one's path."

The deck clanged and rattled. Canvas boomed as sails were raised. I crouched upon the deck and told myself old stories in the language of my birth. I was on my way to a port from which with luck I could hear the sound of Endurance's wooden bell. I was on my way to freedom.

I was on my way home.

Going Back

SRINI PUT me to work in the galley with an elderly Hanchu cook who had only one leg. Lao Jia wore a wooden peg to move about on deck, but he hung that at the galley hatch and spent his time within braced against the inbuilt counters. The peg was carved with flowing dragons chasing a series of black pearls set into the wood. The galley was strung with a clever series of canvas straps to secure him against heavy seas or rising storms. I believe he tolerated me at first only because I was small and lithe enough to duck around him.

I was just as glad to be down there. The deck frightened me. I *remembered* horizons, first from home, then aboard *Fortune's Flight*. Actually seeing them again was profoundly disorienting. Even the streets of Copper Downs had been enclosed by buildings, trees, people. The ocean was nothing but horizon, rippling uncomfortably in all directions.

The old man spoke almost no Petraean, other than shouting the names of some foodstuffs at me. I certainly spoke no Hanchu then. I had never heard the language in my life before being forced to share the narrow kitchen with him. However, he did have a bit of Seliu, a language he shared with Srini and the memories of my earliest childhood.

The steam of pots clamped to the swinging stoves was the smell of freedom to me. Lao Jia made me chop cabbage and carrots under his watchful eye. He soon determined that I would not lose a finger into the food or stab him as *Southern Escape* rolled with the swells. "You will do," he said in Seliu.

Those words from a busy old man were perhaps the first genuine praise I'd received in my life.

"My thanks," I told him.

When I proved to know my way around his spice bottles by sight and smell, he seemed almost pleased. On our second day at sea, I made a very serviceable turnover stuffed with ground pork, cumin, and mashed cress. Lao Jia pronounced me good. "I talk to Srini, you stay here and cook." His gap-toothed smile beamed.

"I go to Selistan," I told him.

He pretended to wail, drawing off his blue cloth cap and folding it to his breast while muttering prayers to his Hanchu gods. Then he smiled, patted me on the head, and put me back to work.

Cooking with him was pleasant. It was even more pleasant to work without ready judgment standing at my back. I did not mind the small kitchen, the limited tools, and the odd ingredients. Best of all, after several more days, Lao Jia began to show me the basics of Hanchu cuisine. The primary techniques revolved around shredding the food, marinating it, frying the results quickly in a hot, shallow pan, then serving everything mixed together in sauce. What was not simple was balancing the humors of the food—Srini had to help me sort that word out in Petraean, when Lao Jia first began using it—as well the complex spices and sauces.

I realized that Mistress Tirelle had left me with a true love of learning.

Bunking me correctly was a more difficult task. "You have not paid for a cabin," Srini told me sternly after my first two nights sleeping on deck. We were still speaking mostly Petraean then. I'd had to kick several sailors away, and wound up awake both nights in fear for my safety.

"I am not a harlot for their use." Mindful of Mistress Cherlise's many lessons, I swept my hand over my mostly flat chest. "I am not even yet grown to womanhood."

He pulled at his broad dark chin, reminding me for a moment of Federo. "I cannot simply give you a privilege. You are quite young to be trading your comforts for the passage, this is true." Srini frowned. "I am sorry to say, but the wounds upon your cheeks will draw the eye away. If you are to be cutting off that great mane of woman's hair and dressing in canvas trousers, they will take less notice of you."

My hair had never been cut in my life, so far as I knew, except for the ends being trimmed to suit the style of my beauty. The Factor's beauty, which I had already sliced away. "I will do it," I told him in Seliu.

"And I will be having a word with the bosun about the night watch on the deck." He smiled. "You walk a long road for such a young woman."

"My path was taken from me years ago."

Lao Jia was scandalized when I asked for a knife to set to my hair. "No, no, beauty!" he shouted. "Not to ruin good knife, either!"

I despaired of explaining the problem that had required such a solution. Still, I tried. Somehow he understood. "I cut," he said. "I keep."

While I'd held some notion of burning the hair or casting it into the sea, I agreed. He would do a better job than I—when had I ever cut hair? Besides that, I could hardly see my own neck.

We decided to stay in the galley for the effort. There was no purpose in setting a show for the sailors and passengers on deck, and they would be less likely to see me as a girl if they had not witnessed my transformation. Lao Jia produced a great pair of shears. "For cutting," he said, then a word I did not know.

I just nodded.

He sharpened them on a tiny grinder, which he turned by hand. Unlike *Fortune's Flight* with its great kettle belowdecks, *Southern Escape* had been built for nothing but wind, wood, and muscle power. No electricks here.

In time, Lao Jia sat me on a little folding stool he kept braced behind a counter and went to work. Each snip of the shears was a heavy pull at my scalp that almost made me cry out. I held still, mouth shut and eyes half-clenched against the drizzle of tears he drew forth from me.

Cutting my hair was in a strange way even more painful than slashing my cheeks had been. I tried to think about why that was so. In principle, I could cover my scars with clays and paints, or even perhaps the attentions of some physician or flesh-healer. My hair, though. I would be faced with the work of another span of my lifetime to grow it out again.

My head felt lighter when he was done. I had never considered what a weight my hair had been, but my neck rose high and strong. "Thank you," I said in Seliu, then again in Hanchu.

"I keep, I keep."

"You keep."

I struggled into the canvas clothes Srini had given me, with my ruined tights and shirt as smallclothes beneath them. My soft leather boots would be worn through in days on these decks, so he had also found me a decent pair of shoes. It seemed easier to remain barefoot. I watched the waves pitch and the birds wheel while the wind rubbed damp, chilly fingers across my scalp. I touched my head. I was not bald, but he had cut me to stubble.

You need a hat, I thought. The air teased a few more tears from my eyes as my scalp grew cold even in the sunlight. Then I went to scrounge a cover for my head.

Freedom had such strange and unexpected prices.

———

My cooking acquired a cachet aboard *Southern Escape*. Lao Jia traded me lessons in Hanchu cookery for my culinary knowledge, especially of baking. Bread was not such a great thing in the Han countries, I quickly learned, and desserts even less so. We prepared ambitious dinners for the captain and the passengers, while also spicing up the sailors' stew and biscuit in different ways.

A fresh catch was brought in almost every day. I knew far more about game than about seafood, and was content to learn from Lao Jia there as well. He showed me how to judge a fish, where to look for worms or other parasites, what to check in the gut to see if it had been unhealthy. Some we threw overboard for the sharks. What he approved of was sliced thin for serving cold or as an inclusion in the fried Hanchu dishes; otherwise thick for me to work with as steaks. I quickly moved toward lighter sauces with sharp flavors to complement the strong tastes and odors of fish.

I brought puddings to the table, pastries, dishes of fruit mashed frozen from the ice boxes below, or mixed into compotes and salads. Lao Jia made his stirred fryings, steamed little dumplings of fish and shrimp, and showed me how to pickle meat until it threatened to rot but tasted divine.

At the same time, Srini came around to the galley or found me on the deck every day and spoke to me awhile in Seliu. He was concerned at how little I knew.

"You are a girl close to grown, but your accent is Stone Coast and your vocabulary has many oddities."

He was forced to explain several of those words.

"I hate that I talk Petraean so well," I told him, "and my own words so bad."

"Then we will talk." Srini spoke of the doings of the ship, the food we'd prepared that day or the night before, pointed out people and described them to me. He talked about the Wheel, which underlies so much of Selistani life, for the people believe it explains the fate and purpose of their souls. His words were like water on a sun-baked pot. I felt Seliu stirring within me. I knew, most unkindly, that Papa would have said little of what Srini told me, but it was still the tongue of my birth. The sounds lay deep inside, waiting only for an awakening such as this.

I also knew from my time aboard *Fortune's Flight* that we would be weeks in the crossing. More, depending on the winds. I also knew from what Federo had told me that I did not want to take passage all the way to Kalimpura.

"Srini," I said one day, a week into our lessons and eleven days out of Copper Downs. "I must ask your help."

"What is it, Green?" He smiled his smile, which lifted the droopy mustache he'd been growing. "I have made you a boy, and carried you across the sea. I am too poor a tulpa to do much more than that."

I laughed, more because he expected me to than because the joke deserved it. "I do not want to go to Kalimpura."

"In truth?" He switched to Petraean. "Lao Jia has asked me if we can keep you aboard as cook's mate. After last night's honeyed smelt in plums, I can say the captain will be easily convinced."

"No, no. I wish to put ashore at Little Bhopura." For a moment, I switched back to Seliu. "I must go there."

"Little Bhopura?" he asked in Petraean. Srini tugged at his chin some more. "I am not even sure where that lies. It has never been a port for any ship I've served aboard. Surely it is somewhere in Bhopura?"

"Thirty leagues east of Kalimpura, I am told." I willed him to hear me and understand my need. "I believe we sail past it on our way. A fishing port, where some bring their rice and vegetables to trade."

"I am only the purser," he said sadly. "I book cargos and passengers aboard, but the ship sails under the captain and his master. Once we have agreed where we will put in, it is not for me to say."

"Then will you do this thing for me." I switched again to our tongue. "When we are close to Little Bhopura, will you tell me? I would swim ashore."

"Swim! In those waters? The greater devilfish would make a morsel of you!"

"I will chance it. That is where I must go." To my surprise, I believed my words.

We made passage over open water for two more weeks after my request. The winds were largely favorable, though our voyage was marked by one great storm and several smaller ones, and once the landing of a gigantic calamar-fish, which was thrown back as an ill omen despite Lao Jia's begging and my own intense curiosity.

Each day, I carefully sewed another knot in my silk. I had taken no bells when I'd left the attic back in Copper Downs, probably because I hadn't thought to live beyond that morning. Though that moment was only days in my past, it already had the unreal remove of some other life's memories. Like something read once, and later misrecalled as if it had happened to me.

It happened that I was on deck immediately after the midday service and shortly before Lao Jia and I would begin cooking in earnest for the dinner.

The lookout shouted something I did not understand. This was followed by a great cheering from the crew, and much pointing off the starboard bow.

I went to that rail and stared. After a while, I realized that the horizon didn't have the same wobbling line that it possessed in the other directions.

Land, I thought. The easternmost edge of this portion of Selistan. Bhopura would be somewhere behind that shore. As would my father. And Endurance.

When Lao Jia called me down to help with the dinner, I begged his forgiveness. "This is my home," I told him. "I have not seen it since I was very small. I must watch the shore." My Seliu had improved under Srini's tutelage.

"You were to make potato leek soup for the captain's table tonight," he grumbled.

"Just go easy on the salt, and none of those red peppers. They will like it well enough."

He stumped away again with a shake of his head. The black eyes of the dragons winked at me from his wooden leg.

I stared at the shore, as if somehow I thought I might glimpse Endurance through some gap in the trees I could not yet make out. This has ever been a weakness of mine, looking ahead to what I could not see, but at that time, it still smacked of honest ignorance and rising hope. Somewhere there was the house where I was born. If I looked hard enough, I would recognize something—even just the shape of the crown of a tree. I wanted a sign that my home would welcome me back.

Unfortunately for me, darkness fell before the shore was anything more than a thickening line on the horizon. The smells from the galley were good enough that I would not be shamed. I let the rising breeze pluck at me and wondered how much time the walk from Little Bhopura to my papa's farm would take. It had been a long road in my memory, but Federo had put the distance at a pair of leagues.

I would walk across the water if I must, to get to shore.

"In the morning, you will see the forests along the beach," Srini said behind me. "This far to the east, they are mostly wild palms and some pine-nut trees. The soil on the ridges behind the shore is too salty and stony to be of use, so no one lives here but bandits."

Being of a practical mind, I wondered who those bandits preyed upon. "Will Little Bhopura be the first port we pass?"

"Yes. I spoke to the navigator. He will plot a course that takes us closer in than we might normally go. It is safe enough from reefs, but the wind is chancier."

"What will Captain Shields say?" I'd been feeding the man at least once a day in the almost-month I'd been aboard *Southern Escape,* and I still had not met him.

"With luck, he will be saying nothing. If he asks, the navigator will tell him that we are checking the charts. Sometimes that is even being true."

"Who am I to the navigator?" Another man whose name I did not know.

Srini smiled. "The woman who makes honeyed smelt. Besides, the navigator is being my lover."

"Ah." Mistress Cherlise had discussed that, in more detail than I'd really cared to hear: how two men might be lovers together. Love among women I thought I could understand, but men were such careless brutes that I did not then see how two of them could love without someone to soften the blows and dampen the curses. This opinion was a legacy of the Factor's house, I now know, but many of those habits of thought were years in the erasing.

"Thank him for me," I told him softly.

"Never fear." He sighed, then switched to Seliu. "I do not yet know how to land you without causing far too much comment."

"The shore will not be far." I felt dreamy, drawn so close to home, as if Endurance were before me, flicking his ears. "I shall stride across the waves like a goddess returning."

"I shall find a need for something in the market there," Srini muttered. "And be taking you ashore to help me select it."

"Will the captain not become angry when I leave your company?"

"He will be cursing you for a ship-jumper, once he knows that the new cook's mate is gone."

"But I never took his tael."

Srini smiled in the gleaming starlit dark. "Of course not. I was never asking you to sign the ship's book, was I?"

I hugged him. He hugged me back. "Go forth and be a man's daughter a little longer, if the turning of your Wheel is allowing it."

"Yes." I went below to pack my very meager belongings and explain myself to Lao Jia.

Two days later, the ship put in close to shore. The navigator was violently ill belowdecks. It had been widely put about that the purser needed a certain fresh fruit from his native land to effect the most immediate cure.

I watched the waters curl and spit along the hull of *Southern Escape.* This part of the Selistani coast boasted clay hills covered with scrub, lined with palms where they descended to meet the water. The port that held the first real buildings I had ever seen in my life now seemed a run-down collection of garden sheds. No dock stuck out into the water, just logs making steps down to the beach.

Nothing looked familiar to me, though I had seen this place before. I now have two layers of memory, like lacquer on an inlaid table, obscuring the grain of the truth that lies beneath.

Children waved and shouted and pointed at *Southern Escape.* Her sails were reefed as she glided to a rest. Anchor chains rumbled when the weights were dropped, while the bosun already had men putting a little boat over the side.

I would go ashore as I might well have left this place, rowed by pale men who cursed their oars at every stroke. With my belled silk rolled tight in a sailcloth bag, I dressed in the worn duck trousers and shirt I'd been given. Underneath, I'd wrapped my chest tight, so the emerging bumps of my breasts would not betray me.

Lao Jai touched at my arm as I prepared to descend to the dory bobbing alongside. "A moment," he said. "I will miss you." He added something else in Hanchu.

"I will miss you, as well." My face bent into a smile even I hadn't expected. "I am going home. Thank you for the lessons in your cookery."

"May the gods carry you where you wish." He frowned. "If home is not what you think, please to keep looking."

I hugged him, then scrambled down the ladder. We rowed ashore, bouncing in a surf I did not recall from my departure so long ago. The children anticipated the boat's arrival. Screaming, they fought with the sailors to draw the keel up the beach. Srini and I tumbled ashore as the bosun's mate began arguing with children who did not share a language with him.

Privy to the curses and taunts flying both ways, I parted company with my friend the purser and walked up the few steps from the beach, as if I were going to market for Srini's fruit.

The town was even less than I recalled, a bedraggled collection of buildings on one side of the muddy track, huts and stalls on the other. I marched into the struggling market as if I knew my way, ignoring the little clicking calls from the stallholders. I understood. I looked the part here, with my skin and patchy hair, but my clothes marked me out as not local.

I will fit in at home, I promised myself. *Papa and Endurance will take me in, and it will not matter how I look.*

That was a lie, of course, and I knew it even then. But I had to see the truth for myself before I could understand the difference.

Passing through the rotten little bazaar, I *remembered* this walk. I could find the farm. The Dancing Mistress had trained me very well in retracing my steps. That the gap between memory and re-creation was a decade long should not stop me.

Passing beyond the last few buildings and a rank pen of bleating goats, I quickly climbed the road that sloped up north and west out of the miserable little town toward the dry upland I remembered from years before. A league or two, and I would be home. In my father's arms again, where I belonged. A few more furlongs, and I could claim my life back for good and all.

The ridgetop was as desolate as memory had made it out to be. I watched for the wayhouse where Federo and I had stopped to eat more than nine years before, but never saw it.

Perhaps it had been a building at the edge of the town, and I had misremembered the distance.

Wooden fences straggled back and forth across the landscape. The plants were a combination of low, scrubby bushes and spiked explosions like balls of thorns. Though I could name a hundred flowering plants and herbs of the Stone Coast, I had no words in Petraean or Seliu for what grew here so close to my home. A few herds of goats as worn and threadbare as their fields eyed me suspiciously when I passed. Otherwise, I could have been on the moon for all that I saw signs of people.

Ahead, a mountain range rose in the morning sun. It was dusty dark, a mix of rose and brown and purple shadow with the light still low in the east. The line must trend north of west, I realized, to keep the shadow so.

After all my years behind walls, I was pleased enough that I could see landforms and understand what they would have been on a map.

The road stayed almost level, still rising a bit as I headed away from Little Bhopura. Nothing changed in an hour of walking except that the fences came closer together and the goats were slightly more numerous.

It all became different within another dozen strides. The road crested and dropped between embankments. An entirely different landscape spread before me, a plain much lower than the ridge I'd been crossing, that stretched from here to the distant mountains. A wide river glinting silver cut lazy curves through an endless patchwork of squares and lines.

Rice paddies. Ditches. Villages. Down there, somewhere close to me, was my home. My foot slipped on some gravel, and to my surprise, I fell seated to the ground. The shock ran through my buttocks and hips, small stones cutting in even past the canvas trousers. The greater shock was how my eyes filled with tears. I felt as if my body had begun to spew hot pepper.

I sat in the road and sobbed aloud as I had not done since the first days of my captivity. Home stretched before me like the Fields of Promise before Barzak the Deliverer in the last canto of *The Book of Lesser Fates*. I was young, alive, and won free from slavery.

Still, I cried. My chest shuddered. My nose filled with heavy mucus until it threatened to drain and choke me. A grief I could not name clutched at my heart. Darkness covered my eyes.

I tried to fight free. I had not cried like this, ever. *What am I mourning so deeply?* Grandmother? My mother, whom I could not remember at all? Mistress Tirelle?

Finally it came to me that I was crying for the girl I could have been. The woman I would never be. My path was bent, perhaps beyond repair. Regardless, I must locate Papa and Endurance and see what could be made right. I was aware my father would not know me, though I'd avoided considering that until now.

I only hoped I could know him.

It took some while for me to reach calm. Finally I stood, dusted off my trousers, and headed down the hill. The river looped not far from the base of the escarpment—I was not yet any decent judge of distance then, but even to my untrained eye it was close—and a crossroads there, which would take me somewhere near home.

If I could not find it, I would ask. If I could not ask, I would walk, quartering these fields until Papa's hut was before me.

Of course, I could not just make my way back. Federo had not been able to give me specific directions. I did not know my father's name. He was just "Papa" to me. So I walked toward the little cluster of huts where the roads met.

The river was a flat, dark presence by the time I got there. The sun's climb toward the zenith had stolen his silver, and paid the land back with heat. My canvas shirt would soon be a punishment, but I had nothing else to wear except the belled silk, and that would not be enough for simple modesty.

A thin-muzzled white dog, a mangy bitch red and gray with dust, slunk out from the first mud-brick hut to investigate me. She growled once, but I stared close into her eyes and spoke some of the simple words Mistress Balnea had taught me, from the language all dogs know in their blood and bone. With a whimper, the bitch sat and began to scratch at fleas, though her eyes tracked me as close as any prey.

Children played in the middle of the pathetic town. They were bandy-legged, with potbellies and slack jaws. Their skins were much darker than mine from the burning of the sun. I could see the dents of ribs upon their thin chests.

Had I been like this? What had Federo seen in me?

I wanted to ask after Papa's fields, but there was no way to make a question. A woman with her belled silk wrapped around her stepped to the empty doorway of another hut to stare at me. She had a wide jaw, and was not so dark as the children, but matched them for her gauntness.

They have little here, except recent famine, I thought. The fields beyond the village were flooded, small green shoots poking above the water. The previous harvest must have failed. It could happen with too little water or too much. Rice cultivation was one of the few topics I had found in Mistress Danae's books that had any bearing on my lost home.

Lost no more, I reminded myself.

I kept walking, giving her a single nod. She did not return it, but stared me out of her little village and onto the road beyond. I headed right, back toward the north, on an instinct that counted as little more than a whim. The dust clouded with each fall of my sailor's boots. The sun pressed down upon my head as I had remembered it doing all those years ago. Except then, it had been my friend, my constant companion, while now I could feel by the warming of the right side of my face that it had become my enemy.

Had I really set out carrying no water? What a fool I was.

I walked, looking for side paths. Brick piles were scattered here and there along the way toward the river. When a man stepped out of one, stretching to his feet, I realized these were huts. Had Papa's been so low?

We'd had a gatepost, and plantain trees nearby with a rich stand of bougainvilleas. These were just wretched hovels amid open fields of rice. I looked ahead at a tree line. My heart raced.

There?

Keeping myself from running, I followed the road. It seemed right. I was getting close.

After passing the shadow of some struggling palms, I looked toward the next array of paddies. They were little different from the last. My heart was a stone.

Eventually I sought out directions. A man with a hoe, wearing only a grubby dhoti, worked in the ditch by the road near the shadow of a familiar baobab tree. I knew I was close.

"Please, sir," I said.

He stopped swinging his tool—a spiked club, really—and stared at me without answering.

"I am looking for a farm. A man of middle years, with a white ox named Endurance."

The farmer shrugged and went back to cutting mud. I knew he would use it to shore one of the paddy ditches. I kept walking, asked my question twice more before a man with a cart filled with short straw pointed onward. "Endurance, hmm?" he said. "Fifth walkway on the right. You are wanting Pinarjee's place, perhaps."

Pinarjee! A name. I nearly cried, instead pressing my hands together, and I bowed. "Thank you, sir."

"Get on, boy, to whatever work it is you are missing."

"Of course, sir."

Counting carefully, I found the fifth walkway. I trembled as I stepped onto it. A stand of plantains rose ahead of me close by a pair of tumbledown huts. A ragged row of stumps showed where my bougainvilleas might once have grown. Cut for firewood?

I walked slowly, my pace dragging more with every step. A crude fence enclosed the huts. I'd remembered the gatepost being almost as tall as Federo, but this was a little gnarled thing that looked as if it had been assembled by a dull-witted child.

Then I heard the clop of a wooden bell. Endurance appeared from behind the huts, rising to his feet from where he had been sitting. He stared at me. My pace quickened; my eyes filled once more. The ox snuffled once, twice, then shook his head. The bell echoed again and again.

Did he know me, even now, after these years? Memory was a pain sharp as any knife.

A woman stepped out of the hut and stared as well. She was thin, dark, and wore only a length of grubby linen wrapped twice around her and then over her shoulder.

"Who are you?" she demanded.

I stopped. Endurance whuffled. Taking a deep breath to fight off the quaver in my voice, I said, "I am my father's daughter, finally come home again."

She approached and took my chin in her hand to turn my face. "Pinar's daughter died with her mother, as a small child. But yes . . . you have his look."

That was the moment when I should have turned and retraced my steps. That was the moment when I should have left the memory of my home as it was. That was the moment when my papa's love was still whole.

Like a fool, twice a fool, I stood my ground. "Endurance knows me. The ox remembers."

She glanced over her shoulder. "That old bag of bones? He goes to slaughter next week." Then she shouted, "*Pinar!* Come out here now."

My father emerged from his hut, shaking, tired, to stare blank-eyed at me as if he'd never seen me before in my life. I saw his face, wanted to run to hug him, but his wife's hand was tight upon my arm as my heart collapsed. Endurance continued to shake his head, ears flapping and his breath huffing as his bell tolled.

The ox had not meant to welcome me home. He had meant to warn me away.

That afternoon, I stood calf-deep in a paddy pulling weeds. The ox was sleeping once more behind the hut that had been his stall in earlier years. Papa—Pinarjee—slept as well. Only his wife was out with me. Shar, her name was.

"If this is your house, then you'll work for your keep like everyone else," she said fiercely.

"Why does he not know me?"

Shar chopped with her hoe, breaking clods and tearing up some of the small waxy plants we were removing. I waited for her to answer, but she kept working. So I worked, too.

Finally she said, "He does not recognize much anymore. Sometimes he cries out for Mira." She looked at me sidelong. "His mother, that was."

"I remember Grandmother," I said softly.

"*You remember nothing!*" Her voice was a shriek as she dropped her hoe. "Listen to you. You don't talk like a woman. Your voice is foreign. Your clothes are foreign. You don't even *walk* like a woman!" Shar leaned close, her voice dropping to an angry hiss. "This is not your home. It is *mine.* Pinar . . ." She swallowed a sob, then continued. "Pinar, whatever is left of him, is *my* husband."

I don't know what I'd hoped for in coming here. Certainly not a frightened, angry woman living with a man whose spirit had already departed from behind his eyes. The ditches where I'd swum and played were filled with dark water and stinking moss. Insects the size of my hand flitted among the plantains of my memory.

Even Endurance was *old.*

My heart crumbled. Before Shar, I swallowed my tears, but she must have read it on my face.

"Go back to your city, little foreign girl. Leave us to starve in our own way. This land is not yours." She spat in the water at my feet. "It never was."

I found a shard of courage. "Wh-what do you fear?"

She looked at me as if I were stupid.

"I d-do not know," I said. "I do not know why you are so angry."

"Because, you fool, you came back. If the village elders believe you are his child, when he dies, all this land will be *yours*. They will marry you to a likely boy, and I will have nothing."

All what *land*, I thought. A pair of rice paddies and a half-rotten stand of plantains? Seen through the eyes of the Stone Coast, it was on the tip of my tongue to ask who would want this. But the answer was clear enough: Shar. The woman who fed and cleaned my father enough that he remained alive even in the grip of whatever madness had claimed him.

Love? Or just inheritance?

Wars had been fought over less, in the history of the Stone Coast.

I understood my mistake then. Everything I cherished in memory had been a lie. If I'd stayed here, I'd have been as fat-bellied and skinny-legged as those children I'd passed. Or already married off, to get my hungry mouth out of the house. I'd spent years behind bluestone walls longing for what had been taken from me.

My captors had been right. Rather, I should have been on my knees thanking the Factor for what he had taken me from.

I reached out to touch her arm, soft as I knew to do it. "I do not want your land, Shar. I thought this was my h-home, but I was very far wrong. Th-thank you for caring for my papa."

Her eyes filled with tears then. "Go, then. Keep him in your mind however you remember him. Don't see him the way he is now."

Shouldering my hoe, which must have been Papa's when he and Shar had worked the fields together, I walked back to the hut. I knocked muck from the blade, then wiped it with my hand, before setting the tool by the door. My father stared from the shadows within. His eyes glinted as if he were an animal in a cage.

I went to see the ox. Endurance still sat upon the ground. His back was covered with flies. I stood by his neck and hugged him. He whuffled. I could hear his gut rumbling.

"You were my guide all those years," I whispered in his ear.

He was a beast, too, of course. Though somehow less an animal than Papa, now.

I went back to the door of the hut. My sailcloth bag was there. I had no other possessions except the memories, which were sliding to dust. I squatted on my knees and looked to the darkness within. His gaze locked with mine a moment, then slipped away.

"Papa," I said. "Pinarjee."

He twitched, but did not look back at me. Flies buzzed, and the room smelled close of sweat and piss.

"I—I love you." I didn't know if that was true. He had *sold* me, after all. How much love was that? Yet I'd been raised with clean sheets and good food and a life of the mind. What of the petty fears of Shar? I might have been a younger copy of her had I stayed here.

Free, but tied to this land by the terror of having nothing.

I had nothing now. Not even a name.

"Papa. Wh-what did you and Mama call me? What was my name?"

He sniffed once, then reached inside his dhoti to scratch at his groin.

"What was my *name*?" My voice was rising despite my desire to control myself, to not frighten him. How could I come this far and not even learn this? This was the one fragment of home I could have carried away.

"What was my name!" I screamed.

He screamed back at me with a wordless yawp of terror, then scuttled into the farthest corner of the hut. That gave him little more distance than he already had, but he must have felt safer there. The hot smell of fresh piss flowed around me.

I stepped back and straightened. "I am sorry," I muttered.

Turning, I was startled to see Shar standing right behind me with her hoe. I slipped sideways away from the swing of her strike before I realized she was not poised to attack me.

"I never knew." Her voice was ragged, but I could hear the regret. "He spoke only of his mother. Baida told me he'd had a wife and daughter, before."

"No one ever said my name?" Tears were down my face now.

"Oh, girl, no—"

"Don't call me that!" I shouted before I realized she had not intended the word as I had heard it.

"You have demons in your head," she snapped. Her moment of honesty was fled in the face of my anger. "Now go."

I stood my ground as she hefted her hoe once more. "What did he do with the money?"

"What money?"

"He sold me for a lifetime's worth of wages."

With those words, I turned away. That was as evil a curse as I knew to lay upon her. She had given me nothing, *nothing*. Papa even less. I cried, walking toward the road once more. Home had been my destination all my life, and it was as lost to me as the past itself. There was nothing for me now, not here or anywhere.

My tears led the way. I followed them into the blackness of my heart, walking onward only because there was no point in stopping.

Alternately starving and stealing, I was over a month on the road westward. I knew nothing of how to find food in a stream or a stand of trees, unless it was ripe and hanging for the touch. On that journey, I killed my second living person. He was a bandit intent on raping me. Instead, I took him with a kick to the groin, then slew him with his own knife, before falling to my knees to vomit what little was in my stomach.

Afterwards, I lit two small fires to him and made a speaking in the manner of the Stone Coast. I had nothing good to say of the scruffy dead man except that his mother had probably loved him once, so I commemorated his shade to her. Then I took his stale flatbread and his good sandals and the knife that I had wedged into him and went on my way.

Killing wasn't easier the second time, even though I'd had cause that no one would dispute. The act was so final. Even now, I cannot look back with anything but sorrow. Nothing was left for forgiveness or vengeance when a person has breathed their last. Papa had been just as dead, but his body had not yet received the message.

I moved on, with no purpose except the habit of walking. Even my bells were forgotten. Eventually, I came to travel three days with a trio of old women who did not say a word for most of that time. They wore pale robes and carried wilted lilies, in honor of the goddess whom I would soon come to serve. They shuffled slowly, but they had food and seemed to know the increasingly busy road. Best of all, they did not try to drive me away when I fell in with them. A few hours later, I flashed my knife at a young man who looked too closely at us. The oldest of the women smiled at me for that. I had no idea then that she was one of the most accomplished killers in this land.

We crested a rise the afternoon of the third day, and there was Kalimpura. It did not look like a city to me. I was used to Copper Downs, first as a place of close walls and distant noises, then as rooftops and sewers, and finally in my last days there, a city of pale stone and slate and copper, squared lines, and narrow windows.

Kalimpura, seen from the Landward Road where it crosses Five Monkey Hill, is a riot of colors and curves and silvered spires topped with the sacred thunderbolts of Rav to ward off the lightning that comes with summer storms. Not that I understood as much when I first followed my feet west out of Bhopura.

So I strode over the hill amid the thickening traffic of the previous days and saw a city that at first looked like a giant tent encampment. The Kalimpuri did not measure their buildings with rulers and plumb lines. Rather, they built in the curves of billowing silk and the lines of prayer flags straining before the monsoon wind.

It was as if the gods of this place had dumped several hundred acres of masonry and precious metal and silk lengths to earth, but forgotten to assemble their toy.

"Ai," said the oldest pilgrim, a woman bent nearly double, who walked with two sticks. The first word I'd heard from any of them.

I was struck by the whim of politeness. It seemed better than drawing my knife and killing again. "Yes, Mother?"

She stopped moving and stamped her sticks into the road three times. A cart behind her swerved to avoid the little knot we four made. The driver began to curse, saw the look in my eyes, and suddenly found great interest in calming his team.

"The Lily Goddess welcomes me home," the old woman said.

"And blessings on you, I am sure." *Blessings,* I thought. *A mockery.* I followed no gods, not at that time. Copper Downs had provided me with none, and Selistan had proven hollow.

"Blessings." She peered close at me. "You're a girl beneath that awful hair, I warrant. You need help, come ask around the temple for Mother Meiko." She cackled, but a strange light filled her eyes. "There's always a place for a woman of a certain bent."

"Thank you, Mother." I let my stride lengthen away from hers quickly enough. Company was good, but I did not want pity. One last hot meal and an hour to work on forgetting my sins, and I would be pleased to leave this turn of the Wheel behind. A line of bearers with huge orange cloths on their heads passed me. I slipped in with them.

People thronged toward the gates of Kalimpura. The portal that admits the Landward Road from the east is shaped like an orchid, tall and graceful and pointed with a set of doors within a larger set of doors. Traffic came in for a while, until the gate warden had seen enough of the flow; then it went out for a while. The gate was too narrow for two laden donkeys to pass one another, I later learned. What I learned that day was there was a terrible jam outside, which created a thriving business in paid line-standing, guard-bribing, and general intimidation.

"You, boy, get away from my patch," grumbled a fat man with no fingers on his right hand.

"I'm not on your foolish patch," I told him as the flank of a horse pushed me within his reach.

His left hand, complete with fist, snatched at me. I tried to slip away, but the fat man was strangely fast. He tugged me close, his breath foul in my face. "My father, and his father, and *his* father, worked this patch. You are wanting to be here, you are paying me, or you are in my pay."

I slipped the knife from my sandal straps and slid the point between his arm and his body. "How much do you pay, then?"

He dropped me, laughing. "That's more like it." Leaning close again, he added, "If you are ever pointing steel at me again, boy, you shall be shitting your own knife out your ass while learning to breathe water through the hole in your throat."

"So?" Reckless, crazed, caring nothing, I stood my ground.

"So go find a few eunuchs to bully, and take their copper paisas to stand in line. Then bring it all back to me." He grinned. "Or I'll have you killed."

Thus I spent my first weeks in Kalimpura without ever passing within the walls of the city. Little Kareen, as my bully-master was known, lived on his patch. At night, one or another of the boys brought him a cotton shelter and his sleeping pillows, while more of us fetched hot wine and cold rice from the carts that never stopped circling out here.

It was an education. I saw every kind of pilgrim, prince, and trader, as well as the endless lines of qulis carrying food, bamboo, hardwoods, and bundled or basketed goods. All of Selistan moved on the backs of little brown men, I realized. Carts were used for longer distances, or loads too bulky and heavy to be carried, but if something could be moved in a day by a man, it was.

Women did not work so.

Some kept their husbands' carts, and many followed as servants of the few wives who passed. There were none who labored on their own.

I had no real sense of how much choice the women of Copper Downs had in their lives, but I'd been raised by Petraean women. Except for Mistress Tirelle, they had come and gone freely from the Factor's house. They gossiped of the city as if they moved about it at will. In my short time of freedom there between my escape and my flight, I had seen women in every crowd. Not under arms, surely, but carrying about the business of their lives as openly as men.

Here women were to be owned, either playpretties much as had once been intended for me, or as servants and tools. Only the poorest women—the cart vendors' wives, the dung-pickers in their ash gray robes and drooping veils, the elderly sweepers who walked before the wealthy to ensure their feet trod on no shit—only they seemed to move with any freedom.

Copper Downs had been a prison for me, but Kalimpura was a prison for all women insofar as I could tell. No wonder Shar had been afraid for my papa's land. There would have been nothing else for her except to be a servant in deepest poverty.

The bullyboys gave me a wide berth at the first. The story of me pulling a knife on Little Kareen was hot on their lips for a few days. Some of them feared my scars, wondering what I had done to earn them from some vengeful judge or village hetman. I made sure they saw my knife, which was better steel than their cheap, brittle iron blades, and I kept my eyes sharp and mean.

The teasing started soon enough. One boy, Ravi, bumped me as we carried food back to Little Kareen's patch for the evening meal. I dropped a pot of warm millet, and was nearly beaten for it. I found him afterwards when he was peeing and thumped him on the back of the head with the butt of my bandit's knife. He fell in his own puddle, from which I dragged him back to our little fire.

"Kareen, Ravi is so drunk, he cannot hold himself," I announced, dropping the boy and rolling him over. Everyone but Kareen laughed. He looked thoughtful, then ordered Ravi dumped in a ditch and banished for three days.

After that, the cuts became more sly, but deeper. I was tripped twice in the dark. Ravi and two friends tried to thrash me, but I danced away from them. Later I slit the soles of their shoes, so they would have blisters on their feet.

Little Kareen did not like this. "It is one thing for boys to tumble and rough one another," he announced one night over a badly made stew of some pale rubbery fish. I could have done so much more with the food here, though the spices were often divine. "It is another for hatred to grow." He looked more closely at me. "Green, step forward."

I did as he bade me.

The bully-master nodded, and someone crashed into my back. Ravi, and his two friends, and then most of the other boys besides. They pummeled and kicked me, the weight of them pushing me down so I could not dance away or draw my knife. I felt my teeth loosen, my ribs ache with sickening pain, as they smacked into me.

Even curled, crying, I knew they were not trying to kill me. Otherwise they would already have done so. On the ground amid my pain and humiliation, I swore I would never be caught beneath a mob again.

"Enough," Little Kareen said. "Green, you are forgiven. Are you to be forgiving your fellows?"

I staggered to my feet. Something was wrong with my right knee, and my breath came with a jagged, burning pain in my chest. I wanted to cry out, *No, by all the sleeping gods, may they burn upon the Wheel!* But there was not enough fight within even me to win what would come next. "All is forgiven," I lied, and cast my eyes down so he could not read them.

"Then lend me your knife," he said. "I have need of it awhile."

"I . . ." I drew a painful breath. "I was told never to bare steel before you, sir."

"Ravi, his knife," Little Kareen called out.

Ravi slid my knife from my legging and carefully gave it to the big man, hilt first.

I went to retch awhile and sleep off my pain behind a compost pile we sometimes used to hide valuables of disputed ownership.

Everyone left me alone for two days. So thoroughly alone I got no food, and had to limp for my water, but alone.

The third day I was back before Little Kareen. The boys were out chivvying the lines and rolling unlucky beggars. Ravi had shouted to me where I slept to see the big man before noon. So there I was, with the sun less than a finger's width from the top of the sky, standing before him.

Today Little Kareen sat on a throne cut from an old wine barrel. His perch was lined with brocade that had come from somewhere across the sea, for it was nothing like the textiles of Kalimpura. He let the sun beat down upon his head as he faced the moving, shoving line of traffic behind my back. His jaw was set, and his eyes drooped as he stared at me awhile. We might as well have been in a closed room, walled as we were by silence.

"If I were a wiser man, I would probably kill you now." His wrists flexed as if his remaining fingers wished for my neck. "As it happens, I am widely accounted a fool."

I knew that was very far from the truth, but I held my tongue. If nothing else, I could outrun him, even with so much tender and sore within me.

"But . . ." He stopped, shifted. "I do not hold the Death Right. Those who push souls along the Wheel guard their privileges jealously." Little Kareen leaned forward. "You have never been among the young, have you?"

"No," I admitted. I'd said not a single word of my history, but somehow he knew.

"I can tell. You lack the way of winning trust. You do not know enough to see when others are showing you their way." He sighed. "You are perhaps the most fearsome boy I have seen since I myself grew to full height. Quick at your work, persuasive of the foolish, rough where needed. But you do not know when to let go of it and be a boy among boys. You will not grow to be a man among men, I am afraid."

I knew why that would be, of course, for I was no man at all, but I was curious as to his thought. "What do you mean, sir?"

"Because someone will kill you for anger or in defense. Given your nature, they will likely be able to argue past the Death Right. If the question is even asked." He pulled my bandit knife from beneath his thigh. "I release you, and suggest with some urgency that you leave the gate. Otherwise Ravi and his little friends might well choose to test the Death Right for themselves."

I found that I sorrowed at that. The regret surprised me. This was the first time since leaving Endurance behind that I'd felt anything besides despair or anger. I savored the emotion like a rare spice as I reached to take the knife from him, hilt first.

"Indulge me in a question." His voice was low with my closeness. "I have already guessed you were raised alone, across the sea. You are like a tiger born in a cage. You know nothing of hunting, or other cats, though your claws and teeth are mighty enough. But tell me this: Are you a boy at all?"

I stared at him, the knife in my hand. "Does the Death Right apply to women?"

"Well . . ." Little Kareen smiled broadly. "You may live awhile after all, Green. Oh yes, it does not apply to women of our city."

The knife fit into my leggings. I tried not to let my stiffness from the beating show. Nodding at Little Kareen, I took up my satchel with my belled silk and walked into the crowd, striding purposefully toward the gate. I knew how to move through this mess now, when to swagger and when to slide quietly sideways. He was right—I did not want to meet Ravi again, not away from the bully-master's protection.

A few weeks' decent food had passed through my gullet, while a few paisas sat in my purse—not to mention I had a purse for my paisas. I even wore clothes fit for the endless heat here. All I lacked was a penis in order to be well set for life in Kalimpura.

The city within the walls was packed just as close as the mob outside. The pinch of the gate itself was gone, but the sheer mass of humanity beyond made up for it. In Copper Downs, people walked as if they expected a path before them. Here everyone pushed like water in flood, and lived within earshot of each other's business.

Buildings were fanciful to the point of foolish, at least to my eye. A great number of people seemed to live their entire lives upon the street. I saw families on little mats surrounded by pots and bundles, as oblivious to the people around them as the surrounding crowd was oblivious to them. There were ox-carts here, too, of a type I had not seen on the road. They never left the city. They moved with a slow and aimless pace. A dozen little shelves were visible inside their open backs. Men of the poorer classes would hand the driver a broken sliver of a paisa, then climb within and arrange themselves for sleep.

These were hostels that roamed the city without ever stopping. Such a strange thing that was, yet curiously practical.

Animals, too. Chickens roosted penned in wicker baskets that took but a small square of pavement while towering dangerously high, so the birds lived in levels and shat upon one another. Dogs ranged free with patchy fur and missing ears. Skinny mules and haughty camels mingled with women carrying snakes upon forked sticks while people cast coins in buckets suspended from the bottoms of their poles.

All classes thronged, too, everyone I'd seen in the multitudes outside the gate and many more besides. Beautiful folk in diaphanous wraps, their trains supported by crab-scuttling servants. Tradesmen in their tunics followed by heralds crying their business with slates waved high—I soon realized an entire commodities market functioned amid the chaos. Laborers, clerkish sorts, men with bundles of scrolls, maids carrying armloads of someone else's purchases, soldiers in studded harnesses and feathered turbans with swords strapped across their backs.

Everyone seemed to have a place, and know their path, but the signs they followed were invisible to me.

I let the swirling movement of the bodies draw me along. It seemed pointless to push in a direction I had no reason to pick anywise. I was dressed well enough like a Kalimpuri not to draw stares, even with my scarred cheeks and notched ears. My gaze was sufficiently fierce that the scuttling cutpurse children avoided me.

As for the smells of this place . . . I closed my eyes for a step or two, to let it into me. My nose found a curdling mix of the steam of tea, the tickle of curry, the damp darkness of cardamom, the sweat of men, the dung of a dozen species, the scent of fires. Where Copper Downs had smelled of stone and saltwater and fires of coal and hardwood, this city was redolent of food and traffic and the overwhelming concentration of people and their animals.

I followed, wondering what I would find that I could do with myself.

———

I circled the city in the course of that day. Two paisas bought me a roasted pigeon wrapped in banana leaves with a pile of reddish rice and a spill of some strangely orange pepper powder that threatened to burn my lips. I had been both overcharged and mocked, I knew, but I accepted it as the price of my education.

The road followed the wall before eventually meeting the docks. There the bizarre architecture settled somewhat, for there are only so many different ways a person can build a warehouse, no matter how creative they are. The docks were crowded with a mix of people, not all of them Selistani by any means. I saw Stone Coast folk, Hanchu, men with skin the red of a tomato, gangrels, massive shambling brutes, and fierce, compact, copper-skinned sailors who wore thin daggers slipped through flaps cut into the skin of their foreheads.

None of the Dancing Mistress' people, though. Just every size, shape, and color of human, mixed through the brown shades of my countrymen like spice in a stew.

Though difficult to judge with certainty, the docks were close to twenty furlongs from end to end. There seemed to be more trade here than what I'd glimpsed in my two trips to the harbor in Copper Downs, which made me wonder why the Stone Coast considered itself the hub of commerce for this region of the world. Beyond, the street was narrower, uncrowded by local standards, though still a near-mob, as it passed before the towering homes of wealth and privilege wrought in the strangest forms of all—high domes and spiraled walls and things that looked like dreams made of ironwood and colored glass.

Once I found another city wall and bent inland, the city resumed its usual crowding. I passed four gates in all before returning to my starting place as dusk fell.

Half a day to make a circuit little more than fifty furlongs around. I felt a stir of amazement. With dusk coming, I tried three of the sleeping carts before one would take me on. I did not know where else it would be safe to rest. Every inch of ground not being actively trod upon here seemed to belong to *someone,* just as Little Kareen had held his patch outside the gate.

By the end of the next day, despair had returned. I was almost drained of paisas. I did not see how to rob people in here without raising a great ruckus. Besides which, it had become clear that the little cutpurses had been set to following me with purpose.

Someone was watching.

I considered seeking a ship, but my only nautical skill was cooking. I was uncertain I could maintain the deception of my gender for an entire voyage. Besides, where would I go? Not back to Copper Downs, where surely there were many who would be pleased to take my head if my role in the fall of the Duke had become known. Where else, besides? In the country of the red men whom I had just passed, I would be a stranger without language or purpose.

Here I had no purpose, either. But also, here I was not so utterly strange. I spoke the language reasonably enough now.

The old pilgrim's words came back to me. Ask at the temple of the Lily Goddess for Mother Meiko. Perhaps they hired toughs there, to defend their altar gold and run the beggars away from the porticos. I thought she might have seen me for a woman. If I were to be exposed, a women's temple seemed less dangerous than the open street. That Little Kareen had guessed my secret meant I had not hidden myself away so well.

Besides all that, I was beginning to feel nauseated. Something stirred in my gut. The pigeon, perhaps, or an injury from my beating that had been awoken by my endless walking.

I began to inquire after the temple of the Lily Goddess. People ignored me, until one of the little cutpurses on my trail piped up. "The Silver Lily. Ahead, at the statue of Maja's Boar. Turn there, and head north to the Blood Fountain."

"Thank you," I said.

"I'm tired of you," he complained. "You go to ground, and I can go home."

I knew better than to ask who had set him on me. Little Kareen had shown me well enough how that aspect of Kalimpura worked. Instead, I followed the directions, wondering what truly flowed in the Blood Fountain and whether it was sacred to the Lily Goddess.

Perhaps she is a patron I could follow, I thought. I had claimed the blood of two people now, not counting the dust of the Duke and his henchmen.

The Blood Fountain was so-called because the water ran over marble of a brilliant red. I paused before the thing, which had seven levels ascending and was covered with a myriad of carvings. Most of them had worn under the water's flow until they looked like so many small, lumpy pillows.

It stood at the center of a circle where the endless traffic went round and round. Five streets radiating as spokes to head to other parts of the city. A number of buildings faced the center. Given the peculiar architecture of this place, I was at first hard-put to say which was most likely to be a temple.

I followed the flow around past an inn that seemed to be in a state of riot on the ground floor. After the challenge of crossing the traffic-choked streets, I found myself before a market that was closing up for the night. The place seemed to specialize in live animals, judging from the smell and the few cages still rattling and thumping next to stalls with their awnings being rolled tight.

The odors of the market revived the nausea I'd been fighting down since eating the spiced pigeon. I held my guts behind my teeth and moved on. Next to the market was a shop selling textiles and clothing. Another time, I might have tried to look. Crossing the next street, I found a more probable building. It was a pointed dome, like a gigantic clove of garlic. The upper reaches were cladded with silver. The lower portions had been built onto with timber and bricks in a haphazard way. Part of a grand marble stair in the same red stone of the Blood Fountain was still visible, though the impromptu walls intruded on its onetime majesty.

That seemed promising. I climbed the stairs, stepping over beggars. They slept clear of the top of the stairs, where the lintels bowed outward so that the entrance was almost round. There were no doors, just an opening to a dusky interior.

I passed within. The scent of incense was so heavy and cloying that I heaved to breathe it. I found myself on my knees on the cold marble, spewing beneath a little bench.

A woman in a pale robe approached and stared me down with a pursed mouth, looking more Hanchu than Selistani in the flickering interior light. She was of middle years, neither old nor young, with a well-bred appearance.

"Mother Meiko said you might find your way here," she told me. "I should, however, have preferred a less spectacular entrance." She helped me rise and gain control of myself. "What you lack in stealth, you have more than made up for in style, my dear."

I woke the next morning in a narrow bed, beneath a tall, thin triangular window. Sunlight blazed in along with the squabble of birds. Mother Meiko sat on a low stool, leaning upon one of her sticks.

"Do not be eating so much of that orange pepper powder," she said. "Hillman's bonnet, it is being called. It will be the death of you."

I gasped for air. My mouth felt like one of those towering chicken coops out on the street. "Not yet, Mistress."

"Not yet, girl." She paused, pursed her lips, then came to some decision. "You *are* a girl, whomever you have killed."

Suddenly I was very awake. I did not even know where the door was, let alone the path out of here. I could run rooftops all I wanted, but not fit through a window small as this.

She tapped me with her stick. "Listen, you. I am not here for anyone's justice."

I tried for straightforward. "My thanks for the night's rest, and the aid. I would like to move onward."

"No, you would not." Mother Meiko tapped me again. "You are being foreign, and though your face is as Selistani as mine, you are knowing far too little of this place to be safe alone. You bear a great burden, and strange skills." Another tap. "Skills that are being difficult to find in most places. Especially for a girl."

Even in Seliu, that word gave me a shot of anger. Clearly such a reaction would not serve me here. "Please call me Green, Mother."

"Green." She leaned on her stick again and watched me awhile.

I watched her back, but I was tired and did not feel well. Curiosity and fear were a potent mix. Finally I had to ask. "How did you know I had killed a man?"

"Hmm." Mother Meiko studied me awhile longer. "A chit of your age has no business with that knife." With her words, I shifted my leg to test that the weight of my blade was still there. It was. "On the road, you looked at it sometimes as if it were being a snake, and sometimes as if it were being your best friend. So I knew the blade had done you a great service. What service could a blade be doing a girl, but to save her life? Or possibly her virginity?"

"Both," I admitted.

"You know of the Death Right?"

"Yes."

"To kill once is hard. To kill again, easier. To kill a third time, a habit."

It was strange to hear this woman who could have been my grandmother talk so casually of murder. As if that were a normal part of life. She was drawing me toward honesty.

"I have killed . . . twice."

Mother Meiko seized on my hesitation. "Only twice?"

"Only twice."

"Hmm." Another long thoughtful pause. "How did you celebrate your misdeeds?"

"By vomiting copiously, then crying great tears." I sighed. "I prayed for both their souls, though likely neither deserved my regret."

She reached forward so far, I feared she would topple from her stool, then took my hand. "In that case, you still have your own soul. There might be a place here for you."

"If I can kill a third time?"

Mother Meiko's smile chilled my blood. My heart slid within my chest. "Yes. If you can kill a third time."

"Wh-what of those who guard the Death Right?"

"My dear Green, who do you think *we* are?"

I wondered then if it was she the cutpurses had worked for. Even Little Kareen might have answered to this woman. Grandmother or no, despite her twinkling eyes and apple cheeks, she was as fearsome as any plotter of the Duke's court back in Copper Downs.

In that moment, I feared her as much as I'd feared anyone. There was nowhere for me to run, I knew. Not from her. Not in this city.

I forced a smile, though surely she knew it to be as false as I did. "I am delighted to accept more of your hospitality, then."

"Never seen them take one so old as you," said the sharp-faced girl. Her nose was as thin as my grandmother's. She'd mumbled her name so fast, I hadn't caught it. She wore a pale robe and sandals, was perhaps a year younger than I, and seemed to have been placed in charge of me. I followed her through a curving hall.

"How old are they . . . we . . . usually?"

"I was a baby," she said proudly. "Brought to the Bone Door."

I was taken as a baby, too. But no one brought me to a secret entrance of a women's temple. "I am twelve, close to thirteen."

"Yes. You're from the east, right? Bhopura?"

"Well . . ."

She shook her head. "I saw your belled silk amid your things. Only the peasants out there do that. It's such a waste, but sometimes you see them on the walls of the great houses here. As if farmers' wives could do *art*."

I took an instant and thorough dislike to this girl. "I've traveled."

"Why would you do that? Everything worth having is right here in Kalimpura."

Then we were in a chamber with a great alabaster bath set into the floor. The hatchet-faced girl slipped out of her pale robe and kicked away her sandals. She had no breasts yet, I saw, which made me ashamed of mine. "Come on, into the water with you."

It took me a little longer to unwind the boy's clothing I'd been wearing. When I kicked free of my sandal leggings and set my knife upon the floor, she whistled. "We don't get metal like that until we've passed the Sixth Petal."

"What?" The question slipped out of me. I didn't really want to talk more than I had to with this awful girl.

"Tests. We have to hunt with certain weapons before we get better ones." Her voice grew admiring. "You must have proved very well to someone."

"Only in life," I muttered. My arm drawn across the odd swell of my small breasts, I slipped into the bath.

The girl dropped balls of herbs and salts in with me before she followed me. The water was soon blessedly milky. She studied me for a while, meeting me eye to eye. "I saw your bruises," she finally said. "Somebody really did it to you."

I didn't see how to avoid answering her. "About eight or ten of them."

The girl leaned forward. "Did you make them sorry?"

"They were already sorry," I said shortly. "That's why they beat me."

For some reason, this impressed her.

We sat awhile in silence. She obviously strained to fill it, but had acquired enough cunning to attempt entrapping me first. Finally she gave up. "I'm to wash your hair and give you robes and bring you to Mother Vajpai. I don't think you're supposed to carry your pigsticker around. None of the Blades do. Not inside the temple."

Blades. That was an interesting term. Despite the slow leaching of my pain and fatigue by the bath, my mind was engaged. "What did you say your name was?" I asked reluctantly. I could hardly call *her* "girl."

"Samma," she answered in a small voice.

"That's a nice name."

"No, it's not." She stuck her tongue out at me. "You are from far away. It's what they call dogs here, mostly."

"What should I call you instead?"

"It's my *name*," Samma said unhappily.

"Names can change. Trust me." I'd killed for mine, after all.

"You're a strange one, Green."

I leaned forward from the rolled edge of the tub. "As may be. My arms hurt. Can you help me with my hair?"

Her touch on my head, the brush of her chest against my back, was like balm for a pain I hadn't known I'd been feeling. Were ordinary children raised in their parents' arms? When Samma began to trace her fingers on my neck and shoulders, I shivered so hard, I nearly passed out.

In time we went to see Mother Vajpai, properly attired. My pigsticker was wrapped in a bath towel so it would not be presented as a weapon on our arrival.

———

She turned out to be the woman I had met briefly on my arrival here at the Temple of the Silver Lily. Today she stood dressed in red silks and chenilles chased with silver threads. Her hair was drawn up in a tight net of rubies, and her eyes rimmed with a powder the same color.

"Mother Vajpai," I said, bowing my head.

Samma touched me once on the shoulder, for luck perhaps, then retreated. She closed the curved double doors through which she had just led me.

This room was taller than it was wide, like the temple itself, with a triangular floor. The point was behind the woman. It held no furniture except carpets and cushions on the floor.

"You are Green," Mother Vajpai said. "Mother Meiko spoke highly of you. She does not often do so."

"We met on the road. I walked beside her for a while. We did not talk."

Mother Vajpai steepled her hands and nodded. "Mother Meiko listens very, very well. Especially to silence."

I realized ruefully how true that must be. "Yes."

"You are a stranger here."

That hadn't been a question, and so required no answer.

"You were raised across the sea," she said after a smooth moment. "Stone Coast. Houghharrow? Or perhaps Copper Downs?"

"Copper Downs, Mother."

"Someone there has spent a great deal of effort to make you into something." She walked around behind me. "We do not make women into something here in Kalimpura. Sometimes, rarely, a woman makes herself." Mother Vajpai passed in front of me again.

Her review was an echo of the Factor's inspection. My anger rose fast. "I am no one's tool. I will be the sword in no one's hand."

"All people are held in someone else's hand." She bent close to meet me eye to eye. "It is the way of Creation. The secret is to choose whose fingers are tangled in your hair."

"Whose are tangled in your hair, Mother?" I asked in my nastiest voice.

Her smile dawned like a sun made of silver-rimmed ivory. I had never seen such teeth, and was caught for a moment in their strangeness. "I serve the Lily Goddess, my little Green. No man wields me. No ruler calls my step. No council reins me in."

"No." I could see this trap easily enough. "Your Goddess wraps her hand around your heart. Whoever she is."

"You are of Copper Downs, my girl. Their gods have been silent far too long. The people of that city follow their own ways with a recklessness that will someday be accounted for. You are not understanding what a goddess is."

"A goddess is a tulpa grown large."

Still bent to face me, she shook her head in dismissal. "Tulpas. Country superstition. Little spirits who are being worshipped by ignorant farmers and disingenuous monks."

I had thought them more like larval gods. Or very ancient ones worn to nothing. Fragments, like in the oldest stories.

Mother Vajpai continued. "No, Green. A goddess is the sum of all her believers, all the prayers and hopes and curses and despair ever uttered in her name. Our Goddess spans the lives of women, from the darkest night of a girl raped and left for dead in a waterfront alley to the silver-bright wedding day of the highest princess in the land. The hand of the Lily Goddess upon my heart is my own hand, multiplied a thousandfold. We serve Her as She serves us. We are Her, and She is us."

I knew that for as great a load of claptrap as any myth out of Mistress Danae's books. Gods were real, surely enough. Septio's silent Blackblood back in Copper Downs had been real. The various theogenies and dieophanies I'd read of during my years under tutelage had made it quite clear that gods were bullies, children, pettifoggers, and taskmasters different only from the worst of men in the degree of the power they held.

The depths of my youthful hubris were staggering.

"As may be, Mother," I said politely.

She stretched to her full height once more. "Of course, you are not believing me. How could you? You come to us from a country of apostates. There is nowhere here in Kalimpura for you. I know of your troubles outside the gates. You—"

"You do not know my troubles, Mother," I interrupted. "You have not the least notion of them."

She shook her head. "A girl of your age has not killed without great provocation. Where will you go, with that habit of anger in your heart and the killing already in your hands?"

That much of my troubles she did understand. "I will find a way," I said, surly and restless now. I was ready to be quit of her.

"There is a way here for you."

"For a killer orphan?" I snapped. "For a lost girl with murder in her eye who knows too much about nothing, and not enough about anything?"

"For a girl who can keep her balance, and knows her way around a knife, yes. I'd wager much that you have other talents as well."

"I can prepare a banquet, sew clothes fit for a Duke's court, and play nine different instruments," I said, almost snarling.

"No doubt is harbored in my mind," Mother Vajpai replied sweetly. "We have an order of guardians here in this temple. The Blades stand behind the younger daughters and widows who serve the Lily Goddess. They wield the Goddess' will to the very hilt if needed. Their way can be yours."

A test? A fraud? Did it matter? "What you offer me is a joining to your temple's Blades. Shelter and fellowship in exchange for my skills."

"Yes." Her mouth wrinkled in a sad expression. "Your skills. There are never enough girls in a generation for what the temple needs. Not at the altar, not in the healing wards, not among the justiciars. Most especially not among the Blades of the Lily."

"To kill once is hard," I said, recalling Mother Meiko's words. "To kill twice is easier. To kill three times is a habit. Most of your girls never take the hard road, do they?"

"No." She sighed. "It is the Blades who oversee the Death Right."

A thought occurred to me. "Who oversees the Blades?"

"Why, my dear . . ." Mother Vajpai smiled. "I do." With those words, she spun into a snap kick that blended into a whirling slash of the edge of her hand.

I had walked for a month, and sailed a month prior to that, but the years before were filled with the Dancing Mistress' lessons. They were in nowise lost on me. I slid beneath her kick and ducked away from the blow before throwing myself toward her balance leg.

Never kick unless you have no other choice, the Dancing Mistress had said. *You are too easily downed with any of your feet off the floor.*

Mother Vajpai had shown off. The hilt of my tight-wrapped knife struck the side of her knee even as I threw my weight against her ankle.

She went down hard, tangling in her red silks, but somehow her fingers caught me on the ear. We wound up rolling to a stop against some cushions on the floor. A slim blade poked into my throat, while the fingers of Mother Vajpai's other hand were clawing painfully in my ear.

"Very good," she whispered. My ear burned with the cut of her nails. The knife at my neck stung. "A new girl has never taken me down at the first lesson. But then you are not really being a new girl, are you?"

"It's very nearly a habit."

"Then you can learn so much more. We are done." She released me. "Are you with us?"

"I have nowhere to go," I said flatly as I rolled away from her.

"Now you do." Mother Vajpai rose to her feet in a fluid motion I did not know how to duplicate, though I could see her knee troubled her. "You are one of us."

I would be no tool. "Am I sworn?"

"Not yet. And not for some time to come. Go with Samma. She waits outside. She will show you the dormitories and introduce you to the teaching Mothers."

Straightening my pale robe, I said, "I will be under no one's lash, not ever again."

"Go, Green. All will be well."

For a while, all *was* well. I quartered with the Aspirants of the Blades of the Lily. Samma was my bedmate and dining partner and, more to the point, the one who guided me through the training exercises, through the winding halls of the Silver Temple, through the endless services filled with chanting homage to the Lily Goddess.

This was a reflection of the Pomegranate Court and the Factor's house, except here was light to those shadows. Where Mistress Tirelle had kept me close within walls and isolated, the teaching Mothers herded their aspirants in a clotted little crowd, the nine of us who were currently passing through the Petals.

Other aspirants trained for the other orders of the Lily Goddess. I soon learned that the Temple took in girls from the great families and trading houses of Kalimpura and the rest of Selistan. Each renounced her social responsibilities and any direct access to her wealth to dedicate her life to the Goddess. In return, the girls were sheltered in powerful luxury and permitted to take up traditionally male arts such as healing and law.

Those girls were of the high and mighty, and they certainly knew it. The healing and justiciary aspirants were paraded about at services and on feast days, sometimes brought before the courts of the city—unlike Copper Downs, Kalimpura had managed to settle on and maintain a reasonable succession of rulership, even if the system was difficult for outsiders to comprehend.

The Blades were another sort altogether. One girl of our nine, Jappa, had come from a trading house, training with the justiciary aspirants awhile before joining the Blades as an older-than-normal Second Petal. Otherwise our girls were street rats and foundlings and natural children of unmarried daughters.

And one foreigner, of course.

Me.

My skin might be Selistani, but my scarred face was not. A small child with my looks would have been drowned. An older girl would have been cast out for a beggar. Even more so, my speech was not Selistani. Most of all, what I had in my head was very much not of this place.

My fellow aspirants quickly came to prize some of that foreign knowledge. Guttersnipes were not so educated in cookery, but they certainly appreciated food. While some among the women made it their business to be in the temple kitchens at all hours of the day, my special talents in that area were quite different.

We had lessons of every sort. My experiences were truckled out of me in those sessions. We also trained with the Lily Blades themselves; they frequently took us out into the city with them.

Some of those excursions were runs, much as I had done by night with the Dancing Mistress back in Copper Downs. The rooftops of Kalimpura were not so useful as in my old city, but the Below was, if anything, more elaborate. The undercity was inhabited by entire gray-capped castes of people who came to the surface only at night. Armories and cisterns and granaries and dungeons and smithies and a whole life could be found in Kalimpura's Below.

This was a kind of heaven to me. I knew how to move underground. My falls and drops and dead reckoning were as good as Mother Shaila's, who led many of the underground training runs, and better than most of the other Blades. She quickly had me drilling the aspirants. I became caught up in reconstructing the lessons once taught me by the Dancing Mistress. How had she led me to my knowledge, what steps had she taken me through to the understanding?

That in turn kept me awake at nights and during our rare free hours, working on paper and slow-stepping through exercises with Samma.

During those months, I also took up my belled silk once more. I had neglected it on the road from Bhopura, lost in my despair, but I had never completely abandoned the thing. I could remake the count of days once more—how often had I lost it before? The other girls mocked me awhile, but eventually they grew accustomed to the momentary sound of tiny bells ringing as I sewed a little while in some late hour of the evening.

As I attached my bells, I thought about children. Federo had stolen me for a special purpose. Not stolen, really. Papa had been paid for me, after all. Here in Kalimpura, there were children on every street. They carried burdens and sold fruit and raced with messages strapped to their forearms and cringed in the backs of carts. How many of them were free? How many of them were with their mothers and fathers?

I could not forget the promises made to myself back in Copper Downs.

Would I somehow save all these children? Could I help any of them? How would I find and best a rich man surrounded by blades and bars?

When I was able to set those thoughts aside, the hardest part of my new life was fitting me into the Blade training. Other than the underground, where I excelled, I had missed much that they expected of someone my age.

"Now try to be stepping below my attack," said Mother Vajpai. Today she wore a simple robe like everyone else, though the waist was cinched and the skirt tied off into legs. We were in one of the lower courts beneath the temple, where the Lily Blades had their passages of arms. When the women of the order were not using it, aspirants were free to collect bruises as we and our training Mothers saw fit.

Mother Vajpai had taken a special interest in me.

Samma, Jappa, and three others of our nine were in the lower court that day. Lanterns hissed with the sewer gas that drove their flames, shedding bright, almost shadowless light across the width of the damp stone room. Straw covered the floor. The edges were lined with rolled bolsters of muslin padded with cotton batting.

I edged around Mother Vajpai. Here we had rules. "Only those steps and movements and blows that are permitted in the circle," she'd told me.

"When will we fight without rules?" I'd asked Samma later. She laughed and told me that was the last Petal, before we flowered into full Lily Blades.

So we had rules, until we didn't. Much like my time in Pomegranate Court. Nine years with rules, and a last few moments without. This was a way I could live.

I backed away from her, letting my eyes follow her feet. Stance was everything, I'd been taught, starting the night that the Dancing Mistress had thrown me down to the stone.

When Mother Vajpai struck, I almost missed it. Her stance had not changed at all. Only the posture of her upper body. She swung that flattened right hand. In the stretching moments of the coming blow, it looked like a sword blade to me. I slipped on purpose, sacrificing balance in order to drop out of the line of the blow. I knew I could roll away to recover before her next swing. It would not be a tactic I could use forever, but at the size of my middle youth, it should have worked.

It might have worked, against the other training Mothers or the working Blades. It would have worked against the other aspirants, only because they were all slower than I. Against Mother Vajpai, who had seen me do this before, it only caught me a handstrike from her left, which swung in just out of my line of sight to slap me in the right temple.

I collapsed in a welter of redness and pain. Even breathing seemed beyond me for a time. When I caught up to myself, Mother Vajpai was speaking. ". . . from the center. Always to be following the eyes of your opponent. There are very, very few who can strike where they do not look." She glanced down at me, smiling so that the silver edges of her teeth gleamed in the lamplight. "Can any of you take that blow as Green has?"

I heard a shuffling of feet, but no one spoke.

Mother Vajpai reached down for my hand and helped me up. "We do not train so much to forms," she told me in a conversational voice, as if it were up to the others to overhear. "When one fights in a form, one expects one's opponent to do so. Most whom you will meet with bared blade and bloody eye are not so obliging."

"Thank you, Mother." I struggled not to stutter as my head rang.

Her voice pitched up again, teaching-loud once more. "Green is being here less than two moons, yet she is better than any of you at defense. She can step out of almost any blow save the very trickiest, as I was just delivering. She can fall and come up again before her attacker has recovered their swing. I am wanting you to watch how she centers her body. I am wanting you to watch how she watches me. Once she learns to read my eyes properly, even I shall be having a struggle to land a blow upon her."

She reached over and brushed her fingers across my face before wagging her index finger in front of me. "Your eyes are being good," she said. "Shall you be attacking me now?"

"Yes, please." I'd only ever touched her once, that first day. Mother Vajpai had limped slightly for almost a week. This was a quiet point of pride for me. Now, the only time we'd sparred since then, I might as well have been fighting the warm air from a bread oven for all I could touch her.

Our usual fight trainer was Mother Anai. She had been working with me on attacks, and I'd touched her three times already. I was getting better, and I thought I was ready to try Mother Vajpai again.

A feint was pointless. She was far more experienced. Likewise her reach of arm beat mine by a good margin. If I were fighting for my life, without the rules of the room, I might have gone for her face. As it was, I bowed, spun left, locked my eyes on her right side, then dove out of my own line of vision toward her left leg.

She stepped right through my attack, slapping me on the head to show the blow she could have landed.

"What is being so strange about you, Green," she said once more in that conversational voice, "is that you are so natural at defense, but are so struggling with offense."

I hopped up from the floor. "I learned in a different school, Mother."

"Were you taught to fight at all?"

"No," I admitted. I'd managed to avoid this question so far, out of sheer embarrassment. "I was taught to dodge the attack, then flee."

"Ah." She looked thoughtful a moment. "I will speak to Mother Anai. We will find a way for you. You are being strong and fast as any Blade we have ever trained. There are merely certain arrows which have not yet been placed within your quiver."

Though I did not glimpse then what this would portend for me, I saw the Lily Goddess for the first time in those months. We knelt to prayers every evening at sundown unless something urgent excused us. There were services every day, at which the priestly aspirants spent almost all their time. The Blades and their aspirants were expected mostly on Monday and Friday. Monday is the moon's day, of course, and the moon governs women during the years of motherhood. Friday is the Goddess' day, honoring the beauty best displayed by youth.

On ordinary days, when there was no feast or presentation, the Temple Mother—an old woman with frosted hair and strangely pale eyes for a Selistani—or one of her senior priestly Mothers would come into the sanctuary before dawn and consecrate the altar amid the sacred circle. The altar itself was a great silver lily, almost six feet wide, sculpted as a flower yet half-opened. The sanctuary stood at the core of the temple building, so that the soaring, tapered roof was like a chimney above the circular walls. Benches rose along the walls, with a steep drop from layer to layer so that we aspirants looked at the tops of the heads of the women below us.

There was always a great deal of praying and incense and scented smoke; then the Temple Mother would address the Lily Goddess directly through the altar. For the first weeks, I thought that just another form of prayer. But one Monday, the Temple Mother was following her order of service when a wind came up in the sanctuary. It ruffled the pages of the prayer books, which I could not read, for the crawling Seliu script was still a mystery to me at that time. It tugged at hair and sleeves and trailing hymns.

This was a whirlwind, I realized, circling on the Temple Mother. She seemed to get larger and larger, until she towered above us all. I understood this even at the same time that my eyes plainly saw her standing before the silver lily just as always.

When her voice boomed, it should have ground stone. The Goddess pronounced words that were not meant for me, but concerned rather justice for a house I did not then recognize the name of. The very sound of Her echoed in my head, made my knuckles ache, buzzed in the stone of the bench on which I sat.

I said nothing when prayers resumed, but as we rose after the final chantry in order to find our way out, I poked Samma. "That was very strange."

She brushed my hand away with a little smile. "What?"

"How the Goddess . . ." My voice trailed off when I saw her blank look. She not only had not noticed, but she also seemed unable to understand what I was telling her.

Later, I sought out Mother Vajpai. Our nine were taking the midday meal down in the dining hall, but I'd skipped the seating to find a quiet moment with her. She was in one of the public offices, reviewing accounts with a bursar from the Court of Starlings. That court dealt with trade in textiles and leather goods, and oversaw justice, banking, and regulation for those trades and their castes within Kalimpura, as well as dyers, scriveners, and the lesser toymakers.

When the old man, bent but bright, shuffled out of the little room, Mother Vajpai nodded to me. I arose from my bench in the hall amid other appointments and supplicants and stepped within.

"What is it, Green?" she asked, not unkindly. "In moments, I must see the adjudicator from the Frutiers' Guild about a Death Right matter, so I shall ask you to be quick."

"This morning, at the services . . ." My words felt strangely foolish, even in my own mouth. "I thought I saw the Goddess."

"You give Her no more credit than you are giving the ice-sellers in the street, Green. Even so, I have no doubt that if you are thinking you saw Her, then you saw Her. She appears within the mind of anyone to whom She speaks."

"She wasn't speaking to me, Mother. Her words were about justice for a noble house. The Temple Mother was tall as a tree, while a great wind bore in circles around us all."

"Really?" Mother Vajpai was rarely surprised, but she seemed so that day. "Interesting. Perhaps you are in the wrong order. I am certain that the priestesses would love to have you on the strength of this report alone."

"N-no thank you, Mother." I turned to leave.

"Green."

I looked back at her.

Mother Vajpai smiled sweetly, the silver edges of her teeth shining wetly. "I am pleased you are telling me such things."

And so began my long troubled journey on the path of the Lily Goddess.

Kalimpura was a city of festivals. The Lily Goddess had Her own, of course, a day that involved flowers raining from the rooftops and women in silver veils pouring from houses great and small. The Temple of the Silver Lily decanted a special violet wine that was carried in trays atop the heads of dancing dwarves and children hired for the occasion from the Mummers' Guild.

Every week, it seemed, some god or goddess or harvest or ruler out of history or famous battle was to be celebrated. Someone was constantly parading through the streets with a bobbling serpent riding the backs of forty men, or a giant ship made of gutta-percha and oiled canvas, or great juggernauts bearing caged tigers and demon statues. Once, I thought I saw caged demons and tiger statues.

The usual crowds were thick as spring mud. A person could run across the heads and shoulders of a festival crowd.

The nearly continuous state of celebration also meant that there were always people in outlandish costumes. To my eye, trained always to the seriousness of state, this was akin to living amid an everchanging field of flowers. Every step outside the temple was a chance to encounter a beaked head larger than the Factor's coach, or stiltwalkers bound for their luncheon from a parade rehearsal, or a troupe of false foreigners in costumes meant to evoke Hanchu or the Saffron Tower or the Smagadine city-states.

The natives of Kalimpura did not need to go see the world. The world came to them. All you required here was a good seat and a cool drink. Eventually everyone would pass by your corner.

My favorite times were within the dormitory. I had always slept alone before my time there, but the Blade aspirants slept together. We shared a room with mats spread out on a floor covered with thick straw slabs. At first, Samma was my bedmate, just to see me through the routine, but it took me no time at all to crave the circle of her arms at night.

We were not yet at the point of playing at lovers, but some of the older girls did. Jappa and Rainai would spread themselves wide in the moonlight from our dormitory's single high window and explore each other with moaning abandon. Samma and I would sit side by side and watch them until we grew bored with the business and giggled ourselves to sleep.

All the girls were close, though, even outside those moonlit trysts. We tended each other's hurts, mended each other's robes, and sat turn by turn when someone took a fever or a flux or a grippe. What Little Kareen had said about me being a tiger from a cage weighed much on my mind, so I tried to laugh easily, take little offense, and ration my words until I knew the substance of whatever took place. These girls had lived together all their lives, after all, while I was still new to the company of anyone other than Mistress Tirelle.

In those hours, I found my anger had sought a level of its own. The fire within was never gone, but where it used to be a stream washing over me, now it was a deep pool. I knew where it was, and I knew it would find me again, but there was a sense of peace I hadn't really known before, except for a few glimpses aboard *Southern Escape* when I had first fled Copper Downs.

Even the fear was mostly gone. The first night Samma's kisses turned to me in earnest, that fear melted completely as our hands locked and my hips began to shiver.

For a while, at least, anger stayed away.

Mother Vishtha trained us in what she called "the black work." She was quite pleased with my abilities at climbing, falling, and moving in nearly absolute darkness. "The Blades are doing many things," she told me one night on the roof of an empty warehouse down by the waterfront after the two of us had scaled the outside wall. "Some of them are to be swaggering with bared steel. Many more are to be quiet."

"Breaking into houses?"

"Well, more usually we are entering places of business. We are not thieves." She sniffed. "You would be surprised how often people are finding it seemly to conceal certain records from us. So there is being a steady need for retrieving files, account books, and the like. It is generally considered very helpful if the Blade doing the work can understand the purpose of her job."

"Cuts down on the mistakes, I'd imagine."

"Oh, yes. And you are being a natural at buildings. With your, eh, facial features, you are soon to be doing the black work, I think. I will be showing you the small havens, so you know where to find help and safety if there is being trouble. You will stand out almost too much by daylight. Only in the night will you ever be moving secretly."

"Or beneath a mask," I said.

"Or beneath a mask. Though that challenges the dignity of our order."

"Mmm."

She stood close. "I am being told you are blooded."

"Blooded?"

"That you have claimed a life," she added.

"Two," I said shortly. I had long since resolved never to discuss my role in the fall of the Duke of Copper Downs, not among these people, nor anywhere else.

"There are being times when the black work is claiming a life by stealth."

"Murder by night."

Mother Vishtha refused to be needled. "Only at need."

"I . . . I killed once in desperation. And once in self-defense." The Duke had been dead before I ever touched him.

"Green," she said gently. "You are even now being a child of only thirteen summers. There are men grown and under arms who could not do those things."

"I shamed myself and my teachers." As I said those words, I realized that they were true. However false my upbringing, the Mistresses of the Factor's house *were* my teachers, each true in her way.

"There is no shame in doing the Goddess' work. Here in Kalimpura, it is being the Blades who extract payments for the Death Right. Her work. Our work."

Anger gathered like clouds against the sun. "I am to climb in the window of some shopkeeper and stab him at his stool?"

"Perhaps. If that man killed his brother to take control of the family business, then refused to stand before his guild and court to answer for it."

I could see the sense of what she said. In Kalimpuri terms, that was justice. Kill without honoring the Death Right, and you were called to account. Conceal the deed or try to dodge the consequences, in time your accounting would come for you with interest. At the point of a Lily Blade.

There was other work, too. Some of it stood outside the peculiar framework of justice in this city. People to be reminded of their obligations, heirlooms and treasures to be removed from one locked room and placed within another, fractious individuals to be brought back to their place in the order of things.

"A bad man in need of justice . . ."

"Listen," she said. "The Blades do not decide. They only take action. You might not know that a man was bad, or why. You might see only a smiling father holding his babe by candlelight, and think, *This is what I have lost. How can I take him from his child?*

"The Lily Blades hold this responsibility before the courts of Kalimpura for a reason. Men are not able to set aside their hearts as women can do. If you follow this course, you will be the hand of the Goddess, and your heart will be Hers."

At those words, I felt a swirl of air around me. My hair stirred as if fingers tugged through it. Words murmured just outside my hearing might have promised salvation or damnation or something else altogether.

Her mention of children awoke me to what might be. I had sworn childish oaths to stop the taking of babies from their families as had been done to me, yet I lived now in a city where half the children on the street were someone's property—bondservants, apprentices, or outright slaves. My own people did not consider it an offense that a child be sold at need, or even a whim.

Goddess, I prayed with words inside my thoughts. *I am the daughter of no house. Not even Yours. Even so, I will follow Your path awhile, if it will join with mine. I wish to strike at those who would take the youngest for toys and mules. If this is Your justice, so let it be mine.*

The wind stilled. I received no other answer. I found my anger quenched, which might have been a reply. Mother Vishtha looked at me expectantly.

"I will choose this path," I said dutifully.

She nodded. We climbed over the decorative parapet to descend to the alley below. I had not realized until then that my fists were tightly clenched. When I opened them, a crushed lily bud tumbled out of each to the tiles of the warehouse roof.

Mother Vishtha had already gone before me, and did not see the sending of the Goddess. I made no mention to her, but my heart was filled with a peculiar joy. Neither did I mention the matter of the flowers to Mother Vajpai.

The next year or so ran before me in this way. There were no more touches from the Goddess, but I knew She was there, just as I might know a bruise was present on my arm even if it did not ache. I caught up to my training within the Petals of the Blade, so that I was equal to or ahead of Samma. This was just, as I was a year her senior. Our affairs of the nighttime blossomed with our bodies, and Jappa called the two of us to her bed together for a while to be taught even more. We fought, too, as I had come to understand that girls will. The moon pulled at each of us in a different way, and the Goddess informed each of our hearts in our own manner.

Making up could be so very sweet.

I taught northern cooking in the temple kitchens to all who would listen. For a while, there was talk of opening a bakery for the breads and sweetmeats

I showed them, but that came to little. I practiced weapons and violence, killing dogs for the practical experience of puncturing a body; learning to shoot with bow, crossbow, and spear-thrower. In this, I was becoming far more dangerous to others than I was to myself. I carried my pigsticker with me everywhere outside the dormitory, as the sworn Blades did.

On my free hours, I watched the children of the city, and learned what I could of the different forms of bonding and hiring and selling. Human traffic varied as widely as the practices of the courts and guilds and castes themselves. I despaired of ever reaching a true understanding of Kalimpura. I took to keeping a great set of lists, modeled after the heraldries of Copper Downs, in an effort to track this. Mother Vajpai found my obsession with authority very amusing.

"It is being the taint of the Stone Coast in your blood," she told me one day in the temple library as I sulked over a wide sheepskin parchment I'd been scratching on with colored inks. "Those northerners have the strange idea that authority should be invested in one man. What if he is being too much corrupted? Or his wits crack? As all stands on a single throne, so all falls on a single throne."

"We have a Prince of the City." I pointed to a sigil of a little crown at the top of my drawing.

"Your drafting hand is being most comely, dear," Mother Vajpai said. She stroked the short ragged mess that was my hair, for I always kept it so nowadays. "But the Prince of the City rules no one and nothing. He is being there as face of Kalimpura for those foreigners who cannot believe we are not savages without they are seeing some crowned head."

"Yet his name is on our trade treaties and guild charters."

"The poor dear has to be doing something with his time."

I ran my hands down the parchment. There were the courts, which were not so hard to understand. I saw them as little governments within the city, responsible for groups of people rather than tracts of land in the northern fashion. The guilds were more troublesome. The word was misleading, for it did not hold quite the same sense as the Petraean word used in translation. They controlled their trades, to be sure, but they held sway far more than that—for example, ruling over disputes that occurred on streets where their trading houses or factories were located. Castes were responsible for certain trades as well, and also ruled over individual families. One could be sponsored to join a guild, for example, but had to be born into a caste. The courts functioned much like a caste for the very wealthy and powerful, but one could be sponsored into them as well, which made them more like a guild.

"Everyone is doing something with their time." I rolled up the parchment. "No one is idle in Kalimpura. Not even the smallest beggar child."

"Nor the most contentious Aspirant to the Blades of the Lily." Her hand pressed hard into my shoulder. "You will never truly be a Kalimpuri, Green. You are fitting better with time, though."

"I am Selistani," I told her quietly. "These are my people, even if I am not one in their eyes."

"We are all daughters of the Goddess."

The last Petal of the Blade came in my fourteenth summer. Jappa had recently sworn to the Blades and left our dormitory. Rainai was preparing to follow her. The next oldest girl was Chelai, who struggled with her head for heights and poor strength of arm, and so might never take the vows. Then me.

I was not the newest, either, for two little ones had come from the temple nursery. Ello and Small Rainai, aged four and five summers, were not much older than I had been when first taken to the Factor's house. I spent time with them, trying to see the girl I had been in their little round faces. At first, they were frightened of my scars, but we became friends of a sort.

When one, or sometimes both, of them cried late in the night, it was my bed they came to. Samma would roll away from my shoulder with a grumpy sigh as the little girls squirmed in. Comforting them was more than anyone had ever done for me.

All I could learn of their history was that Ello had been a foundling at the Ivory Door. No one would speak to me of Small Rainai, but from scarce hints, I decided that she had been taken from a scene of violence. Our doing or someone else's, I did not know, but I kept thinking of Mother Vishtha's words about a father and his babe by candlelight.

We were ten for a while, until Rainai moved on. All I lacked was my last Petal, and the seasoning to follow it, before I could join her and Jappa in rooms kept by the Lily Blades—scenes of raucous riot and debauch, if the mealtime gossip from the Mothers of the other orders was to be believed.

Given how we passed our nights in our dormitory, I was become quite curious as to what it would be like to live among the full Blades.

One day Mother Vajpai called me out of a lecture on dockside rules and the etiquette of trading captains. This was the month of Shravana, which would be the beginning of August back in Copper Downs—even after two years here, I had to make a conscious effort to keep track of the Kalimpuri calendar. The day was brass-hot, much as I recalled from my earliest youth. Even within the Temple of the Silver Lily, where the architecture drew the warmest air upward, the air was beastly.

I'd spent more time aboard ships than everyone else in the lecture room combined, including ancient Mother Ashkar of the justiciars who was holding forth, but I knew that was not the same as bargaining with a captain. My experience lent me a sense of easy contempt for a subject that truly should have been interesting. That contempt, even in its wrongness, had mixed with the heat to make me irritated and distractible.

In short, I was glad enough to leave the little room and walk.

"Mother," I said, folding my hands as initiates of the temple did to greet one another and honor the Goddess.

She returned the sign. "Green."

Though some of the patience so carefully beaten into me by Mistress Tirelle had left me with my monthly flows, I still knew enough to follow Mother Vajpai and wait for her to speak.

To my surprise, she led me out a side door and onto Six Chariots Street. We moved into the currents of traffic. I contrasted what I perceived now with the mob I had seen on first arriving in Kalimpura. Then it had been all shouting tradesmen and lowing beasts and a great stream of people; now I understood them as threats, as powers, as problems and opportunities.

Here was a line of children from the Upper Sweeper caste, with their saltgrass brooms and brightly dyed sacks. Their caste had sole rights to the dung of certain animals, and these would not hesitate to shriek theft if some beggar made off with a handful of elephant scat. A trader from the Court of Herons passed, his silver bird clasp affixed to the crown of his hat to show his privileges in glass and food beyond three days fresh, with a brace of swaggering guards from the Street Guild following behind to protect the coin and papers on his person. Beyond him were a pair of fruit-sellers enmeshed in an argument concerning whose cart took precedence in the roadway.

In two years, I'd learned to read all these people, and almost everyone else around them. The foreign, the foolish, and the lost stood out to my eye like candles in a cistern. Much as I must have done to Little Kareen on my arrival, and to everyone who cared to look my way when I first passed the walls after he expelled me.

Perhaps this was what Mother Vajpai meant for me to see: that I belonged here among these people.

She led me by a wandering route down to the Avenue of Ships. That was the dockside leg of the route that otherwise circled inside Kalimpura's walls.

As always, it was lined on the seaward side with a thicket of masts and bowsprits and the occasional smokestack. The landward side was a mass of warehouses, office fronts, trading carts, booths, stalls, windows, and the everpresent throng of people.

"There is a ship in." Mother Vajpai pitched her voice in that manner we trained for in the temple, which made us hard to overhear.

She had finally found the borders of my patience. "A hundred ships are in, Mother."

"Then perhaps you can tell me which vessel is to be drawing my interest today?" she asked in her sweetest voice.

I looked carefully, letting my eyes rove quickly just as if I were picking a pomegranate from a tree in the moment of being unblinded. The secret to that had always been to let your sight do its own thinking, and judge afterward.

"Arvani's Pier." I wasn't sure what I'd seen, but it was something. Then I realized that a pennant from Copper Downs rode among the masts there. "A ship from the Stone Coast."

"Mmm."

We walked on past Arvani's Pier in silence. I hoped her quiet meant that I had found the truth, but with Mother Vajpai, it could just have readily been the opposite. A pair of foreign sailors, men with skin the color of liquid brass and a strange squareness to their eyes, lurched toward us with leers upon their faces, but three beggars drew them urgently off.

No one of Kalimpura would so much as spit on one of the Lily Goddess' servants. Priests and their helpers were sacred in general, but the Blades were as widely feared as they were poorly understood.

"It is time for you to decide what habits you will make of your life," Mother Vajpai said, as if there had been no lapse in our conversation. "A matter of the Death Right is being laid before us by the Bittern Court. It concerns a man of Copper Downs who killed two members of the Street Guild, and has refused justiciary mediation on the grounds that he is a foreigner."

The Bittern Court concerned itself with the wharfingers and warehousemen and chandlers of these docks, as well as those affairs of the harbor that did not fall within the Boatmen's Guild. The Petraean in question must have been directly associated with a docked ship, or the case would not have come before a Bittern Ear.

"Why has the Street Guild not taken their own action?" I asked. "They are quite pointed in their discourse, and Death Right would not seem to be difficult to argue."

"The victims were not acting in a manner that reflects well upon their guild," she said. "It is being a matter for the Bittern Court because of the killer's ship in port."

Which meant the unfortunate bullyboys had tried to roll a stranger who was far more dangerous than they'd realized. But the Petraean had not answered whatever summons he'd been sent by the Bittern Court, and so fallen in default to the sentence for violating Death Right without cause.

"Would it not be easier to send someone to convince him to speak before the Court?"

"We do not judge, Green." Her voice was sharp. "The Blades do not advise, except in the narrowest matters of our art. Should the Goddess wish counsel dispensed, She will move one of the justiciary Mothers to go to this man."

That I knew before I'd spoken. It seemed unfair to kill a man who did not even know he was under a death sentence.

"And me?"

"It is the season for you to take the last Petal. You are the only aspirant who speaks Petraean. This may be an advantage should you be spotted or questioned while at your purposes—you might be able to turn away suspicion for a key moment, where none of the other girls could."

"Very few of the sworn Blades as well," I said.

"You have the right of it."

We walked on, then circled the statue of Mahachelai on his Horse of Skulls and began to pass the other direction down the Avenue of Ships. Arvani's Pier was now ahead of us. The lane in the crowds opened for us as always, though suddenly I was conscious of it in a way I had otherwise long since ceased to be.

"So, I shall make my way aboard this ship, find a man, and slay him for a crime he does not understand, as he believes himself to have killed in defense."

"No," she corrected me. "You shall express the will of the Goddess and the judgment of the laws and customs of Kalimpura."

The whimpering pleas of the dying bandit had long since ceased troubling my dreams, but I still vividly remembered the crack of Mistress Tirelle's neck. In our training, we had attacked each other, attacked straw dummies, wooden stands, squealing pigs, and dogs first defanged, then later with all their teeth. I had shed blood, spilled blood, and stanched it in myself and others.

Mistress Tirelle filled my imagination now—the spittle on her face, the damp slump of her body on the cobbles of the Pomegranate Court. Would I do this thing a third time? Would I make a habit of what had begun in fear and desperation?

Would I be a Blade?

Will I belong here?

"Who is this man, and what is his appearance?" I asked. For one brief, dizzying moment, I imagined that the Lily Goddess had somehow set me to kill Federo. That would either be the most satisfying vengeance, or murder of my oldest friend.

Both.

"His name is Michael Curry. He is a man of Copper Downs who is being a factor of House Pareides out of Smagadis, aboard the vessel *Crow Wing* as a spice buyer for the Stone Coast trade."

I felt an immense sense of relief every bit as irrational as the concern that had preceded it.

She continued, her mouth flashing silver as she spoke. "He is a small man who keeps his head shaved bald, and favors dark velvets with puffed sleeves and leggings."

"It's called a Sunward doublet," I said absently. "A style popular in the Ducal court a generation past."

Mother Vajpai looked at me strangely a moment. "You may know him for certain by the iron key he wears on a silken thread around his neck. Its head is wrought as a snake's, with an emerald for one eye and a sapphire for the other. This key unlocks his strongbox."

"Am I seeking anything within the box?"

She hesitated slightly. "No. Bring the key, that one of the justiciary Mothers might present it before the Bittern Court as proof of justice done."

That was far too easy to unravel. *Crow Wing* would stay tied up while the killing was disputed and discussed. Someone in the Bittern Court would make use of the key, I was certain. Had this Michael Curry asked too high a price for the cargo he'd sold here?

I wondered at her hesitation, and my own sense of disgust. "If I cannot fetch the key for some reason, will another proof suffice?"

"As the Goddess works within you, Green." Relief stood in Mother Vajpai's eyes.

What test had I passed? Or failed?

"When?"

"Now."

Here was Arvani's Pier. I nodded at Mother Vajpai and trotted up the stoneway as if I had every business in the world there.

There were no more rules now. Just as Mother Vishtha had once promised.

Crow Wing was the third ship moored to my left. I wondered what would happen if I stepped aboard and asked in my most formal Petraean to be taken back to Copper Downs.

Likely I'd be thrown into the harbor.

A deckhand idled at the bottom of the gangplank. Someone with that slouch and such a grubby shirt could not possibly be the purser. I made a mental apology to Srini, who had treated me so well aboard *Southern Escape,* and shouldered past the sailor to walk right up the plank.

"Oi, there," he snapped in Petraean.

"Don't you people remember anything?" I demanded in the same language, haughty as my very well trained voice could manage. "I'm back with an answer for Master Curry." I winked. "One he's quite anxious to hear."

"Figured you dogs only spoke yer own yap here," he muttered. "Go on then, boy, if old Malice is expectin' yer."

Patience, I thought. No Death Right penalty had been pronounced against this one, nor was the Right itself now in place for his behavior. I wondered how many dockside bar fights he had started and lost.

I trotted aboard *Crow Wing.* Another reason to send me on this job was that I knew something of the layout of ships. Curry would be belowdecks in the stern, near the captain's cabin. All officers and important passengers traveled behind the mast. That had been pounded into me aboard *Southern Escape.*

Also, I was just as pleased to be a boy in the eyes of the oaf at the dock.

Stepping down the short companionway, the enormity of what I was about to do struck me like a blow to the gut. I staggered into the hot shadows of the corridor beyond and tried very hard to swallow down a heave. My mouth filled with bile, which I was forced to spit out upon the deck.

I was set to kill a man who did not know he was to die. Who probably did not deserve to die, truth be told. Especially not if someone in the Bittern Court was so interested in his strongbox key. The stink of politics was strong enough even for my indifferent nose.

Goddess, I prayed. *Lend my heart strength to know the path.*

The hot, close air within the rearcastle stirred. I heard for one moment the sharp peal of a child's laugh. Was that meant to draw me on, or to send me away?

I walked aftward. No doors were marked, of course, but no one was about, either. The widest door at the back would be the captain's, I supposed. I tried the one on my left, but it rattled, shut tight. An iron lock below the knob told that story. Stepping to the portside, I tried that. Locked as well. I heard a scrape within.

That was most likely him. I drew my bandit knife from the leggings beneath my robe and kicked at his door. It sprang open with a crash that was sure to draw someone to investigate.

My remaining time would be measured in seconds.

Curry was already rising to meet the threat. He was easy enough to recognize from Mother Vajpai's description, though she hadn't said that his eyes matched the eyes in his key—one was green, the other blue. He paused when he saw me, and the pistol in his hand drooped away.

"They send a boy?" he asked in Petraean, then laughed with the same cruelty that the Factor had, just before I slew him.

The capped well of my anger broke in a rush like lamp oil spilled over open flame. I would not be mocked.

Firearms were almost unknown in Kalimpura. Even those used on the Stone Coast were as likely to flash in the pan and blind their owners. Some of the best hand-built guns had another system of cartridges and shot, of which I'd been told by Mother Vishtha but had never seen for myself.

This pistol had no pan, so it was one of the new ones.

To cut my risk, I sprang straight toward the weapon. *Mother Vajpai might have mentioned the gun,* I thought, just as Curry and I collided. I snapped his wrist back, forcing him to drop the pistol as it fired. The noise slapped at my ears, but no bullet pushed me down. Curry tumbled over with a shocked expression, fetching up against a brass-handled cabinet behind his desk.

"You should have answered your summons," I said through clenched teeth, using Petraean so he would understand me.

He glared as my bandit knife entered just behind his collarbone, striking downward. It took more pressure than I had expected—men had thinner skin than pigs, as I'd been told—but I knew when I'd pierced his heart.

In that moment, I learned I could kill at need, whatever my later regrets.

"You're the one who . . ." he began. Then he was just so much meat.

"One who what?" I growled, but my words were moot. Voices rose in the corridor as I slid my knife free. Blood followed, but not in the rush it would have if he'd been still alive. I wiped my blade on his shirtfront, then tugged his key loose and slit its string of silk thread and pearls.

If I brought this home, whoever within the Bittern Court had engineered this man's death would prosper. The law is the law, as they said. A Blade does not judge.

My knife popped his odd-colored eyes free of their sockets, one after the other. I severed the optic nerves, then slit a length of velvet from his sleeve to roll them tight in my hands. I then tore down the drape behind him. A porthole, as I'd hoped. I would not have to fight back to the dock, where a man was even now shouting Curry's name.

The window was slender and square, relieved with leaded glass in the manner of a ship's stern lights. I swept up Curry's pistol and smashed out the glass with the butt. The weapon went into the harbor. Being slender myself, I followed it. His eyes I clutched tight in one hand, my knife in the other. The key I trailed in my fingers, so that the water tore it from me when I splashed hard a dozen feet below.

Much as I had done in my earliest childhood, I kicked like a frog to swim away from *Crow Wing*. I could pass under Arvani's Pier where the stonework was arched to let the tidal swells through. This was less a bridge and more a sewer, but it was enough for me. I slipped into shadow with the garbage and the flotsam. There my feet found stone to cling to amid the tidewrack stench. There I cried for the death of a man I'd never known.

Yet somehow he knew me.

I waited in the shadows. A great deal of shouting went on above in both Petraean and Seliu. Whistles blew, and at one point I heard a clash of sticks and fists, followed by someone being thrown cursing into the harbor. Eventually the combination of being soaking wet and the rank odors began to irritate me sufficiently to risk moving. Besides that, something had tried to nibble on my legs.

Tucking away both knife and eyeballs, I slipped out the far side and clung to the stonework as I clambered toward the footings of the Street of Ships. I was forced to pass two close-moored vessels as I did so. The first hull towered above me, rocking less than two feet from the stone of the pier. A shadowed wall of mossy barnacles threatened my skin. I tried not to consider what would become of me if a swell pushed the ship toward the dock.

The second such passage terrified me as well, but it was already becoming familiar. I could not just climb up. Too many people with official business were on the dock disputing recent events. Surely the Bittern Court would send its word. Though not, I realized, until I returned with my proof.

I found a series of rotten grates in the wall below the street frontage. Clearly I was not the first to pass this way, for two had been twisted open.

Figuring on the tunnels they covered being stormwater outflows for the streets beyond, I slipped in the first and followed the pipe at a low crouch. If I had been given to fear of tight places, that one might have panicked me, but in less than two hundred paces, I was inside a catchment. I knew from the distance and direction to Arvani's Pier that I must now be under the Plaza of Broken Swords. With a deep breath, I found my bearings. There would be an access in the little park just north.

Once among the mango trees, I squeezed what water I could from my robes. I looked beyond disgraceful, but I still knew how to carry myself. Slipping out into the street, I slunk toward the Lily Temple. A few people stared. Most knew better.

When I passed a fireseller's cart along the curb, I stopped. She was a woman of middle years, plain-faced and worn with the effort of her life. She was also visibly frightened at my appearance.

"I would have a black candle and a white one," I told her. "And some punk or matches to light them. I . . . I have no money with me, but can leave my good steel knife as surety. The Temple of the Silver Lily will stand for it."

"N-no, Moth— . . . sister . . ." Her fright deepened. Hands fluttered like birds as she began pushing candles at me. "Take what you will. I offer to the Goddess."

I opened my mouth to thank her, but a whirlwind overtook my words, and left something distant and calm within her eyes. I nodded, claimed the box of lucifer matches and two candles that suited me best, and stepped into the next quiet alley.

Three boys rolled a drunk there, while a thin dog tied to a drainpipe barked weakly.

"Out!" I roared. Their sneers broke as they saw my face, and they fled. The dog whimpered as it tried to hide behind the pipe. The drunk just moaned.

I knelt in the stinking slime that scummed the bricks. There I scraped clean a patch with the edge of my hand and set out the two candles. I placed the sorry, ragged mess that was Curry's eyes before them.

The black candle I lit first. "H-he violated the Death Right," I told the alley. Curry's shade as well, should the man still be listening. Perhaps his gods heard me, if they were not resting silently far away across the Storm Sea.

His surprise loomed large in my memory. Curry had not protested his death. Rather, he had thought to find it at a different hand. Perhaps there were games played here that went beyond strongboxes.

I found that I did not care. Curry and I had played but one game: the game of life. He had lost. *So have I.*

Then I lit the white candle. "His debt to the Death Right is settled." That did not seem to be the sort of kindness that should be said to send a man's soul back onto the Wheel. I knew nothing of Michael Curry but his contempt for me. Like the nameless bandit whose life I had claimed, he must have had at least one grace. "Surely his mother loved him."

I threw up once more, filled with the awful sense of having done something beyond retrieval. When that finally settled, I reclaimed the packet of my victim's eyes. Then I stood and wiped my hands against the ruins of my robe. The drunk stirred. "Lost a friend of yours?" he mumbled.

"Yes," I said. "Though I knew him only at the last."

Heading back for the temple, I wondered what would be done with me.

Mother Vajpai took the crumpled mess of velvet. She eyed it with speculation, then looked me up and down. I stood before her in one of the belowground practice rooms. We were at little risk of being overheard or interrupted there.

"Did the Goddess guide your hand?" She chose her words with care.

I did not feel up to liturgical games. "She guided me in my progress, at least. I struck true. He *did* have a pistol."

"Mmm." She turned the ragged bundle over to inspect it from all sides. "I am sorry we did not know to warn you of that. What of the proof demanded?"

"You will find a blue eye and a green eye within that," I said. "Also, I need to deliver a handful of copper paisas to a fireseller on Longspear Avenue."

She waved that aside with a flip of her hand. "I'll send a girl. You should not go back out for a while." Then Mother Vajpai opened the damp, sticky bundle. She looked at the eyes crushed within, then began to laugh. "Green, my child, you have the makings of a Mother Justiciar."

"I did as I was asked, Mother Vajpai."

"Did you find the strongbox key?"

"Yes, Mother."

"What became of it?"

My feet suddenly became very interesting to me. "The Goddess snatched the key from my hand as I escaped *Crow Wing*. She sent it to the bottom of the harbor. Alongside Michael Curry's pistol."

"And you?"

"I am here."

"After being aboard a ship that could have carried you back to Copper Downs," she whispered softly.

"I will *never* return to Copper Downs!" Tears welled, my chest hurt, my body ached, and I was covered in slime. "I go to the baths."

"Go, Green, and take my blessing with you."

I stormed from Mother Vajpai's presence in search of some way to clean my hands. The stain on my soul would be much harder.

In the baths, I poured the water as hot as the boilers would make it, until my skin puffed shiny and pink. Blood still stained my hands, crusted under my fingernails. None of the body brushes would clean it off. I was crashing through the little mop closet in search of something stiffer when Samma came in.

"Green, Green!" she shouted, and tugged me away from my effort. When she saw my hands, she shrieked. "Come with me, now, please. Jappa said this might happen."

I raised my hand to slap her away, then stopped myself. "What does Jappa have to do with this?"

"Sh-she said you might . . ." Samma sniffed, swallowing her next words. "Please, dearheart, just come with me."

Glowering, I allowed myself to be led. I was wet and naked, and shivering despite the heat. The pain in my hands was the only thing that mattered. Maybe *that* would cleanse me.

Samma dragged me down a hall, shouting for help until Ello came. "Get Jappa, and have her meet us in the small practice room below," she told the little girl. Her voice broke.

"Are we to f-fight?" I asked.

"No, no, sweetling." Samma stopped pulling me to kiss my forehead a moment. "Something else. Completely else."

Jappa somehow found the small practice room before we did. I stumbled in, shivering cold, to find a fire in a glowing brazier. We never had open flames in these rooms. They were underground, and any blaze that escaped was too far from water to fight easily.

"Over here, Green," Jappa said, taking me from Samma. "We'll make it all right."

A sword frame stood in front of me, a heavy-legged tripod to support a wooden practice dummy. I saw the dummy was off its mounts. Jappa leaned me face forward against the frame and drew my hands above my head. The skin of them burned. Was that Curry's blood?

"Are you going to slash me now?" I asked.

"No, darling," she said. "I will give you the gift that Mother Chapurma gave me when we were both aspirants, and I came back from my first killing."

She tied me to the frame with small leather straps. "What do you feel?" Jappa whispered in my ear.

I heard Samma whimpering Jappa's name, then mine.

"Nothing," I said. "Only blood on my hands."

"You killed a man you didn't know."

Like Samma, I whimpered, then nodded.

"Now you are so cold, you burned yourself with water, just to feel something."

"M-Mistress Tirelle," I gasped.

"I am going to hurt you now." Jappa's voice was husky, low as it got when she was ready for her release after I had ridden her sweetpocket hard. "Only a little, but when you feel the pain, you will know that your other feelings will follow it back home to you."

Closing my eyes, I whimpered again.

A crack echoed as I felt a lash across my naked back. I jumped against the frame, but truly it did not hurt even as much as a solid touch when we sparred in this very room. Samma shrieked once more.

Another crack, another touch of the lash—lower, across my buttocks. I jumped. She was right. The hot welt where the leather scored my skin reminded me of who I was.

A third blow, then Jappa leaned close. "Do you feel it?"

"Yes," I gasped, then began to sob as she slowly flogged me. Blow after blow, driving me back from my cold place and into myself once more. Driving out the shade of Michael Curry. This was like the old beatings from Mistress Tirelle, except these were for me, to draw me in rather than push me away.

Somewhere in the middle, I felt the heat build in my sweetpocket. When Jappa set down her whip, I bucked, finding my own pleasure even as the splinters of the frame pushed into the front of my thighs, the crest of bone above my groin.

I had sworn I would never live under someone's lash again. Now I swiftly came to love making a liar of myself.

Finally I lay shivering, my feet barely holding my weight against the pain of my binding. Jappa took me down. She and Samma drew some cloth around me and carried me weeping back to the dormitory. There Samma gave me suck against her breast while Jappa rubbed creams into my back and my poor burned hands, until I fell into the deepest, most dreamless sleep of my life.

The next morning, I was taken before Mother Vajpai, Mother Vishtha, and old Mother Meiko. They were in a room high up in the temple, where I had never before been. The space was more strangely shaped than most here, a teardrop with a floor across the bottom curve. The three sat in lotus on cushions. A single joss stick burned before them.

I was given a low stool with some quilted cotton folded across it.

"I . . . I might prefer to stand, Mothers," I said when Mother Vajpai waved me to the seat. My buttocks still had welts. I was ashamed of everything I had done, or allowed to be done to me, the day before. That my hands were wrapped in oil-soaked cloth was the most direct evidence of my failings, but far from the only one.

"As it is to be pleasing you," said Mother Meiko. "The chair is yours if you need it."

"Thank you." I bowed, but did not try to make the sign of the lily. Not with these hands, not in this state.

"When I took my first life," Mother Vishtha said, "I did not return to the temple for three days. I was hiding in the banyans of Prince Kittathang Park the whole time, suckling eggs and chewing on leaves to banish my hunger."

"I was finally bringing her home," Mother Meiko added with a smile. "She was being my student, and time had come for her to return."

Mother Vajpai spoke up. "When I took my first life, I came back and tried to assault my teaching Mother. She was eating at table in the refectory. I nearly caught her between the shoulders with a knife, when one of my sister Aspirants of the Blade stopped me."

"Hah!" Mother Meiko glared at her. "You would never have been catching me. I watched the reflection of my wineglass as you were to be approaching."

"And you—?" I asked her, the oldest. I saw clearly enough what they were doing.

"Me? I took a boat from the docks and rowed out to sea, until I was losing sight of the city." Her eyes looked at something far away. "There I wanted to be in the world without a scrap of our land. The Goddess spoke to me from the water, and sent me home again."

Mother Vajpai looked at me carefully and nodded slightly.

"The Goddess spoke to me yesterday," I told them slowly. "Though I am not sure what she said. Once She used the voice of a child, and once Her words came from my mouth to a fireseller, though I could not hear them."

"Now your hands are bandaged," Mother Meiko said, "because you were being so diligent to scrub the blood away. You cannot walk well because you were having the sense beaten back into your body."

"I needed to feel something."

"Not all of us turn to the lash, Green," said Mother Vishtha in that quiet voice. "But it is still being an honored road among the Mothers of this temple. The Blades especially. If you are moved to bend yourself over again, or to bend another girl to your will, please to be speaking to me first. I will show you what can be safely done without undue harm." She smiled shyly. "Also how to find the most pleasure in what you do, at whichever end of the lash calls you the strongest."

"All of that is between you and your heart," said Mother Vajpai. "We will be aiding where we can, or when you ask. Something else is being between you and us, however."

"She knows," Mother Meiko added. The old woman laughed. "Her road has been harder than any of yours. I will be most surprised if it does not turn hard again along the way."

"You want to know if I will be able to k-k-kill again. When asked . . . told." Beneath my bandages, I flexed my fingers.

Mother Vajpai fixed me with her smoldering eyes. "Will you follow the will of the Goddess in this? Or do you need to turn to another path?"

I wondered what would happen if I declined now. Quite possibly I would not leave this room alive. They could hardly turn me to the street once they'd made me a killer. But I was yet unsworn. This must be a dangerous time for them.

With that, the fog that had wrapped my mind since stumbling home yesterday lifted. I was clear-eyed and clearheaded once more. A most welcome feeling.

There was time between the last Petal and taking vows. As much as a year for some girls. I could not yet swear to the Lily Goddess and her temple, did not know if I would. That meant I was not forced to tell a lie today in order to remain here a bit longer.

"Yes," I said. "At need, when called. I have killed three times. As Mother Meiko said to me, it becomes a habit."

"You are excused from all lessons and obligations until the next Monday," said Mother Vajpai. "Rest, think, pray. You may wish to spend that time at services, but no one will look to count you in the sanctuary."

It was not credible that I would be anything *but* closely watched. I would do the same in their place, after all. This was like the Pomegranate Court, without the walls. Except that I could choose what came next, which had never been in the way of things within the Factor's house.

Whatever the Goddess wanted of our uneasy relationship, I would remain here awhile and listen. I might yet choose not to be used, but I would be here until then.

For a time there was no more killing. It did not take me long to realize that my unique circumstances were why Mother Vajpai had sent me for Michael Curry. Any sworn Blade would have found a shipboard killing on a northern vessel difficult. Whatever machinations had been upset within the Bittern Court did not flow back to me. Nor did I hear of the Temple of the Silver Lily suffering consequences.

I gathered some copper paisas and a beautiful flower from the altar and went to find my poor, frightened fireseller. Her cart was not where it had been. I searched every day for a week, but while finding people in Kalimpura was like finding birds in the sky, finding one person in Kalimpura was like finding a single, particular bird in the sky.

That was a disappointment.

Samma and I fought far more than before. I came to realize how much of a child she still was. She in turn was frightened by my flirtations with the lash. She soon kicked me out of bed. I took a pallet down by the end, sleeping by myself. Even the little ones began to avoid me.

I told myself I did not care.

I told myself I was a grown woman now, fourteen summers behind me and a fifteenth coming. I'd traveled the world and killed people, while these arrogant daughters of privilege knew nothing.

I told myself I was happy. Sometimes I even believed that. Killing Michael Curry had changed something else within me, though. His death had once more torn the cap off my well of rage. I took offense too easily, and used my prodigious strength to bully the other girls, to swagger in the streets and brush into the sort of boys who would fight a stranger without question. I kept my hair short and choppy. No one took me for a girl of the temple unless I walked pale-robed with the Mothers or some of the other aspirants. When I went out, I resumed binding my breasts, though they were never so large to begin with.

Once more, I was the tiger in the invisible cage that Little Kareen had seen around me. I lost the trick of being with people, of being one of them and one with them. In time, even the hard, old women such as Mother Argai liked me less, for I was more trouble to them than my lithe body and violently explosive passion were worth.

I still sparred with Mother Argai even after she stopped playing at sex with me. The same hardness that she disliked in me as a lover made me a good one to fight with, she claimed. "You're not afraid for your face," she'd growled. "Most young ones are. Ain't been being roughed up enough yet."

"I am what I am, Mother," I told her with a leaping swing that touched the top of her head. This did little for me, as she scored on my ribs in the same pass.

"Who was it cut you so?"

"Me." I grinned at the lift of her eyebrows. "I did it to *myself*." As I spoke, I drove a hammerstrike with closed fist into her thigh.

We went to the baths after. Even though we no longer played at the flogging frame together, Mother Argai still liked to watch me wash. After all, we'd worked up the sweat side by side.

I lay stretched in the warm water, wondering if my breasts would ever be large enough to bob as Jappa's did. Mother Argai's had never grown so. She sat next to me with her eyes closed. I resisted the temptation to touch her on her certain spot along the hip. Instead I asked her about how best to get about in the city on my own.

"There's something I'd like to do," I started.

"Hmm. Ask someone else, girlie mine. I'm out of the business of doing you."

Oddly, I found myself blushing. "No, no. I want to go outside the temple."

"Our Goddess' house is full of doors." She yawned. "No woman is trapped here, least of all you who walk the streets every day."

"Without people knowing it's me."

She cocked one eye open. "People here, or people out there?"

"People out there, Mother. I don't suppose anyone's business is private inside the temple."

Mother Argai laughed. "Take two hundred and more of the most ornery, independent women in this city and put them under one roof? With the Goddess in charge, lurking in every corner like a fart in the Courts? No one's business will ever be private. One grows accustomed."

Her casual words surprised me. Women in the Lily Temple tended to be comfortable with their divine patron, but I rarely heard someone speak so crudely of the Lily Goddess.

"As may be, Mother. Still, I would pass the dockside unnoticed to hear news of the world."

"Missing your other home, eh?" She slopped through the water to draw me into a wet hug. "Then don't go as a Blade, or as Green. Go as someone else."

"Who?"

"Put on a veil. Or mask, girl. You are your face to everyone who sees you. Most notice nothing else about you. Hide your face, you've hidden yourself."

I curled closer into her arms, my fingers seeking that spot on her hip. "I shall think on it."

Some time had passed since I had sewn more than my bells. I found the workshops on the ground floor of the temple, where I begged supplies for what I had in mind. The Mothers there were willing to give me black-dyed muslin, a bit of leather, and the appropriate needles and thread. "Ain't nobody ever taking a liking to our work," a white-haired woman told me. "If you are not being at the altar or the justiciary, you are being unseen hereabouts."

"My interest in cloth and clothing has been with me most of my life, Mother," I said politely. "I wish to take it up again as I approach my vows."

"Such a sweet girl. Come see me at the end of my day. I'll find something special to wrap you in."

"Of course, Mother."

Up in the dormitory, I began sewing pants and a tunic, with a cape and mask to go with it. I based them on my recollection of an illustration of the Carmine Flaxweed from one of Mistress Danae's storybooks. He was the youngest son of a noble house that had been overthrown in Houghharrow, and had fought in secret to restore the fortunes of his brothers and his lover. I figured the look of a theatrical Stone Coast would-be assassin might pass well enough in this city of endless festival and spectacle.

While I made no great secret of my project, I found I preferred to work on it alone. It took me several weeks. When I was done, I had flared leggings, a cinched tunic with long sleeves puffed at the wrist, a leather half mask, and a tatted veil. I was forced to buy a hat—making such a thing was not among my skills. Brims were not popular in Kalimpura, so that was round with a pointed leather crown.

People would see only the gleam of my eyes. All else was dark and dramatic. Exactly the sort of outfit no working troublemaker would be caught dead in. I was trying for a naïve but possibly dangerous dilettante. If I could not be anonymous, I would be memorable for something other than who I really was.

Taking a small sack of paisas with me, I went down to the Avenue of Ships late one afternoon dressed in my handmade blacks. I'd received a few stares leaving the Temple of the Silver Lily. The little space that followed the Mothers of the temple through the crowds of Kalimpura didn't attach to this costume. Rough customers stayed away from me regardless. I saw pickpockets turn aside, as well as a pair of footpads. Perhaps it was the set of my shoulders.

Along the Avenue of Ships, I drew no stares at all. Enough strange costumes came off the ships in harbor that I fit in as just another oddity. I walked the length of the street as the sun was setting. No one bothered me.

I stepped into a tavern when dark fell. The signboard was at a slight angle, one chain slipping down. It read FALLEN AXE, with a crude painting of a black hood with two eyeholes. Somehow, that drew me.

Within was a wide room with a low ceiling supported by rough-hewn tree trunks. Tables encircled each trunk. A trough of water stood against the far wall, chunks of ice floating in it.

Sailors in the dress of half a dozen nations clustered at those tables. Few enough Selistani were here, which suited me fine.

The barkeeper, a local man with no hair, nodded.

I wondered what to do next.

Money. Money. I had never really *bought* anything. I slipped half a dozen coppers onto the bar.

He nodded again, then laid out a bowl and poured something dark and foamy from a jug.

I sniffed it. Bitter, almost loamy, mixed with yeast. Ale? There had been wines back in the Pomegranate Court, and also at the table in the Lily Temple. Little Kareen had preferred a beer that smelled of swamp water, back when I'd worked for him outside the gates. I'd never tasted it myself.

Taking my bowl, I retreated to an empty table and listened. Sailors chattered in several languages I did not speak, though one table muttered along in thickly accented Petraean.

That was sufficient. I listened awhile longer to sounds that felt oddly like home to me, and drank from the edges of the thick unpleasant brew. I knew I looked like something from a festival dumb show. No one here cared, as half of them were equally out of place.

Eventually I headed back to the temple, smiling beneath my mask.

"Green." Mother Vajpai stood at the door of the practice room where I fired arrows as fast as I could into a mudball target.

I turned with an arrow nocked.

She ignored the weapon to step toward me. "How are you, my girl?"

We hadn't spoken much in the past few weeks. "Well enough, Mother."

"You are growing closer to the need to take your vows." She reached down and pushed the bow away, her fingers on the arrow shaft just behind the razored head.

I slipped the arrow loose and let the bowstring relax. "Yes, Mother." I was growing ever further from any desire to take my vows. The Goddess had not spoken to me since Curry's death. My quarrels with the older Blades were weakening the bond of sisterhood.

"We have let you be too long idle. Your . . . obsession . . . with costuming is unseemly."

In her present mood, my temper would do me no good at all. "I would walk the city unnoticed, Mother. With my face, I cannot simply pull on some bright sari and pretend to be a merchant's daughter. A costume draws attention to something I am not." I smiled. "Mother Argai first gave me the idea."

"I have spoken to Mother Argai concerning the wisdom of her suggestions." She sighed. "You need to work more. Play less."

I gestured with the bow. "I work all the time."

Her voice was gentle. "To what end, Green? We serve the Goddess here. You have not recovered your sense of purpose since reaching your final Petal."

"To whatever end seems best to me. The Goddess moves us all, you say. Perhaps She moves me in a direction you cannot see."

"As may be." Mother Vajpai's tone was bare steel. "For now, you run with the Blades. I'm assigning you to Mother Shesturi. Her handle patrols the city six days a week, on whatever schedule she chooses to set."

A handle, of course, was a group of Blades.

"I am not yet sworn."

"You will be soon."

We shall see, I thought. "What of my dockside forays?"

Long silence. Finally she said, "I will not forbid you those. The Lily Goddess does not hold Her followers prisoner within these walls."

The implied *yet* hung between us like a slow curse.

The women of Mother Shesturi's handle were a mixed lot. All Blades stood outside the norms of the Temple of the Silver Lily, let alone the standards of the women of Kalimpura. I quickly realized that Mother Shesturi had the running of me because her team were the misfits among the misfits.

We gathered in one of the running rooms that let out onto the back of the temple, where the building faced an alley. There were three of these, long and narrow with benches along each side, and rows of racks and hooks. Today the rooms were empty, though I knew from my training they were used to store weapons or equipment for the Blades as needed.

Mother Shesturi herself was a quiet woman. She was compact with an efficient way of moving, which told me I'd likely have trouble taking her down in the practice rooms. She patrolled the city with four other women in her handle.

One was, to my surprise, Mother Argai. The other three I knew, but not particularly well: Mother Adhiti, Mother Gita, and Mother Shig. Mother Adhiti was by far the largest woman in the Blades, and one of the biggest human beings I had ever met. She was mostly muscle. Whipcord-thin Mother Gita rarely spoke. A pink scar seamed her face, giving me a sense of kinship which I immediately recognized as false. Mother Shig was harder to understand. She was small, her complexion almost gray, and she bordered on the misshapen. Even so, she climbed better than I—one of the few in the Temple who could.

Mother Shesturi only nodded and said, "Welcome." The others muttered, except for Mother Gita, who stared a long moment and then seemed to forget me.

Blades on patrol dressed to be noticed. We wore light armored skirts over leather trousers, blouses of a triple-woven fabric slick to the touch, and knee-high boots. Everything was black. We didn't strut abroad like members of the Street Guild working protection, or the Claviger Caste searching for criminals escaped from bond. Our patrols were in alleys, through potshops, down into the Below, and back up again.

At first, I didn't know what we were looking for. I followed Mother Shesturi and her handle high and low through Kalimpura. I already knew how people on the street made way for the Mothers of the Temple. Now I understood why.

A Blade handle on the move was frightening even to me, and I knew these women.

We returned home that first evening with not a dozen words exchanged. We touched no one, caused no fights, ended no fights. We had simply been *present*, at different times and places all over Kalimpura.

"Target practice in the shooting hall a span before sunrise," Mother Shesturi announced as we sat in the running room to change into our Temple robes.

That night I had little time to do anything but sleep. I didn't touch up my costume, or consider venturing out.

The next morning we shot early with bows and crossbows. Mother Shesturi worked us until we had each achieved a tight group with both weapons on all three ranges.

"Run at noon," she said when we finished up. Time for a bath, then we were on the street again.

So it went for a week straight. The other women of the handle began grumbling, except Mother Gita, who continued to keep her own counsel. After several days, Mother Adhiti looked me over closely. "Surely you are being old enough to mind yourself. How dangerous are you?"

One night we ran to a dozen small havens. Mother Vishtha had told me of them—lean-tos and sheds and hollows, and occasionally entire apartments or offices, scattered across Kalimpura for Blades to seek out if they met with trouble. Our handle checked them from a distance, then sent someone sidling close to certain ones. Being small and swift, that usually was me.

"It is death, you know," said Mother Argai as I shimmied down a drainpipe from checking a rooftop.

"What?"

"We tell no one. Not even the rest of the Temple. The Blades have very few rules, but one is that we never tell of the small havens except to other Blades." She leaned so close she could have kissed my ear. "That rule may save your life someday, Green."

The eighth day we ran, this time well into the evening, was the first time I'd seen a handle meet with trouble. Mother Shesturi brought us up out of the Below behind the Plaza of Broken Swords, right where I'd come up after killing Michael Curry. We came to ground in front of the mango grove I remembered all too well. A group of men squatted beneath the trees with bare steel in hand.

Twelve men, I counted quickly, and noted the best three swordsmen by their stance. Six of us. I was too short-armed to face any of these in a stand-up fight. I wasn't sure about Mother Shig, either.

Mother Shesturi made the same assessment. She barked our names in order, pointing as she spoke. I was on the right edge of the group, with Mother Shig. I carried only my pigsticker, though the sworn Blades all bore swords.

"Go away home, boys," Mother Shesturi told them. "Your beds are getting cold."

The leader held his sword loosely at his side. "The soldier women of Kalimpura." His Seliu was terribly accented, though the words were right. "I wondered if you were real." He called out to his men in some language I did not recognize.

Their blades came up.

Mother Shesturi nodded. "No one walks away." She meant no rules. Faces, joints, necks, hearts, guts. However the enemy presented himself to you. Whatever you needed to drive him down.

Mother Adhiti waded in first. Three of them fell back to draw her on. She kept moving past the springpoint of their trap. Then I lost sight of the others because Mother Shig and I were closed on by two grinning men. They laughed to one another as they came for an easy kill.

Mother Shig sprang into the air, legs splayed wide, and brought her sword down above the guard of one of the attackers to split his face open. He fell screaming as she hopped onto his chest, her heels drumming into his ribs.

His partner turned with a snarl. I slipped the pigsticker in below that crest of bone that rides at the waist, in front of the hips. His armored berk ended a little too high for its intended purpose. The man shrieked and tried to swing back to me, but my blade grated against his hip. I slugged him right next to the embedded blade, then kicked him in the back of the knee. The fighter went down in time to receive Mother Shig's sword point inches deep into his ear. He kicked twice, then died noisily.

I pulled free my bandit blade and went for the back of another man engaged with Mother Argai. He never saw me coming. I took him with an upthrust to the kidneys—they obviously did not think to be fighting people as short as I still was then. Mother Argai used the momentary respite to slash the throat out of her second attacker. Her third caught her in the shoulder, a rage-filled blow that tore through the black shirt and opened her to the bone.

She collapsed with clenched teeth sucking in a shriek. I stepped close inside her attacker's swing and took his wrist on my own shoulder. His sword flailed as he punched with his free hand. The knife that I hadn't seen snagged on the left sleeve of my shirt. I smacked my head hard into his chest, then smacked him there again, trusting Mother Shig to arrive.

Arrive she did, announcing herself by shattering the man's sword arm. He fell screaming next to Mother Argai, who put her dagger in the soft underpart of his jaw with her off hand.

Then it was over. I couldn't have counted to twenty through the entire length of the fight. Eight men were dead, one more dying with a wet, wounded bubbling squeak. Three would continue to breathe so long as Mother Shesturi was moved to allow them.

Mother Argai was down with the slashed shoulder, bleeding very badly. Two of Mother Gita's fingers hung by a flap of skin. She silently pushed them more or less into place, then wrapped tight a strip of cloth.

I tore a cloak from one of the dead men and began to bind Mother Argai's shoulder. Mother Shig sprinted away at a word from Mother Shesturi.

In this city, even the cutpurses would stop to aid a fallen Blade. Unless she was alone and there was no chance of being caught. Now that the fighting was done, people were drifting into the park. Mother Shesturi deputized half a dozen good-sized men to stand on the necks of the survivors.

Then I realized I was hurt, too. Blood was spattered all down my left sleeve. That side was growing numb.

Mother Gita squatted down next to me and touched the wound on my upper arm with the fingers of her good hand. I nearly passed out from the pain. "Good work," she said, then began packing dirt into my wound.

Dirt? I thought.

The world whirled in darkness.

"We run as we do so no one will know where to find us," said Mother Shesturi to me three days later.

"That hardly seems effective," I mumbled.

"If we are nowhere, we are everywhere. You, Green, were everywhere that night."

"Wh-who were they?"

"The men we killed?" Her smile was grim. "No one. Nothing. Men bent on stealing something that didn't belong to them. We found them on accident."

"Th-then why do we care?"

Mother Shesturi took my hand. "What happens to Kalimpura happens to the Lily Goddess. When the city suffers, She suffers. When we defend everyone, we defend ourselves."

"We killed a dozen men in the park." My stomach flipped.

"So we did." Her tone was even.

The wounded had not survived. Should I sorrow? "Please," I said. "I would like a dozen black candles, and a dozen white candles. Matches. And if you know, their names."

"This is not our way."

"It is *my* way," I insisted, feeling my temper bubble.

Eventually she said, "Fair enough."

I waited for my candles and considered the nature of souls. The air circled in the healing room as if the Goddess had something to say. I glared at Her, wherever She was. "I will be going down to the docks. I wish to hear more of Copper Downs. If they are still buying children, I will know of it."

No answer came but silence.

It took ten aching days for the slash through my left biceps to heal well enough that I could pull weight with that arm again. The candles had brought me neither peace nor release, but still I felt better for them. I sat in on training with the younger Blade aspirants. The kitchens took more of my time, as I dictated recipes and tasted new experiments in their version of northern cooking. "Bland," Mother Cook said of a lamb stew, "but we can build on it." They still liked my baking best.

I also haunted the docks every day in my hand-sewn costume. The leather mask was a bit theatrical, but no one ever saw the slashes on my face, and it diverted attention from the Petraean accent I could never quite shake off.

Drinking among the tars required money. While the Blades drew no salary, let alone their aspirants, the Temple of the Silver Lily was more than wealthy. Since my part in the stand beneath the mango trees, the women of Mother Shesturi's handle had made it known that my wishes were theirs. No one said anything more about my choice of clothing.

The Fallen Axe quickly became familiar to me. I spent time in winesinks with names like Risthra's Nipple, Three Bollards, and The Bunghole. It was the barkeep at the Fallen Axe who named me, early in my adventures.

I walked in for the third day in a row, carrying a small purse of copper paisas and a few silver ones. "Oi," he said. "If it ain't the Neckbreaker back again. You must be liking of our brew."

"Deep stuff, my friend." I let the pain in my arm burr my voice. Likely enough they thought me some younger son of nobility skylarking about in a festival getup.

"I am giving you the better cask today," he whispered so loudly, the rats in the alley behind the building probably heard. "On account of you almost being a regular customer and all."

"Mmm." I made it a point never to thank people when dressed in my blacks.

His barmaid smiled as she brought me a bowl. Even with her missing teeth and the sores at the corner of her mouth, I could see the beauty she would have been. "Here is being your brew now, Neckbreaker." Her wink was meant to be flirtatious.

If I were in fact the younger son of a great house here in the city, I would be quite a catch. An hour's dalliance could bring her more reward than months of working drudge at these tables.

I smiled at her, knowing that she would glimpse the crinkle in my eyes.

The stuff was somewhat less foul than his earlier bowls. It slipped up easily enough beneath the edge of my veil. I sat and listened.

Over time, since I had begun haunting the docks, I realized just how many tongues came to this port. Seliu was always spoken to some degree—it was the local language of coin.

Of course, I listened for Petraean. I spoke it better than Seliu, even now, and no one around me would think it my language to look at me. Hanchu I could follow a little bit, and I quickly came to recognize the quick, pattering consonants of Smagadine. There were half a dozen more languages I heard almost every day, and a dozen more than that passed in a given week.

I would never know them all.

Seliu and Petraean were the two most important. Selistan and the Stone Coast stood at each end of the child trade, at least as it had taken me. I had promised myself to stop that somehow, someday.

Yet a ship might have sailors from anywhere within ten thousand leagues of whatever water it sailed upon. Given that the plate of the world was wider than anyone had ever compassed, it followed that the tongues were just as widely scattered. Presuming that the gods had not played some joke and fastened the ends of all things together in a great circle, of course.

We often drilled at our violence on dogs, in the practice room with the channels in the floor and the good drains. Strays were like sand on a beach in Kalimpura. The larger ones took wounds much as people did. Pigs were better for close work, due to similarities that their arrangement of skin and organs held with those of humans. In sparring with spear and short knife, though, I became convinced that I wished to best a bullock.

"You are cracked," Mother Adhiti told me one day after a grueling session. We'd bruised each other blue and green, like so many orchids tattooed upon our bodies.

"No, no, don't you see? A bullock would draw out all our strength." I could see it as a certain man, implacable, powerful, and just as subject to death as any dumb animal.

She looked at me strangely. Even at my current growth, the woman outweighed me twice over and more. "A bullock in a small room like this would draw out all *my* fear. You would be trampled like plum paste beneath a child's feet."

"Then we can fight it at a festival. Make a show of things." I had not set to with a blade in earnest since the night we'd fought under the mangoes, though months had passed. There would be no more black work until I had sworn my final vows—that was sound-enough policy. Besides, at the moment, I was neither well liked nor widely trusted outside my own handle.

Mother Adhiti mopped her neck. "The temple does not concern itself so much with that sort of spectacle, as you well know, Green. Like all sharp weapons, the Lily Blades are most effective when still in the scabbard."

"Sheathed, we must always be sheathed." I flexed my knuckles, which ached deliciously.

"If you want to fight so much, go pick trouble down at those docks you seem to love." Now she was grumpy. "Forget this foolishness with a bullock. No one would let you fight one even if it was our way. You are the youngest and smallest of the Blades."

With that, she left me. I was no Blade at all, of course.

I shook off my fantasy of fighting such a large animal and followed Mother Adhiti out into the hallway. It was always warm and damp down here, where the temple extended out beneath the buildings and grounds around it. Really, all they'd done was lay claim to some of Below, walling off passages and bringing light and water where they could.

When we reached the stairs that spiraled up into the main part of the building, I found Mother Meiko sitting on the bottommost step. Her walking stick was propped beside her. She drew from a short, stumpy pipe. Today instead of our usual pale robes, she wore the oil-stained pale blue muslin of a woman of the Bucket Carrier Caste.

"Good day, Mother." I set down my weapons and made the sign of the lily toward her.

"Green." She sucked noisily on the pipe a moment, then cupped it loose in her hands. "Girl," she added.

I waited. This woman had come down here for me. She would tell me what she came for when she was ready to do so.

"You desire to fight some great cow, or so I am overhearing."

"A bullock, Mother."

"Mmm." Mother Meiko studied the smoldering wisp within the bowl of her pipe. "An animal. Tell me. What are you?"

"An Aspirant of the Lily Blades of this temple."

"No. You are not that."

I was surprised. "Nothing else, Mother."

"If you were an aspirant of my Blades here, you would be sleeping in the dormitory. Attending, or teaching, the classes with the other aspirants." She leaned closer. "You would be helping the children of our temple instead of mooning after those whom fate has swept away."

My desire for an end to child selling was hardly mooning, but I was not willing to argue that with her. "I am what I am."

"The Goddess has ceased speaking to you." That was not a question.

"Yes," I admitted. "I have not heard Her since before I fought alongside the rest of Mother Shesturi's handle."

"The *rest* of Mother Shesturi's handle." She snorted. "To be listening to yourself. You claim you are an aspirant in one breath, and a Blade in the next. Here is what you are, Green: You are being neither this thing nor that. You are being a girl who will not choose which of her fates she is to follow. You are being nothing at all."

"Mother." I tucked my chin low.

Her pipe tapped my forehead. "We are nearly upon the moon that brings us Vaisakha month. You are nearly being to your fifteenth summer. That is old enough to be an auntie or wife. Or a sworn Blade. When the month of Vaisakha ends, come back and be telling me if you will swear your vows."

"Otherwise?" I asked, my voice barely above a breath.

Nothing pleasant rode in Mother Meiko's smile. "Otherwise you will be cast upon the goodwill of the Goddess. Ask yourself how much care you have been showing Her, girl. Ask yourself how much care She is to be showing you in return."

I was reminded then that this was the Blade Mother, who stood over all of us. She could kill as easily as she could count the days of the week and with no more remorse. Throwing me out of the Temple of the Silver Lily would be nothing for her. In a strange way, it might even be fitting. Mother Meiko had invited me to come in the first place, after all.

That evening I nursed my resentments as carefully as any babe at the breast. *I will show them!* I could free the children in the thrall of the Beggar Caste, race to the harbor to confront the most corrupt captains, fly over the curled and pointed rooftops of this city in search of some crime so foul that my redressing it would bring undeniable credit on the temple, along with the sweet revenge of my repudiation. Or perhaps just slink away into the night, leaving them to question where they had wronged me and wonder what had become of me.

In the end, I did what I always did these days. I slipped into my blacks and walked out a side door of the temple. Sometimes my trips to the docks were more about the drinking than the listening.

This was one of those nights.

———

I had a month to make up my mind, so naturally I spent the next few weeks declining to think about the problem at hand. My days and nights were full enough, and I suppose I must have believed the Goddess would move me somehow. The needle on the compass of my purpose had been spinning for a while.

Down along the Avenue of Ships, in the middle of a warm, rainy Wednesday, which happened to be the Festival of Coal Demons, the Goddess spoke to me again. I did not feel Her presence as I had in the past, but there was no mistaking the furred, rangy shape that stepped through the crowd near me.

A Stone Coast pardine.

I had never seen one of that race here in Selistan. Sometimes the Lily Goddess made Her will known through unlikely chance.

As I took a few strides more, I realized this was the Dancing Mistress. Only strongly drilled habit kept me moving when I wanted to stop and stare. She was bare-handed and barefooted, wore a light toga of some open-weave fabric, and carried a satchel over her shoulder—almost as she'd looked back in Copper Downs, except dressed for our weather.

I brushed past her, close enough to touch. Her pace faltered as if she'd noticed me, but I was clothed as Neckbreaker, not to mention three years older and taller than when last she'd seen me. The small riot of beggars and children who jostled in her wake kept her moving, or she might have turned to stare.

At least, so I fancied.

What is she doing here?

I took half a dozen more steps. Then I rounded a bollard, using our distance to keep her from noticing. I could follow this woman far better than she could follow me. Especially on these streets. With the Coal Demon festival in full swing, there were firecarts everywhere, people in blackface or redface, and vertical firepots of glazed terra cotta at almost every corner, burning even now with their rain chimneys on.

She was a canny woman, perhaps the most so I'd ever met, but this chaos would defeat her. At least so long as she was new to the city.

The Dancing Mistress *must* be new to Kalimpura, I realized. Else I'd have heard tell of her in the taverns. Possibly even as gossip in the temple. When one of the Red Men of the fire lakes had come to the city in the cool season, they had talked of nothing else at table for days.

For a pardine, they would gossip a whole season long.

I followed, watching the crowd that surrounded her. She walked as one did in Copper Downs, as if one's business was one's own and there could be an expectation of privacy. I recalled the shoving, crowded madness of my arrival here, before I had learned to move among the Kalimpuri. I further recalled how little the Dancing Mistress liked to be touched.

They were *plucking* at her fur, by the Goddess. I almost began to laugh. No one here had seen her claws, certainly, or watched her teeth bare as she worked through the angry hurt of a bad throw or a low blow.

She tried to step around the statue of Mahachelai on his Horse of Skulls, keeping the plinth close to her left hand. Two of the smaller beggar children slid between the Dancing Mistress' thigh and the granite base. She kicked them away, and they began to squeal.

I immediately recognized the Broken Wing. It was a beggar's takedown, which rarely worked on sailors or soldiers, but was sometimes effective on traders or captains in the company of their wives. Those unfortunates could not show the flint in their hearts with their women at their sides, and so while one child squalled and pretended to have been hurt by the horse or carriage, the other quickly insisted on a small sum to see his sibling home without trouble, otherwise the militia would be here quite soon, begging the master's pardon.

That Kalimpura had no militia—and no particular interest in maintenance of the public order as the Stone Coast understood the idea—was not something that every traveler knew in the moment of confronting a frightened, crying child. Some of the little ones in the Beggar Caste were so good that I'd seen the Broken Wing run through to the payoff even when the touch had spotted the initial dive.

The Dancing Mistress made the mistake of turning and kneeling to see what she had done. I pushed forward through the crowd, growling from behind my mask, just as a cutpurse plucked at the satchel on her arm. She whirled, and blood spattered.

The claws were out.

Drawing my pigsticker, I ran toward her. I had to stop her before she killed one of these beggars, or the other citizens stepping *into* the fray like the fools that they were.

If they lost their lives on my blade, it would be a matter for negotiation. If they lost their lives at her hands . . .

There were too many backs in the way, too many bobbing heads. I scrambled up a big man's shoulders as he cursed me. In that moment, I had forgotten that I was masked and in black. No one but me knew I was a Blade.

"Out, away," I roared, my voice screeching far too high to gain their attention. I jumped past my perch and onto a woman, knocking her down and me with her. Her neighbor in the crowd saw my knife and wiggled away as I regained my feet.

The Dancing Mistress was clinging to one of the Skull Horse's legs, swinging a stick she had not been carrying moments before. I thanked the Goddess and the tulpas of my lost home that she hadn't snatched a blade. Still, there was blood and people screaming for more blood. The Death Right could yet be at issue.

With fists and elbows, I fought through to her. A pair of toughs from the Street Guild were closing on the Dancing Mistress. I popped one of them behind the ear with a stiff-fingered jab. He stumbled backwards, howling. She tried to kick the other away, but caught him in the throat and soft under-part of the jaw with her foot claws.

His skin tore open in an impressive spray of blood. His fellow grabbed at me. I turned, blocked a stab from a dagger, then drove my own knife into his gut. The tough went down for good that time, vomiting blood and bile. The other staggered as people around us panicked. Those in the front tried to push backwards while those behind tried to push forward.

I grabbed at her wrist and called out in Petraean, "With me, with me."

Though there was the light of battle in her eyes, the Dancing Mistress responded to the words. She jumped down onto the two bodies, one still moving and groaning, and shouted, "Where?"

Pointing ahead, I charged with elbows and knife butt flying. People moved quickly enough.

She followed.

Our saving grace would be that the street was so crowded with festival traffic. The entire screaming mess of the riot had probably gone unnoticed twenty paces away. I shoved and prayed, counting on the Dancing Mistress to remain close on my heels.

What I didn't count on was the mass of children following us, shrieking about violence and the Death Right. I was certain that the Street Guild man whom I'd stabbed was dead. The other likely so, and him by the Dancing Mistress' hand.

I was protected from the Death Right, but she was not. If a child with any family of substance had been hurt as well, her fate was probably sealed.

Realizing what I was thinking, I nearly dropped to my knees in disgust. Children. Whom I'd spent so much time claiming to worry about and fear for. How easy it was to see them as an obstacle, an inconvenience, when they were not of my own accounting.

Ahead of us, a writhing line of coal demons chased a fire snake. I turned with bared blade and shifted the Dancing Mistress past me. I showed the mob of children the bloody edge. "Get away from the docks," I screamed at them in Seliu, "before any more of the child-takers come!"

That was a stupid lie, but it gave them pause. A moment was all I needed. "Keep close!" I shouted in Petraean. The snake dodged and twisted right before us in a clash of gongs, spewing nose-searing red and orange vapors from censers dangling below his frills. Underneath, a line of sweating, nearly naked men worked poles and spun back and forth on their heels. They were a storm of legs and wood, with the crowd pressed skin-close on the other side.

This was the woman who'd taught me how to move. I moved. With a quick tumble and a screamed apology, I slipped between two of the snake dancers. The Dancing Mistress was so close behind me that she must have slipped between the next two. I heard an angry shout, but already a twelve-foot coal demon roared and vomited black smoke amid the crashing of *his* gongs.

Shoulder first, I pressed into the next part of the crowd. These people were a shift from one of the green-wallah houses, for the group of them smelled of garlic and onions. *Not so much different from lily bulbs,* I thought, and wondered if the Goddess had sent them.

I wasn't concerned now about whether the Dancing Mistress could follow me. She still was my superior in the art of swift, graceful economy of motion. I was worried that some ripple of outrage would pursue us both, even through the snake. The street was a peculiar thing, and rumor traveled by strange paths.

While I could slip away easily enough, it would be impossible to deny her part in the fighting.

Amid a hail of firecrackers, with their red-and-gold flurry of shredded paper and stink of pouther, we slid into an alleyway. Though the din was magnified here by the confined space between the walls, there was no one with us.

I stepped back into the shadows and looked up as she loomed behind me. "My thanks, stranger," she began, but I put up my hand for silence.

This had to be the Ragisthuri Ice and Fuel bunker house on my left, and the Wheelwright's Guild Storehouse on my right. A small haven was located in a shack atop the bunker.

"Up," I said, and began climbing the drainpipe.

Once again, I did not need to look to see if she followed.

She scrambled up behind me, then across the roof toward the little shack. I opened the ill-fitting door. No locks on this small haven. Inside was a collection of ladders and rags and buckets—stuff too difficult or worthless to bother bringing up and down for use whenever the roof needed cleaning or maintenance. Many of our small havens were as anonymous as this.

The junk was out in four armloads. I opened a folded piece of canvas, then reached behind a loose board to find a pouch that would contain needles and thread and a few other healing essentials. There was also a clay water jar. The place reeked of old paint and moldy cloth, but it was quiet and hidden.

The Dancing Mistress stepped inside with me. Together we filled the space. Small havens were for the most part, well, small. They were intended for one Blade to go to ground until help could arrive.

I had just betrayed the location of this small haven to a foreigner. Not to mention their very existence.

Putting that aside, I touched my face. After all our dodging and leaping, the mask was still on. My blood pounded in my ears, and I found I was trembling. I took a deep breath and tried to relax. "You nearly forfeited your life down there, Northerner," I told her.

"My thanks again, sir." I realized her breathing was quite ragged. "That was very poorly played on my part."

She'd never spoken much of her people, but I knew they came from woodlands high in the mountains. Five was a crowd and ten a mob. I remembered how Kalimpura seemed to me when I first came, and I had not arrived during a festival. "You've never seen so many people in one place in your life."

I was not quite ready to reveal myself, not until I understood what it was she did here. The Lily Goddess had not pulled this woman all the way across the Storm Sea merely for my bedevilment. Something else was afoot.

She sighed. "I have never seen so many people, even adding up all the days of my life. Now, who are you, please?"

Think like a Blade, I told myself, *and not a former student of this woman.* "This is my city. You will answer first. Who are you, and what is your business here?"

"I am . . . searching for something." She took a long look into my veiled eyes. "A priceless emerald stolen several years ago in Copper Downs."

Me.

A chill stole across my spine, counterpoint to the redness in my eyes and ears. *Me.* What did they want me back for? Enslaved, boxed up for years, then turned loose to kill, after all the use they'd made of me, after all the ruin they'd made of my life, why call me back now?

Betrayal flooded me like bile in my sleeping mouth. "You will not find it here!" I roared in Seliu.

The knife was in my hand now. She kicked me with those powerful hind legs—so hard, I slammed against the door of the small haven and tumbled out to land among the jumbled trash and equipment.

My back hurt, my legs shivered, and the wound in my upper arm felt raw all over again. The Dancing Mistress leapt out of the little shack just in time to meet my arms coming up. I threw her past me, then followed to jump on her legs and scrabble for her neck from behind.

She twisted, sloughed me off, then caught my right thigh with a handful of claws. I kicked at her, scooted backwards and onto my feet as I brought the knife out far enough to make her rethink her next lunge.

We circled a moment, both panting. Neither of us had gone for the eyes or the throat. There were some rules here, then. At least until one of us discarded them. I would not let her kill me, and I would not let her take me back to Copper Downs.

I had slain a teacher before.

She spun on one heel, whip fast, but I knew that move from the old days. The Dancing Mistress had never taught me to attack, but she'd taught me to defend myself, and I still defended best from her. Shoulder first, I leapt inside the swing of her other leg and slammed into her chest. The knife could have gone into her gut, but I pulled the blow and scored a deep cut on her thigh.

We separated once more.

"You did not make the kill," she gasped.

"A mistake I shall not repeat."

We circled a moment longer, both catching our breath, before we met in a flurry of blows. I tapped her hard, half a dozen times, but she tapped me harder, twice on the side of my head so that she drove me to my knees.

This time, the Dancing Mistress bore me down with sheer weight. She let the claws of her right hand extend for her kill as she whipped away my mask and veil with her left.

The shock of recognition was written large and plain upon her face. *"Green?"*

"Never Emerald," I spat. A sob caught up with me then, overwhelming the red river of my anger.

"Up," someone said in Seliu. I looked to see Mother Vishtha leading a handle. Five women with swords out. One of them was Jappa, at that.

I staggered to my feet. "You came just in time, this—"

The flat of Mother Vishtha's blade darted in and caught me on the side of the head, right on the bruise the Dancing Mistress had raised. I whimpered and dropped back to my knees.

Her voice was hollow, and came to me from a distance I could not measure in that moment. "There is a riot below. Death Right has been cried. Worse, you have exposed a small haven to a stranger." Mother Vishtha's breath was hot on my face then as she leaned close. Even in my blow-addled stupor, I could read the fury in her eyes. "You have broken too many stalks today, Green."

They bound our hands and marched us to the edge of the roof, where we were lowered on ropes from one hostile set of hands to another before being taken away as prisoners through the roaring city. Every step was misery, every glance from the Dancing Mistress a murderous accusation.

Soon enough, we were in a cell beneath the Temple. I did not recognize the room, though it was off the same damp hallway as our practice rooms. I had always thought the little door led to a closet or some such.

I sat with my back to mossy stone. The Dancing Mistress sat facing me against the other wall. A large ewer of water stood between us, and a smaller metal bucket for slops. Some light flickered through the window relieved within the door, and beneath the crack at the bottom, but we sat mostly in red-laced shadow. I ached abominably, as after a very rough round of sparring. Which was unsurprising, of course. The Dancing Mistress winced also.

For a very long time we just looked at one another. Even in the deep shadow, I could see that her eyes were tightened and her ears set low. That meant she was angry. I knew my own face must be hard as well. All the doubts that had flooded into me when she'd mentioned the word *emerald* were back, deviling me.

I would not restart the fight with her, but neither would I treat with her. Mother Vishtha said I'd broken too many stalks. Quite possibly that was true, and a great pity besides. But where the Dancing Mistress had come from, I'd not only broken stalks, I'd set fire to the entire plantation.

Whoever wanted me there, whatever they wanted me for, it could not be to the good.

Everything was broken; everything was ruined. I did not fear the Death Right, but I was finished in this city. Even if I hid my face for a few years, whenever I reappeared, people would mark the scars and remember scandal and old disgrace. I knew how these Selistani were—tongues sharp as adders' teeth and a memory for insult that could extend across generations.

As for the traitorous wretch across from me, she had everything to fear from the Death Right. I'd claimed the life of one Stone Coaster who had killed in self-defense. My privilege, such as it might be now, was no shield at all to her.

She could keep her damned emeralds and phony stories about stolen valuables and the preciousness of whatever had been snatched across the sea against its will.

They will kill her.

"Green." The Dancing Mistress' voice was soft.

That was when I realized I was sobbing. "Leave me alone," I said in Seliu, barely able to speak through the tears.

"I'm sorry," she replied in Petraean.

My heart roiled along with my gut. I took a few breaths to calm myself, then answered her in that language. "What are you doing here?"

"Looking for you."

"Well, you found me. More fool you." Bitterness infused my voice.

"No fool at all. The first hour I was here, I found you." She smiled, lopsided with some pain in her neck or jaw. "As if my steps had been guided."

Perhaps they had, if the Lily Goddess' hand was to be discerned. "Don't be so pleased. You are about to be charged under the Death Right."

"I was attacked."

"You killed, without privilege." I shrugged, which sent a stabbing pain through my old wound. "It is our way here."

She stepped across the cell and knelt before me. "Nonetheless, I am glad I found you. Such a fight you made. I am proud of you."

"Even though I landed blows on you?"

"Especially because you landed blows on me."

I laughed through the bitter tears. The Dancing Mistress tore a strip off her toga and dipped it in the ewer. I wondered what she was about when she turned back and said, "Let me bathe your hurts."

For a moment, I wanted to send her away with my words and with my hands, but I stopped myself. Whatever she'd come for, it hadn't been to push me once more into the confines of the Pomegranate Court. The Duke was vanished to dust, and the Factor with him. Mistress Tirelle was dead. No one remained to keep me in that place.

I began to slip free of my blacks. "Why did you ask for an emerald? I thought you were here to take me into captivity once again."

"No, no, no," she said, brushing my face tenderly with her fingers. "I needed to inquire cautiously at first. I did not know if you were alive, let alone here in Kalimpura. This was no more than where the ship I took brought me."

"You are a traveler very far from home."

"So are you, Green, for your home is lost to all but memory."

That she had the right of. We had much in common, the Dancing Mistress and I. The thought saddened me, so I bowed my head and tried to will myself toward peace as she slowly dabbed at my wounds. I was cut in a dozen places, and bruised in twice as many. Not to mention the hurts to my soul. My skin was marred with friction burns and smears of coal dust. Pains plagued me just as after the roughest workout, which the cool touch of the wet rag soothed.

Her fingers were lithe enough, for all that they were stubby and broad. The caress of her hands was so gentle as the fur slid over my skin. I let myself be eased into the Dancing Mistress' arms while she cleaned and comforted me.

After a time, I realized that she was singing softly to me in some language of her people. I did not understand the words, and could barely hear them besides, but the sense of it seemed to be a chanson of peace and rest.

When they came for us, her life could be at an end. Mine was likely in peril as well, depending on how many of Mother Vishtha's stalks I'd broken. Here in the shadowed cold and damp of the cell was as close as I'd felt to cared for, at least since the night Jappa and Samma had helped me back to the dormitory. Possibly ever.

I curled in the Dancing Mistress' embrace. Her silvery fur was the softest of blankets. Her hands slipped over me like night wind through a garden. She traced the patterns of my bruises, giving me a little jolt of delicious hurt without it being so painful as to draw me to full wakefulness. I moaned so slightly at the touch, and so she did more of it.

We were entangled a very long time. It never passed into the pounding sex I had enjoyed with the older Mothers. More like the early exploration with Samma. Nothing was pushed or opened or thrust within, but the endless circling of her hands, and then her tongue and tail, brought me to a wet, wishing tremble all the same.

I wanted to stir myself, to wash her, to stroke her fur and tickle her back and find a way to return the jelly-legged feeling she gave me, but the Dancing Mistress was too giving, too kind, too gentle as she folded me closer into her arms and laid her head across my shoulders.

What came next was a dream, I supposed later on. Or possibly a visitation from the Lily Goddess. She was not shut of me, nor I of Her, for all that we had so tenuous a connection. She is an autochthonous deity, as Septio explained to me later—meaning that she is rooted in her place and time. Even Bhopura to the east within the same lands was beyond the purview of such a goddess, let alone the doings of a girl across the Storm Sea far to the north.

Yet there are those who ascribe much to the tales of the Splintering of the

Gods, the so-called theogenic dispersion, the birth of the gods in the First Days when the course of suns had not been laid in the sky and the plate of the world was silent as any table the night before the feast of life was laid upon it.

Mistress Danae might have said that the Lily Goddess was a splinter of one of the titanics in the leviathan times before, one of Desire's children. As a nephil-daughter of their shattering, She would have sister shards in other times and places.

I stood in a rainfall. Not the straight, warm rain of the Selistani monsoon season, but a whirling bluster of cold water and dissonant wind as autumn might bring, back in Copper Downs. A city lay in ruins around me. It stretched beyond the horizon. Most buildings were rubble and foundation posts, but a few stood higher and nearly unharmed. One of those was the Ragisthuri Ice and Fuel bunker. Another was a looming bluestone fortress, which might have been the Factor's house.

Plants grew around my ankles, rising from the soil even as I noticed them. I looked up again to see the ruins being strangled. Already the works of generations were being lost in a curling jungle. The leaves were broad and shaped like hands, with a low nap of silver fur on the underside and a pale, fleshy aspect above. They moved, their fingers wriggling, and each showed me a silver lily before the rain washed the flowers away.

In time, I stood alone atop a rock amid a wind-tossed lake. The city was gone, but for the bit beneath my feet. The twining vines had become roots for plants that floated like water lilies. I was amid a sea of hands. They began to curl one by one, then all of them, to the horizon, forming fists that reached for me.

I awoke with a sharp gasp, unaware that I had been dreaming. My head jerked back and jammed into the Dancing Mistress' jaw. She mewed in pain, but hugged me tighter.

"I am sorry," I mumbled in Seliu. "Was there a wind within our cell?"

She stroked my hair. "I cannot understand you, dearest, when you speak the tongue of this place."

Though I did not want to leave the circle of her arms, I sat up. The stone floor was cold. I pushed my blacks beneath me for a seat and leaned close to her from the side, as friends will.

"Nothing came as I slept?" I asked in Petraean.

"Nothing and no one."

"Mmm." I hugged her closer. "I am sorry that we hurt each other."

She whispered in my ear, her left hand on the skin of my right thigh. "You have learned so much."

"And more I would show you, if times were different." We both giggled at the tone in my voice. "Now that you have found me," I finally said, "will you explain what it is that drove you so far from home to search for me?"

She folded her hands and stared at the floor a little while. Embarrassment or simply lost in thought, I could not tell. Then she looked up. "These are dire times in Copper Downs. Much that the Duke had bound away was loosed when you struck him down. Trouble has unfolded on trouble. Some . . . some of us . . . feel that your part in the fall of the Duke might give you powers of both resistance and attack in the problems at hand."

My heart skipped. "Some of who? Only you and Federo even know of my role, yes?"

"There are others. Septio. Mother Iron."

"Septio and Mother Iron sent you across the sea?" I was baffled. "What did Federo have to say about it?"

"Federo does not know." She took a great shuddering breath. "It may be that he stands at the center of these difficulties."

Then I realized *she* was weeping. I drew her head into my lap and began to stroke at her cheek, her neck, her little round ears. The Dancing Mistress did not cry, exactly—I do not even know if her people can cry as humans do—but she was a knot of fear and sadness. I knew that mix well. Even though these troubles were not mine anymore, my heart opened to her.

I held her close, kissing her head and calling her sweet names in Seliu. In time she sighed and drew me down, and we kissed mouth to mouth. Her breath was no worse than any other woman's, and her arms were familiar.

For a while we managed to forget what was soon to come.

When the door banged open, the Mothers were angry. The Dancing Mistress and I tried to untangle, shielding our eyes against the invasion of brighter light. They became angrier.

"Get up," barked Mother Vishtha. She had Mother Argai beside her, the other woman with a crossbow in her hands. I could see several more Mothers in the hallway beyond. Had they expected me to grow violent and give battle to them all?

I stood, all too aware of my nakedness. Both these women had many times taken me into their beds, but now the revulsion was plain upon their faces. The Dancing Mistress found her feet beside me and slipped into a fighting stance that would let her use the immense leverage of her hind legs.

"Where is it written that you should lie with animals?" growled Mother Argai.

Mother Vishtha waved her to silence.

"She is not an animal," I told them, speaking urgently to overcome the glittering danger of the moment. "This is my best and oldest teacher!"

"Then let her speak." Mother Vishtha pointed at the Dancing Mistress and snarled, "Defend yourself, miserable creature."

"Wh-where is lodgings?" the pardine stammered in horrendously accented Seliu.

I glanced at her, amazed. *"What?"* I demanded in Petraean.

"I only know a few phrases," she snapped, not taking her eyes off the crossbow. "I'd figured on having more time here to learn before things grew difficult."

"The yowling of an animal," Mother Vishtha announced. "Just as a bird may be taught to speak, so has someone taught this one." She glared at me. "How could you?"

"Why did you come here?" I demanded hotly of the Mothers. Surely they had not trooped down the stairs to harass me over this.

Some of the anger left Mother Vishtha's face. "To bring you before the Mothers in assembly."

Mother Argai's crossbow wavered slightly as she spoke. "The Street Guild and the Bittern Court both seek charges. One of the dead is a Master's son."

"Your little adventure today was badly played," Mother Vishtha said. "We should have barred you from those blacks when you first made them."

Only I'd done too well as a Blade, I realized. The runs, which were meant to embarrass me and turn the sentiment of the sworn women against me, had induced the opposite effect.

"Green." The Dancing Mistress' voice was thick and low.

"They are here to conduct us upstairs," I told her. "To a hearing before the Mothers of the Temple of the Silver Lily. I do not know how this may go."

"Will they kill us?"

"Likely not." *Not me, at any rate.* Would that I knew more than "likely." "I am going to dress—"

"No," Mother Vishtha interrupted. "Not in your ridiculous costume." She threw me the pale robe of undyed muslin of an aspirant.

I slipped myself into the robe, directly over my skin.

"Will your animal need a collar?" asked Mother Argai in a nasty voice.

I waited until my head was clear and she could hear my words. "No more so than you."

Her face tightened, but her finger on the crossbow trigger did not.

The Dancing Mistress gathered her torn, muddy toga close and followed me out. We went up the stairs with Mother Vishtha in front of us and weapons at our back.

We did not go to the little room high in the temple, as I had expected. I'd thought to see an inner court as I had once before, Mother Vajpai and Mother Meiko besides Mother Vishtha and one or two of the other senior Mothers.

Instead we entered the main sanctuary. Wednesday afternoon wasn't time for services, but still the galleried seats were nearly full. Mothers in the robes and sashes of all the temple orders were present, as were a number of women from outside. I saw more than a few in the colors of Street Guild wives or the Bittern Court.

Of course the Bittern Court. I'd done them a bad turn, in the death of the man Curry when I'd dropped his key into the harbor. Whoever had arranged that killing now saw a chance to pay me out for my insolence.

"We are to be made an example of," I whispered to the Dancing Mistress. "You don't say."

Despairing of her fate, I fell silent then. There was little I could tell her, unless it came time for me to translate some speech or exhortation. *Or sentence.*

The Temple Mother waited before the altar at the center of the sacred circle. Always the woman in that role was the senior Mother of the priestesses, though she was advised by the Justiciary Mother, the Blade Mother— Mother Meiko since before I'd been here—and a few of the other senior Mothers from the healing and teaching orders.

I had never had much to do with the Temple Mother. She had lost her color with age, rather than never having had it baked into her in the first place as with a northerner under their tiny pale sun. Her name was Mother Umaavani, though I knew no one who called her by that name except Mother Meiko.

Today the Temple Mother stood and stared at me with those pale eyes as I walked downward among the ring of seats. The Dancing Mistress followed half a pace behind me. I knew from the prickle of my back that Mother Argai still stood at the top of the gallery with her crossbow, and probably the rest of the impromptu handle that Mother Vishtha had put together to come fetch me.

It was strange to be stared at by the old woman, who normally attended only to the altar and the progress of the prayers. This truly was a hearing and not a service—no incense, no bells, no scurrying priestly aspirants.

Just a very angry Temple Mother, me, and the woman who was both my oldest teacher and newest lover.

I stared back, gave her my hardest glare. Where I could make even Mother Gita look aside when the anger was upon me, there was nothing in me that would push away the Temple Mother. No more than I could push Mother Meiko, I realized.

In moments, I stood at the bottom of the steps in the circle of the altar. I had never walked here—never expected to, except when it came time to take my vows as a sworn Blade.

She must have been thinking the same thing, for the first words the Temple Mother said to me were "I had hoped to meet you differently, Green."

"Mother." She was the only Mother in the entire Lily Temple who required no name or title beyond that honorific.

"You seem to have been a great deal of trouble, dear."

Though her voice and words were sweet enough, I knew the look on her face. This woman might well have run with the Blades at some time in her life. Not that I'd ever heard such a rumor, but the hardness was there.

"I have done what was needed, Mother."

"Oh, yes." She began to pace in front of the great silver lily as if the two of us were having a conversation, without the Dancing Mistress at my side and more than two hundred others looking on. "How did you know these things were needed? Did the Goddess speak to you?"

"At times," I said baldly. If I could keep them talking, we might somehow both walk away. "But I never understood what was required of me. Her voice is like distant thunder, Mother, telling me of rain, but not how much water will flow across my doorstep."

"So it is with the Goddess sometimes, child." The Temple Mother's voice was filled with sadness. "If She herself did not tell you what was needed, how did you know Her will?"

I took a deep breath. I did not know where these questions might yet lead. All I could do was follow, and try to jump where she pointed. "I judged for myself, Mother."

"And did Mother Blade and your other teachers not tell you the one true rule of the Lily Blades?"

This trap I knew. I'd stepped into it as casually as a child walking into a mud puddle. I saw no point in pretending to coyness. "We do not judge."

"She has judged," the Temple Mother called out in a voice that rang to the heights of the sanctuary. "Even where we have taught her to do no such thing."

Applause smattered above me, followed by the buzz of voices. The Temple Mother was speaking to the Street Guild, I realized. And the Bittern Court.

I *must* push, I realized. If they'd intended me to remain silent, Mother Vishtha would have said so coming up the stairs. "We judge every moment, Mother," I called out loudly. "We are taught to judge when not to bare our weapons. We are taught to judge when to step into one dispute and when not to interfere in another. We judge all the time, for to make no judgments at all is a far worse error than to sometimes be wrong."

"You . . . do . . . not . . . judge," said the Temple Mother. "And in your pride, you brought a dangerous foreigner to our city."

On this, much of the matter hung. I turned to the Dancing Mistress. She was strangely relaxed, given the trouble unfolding around her. Surely the general meaning of the Temple Mother's words were clear, even if their specifics were hidden in the sounds of an unknown tongue.

If the Dancing Mistress had been a woman of Kalimpura, she would have been safe from the Death Right. As a foreigner, she was at risk.

Another strategy occurred to me. I almost laughed. All was already lost, how could another throw of chance deepen the well? "She is not a dangerous foreigner, Mother. I have been told by Mother Vishtha and Mother Argai that this is an animal." I cleared my throat and cast my voice as loudly as I could. "Animals are not subject to the Death Right."

Someone yelped with startled laughter high in the gallery, but was quickly hushed.

"Be careful what you ask for," the Temple Mother said in a conversational voice. "If she is an animal, we are free to chain her in the training rooms and spill her life for weapons practice."

Like the pigs and dogs I had killed, and the bullock for whose life I had asked so recently. I felt slightly ill. The time for a simple plea for forgiveness was long past. Not that I'd known what to ask. Mercy, perhaps, but I'd had little mercy shown to me in this life, nor held much in my own heart.

I pitched my voice high again. "Am I wrong, Mother? To aid my oldest teacher in her time of need? In the cities of the Stone Coast, we do not have Mothers, but she was a Mistress to me. Much the same. I bared my blade for her just as I would have done for you."

She gave me a long sad look. "*We* do not have Mothers? Surely you meant to say *they* do not have Mothers."

The gallery broke into a roar of voices. A drop of water hit my face, then another. I looked up, but there was only the towering point of the sanctuary's distant roof.

"You do realize what this place looks like," the Dancing Mistress muttered. I glanced at her as she made a vagina sign by nearly crossing the webs of her thumbs until a curved slit showed between them. Crude as that was, in that moment I was very glad that no one around us spoke Petraean. She'd intended the insult, and she'd intended it to be understood.

Nothing was above me to send the water down. Another spray of drops swirled around me on a wind. I recalled my dream, down in the cell below, of rain and lilies and the death of cities.

"I call . . . ," I shouted, then stopped. The gallery began to calm at the echo of my voice. I stared at the Temple Mother, but she was not focusing on me. From the fiery glare in her eyes, she had caught the gist of the Dancing Mistress' remark. My last gambit had failed; now I would play for all. "Mother Umaavani," I said, adding to the Dancing Mistress' insult with deliberate disrespect of my own, "I call upon the mercy and wisdom of the Lily Goddess to pronounce upon my case. Lay your charges before Her, if She does not already know them, and let us see what She says of both me and my teacher."

I heard another laugh in the gallery, this one loud and clear. The voice sounded like Mother Shesturi. There were some here who still cared for me.

"Very well." The Temple Mother's tones were ice now. "So it will be done. On your soul the burden rests."

The gallery erupted again. Protests were shouted from higher up—by the outsiders, I was sure—but they were drowned out by the chatter of the women in the lower seats.

The Temple Mother pointed the Dancing Mistress and me to a low bench at the edge of the altar circle, just beneath the bottom tier of the gallery. It was normally used by aspirants awaiting their vows, or others sitting out a service until their special role was called upon.

This bench also had the advantage of being out of the line of fire of Mother Argai's crossbow.

"What takes place here?" the Dancing Mistress asked in an urgent whisper.

"We are to be judged by the Goddess."

"Really?"

"Yes." I frowned at her. "I have made the best play I know for our lives and freedom. These women have no mercy, but the Goddess has been speaking to me. And Her power is very real. This is not Copper Downs. The divine does not drowse the years away here. There is risk, though. Most dicta from the Goddess are as She inspires the Temple Mother."

"The Temple Mother says what she wishes, then credits your Goddess?" The sarcasm in her voice could have been scraped off with a spoon.

"Well, yes." Put so baldly, the flaw in my plan was obvious enough. "Yet there are times when the Goddess speaks directly through her. Our gamble is that the Goddess will personally engage this matter, as she has been with me at times."

"Why do you *think* that, Green?" I could hear the fear in her voice. The end might come at any moment, and the Dancing Mistress could not fight free of so many.

"Because I dreamed of rain, when we were below, and rain fell on me just now at the altar."

She sighed. "She is not a rain goddess, is she?"

I shook my head. My Mistress' life hung by far too thin a thread.

"Then let us hope your dreams are far more powerful than mine."

As the altar was set up, a woman of the Bittern Court finally forced her way down to the sacred circle. Several Mothers from the Blades trailed protesting in her wake. The Temple Mother was having her sacred robes drawn over her by two aspirants.

When she turned to face the woman who approached in the harbor-gray silks of the Bittern Court, exasperation was plain upon the Temple Mother's face.

"You cannot do this," the Bittern Court woman said quietly. That there was no greeting or introduction told me they must have been speaking earlier, and were once more taking up the conversation in this awkward moment.

"I do not strut into your Great Room and tell the Prince of the Bittern Court how he may dispose ships in the harbor," the Temple Mother said sharply. "It is not for you to come to my altar and tell me when and how to petition my Goddess."

"We have an agreement." Though she stood with her back to me, and might as well have pretended I was made of air and smoke, the Bittern Court woman's wag of her chin to indicate me was clear enough from behind.

"We have an agreement to pursue the deaths today," the Temple Mother said. "I am pursuing them. You will have your turn."

"My turn is *first.*" There was venom in the other woman's voice.

"Not when the issue is at prayer before the altar of my Goddess." The Temple Mother's tone matched the poison of the Bittern Court woman. "Now I suggest you go back to your seat before your daughters are made barren."

When she turned, the woman finally looked at me. If a cast of the eyes could cut, I would have departed in a basket. I smiled broadly at her and nodded as though we were friends meeting in the market.

She left, shaking. I wondered if she would resume her seat in the gallery. More likely, there would be bullyboys in the pay of the Bittern Court lying for me, should I pass out the doors of the sanctuary with my freedom intact.

Though it would take a particularly foolish or ignorant street fighter to take on a Lily Blade. Any Blade had a number of very well armed friends.

Assuming, of course, that vowed or unvowed I was still a Blade when this proceeding ended.

One of the priestly aspirants began to light the thuribles hung around the altar. The look she shot me was full of worry. *Interesting.* I was still not convinced that my life was at stake, but the Dancing Mistress' certainly was. We had upset whatever their plan was for this convocation.

The incense smoldered. At this time of year, there was saffron crumbled into it, which gave the smoke a strange smell of wormwood and sunflowers—nothing like what the spice did in food. A chanted prayer began among the circling aspirants, who were joined by two Priestess Mothers whose faces I recognized but who I did not know by name.

The prayer went on, calling on the Lily Goddess for Her strength in times of strife. I hadn't heard this one before. It sounded more like a war prayer than an invocation of wisdom. The women's way was not to stand to a fight. Even we Blades ran secretly, or did black work.

Still, they prayed the virtues of arm and shield and bright helm. The Temple Mother stepped forward, spread her arms, and led the gallery in the Hymn to Change.

> *O Lily, Mother of us all*
> *Here in Your sacred hall*
> *Watch over us as we age*
> *From cradle to the grave*
> *From child to maid so gay*
> *To mother then crone so gray*
> *Make us better than our fears*
> *Down the course of bitter years*

The singing died down with the last notes of the peti being played above the gallery. Its bellows eased to a stop with a familiar creaking wheeze. The Temple Mother turned to her altar, dropped her chin, and began to pray again, this time alone. Her voice ran in a long wavering chant, never pausing for breath.

The Dancing Mistress clutched at my arm. "Something comes," she whispered so softly, she scarcely had voice at all.

The Temple Mother's vestments began to stir in a familiar swirl. I felt a chill down my own back—fear or something else, I did not know. A great wind rustled, even though it did not pass through the hall except to send the smoke from the thuribles circling the Temple Mother.

I thought of rain, and the death of cities, and slipped the Dancing Mistress' hand within mine. This was to be a channel, direct possession by the Goddess, rather than "inspiration." What I had gambled for, but all I'd really done was change the rules. I could not say what profit this would bring me, or whether I would be right in the risk I had taken for both me and my teacher.

The wind suddenly turned furnace hot. Screams echoed in the gallery above as doors slammed open. Some of the altar cloths whipped loose to catch upon the great silver lily. My groin ached like a stab wound, and I felt a sudden, terrible flow of blood from within my vagina. Doubled over against it, I could see red-brown spots emerging on the robes of the aspirants near the altar. A fearful wailing erupted from above.

All the women in this place must be bleeding.

SILENCE, said the Temple Mother in a voice that was much, much larger than she.

The air stilled in an instant. Even the thuribles stopped shivering on their chains. A moment later the sanctuary was quiet enough you could have heard a flower unfold.

I AM CALLED. The Lily Goddess slowly turned the Temple Mother's body so everyone in all the galleries could see Her divine aspect. If I focused my eyes on Her hand or Her hair, I still saw Mother Umaavani. Except for the dark blood flowing down one sandaled foot, she looked the same as ever. If I tried to see Her as a whole, She filled the sanctuary. More to the point, She filled a place in my head.

I AM COME. Dust sifted down from the ceiling. I WILL SPEAK TO THE GIRL GREEN. The Lily Goddess said something else, in a language I did not know.

I realized I was kneeling on the floor. I did not remember falling forward. Everyone I could see, from the aspirants in front of me to the back of the gallery beyond them, knelt as well. Everyone except the Temple Mother in her theophany as the Lily Goddess.

I stood and took the half dozen steps to present myself before Her. I could not look at the Temple Mother's eyes, and found myself drawn again to the blood on Her foot. My own loins felt both hot and empty, in pain like the worst of a monthly.

The Dancing Mistress stood with me. Out of the corner of my vision I could see her head was held high. She addressed the Lily Goddess in her own language. The Goddess answered likewise, in that gigantic voice. Then She spoke to me.

GREEN. YOU ARE A POOR SERVANT, BUT A BRILLIANT TOOL.

Drawing my shoulders up a bit, I nodded toward Her feet. I felt like a kestrel before a typhoon. Why had I thought this better than the simple judgment of women against women?

There was nowhere to go, nothing to do, but stand in place, even against the tearing feeling within me.

YOU HAVE SINNED AGAINST MY HOUSE, THE HOUSE OF SHIPS, AND THE HOUSE OF STREETS.

I fell to my knees once more and wept.

I LOVE YOU TOO MUCH TO LET YOU BE THROWN DOWN FOR THIS.

My weeping became tears, from the base of my stricken heart.

DANGER ARISES TO SELISTAN, TO KALIMPURA, TO MY TEMPLE. YOU ARE THE BLADE I WOULD TURN AGAINST IT. IN ANSWER TO THE PLEAS FOR JUSTICE AMONG THE WOMEN OF THIS CITY, I BANISH YOU FROM THESE SHORES TO THE COLD NORTH, ACROSS THE SEA. THERE YOU WILL STOP WHAT HAS BEGUN BEFORE IT CAN STRIDE ACROSS THE WATERS AND STRIKE HERE.

I was on the floor. Drool ran from my mouth across the marble. My ears were bleeding. I realized that I must know one thing. "Wh-where, Goddess, does this d-danger lie?"

The Temple Mother's hand trembled as she pointed to the Dancing Mistress. WITHIN THE COILS OF THIS ONE'S HEART.

A great thunderclap echoed. The thuribles fell; some crushed or shattered even though they were made of silver and brass. The Temple Mother staggered forward, slipping on the pool of blood beneath her left foot. I tried to gain my feet, but it was the Dancing Mistress who caught her before she tumbled to the floor.

"Th-thank you," the Temple Mother said.

Wailing and screaming rose all around. It took all the Priestly Mothers, and the Blades besides, to calm the gallery this time.

———

The Dancing Mistress and I stood in the sacred circle surrounded by Blades. Mother Argai was there with her crossbow, and a dozen more, including Mother Shesturi, who would not meet my eye. The gallery was being cleared of visitors, aspirants, and some of the vowed Mothers.

"Mother," I said.

The Temple Mother looked up at me. In that moment, I could see within her face all the women she had been—the girl aspirant, the young priestess, the training Mother of middle years, and now the wise old woman who led us all and took the Goddess into her body at need. I wonder what she saw in me. Scars? Rebellion? Perhaps a foreign fool pretending to be a good Kalimpuri.

"It is too late, Green." A sick smile quirked her face. "That was being a shout from the heavens as surely as I have ever heard in my life. The Goddess' command was clearly stated. You will go."

"I . . . I am not ready." True as it was, the admission surprised me.

"Your time is done." Her face hardened as she pulled herself wearily to her feet. Pitching her voice loud to the gallery, the Temple Mother announced, "I will have order. We are in convocation now."

The room fell silent again. Not the stunned silence of the Goddess' departure, but the rustling, noisy silence of a group of unhappy people waiting to hear what might come next.

"We have been told what must be done," she said. "We have not been told how to go about it."

"If the danger is in her heart," shouted someone whose voice I did not know, "cut her open and still the threat while we can."

I glanced at the Dancing Mistress. Certainly she knew she was surrounded by women who would have her life in a moment if they could.

"Do we remain at risk?" she whispered.

It took me a moment to understand that she made a joke. I snorted, then turned my attention back to the Temple Mother. She was speaking to the gallery directly above and behind me, where I could not see the seats or know who was asking for the Dancing Mistress' life.

". . . not so much a fool," the Temple Mother was saying. "Even our youngest aspirants would know better than to think the Goddess meant our troubles were literally coiled within this one's heart like worms in a dog."

"It is a clean solution," the woman called back down. "And does not turn against the word of the Goddess."

"Do not be stupid," I called out, surprising myself.

The Temple Mother gave me an angry look.

"We are in convocation," I told her. "Surely I am given right to speak."

"You are not vowed or sworn," she said. "Even so, the Goddess called you by name, so you stand tall in Her sight. Speak if you must."

I stood and stepped to the center of the sacred circle. Turning around, I saw a knot of women in justiciary robes. One of them had loudly called for my friend's death.

"You insult our intelligence," I said, "and betray the clear intent of the Goddess. My oldest and greatest friend has crossed the Storm Sea to bring me word of a disaster in the north. The Lily Goddess has joined Her voice to this foreign news to ask that we return there. The Dancing Mistress holds close some deed or choice or hope or love that will play a part in the unfolding of this."

"There is no argument here." The Temple Mother looked around. "We have been given as clear a directive as has crossed this altar in my lifetime. There will be no appeasement of the Bittern Court. There will be no killing of this stranger." Her gaze settled on me. "You have been banished from the shores of Selistan. From these shores you are being cast."

She then gave her orders to Mother Vajpai. "Wrap them both in beggars' robes and march them to the Avenue of Ships. There you will throw them into the sea, with three handles of Blade archers to see that they do not return to Kalimpura. If either of them sets hand or foot back on land, pierce it with an arrow."

Mother Vajpai bowed her head. "So it shall be done, Mother."

"This is the will of the Goddess," the Temple Mother called out.

The answer echoed in a mix of voices almost as loud as the Goddess' voice had been: "This is the will of the Goddess."

I had never seen such a run. As crowded as this city ever was, almost forty women with weapons in their hands and murder in their eyes cleared a path through which you could have driven an elephant. A knot of toughs in Bittern Court colors were shoved back just in front of the Blood Fountain, and I saw a great many disappointed Street Guild men as well.

We moved through the late afternoon like the blackest, most dangerous festival processional. Blades and prisoners swept down Jaimurti Street toward the Avenue of Ships. People scattered, but followed to see what the fuss was. Everything on the streets of Kalimpura was a show for someone.

I watched children racing along, the little cutpurses and beggars. How many of them had been sold already? How many would live long enough to grow into their lives? How many was I leaving behind?

"Green."

I looked over at the Dancing Mistress and found my eyes full of tears.

"This is change, not death," she said. "The path remains open before you."

Then we spilled out onto the docks. Mother Vajpai was taken up onto the shoulders of Mother Adhiti. She stood there—a trick of balance I'd shown her, I realized with a strange, quirky pride—scanning the waterfront. A crowd gathered around us, ringing my escort of Blades with shouting faces. Someone tossed a rotten fish over the heads of the Blades. As I did not dare raise my hands to block the missile, it struck me with a wet, stinking slap.

Mother Vajpai jumped down and, using our battle code, called for fighting as needed but to cause no deaths. She then pointed east, curiously enough toward Arvani's Pier. We hustled along as fruit, fish, and stones began to shower down. The women did not strike back, though they could have. Riot was unfolding in our wake.

I saw the purpose in Mother Vajpai's plan quickly enough. The Blades took the base of the pier, where it met the waterfront, pushing the Dancing Mistress and me out onto the tongue of stone. A single handle scrambled ahead, forcing anyone working there up the gangplanks of the moored ships and effectively clearing our path.

"You will leap from the end." Mother Vajpai pointed. "The Blades will stand over you as directed, but there you will be free of thrown cobblestones."

"Thank you," I said, though it seemed foolish.

"I suggest you speak quickly to whatever captain will listen first as you swim alongside." Her face clouded. "I should hate to have you killed."

"So would I."

The Dancing Mistress took my hand. The sense of Mother Vajpai's words must have been clear enough.

Followed by twelve archers, all women I knew, and some of them women I had been very close to indeed, the Dancing Mistress and I walked to the end of the dock. The rails of the dozen ships we passed were crowded with sailors, longshoremen, and idlers being harangued by panicked pursers and mates. The onlookers were all too busy laughing and jeering in the dozens of languages of the sea.

This show would be remembered in the taverns for years to come. I waved broadly, pretending a bravery I did not have.

Then we were at the end of the pier, and the women were driving us forward at arrow point without breaking stride. I went into the ocean with my teacher beside me, wondering if we would come up whole and how many dead-eyed monsters awaited us here.

Returning Once More

SOMEHOW I took in a mouthful of harbor water. It was foul—not just the throat-closing saltiness of the sea, but a mix of stagnation and bilge and whatever had flowed out of the bottom of Kalimpura as well. I found the surface and kicked hard to keep my head and shoulders in the air, spitting the whole time.

The Dancing Mistress struggled, though the tide was slack and there was almost no chop. I launched myself into her and tried to buoy her up. "Breathe!" I shouted in Petraean. "And do not thrash so!"

She calmed a bit. I tugged at her as I kicked in a backstroke toward the footing of the pier. Up along the top, I could see Mother Vajpai frowning at me. She was surrounded by drawn bows.

Time for a better plan, I thought. A ship was moored to the left, in the last tie-up along Arvani's Pier. She was a low, wide, open-topped coastal trader, in truth an overgrown longboat. Half a dozen Selistani men lounged at the taffrail. They stared as they passed a pipe.

The Dancing Mistress' struggles slackened. Dragging her with me, I grasped hold of the ship's rudder for support.

"Here," I said to her, "hold on to this chain."

"You there," one of the men called down in Seliu. He spoke with a thick Bhopurti accent. "Hands off. You might break something."

They all laughed at this wonderful joke. An arrow shot right in front of them to splash in the water beyond. The men and I looked at the pier to see Mother Vajpai there, shaking her head. Mother Gita winked at me.

So it truly was not the Blades' desire that I die today. I drew some small comfort from this prospect. Even in the heat of the afternoon, I was shivering. The water wasn't cold, but I was. The Dancing Mistress' condition grew worse, shaking and coughing. I'd never before seen her frightened.

"Man, bring us aboard," I said in my best imitation Bhopurti accent. Hiding the Stone Coast in my speech had been harder.

The leader glanced at the array of bowwomen, then back at me. His laughter was gone. "You are a danger, little boy."

I had to get out of the water. "I am far more than a danger. I am an opportunity."

"For what?"

"Bring us aboard, and I shall tell you."

He looked at Mother Vajpai again. I saw her nod. Reluctantly, grumbling, his men threw down a pair of ropes. We both climbed in our sodden beggars' cloth. Hands helped me over the rail, but they stayed well away from the Dancing Mistress.

I lay gratefully for a moment on the sun-warmed deck. My breathing was ragged and my heart raced, but I was no longer in danger of drowning. The Dancing Mistress coughed until she spewed, spraying her guts across the deck as the sailors jumped back cursing.

"Speak quickly," the leader said. "I don't like those arrows over there. I like you fouling my ship even less."

After opening my mouth, I stopped. The truth would not impress a man like this, who probably worshipped his great-grandmother or some little crocodile god. I could not readily imagine a lie that would be convincing from me, ragged and wet at his feet.

So I stood.

"I will not tell you I'm no trouble," I said. "But I will tell you I'm the kind of trouble you want."

He laughed. "How's that, little boy?"

"A boat like yours calls at ports all along the coast. Smart people sometimes think they don't have to pay, right?"

Now his face closed, suspicion dawning. "It is happening."

"I'll face down any of your men. Any two of them. If I throw them to the deck, take me on as a tough to watch over your cargo and defeat your enemies." I nudged the Dancing Mistress with my foot. "My friend here is allergic to water, but on a dry deck, dock or beach, she can fight all of you."

She groaned miserably, but rolled over and showed him the claws of her left hand. He looked impressed, then laughed. "You are being a great fool, whatever else may be true."

"I am the one it takes a dozen archers to keep at bay," I said quietly. "And I cook very well."

"Enough!" shouted Mother Vajpai from the docks. "There will be no fighting today." She tossed a small leather sack on the deck. It clinked in a manner the captain seemed to find promising. "I will hire you to sail east, to Bhopura, if you leave now with all your hands. Especially the newest ones."

He scooped the sack up and opened it. A greedy smile dawned. "We will be gone within the hour."

The captain's men put a boat over the side and rigged a tow line. That took much shouting and splashing. The vessel began to edge away from the dock. Mother Vajpai stood at the end of the pier, making the sign of the lily with her hands. Beside her, Mother Gita winked at me again.

Then we were turning away from the docks of Kalimpura. With much cursing and shouting, we headed out to sea.

Utavi, the captain of the little coastal trader *Chittachai*, agreed to sail us well east of the city, then out to sea and into the shipping lanes, where we would try to hail a vessel bound for the Stone Coast. The price of our passage paid by Mother Vajpai could probably have bought the entire boat.

The Dancing Mistress and I had little enough chance to talk as our new, temporary home was hugging the coast. *Chittachai*'s deck was open, except for a small space under the poop and an even smaller space under a little foredeck, which the crew used as an equipment locker.

After a day aboard in my right mind, it was clear enough to me that she either had a hidden, shallow hold, or truly vast bilges. These men were smugglers, moving goods past whatever taxmen or customs officials might be working the port towns of this coast.

Now *we* were their cargo.

Other than being out from under the threat of imminent harm, we were little better off than we had been back at Arvani's Pier. Warm, dry, fed, but still much shorter on prospects than on intentions. In the evenings, I missed my belled silk. That was more of a habit these days than anything serious. Keeping count in my mind all anew, and sewing those many bells yet again, seemed more than I could bear.

How had the women of my home kept theirs? By never moving far from where they started, of course. Like Shar, a woman there was born in one hut, living in a second with whatever man would take her in, and perhaps a third with one of her children after another son's wife did not want her around. All of them within a few furlongs' distance.

Girls who strode across oceans as I did could not expect to maintain tradition. I mourned my loss. Perhaps the Blades had kept the silk against my return, though more likely Samma had burned it.

Every step I'd ever taken toward home had only led me farther away. Just as I myself had been taken away.

"I killed a man, back in Kalimpura," I told the Dancing Mistress the first evening of our coastwise voyage.

"When did you become a killer?" Her voice was heavy with sadness.

I never did, I told myself. I thought of Michael Curry, sitting in surprise as the light vanished from his eyes. "You taught me to stand against the ill in the world." The excuse sounded horridly weak, even to me.

"This man you killed? Was he responsible for the ills of the world?"

"No." I picked at a splinter on the rail. Monkeys screamed in the dark trees a few hundred yards to the north, where the jungle came down into the water behind a great bar of sand. The evening brought a shift of the breeze, which caused the boat's heading to change. The smells changed as well, to rot and the sickly sweet odor of fruit going bad. No wonder the monkeys were screaming. They were drunk on ferment. "It was in the service of what I was told was justice. I have found a great interest in such things since returning to where I was sold."

A long silence followed. Eventually the Dancing Mistress spoke. "Federo does . . . did . . . does many things I do not understand. The buying of children was one part of his duties in the old days, when he carried the Factor's seal and purse. As I heard the tale, he bought you from your father at the gate of your farm."

"Trade," I muttered. "That wasn't—"

She interrupted me, still soft and careful. "Trade is not like a snake. You can cut the head, even gut the body, burn all the ships and warehouses. Someone will come along on the next quiet day and begin it anew. You cannot kill trade. Not at the point of a blade, not with all the fire in your heart."

Spitting over the rail, I said, "I am not *trade.* I am a person."

"People are traded everywhere. Apprenticeships, betrothals, the swearing of soldiers and hiring of sailors."

"They *chose* their fates."

"Green." Her tone grew pitying. "How many brides select the man they marry? How many apprentices looked across the trades of their city and decided which they would pursue? Most people never choose anything. They are chosen for, or they follow what is left to them after their choices have been eaten away by time, by ill fortune, by their own actions or the deeds of others."

I wanted to slap her, to restart our fight and give the Dancing Mistress the beating of her life. She didn't know; she didn't understand. She didn't *care*.

"Green."

Turning my back to her, I stared at the stern. The man at the tiller—I did not yet know his name—waved and smiled. He seemed impervious to the thunder that must have hung in my eyes. Or the last, failing light of day had cloaked my face too much for him to see.

"Green." She touched my shoulder.

I swung around with a hard block, then pulled my blow before it landed. *"What!?"*

"You are not wrong. It is just never so simple as we would like. Children should be free to grow and prosper and choose. So should adults. All persons, of any race or kind. That you would keep more children in their homes is a noble ambition. Do not forsake it. Just learn what it will mean. Should the prettiest girl in a family that starves stay home and starve with them? What if her price will bring her to a comfortable house, and feed her brothers through the next failed harvest?"

My tears continued to flow. "That cannot be *right*."

"Many things are not right. You can dedicate yourself to repairing some wrongs, but not even the titanics could have repaired all the ills of the world. In their time, they sundered, and from them have splintered all the folk of the world. We each carry a measure of grace, and we each carry a measure of evil. There is never enough grace to banish the evil, and there is never enough evil to smother the grace."

"So no one does anything." My heart was leaden. My throat had closed. The very words were bitter in my mouth.

"People do what they can." Her hand on my shoulder squeezed tight. "When you strode into the Ducal Palace, you threw down more evil than a generation of child-sellers could possibly wreak."

"That was not my evil." I felt very small in my shame and anger. "It belonged to your people, and to Copper Downs."

"No, it was not your evil, yet you fixed what you were able to." Her smile was tender by the rising moon.

"Then why have you come to call me back?"

"I have already told you. More evil is afoot. Many of us believe your place in the breaking of the old order gives you power in the new."

"It isn't power I want."

She knelt. "You could still leave this ship and take foot back to your temple. When their anger has banked to coals, they might even take you in once more. That choice is yours. But I beg you to come and help, for my sake. For the city's sake."

"Get up, get up." I flushed with embarrassment now. Goddess only knew what the tillerman thought. "The Goddess has sent me. I am going."

"When you released the spells upon the Duke," the Dancing Mistress said late the next afternoon as a pot of fish soup bubbled between us, "what did you see and feel? Where did this take place?"

"W-we were in a counting room." The memory was intense and difficult to frame into words, for then I had not yet taken up this habit of writing my story behind me. "There was no throne—it was not an audience chamber, but rather a place where men would meet to talk over numbers until their arguments turned to agreement. He toyed with me awhile, then I jumped at him and spoke the words you gave me." I paused for a deep breath of air, which despite the baking sun tasted almost chill for a moment. "Then he was gone."

"I know he is gone. His power is not."

"It must be. That might swirled around me like a storm of dust and air, and plucked at me with a thousand small fingers. Then his power wailed away, taking him with it."

"We did not study our war so well." The Dancing Mistress' voice was sad and slow. "People came as claimants to a vacant throne. What they sought was not his Ducal coronet, but the power that hung like a pall over Copper Downs. I was forced to deal with one of these shamans myself." Her eyes were haunted a moment. "At great cost."

"I am sorry," I said.

"No, no. It must be done. In the Duke's absence since, the gods have stirred from their long silence. At least one has been slain out of hand—"

"*Slain!?*" I paused. "I am sorry for the interruption, Mistress, but gods are not meant to be killed."

"They certainly do not think so." Her smile was crooked. "It is something that can be done. With the right preparation and the right powers."

"Small wonder the Lily Goddess fears," I said. "If even that idea crosses the Storm Sea, She is at risk. Let alone someone with the sort of weapon that can do the job."

"Oh, it is far more complex than possessing a mere weapon." The Dancing Mistress frowned. "I do not have the secret of it myself, and wish nothing to do with such knowledge, but the Interim Council had discussed it more than once."

"Interim Council?" The sound of that title bothered me. I had read enough history to know better.

"When the Duke fell," she said heavily, "Federo stood forward, with a few of the great trading factors. Our little plan was secret enough, but general discontent was a club sport in Copper Downs under the Duke. It was not hard to find people who thought they knew better."

"I suppose after four hundred years, there was no heir to come forward."

"No. Not a trace of the old ruling house. The Duke had been a collateral cousin, but he'd killed them all long before they could die of old age. To keep there from *being* a claim. That was part of his own grip on power."

"Your council rules the city now?" I was fascinated at the idea of the Dancing Mistress—a quiet woman who walked in shadow—sitting at the table of government.

"To some degree. The gods have bestirred themselves after long silence, the priests bicker, and our sister states along the Stone Coast have asserted all manner of baroque rights and interests."

"Were you sent on this errand to get you out of the city?" I asked her gently.

"I claimed this mission for my own." She smiled again, this time with genuine affection. "The council would have sent an embassy with edicts to claim you, if you yet lived. We had learned from the captain of *Southern Escape* where you went, and were set to petition the Prince of the City to proclaim you free and seek you out."

That made me laugh. "The Prince of the City? He is a fop with less power than a decently successful chandler. He sits on a throne of lapis and silver to impress foreigners, and spends his time seducing their wives."

"This is not so clear from Copper Downs," she said with asperity.

"No. Petraeans see a title and think it makes the man."

She returned my laugh. "You have become one of your country."

"No more than you are."

"No, I suppose not." With a gathering of breath, the Dancing Mistress resumed her tale. "A claim has been made upon the Ducal throne. A threat, really. A bandit chieftain in the Blue Mountains campaigns ever closer to the city. His name is Choybalsan. He has taken up some of this old magic of my people, and wiped out half a dozen prides of us when we tried to fight him."

"Oh . . ." I stepped around the fire and reached for her hand. "I am very sorry. So many soulpaths clipped to nothing."

"To be sure." She pulled away from me to stir the pot awhile. Then: "We are not numerous now. We never were, in truth. It would not take much more to drive my people from the world as anything but a memory."

I sat with her in silence, until the Dancing Mistress was ready to resume the tale. Finally, she was. "Choybalsan is as deadly to my race as a fire to a forest. He has upset the gods as well. He seems likely to rise on the back of this freed magic to oppose them."

"Did he kill the god who was slain?"

"Goddess. Marya, who watched over women's desires. No, not him. We are not sure who did the deed—agents of the Saffron Tower acting in secret, or some darker force. That is what most disturbs the priests of Copper Downs."

I could imagine.

"So," she went on, "we come to you. The only person alive besides Choybalsan who has controlled that magic he now rides."

Recoiling with horror, I nearly shouted, "I did not control it!" The tillerman Chowdry looked up to see what we were about with our arguing.

The Dancing Mistress shook her head. "Oh, surely you did, when you unbound the spells from the Duke."

This so distressed me that I went and exercised myself with a boat hook for a very long time, until the captain came to beg me to stop destroying the rail.

We avoided each other most of that day, but the sense of the Dancing Mistress' story was clear enough. I had touched it last before this Choybalsan. If anyone could turn him, it might be me.

Such reasoning smacked of idiotic desperation. The Duke had spent four centuries suppressing all other powers in his demesne. He'd even cowed the gods to silence. Who else could rise up now to defend Copper Downs?

Not me. Toppling one magic-ridden despot was more than enough to last me this lifetime and my next several turns on the Wheel besides.

In time we reached the shipping lanes. I'd grown accustomed to Utavi and his sailors—the nervously smiling Chowdry, Utavi's giant catamite Tullah, the rest of the sullen crew, but I was eager to be on to the Stone Coast. Loitering in the shallows along Bhopura gained us nothing. Along the way, our hosts had argued several times late into the night, making me nervous, but always they hid their words from us.

The captain did not hide so much. He grumbled time and again. I think Utavi would have sold us out even then if he could have found a buyer, though our swaggering ways and his fear of Mother Vajpai should have discouraged him from that plan.

In any case, he took us out into the deeper water, away from *Chittachai*'s natural habitat, where we could find the big oceangoing traffic. The men grew nervous in the open sea, but money was money, and they were making well more than a year's wages with the work of little more than a week. We hailed two ships before we found a third who would both answer and admit to being bound for the Stone Coast. *Lucidinous* was a high-sided iron-hulled vessel flying a flag from Dun Cranmoor.

When we'd finally talked ourselves aboard, Chowdry scrambled after me up the ladder.

"Where are you going?" I asked him roughly in Seliu.

"Utavi has threatened my life," he replied with a quaver in his voice. "I would not agree to bind you over for sale back in Kalimpura."

Bastards, I thought. It had been Chowdry who seemed at the disdvantage in their whispered disputes.

"You have no place where I am going," I hissed, but already Utavi was cursing loudly from below, and pale-skinned sailors were tugging me over the rail. They glared down at Chowdry, then heaved him aboard as well when Utavi showed them a long curved blade.

The decision was out of our hands.

Chowdry stood at the rail and cursed in some dialect of Seliu that I could barely follow, until a pair of bulky men took us all to see a ship's mate.

He was as pale as the rest of them, which was to say in these latitudes red as an apple above his sweat-stained whites. "You ain't armed, I trust."

I was mortified at how pleasing I found a Petraean voice. "Only a work knife, sir," I said.

The Dancing Mistress bowed and flexed her claws.

"You don't worry me, ma'am," he told her with a tight smile. "Come on, then." The mate waved us out.

We followed, Chowdry reluctant in the face of new authority. We were swiftly brought to a small mess. Looking at the four men waiting behind the table, I realized this was a hearing.

Then I saw that one of them was Srini, the purser from *Southern Escape*.

His astonishment was even greater than my own. "Green," he said in Seliu, half-rising from his seat. He took it again in some embarrassment as the fat man at the end of the table glared him down.

"Srini," I said in Petraean. "It is good to see you again."

"These people are known to you?" the captain asked Srini.

"Only the gi—" He took in my cropped hair and sailor's clothes, then corrected himself. "Only Green."

The purser's slip might as well have been a thunderclap, but no one else seemed to notice.

"Not many of you southern lads speak so well," the captain said. "What are you doing with this pardine?" He turned to the Dancing Mistress. "Begging your pardon, my lady."

"No pardon required," she said graciously. "Green was my very apt pupil in Copper Downs."

The look in his eyes told me I'd just risen considerably in status. "We're well under way, even with stopping to take you on. So you'll all be coming north. We call at Lost Port, then Copper Downs, then home to Dun Cranmoor."

"I can guarantee you triple fare when we land at Copper Downs," the Dancing Mistress told him.

"Or we'll work for it now," I added. "I am an experienced cook, both in palace and aboard ship."

"What of your father here?"

Father? I wondered for a brief desperate moment, before I understood the man's assumption. "Chowdry?" I looked at him. He stank with fear sweat. How had I let this happen? The Goddess had her purpose for Chowdry, of course, but it would be a long time yet before I could glimpse Her plan. "We will account for him."

"Sir," said Srini. "I am speaking for Green and her companion. If they stand for the Selistani, I would consider him stood for."

The captain frowned. "You three are on your parole. Srini, if they jump, you'll meet their fare out of your own pay."

"Yes, sir," the purser said.

"Thank you," I added.

The Dancing Mistress simply bowed her head.

With that, the hearing was ended. We were now aboard *Lucidinous* as something midway between prisoner and passenger.

We were shown to quarters. Chowdry bunked with the deck idlers with their hammocks slung near the bow. The Dancing Mistress and I were given a small space below, amid a crowd of grumbling servants within a windowless cabin that stank of sweat and old hair.

Copper Downs was my path home to Kalimpura once more. Perhaps my life was to be traced in a circle. At my quiet request, Srini found me supplies from the sail maker—even with a kettle, *Lucidinous* spread canvas when the winds favored her. During the quiet watches I sewed another, cruder version of the blacks I had worn as Neckbreaker.

As the voyage progressed, the Dancing Mistress and I continued to discuss the politics of the city. I could tell that she suspected Federo of something—old trust breached—but it was just as clear that she wanted me to make my own judgments. Chowdry joined us often enough, but he was sullen and withdrawn, obviously lost in regret over his impulse to follow us up the ladder.

All in all, it was a better voyage than I could have asked for.

I did not leave the ship at Lost Port. Neither did the Dancing Mistress. Captain Barks hadn't forbidden it, but I saw no point in risking his wrath. Instead we remained unusually at leisure, and talked about cities.

"My people do not raise stone halls," she told me. "We never have. Whatever god first set monkeys free with fire in their hands and ideas in their heads created city builders. It is humans who do this. That is why you outnumber all the other races of the world combined."

"In all the plate of the world, do you suppose that is true?"

The Dancing Mistress looked at me sidelong. "Perhaps not a hundred thousand leagues east or west, no. But you could not travel that far in your lifetime."

I smiled at her. "A fast ship and a good crew." Far away from Choybalsan, the Bittern Court, and all the ghosts already following me, though I was not yet sixteen summers old.

"Until you reached a desert or a mountain spine your hull could not cross. There you would not speak the language, or know the money. You would wind up begging beside some purple dock amid people who speak with feathers and curse one another with flowers."

I could imagine worse fates. I'd *delivered* worse fates. Even now, her words that day sometimes call to my heart, though I've long since set myself a different course. Then, I merely said, "I am not made to be a sailor on the seas of fate in any case. The Goddess has sent me, you have called me. Someday I will go back to Kalimpura. I know my life."

"No one knows their life, Green. Not until it is done and some grandchild marks a line or two upon their grave."

When landfall at Copper Downs was upon us, I begged a favor of the Dancing Mistress. "Do not yet tell Federo I am returned, please."

"I am not so certain what is the right thing to do here."

"Nor am I. So let us start with the simple things. You are going to find or send for funds to pay our passage. Chowdry is going ashore with us. You will need all of our fares."

The Dancing Mistress frowned thoughtfully. "That might make it easier, if I can speak of him. I will need to send word."

An idea occurred to me, something between fatal idiocy and clear-eyed brilliance. "I will go. As Neckbreaker. My Petraean is as good as any native's."

A strange smile crossed the Dancing Mistress' face. "It will be a test of your ability to pass."

I nodded and set to dressing. Sometimes I still missed my belled silk, but I'd tried to remake it so many times that the cloth seemed to exist only as effort, not as a reward.

With my face covered, I climbed back to the deck and stood by the rail. We approached Copper Downs in the watery gray light of a lowering rain.

Even with the weather, I could see much of the city as we edged into the harbor. My memory of the bells proved true—buoys, other ships, warnings ringing from rocks, welcomes sounding from the shore.

All that was missing was the clop of Endurance's bell. The ox was so far away now, dismissed from my dreams along with everything else from those days once I'd gone back and found the misery in which my papa lived. The sound of the harbor reminded me of how much I'd missed them when Federo had first brought me across the sea almost thirteen years ago.

I had few tears left, but the rain made my cheeks slick all the same.

Copper Downs spread before me. Metal roofs gleamed in the rain. Masts bristled along the docks, though not half what I was used to seeing at the Avenue of Ships in Kalimpura. Many moorings were empty as well. Some of the warehouses had burned and not been rebuilt, though judging from the waterfront bustle, that fighting was long since settled.

Two years settled? I wondered.

The Dancing Mistress found me again as *Lucidinous* slowed to dead in the water just off the docks.

"Srini gave me a chit of our accountings for the voyage." She passed me a pair of papers folded together, which I slipped within my blacks. "I have written a note requesting the disbursement."

Making a new port was one of the busiest times for a purser. That Srini had found any moments to spare for her was good. Well, good and the captain's orders. "Where do I go?"

"The treasury is in the Ducal Palace—the only place with strong rooms not serviced from the payroll of some trading house or great family." Concern edged into her voice. "Will that sit well with you?"

I felt a rush of memory. "The palace is just a place like any other." Untrue, but it was also what I must say.

She blurted her next words. "Find the Spindle Street entrance, and ask there for Citrak or Brine. They will know my hand and sign."

"What surety will they require from me?"

"My note should be sufficient. If they ask, your name is Breaker."

Bells rang from the poop. The kettle belowdecks shrieked as *Lucidinous* crept to her tie-up. The rail was lined with sailors and passengers. Copper Downs might as well have been the vessel's home port. Longshoremen and dock idlers crowded the quay—crowded in the northern sense, at any rate— while vendors and prostitutes and others of the usual dockside sort waited close behind with their colored rags and bright slips of paper.

Once we were secured to the bollards, a plank went down. Srini and two burly hands stood there to watch who and what came off and on. As I under- stood it, they would first let the crush of people clear, then release those hands that were to take leave in this port. After that, the dockside cranes would bring out the cargoes. *Lucidinous* might be on her way by tomorrow.

I had a few hours to fetch money back. Shouldering through the crowded deck, I nodded to Srini. He returned the nod; then I set foot once more in the city of my long captivity.

Perhaps I expected the heavens to open, or the Lily Goddess to speak, or ghosts to rise from the stones. In truth, three paces after clearing the plank, I was the same woman I'd been three paces before. The crowd was simple to thread through after my time in Kalimpura, while my air of swaggering menace came back to me easily enough. All my costume needed now was a weapon to back up the implied threat.

I was Green. I was back in Copper Downs. So far, no one had noticed.

Spindle Street was not difficult to locate. I followed it away from the harbor and through a succession of neighborhoods.

Copper Downs was infected with a furtiveness I did not recall from my glimpses of street life in prior years. Our night runs from the Pomegranate Court had been among people laughing, drinking, following their business through the darkness. From Federo's hidden attic, I'd observed a city of tradesmen and laborers hard at work. There had been no sense of desperation. People did not spend their time checking over their shoulders, or hesitate to round corners.

Here, now, they did. The only ones who walked with confidence were swordsmen, and the few protected by such guards. Ordinary people—baker's boys, mothers leading their children, clerks, carters, and messengers—seemed fearful.

Of what? I wondered. The riots were several years past. The Dancing Mistress had not mentioned attacks in the street.

My concept of the geography was still sketchy, but I knew the temple district was off to my right, and the Dockmarket behind me, not far east of the Quarry Docks. The old wall rose some distance to my left. Beyond it lay a district of quiet streets and iron gates, where the Factor's house stood. That was one place that riot could have claimed and I would not have mourned.

I crested a low rise where Spindle Street bent slightly west of north. The Ducal Palace rose before me six storeys tall, not so much a castle or a fortress as a manor house grown impossibly large. As I recalled, there had been no wall, just a garden. That had become a flowered overgrowth in the cool climate of the Stone Coast. A wooden gate of obviously recent construction stood open where Spindle Street met Montane Street running alongside the palace grounds.

Here was the Interim Council's treasury.

As I approached, I found my stride slowing. I had exited the palace at this point the day the Duke fell. Could I locate the window in the Navy Gallery through which I'd slipped? From there, I might even retrace my steps. I wondered who was inside besides Citrak and Brine and whatever toughs protected them.

Instead I marched through the wooden gates and up a muddy path to a doorway that had once served the palace as an ornamental entrance to the garden. There I found a young man in poorly tanned leather armor, chewing on a reed. He seemed unconcerned, in contrast to the fearful state of the rest of the city.

"I am looking for Citrak or Brine," I announced.

"Mikie's gone off to his mum's for grub." The young man's eyes were hazel. He was as pale as a fat man's belly, just like the rest of his countrymen. In a few days, they would come to seem normal to me, but not yet. "Brine's over at council chambers on a hearing."

"I have urgent need of funds."

"Ain't we all, boy, ain't we all."

I leaned close. "The Dancing Mistress has returned across the Storm Sea and must buy her passage off the ship *Lucidinous*."

"Who?"

Holding in my next words, I showed him Srini's chit and the letter from the Dancing Mistress. His lips moved as he traced the words with a grubby finger before giving up after two lines. He looked up at me. "You'll want Citrak or Brine for this, boy."

There was no reasonable reply to that. So we waited in shared silence for Citrak to return from his mum's.

When the man did come back, he was annoyed to find me waiting. He was annoyed at the guard for making me wait. He was annoyed at the counting-men within the building for waiting.

I soon realized Michael Citrak was annoyed at everything. He even *looked* annoyed—slim and fussy with a pursed mouth and frantic eyes that never quite rested their gaze on anyone or anything. His clothes were fussy as well; a maroon cambric shirt that had been pressed to creasing with a flatiron, over tapered wool slacks in a pale gray without a speck of dust on them.

"This is enough money to find you trouble," he told me. "I know *she's* good for it. You lose it, someone will have your head. Probably mine as well. Trusting such a sum to a foreign boy, I don't know."

"I shan't lose it," I said in my snootiest voice.

He gave me a small velvet purse stitched quickly shut with a silvered thread that had been finished in an ornate knot, then sealed with a lead slug and a wax stamp. Clearly it was not for the likes of me to open such a precious burden.

I tucked it away and bowed once. "A wasting upon your goats, and flux on you and all whom you love," I told him pleasantly in Seliu.

"Foreigners," he sniffed.

Grinning, I walked out through the garden, past the guard, and down Spindle Street once more. I was fifteen minutes from the ship. There I would be free of my burden.

Four men, rough-faced and thick-bodied with middle age, dropped off a wagon tailgate as I approached. They didn't even bother to flank me.

"Give it up, boy," the one with the thickest beard said. "Whatever you came up this road to fetch from the palace. We don't got time for foolery." He held a cudgel. The man to his left was armed with a short knife, similar to my lost bandit blade. The other two flexed their hands like stranglers.

"Are you with Choybalsan?"

"Huh. Smart one, are you? We're making a living here. You're losing one."

"No. I don't think so." I took a step back. This would have to be quick, for I needed to return to *Lucidinous* before Srini thought me a deserter.

"Pound the kid," the leader said in a tired voice. "Break whatever you want."

Rushing three steps toward the knife-wielder, I took a high, showy leap. I crashed into his face with my elbows. He was fat and slow on his feet, and tumbled back. My weight went with him to drive his head into the cobbles. I snatched his knife up and turned in one motion to bury it in the gut of their spokesman.

"Good luck making that living," I snarled. His eyes were wide with shock as he swayed on his feet. Yanking the knife free, I swiped it clean, left and right across his leather shirtfront, then pushed him over with a tap of my fingers.

The other two backed away. I saluted them with the blade, then trotted off to bring the money to the Dancing Mistress.

It was obvious now what the people of this city were afraid of. They didn't need a bandit king here in Copper Downs when they had each other.

The rain had picked up by the time I returned to *Lucidinous*. It bore the sharp, dark scent of the ocean. The Dancing Mistress waited at the ship's rail with Srini. Having a knife in my leggings once more made me happier, though this one was not balanced as well as my old blade. Energized from the mugging, I walked on the balls of my feet.

I *might* have killed one or both of the two I'd tangled with. Only if the others didn't fetch some help for their friends, though. In this city, I could be the terror that both the Dancing Mistress and the Blades had trained me up to be.

Stopping next to the base of the plank, I tossed the sewn purse up to the Dancing Mistress. She seemed surprised as she grabbed it out of the air. I scanned the crowd, now mostly sailors and laborers as the debarking passengers and their natural predators had moved on to other business. The Dancing Mistress and Srini counted out the funds, murmuring together. Then she came down the plank followed by Chowdry, who carried a ditty bag he must have cadged from among the crew.

She looked me up and down. "What happened?"

"Someone tried to make trouble."

"And? . . ."

"And I made trouble for them." I grinned manically. "Let us be away."

"Green . . ." Her voice trailed off. She and Chowdry followed me off the quay in silence. The Dancing Mistress plucked at my arm. "If it is your aim not to be known, perhaps you should be discreet."

She had the right of it. I could have outrun those oafs easily enough. Simply sprinted the other way, then dodged down a cross-street or taken to the roofs. It had felt good to stretch out and really *work*. I hadn't cared to play the victim.

"As may be," I said.

She let it drop and so did I. We stood in the street, Chowdry close by.

"You do not want to go to the Council yet," the Dancing Mistress finally said. "We have landed almost without notice. What would you do instead?"

I'd given that some thought aboard *Lucidinous*. Wandering streets almost unknown to me wasn't a worthwhile way to learn anything of value. While the empty halls of the Ducal Palace had certainly been tempting, I knew my earlier logic about venturing there held true.

"Let us visit the Pomegranate Court," I told her. "Look over the Factor's house. See some of the city. Then if we find nothing, go Below. You told me time and again that the underground was the dreaming mind of the city. Let us learn what Copper Downs thinks on now as it drowses."

Two years of running the streets of Kalimpura had taught me something of how to read a city and her people.

"We will need to settle Chowdry first," the Dancing Mistress replied. "I know a tavern where he can work the kitchen, sleep beneath the tables in the mornings, and be out of harm's way."

Turning to him, I said in Seliu, "You are ashore now. Will you cook in a tavern for a time, to stay hidden?"

"I—I will." His voice was stricken. "I did not know we came so far. I shall never go home."

Clapping him on the shoulder, I felt in his sorrow an echo of my own despair. "We will see you settled for now, and return in a few days' time to figure a better arrangement." My attention back on the Dancing Mistress, I added, "Is this tavern peaceful, or full of brawls?"

"Oh, very peaceful," she said. "Let us both take him there, so you can explain to the keeper. Then we will go on together."

The place she had in mind was run by one of her people, mostly for her people. The inn had no sign, and it stood off a quiet alley near a district of breweries. Chowdry was made welcome with little fuss. I met the first man of the Dancing Mistress' people I had ever seen.

He kept the bar, though in this place, that did not mean quite what it did elsewhere in the city. Scattered tables held deep stone bowls filled with scented waters. It felt welcoming. Like returning to a home I'd never known.

The bartender, whom I was to know only as the Tavernkeep, stood taller than the Dancing Mistress. His shoulders were no broader than hers, but he was rangier, with longer arms and legs, and larger hands and feet.

"You are she." He studied me. My costume meant nothing here. Besides, I was fairly sure these people saw almost as much with their noses as with their eyes.

"I am who I am. I am also responsible for this sailor far from home. He believes he may already be in the land of the dead."

We settled the former Selistani pirate into a very quiet house after some small chaffer. I gave him his duties in his own language, made sure he and the Tavernkeep knew one another's look—and smell—and then we were back out into the rain. That had turned from the earlier curtains of mist to a vigorous shower, a cold cousin of Kalimpura's monsoon.

Together we passed through streets vacated by the rain. Another difference: in Kalimpura the traffic barely changed for the weather, except in the face of the occasional full-on typhoon. Here we might almost have been alone in the city.

We passed close to the remains of the old wall with its cap of strange wooden structures, then into a neighborhood of wider streets that showed little sign of regular use. A district of wealth. Finally we found a street with a very familiar block of town houses. A bluestone wall rose on the other side. I drifted to a stop and stared upward.

"I should think we may use the gate now," the Dancing Mistress said.

"Perhaps. That somehow seems less fitting." I sprinted for the drainpipe at the far end of the block and swarmed up, much as I had on our night runs long ago. She was half a dozen heartbeats behind me.

On the broad walkway atop the outer wall, I looked down into the yard next to the Pomegranate Court. Whatever tree had stood there—I could not remember now—was gone. Even its base had been torn out. Weeds thrived in the jumbled pile of soil and stone where it had once grown.

Copper had been stripped from the roof beneath my feet. The exposed beams sagged, covered with rot and mold.

Something inside me fell. "This place is empty," I whispered.

"Which is why we could have used the front gate."

"Still . . ." I don't know what I'd thought to find. Girls in captivity. Perfidy. Bandits living in the rooms of my youth. This was almost as bad as seeing

Papa in his hut, Endurance dying in the mud beyond, while that desperate woman Shar looked on me as the thief who would steal her tiny, tiny future.

I had learned cooking and dance and the stories of old here. The swell of regret was surprising.

With dread I stalked down the wall toward the Pomegranate Court. I didn't want to compass the strides. Rather I wanted to remain safely distant, closed off from whatever had happened there.

You left the place with a corpse cooling behind you, I thought. *What do you expect now?*

My home had burned. My tree was shattered, spread across the court to rot. The horse box still stood, fairly intact and apparently spared from the fire. The building below my feet was a total loss. There was no body in the yard, at least.

The Dancing Mistress folded me into her shoulder. I was the scourge of this city. I had come to defend, to attack, to right wrongs—not to shed tears for a hated youth from which I had struggled to escape every minute I'd spent here.

"Wh-what happened?"

She hugged me tight, then set me at arm's length. "His men mutinied." Her voice was quiet. "The day you met the Duke, once the spells were gone and the word flew across the city on wings of rumor, the guards slew the residential Mistresses. They raped the older girls to death. For their beauty, I suppose. A few of the younger girls escaped. A handful of the visiting Mistresses were trapped as well. Of them, I believe only Mistress Danae emerged alive."

I was on my knees, heaving as I had done the night I killed Mistress Tirelle. Oh, Goddess. All I had meant to do was find my way out, not call down death on a house full of women. The girls were innocents, just as I had been. Even the Mistresses . . .

Goddess, have a mercy for their souls, if it is not too late, I prayed. *These people do not follow the Wheel as they do in Your south, but there must be some balm for them.*

The rain fell on me like a benediction. My hair was plastered to my head. It felt as if the Goddess' hand were pressing down on me. I listened for a long time to see if She would guide my heart. She told me nothing that I wanted to hear. That silence meant more than words might have been able to say.

"It is my doing," I finally said, wiping the bile from my mouth. My heart felt ground to shattered glass. "I wrought this."

The Dancing Mistress knelt before me. "Green. We know now that the Duke created this disaster, in his guise as the Factor. He set men to guard these girls as if they were treasures out of legend, and treated the guardians harshly. The girls were doomed the moment he was gone. If someone else had done the deed, you would have met your end as well."

"I did it," I repeated stupidly. Killed them all, with a few words.

"They died." Her voice was hard now. "With and of the Duke. Come now, we must move on. Nothing is for you here."

She was right, though my legs protested. Whatever I might have found in the rooms of the Pomegranate Court had been wiped out by fire and weather since those first days of riot and blood. *Perhaps that was just as well,* I thought. The ghosts I could meet down there would be very unpleasant.

I was too upset to climb down the drain. The Dancing Mistress led me to the main gate and a little stair choked with leaves and debris but still passable. We descended into a narrow alley that must once have given access from the street to the blank-faced central tower.

Looking up, I tried to imagine the men who had lived there. How they had thought, felt, why they had taken the lives of so many girls and women with such pain. I knew what sort of men they were. Like the four who had tried to rob me of my purse today. Not the elegant guardians who'd ridden blindfolded with the Factor's coach, but angry brutes who believed their strength made them right.

What did men like that think would happen to them as they grew old and frail? To their wives and children? Did the world only ever belong to the strong?

The tally of my dead had just more than doubled, with the women and girls of the Factor's house to my account.

I realized the Dancing Mistress was plucking at my arm. "We go Below now," she said. "It will be good to be out of the rain."

"It is just water." I tried to smile. "I've been told that washes away sin."

"My people do not believe in sin." Her voice was serious. "There is only circumstance, and choice. Green, you had neither circumstance nor choice when great harm befell this place."

I nodded, because that was what she expected. As we turned toward the street, something caught my eye. I looked back toward the blank-walled central tower. Someone stood there, half-hidden in the pouring rain.

Tapping the Dancing Mistress' arm in battle code for rapid reconnaissance, I sprinted toward the figure.

I heard her curse, and realized I'd used a signal of the Lily Blades. Which she would not know. Still, she would follow.

Whoever it was seemed to retreat as I approached. At the same time, they did not move at all. I burst through a swirling curtain of rain to find the Factor—the Duke—standing in the shattered doorway of the tower. The skin of his face was as gray as his rotten clothes. He appeared surprised to see me, then backed into the shadows with one hand raised before him.

He was gone.

The Dancing Mistress caught up to me. "What?"

Shivering, I found my voice. "The Factor was just here." And why not? "He was dead long before I slipped your words within his ear, Mistress. Surely he still is."

Like a god, I realized. Ghosts and gods were not so far apart. Especially as the greatest part of their power came from how much a person believed. As with tulpas?

"A glamer." She touched my face, peering into my eyes in the graying light of the rainy afternoon.

Staring up at the blank bluestone rising between the closing walls of this gateway, I was inclined to agree with her.

Over the next few days, the Dancing Mistress and I visited different parts of the city. I wanted to see Copper Downs by daylight, without riot on my heels. I wanted to understand more of what there was here. At the same time, we set about purchasing various neccessities with her recently procured funds.

"I cannot put the Interim Council off long," she told me. "Only Federo's absence has allowed me to avoid them more than a day."

"Where is he?" We were down in the Dockmarket eating a watery northern curry of some lumpy squash mixed with stewed fowl. I thought these Petraeans should be barred from using the word *curry* to describe it, even if someone had waved masala powder near the pot as they thought about cooking it.

"Off on an embassy chasing after help to fight Choybalsan."

"Houghharrow or Dun Cranmoor?"

"Would that it were so. No, he makes a circuit of fishing villages and farming towns. The other cities of the Stone Coast have yet to take this bandit seriously. Federo is begging his spearmen in tens and twenties from little men with little troubles who cannot see past their own bend in the road."

"A pretty problem," I said. "But not mine. I would still prefer to hide my face a while longer, in case anyone has a particularly keen memory or a thirst for old vengeance."

My ship-made blacks were wearying, the wrong texture and weight for my comfort. I would owe the Dancing Mistress a double hand of silver taels for the new ones she ordered for me.

While we waited for my purchases to be ready, we quartered the streets. The

Dancing Mistress showed me the compound where she had met a shaman in the days after the Duke's fall. She told me the story of how she and a Hunt of her people had run him to the ground.

"More of our magic on the loose," she said sadly. "A forerunner of this Choybalsan."

I did not sense any stirrings of either the divine or the profane as we passed through the little squatter village beneath the willows of the long-abandoned estate.

So it was. I saw granaries and slaughterhouses and the five armories around the city and streets full of the most ragged poor—they did not call themselves beggars here—as well as the quiet boulevards surrounding the high-walled gates of wealth. We walked the docks, for there was no single Avenue of Ships here as in Kalimpura. We passed by warehouses, factories, bourses, markets, exchanges, moneylenders, public strong rooms, and all the appurtenances of commerce on which a great city must run. Likewise the slips where ships were built and refitted, the parks, the rubbish heaps, the old mineheads now walled in and nearly forgotten, and the Ducal Palace from the outside.

I felt like a traveler coming back to his own home for the first time. Neither was true here, of course—I was no mere traveler, and while this city had been my residence a long while, it was never my home.

Perhaps most odd, all the traveling and talking of places and names made me long for my belled silk. More understandably, at night my empty sheets made me wish for a woman's arms and a place where I might be whipped freely and in safety.

"Where do women find one another here?" I asked the Dancing Mistress as we walked down the Street of Advocates.

"Wherever they are, I suppose."

"No, I mean for sport. If a woman desires to be scourged, or loved, by another woman, where does she go?"

"I am not sure."

The Dancing Mistress was embarrassed. I laughed at her, and began making it my business to catch the eye of the tougher women I met. Some looked back with a certain glint, to be sure, but I would need to work out the safe approach for these people and this place.

I had not appreciated what riches of sisterhood the Lily Blades had offered until they were lost to me.

Changing the subject, I said, "I have seen a few of Choybalsan's posters, but mostly what they tell me is that this bandit king has a friend with a printing press. The city is fallen on hard times, but nothing desperate."

Waldwick Public Library
19 East Prospect St.
Waldwick, N.J. 07463

"Times will be desperate soon," she said. "Did you see this morning's broadsheets when we passed the bookseller on Finewire Street? Choybalsan's men have broken the altars at the Temple of Air in the Eirigene Pass."

I knew more of Stone Coast geography than I really cared for, thanks to my lessoning. "That would put him less than three days' ride from Copper Downs, should he come down the Barley Road by horse."

"Yes. Have you noticed all the lading down at the docks is *onto* ships? Almost nothing comes off."

I thought about that for a moment. "Yes, I did, but I do not recognize the significance."

"Lading is work for the longshoremen and dock idlers either way. Yet if one sits in a seat of government, that is terrible bad news. There are quiet men with account books who will lecture you about balance of trade. Even the broadsheets talk of it now. In years past, you could not get most Petraeans to understand why money is not the same the world over. Hard times make for sharp thinking."

"Why have the people not fled?"

"Some have." She shrugged. "Others . . . where would they go? It is a hard road overland to either Lost Port or Dun Cranmoor. There are not many berths aboard ships. People stay, scavenge wood scraps to board their windows, and hope they have enough coal and potatoes to last if the markets are shut down for a while."

"And no ghosts," I replied. "I have not felt a prickle of the spell of release that I spoke. No strange power of any sort since spying the Factor's glamer the first day. If we do not find wisdom in the Temple Quarter, I think we must again go Below."

Even from a distance, the houses of the gods were clearly in disarray. Broken domes were visible from halfway across the city. The gods might have stirred from their long silence, but they hadn't yet concerned themselves with matters architectural.

Closer in, the Dancing Mistress pointed out to me the fat iron posts scattered along the east curb of Pelagic Street, which bounded the west edge of the Temple Quarter. "For many years, no one passed within except the consecrated, the very brave, and the foolishly suicidal. Offering boxes were set here for such temples as remained active through the Duke's reign. People slipped their money in, or hung bags of food for the priests. Sometimes they even prayed. No one crossed a temple door without good reason."

I remembered Septio from our underground runs. He had been a strange young man, not much older than myself, who had hinted at rivalries and jealousies among the priests who served his god Blackblood.

"Why were they so dangerous?"

"Were?" She laughed as we passed a building faced in slick black tiles. A pair of rusted iron doors stood open, much too tall. "They are more dangerous now. Better organized. In the quiet times, there were—well, tulpas perhaps."

"Mother Iron and the like?"

"Yes. What do you suppose happens to the dreams of a silent god?"

I considered that. "They might walk into the world, if the god were great enough."

"Exactly."

As opposed to someone from the world walking into a dream, as her people did from time to time. "It is tempting to wonder if our world itself is the dream of an even greater mind."

"As I recall," she said in her teaching voice, "Mistress Danae had you read Gnotius. That was one of his favorite ideas."

"Gnotius believed he himself was a dream, Mistress. I am not so sure he passed such judgment on the world, as he did not trust in its existence outside his own mind. That mind was what he doubted."

She laughed. "Now you know why I instructed you in dance and defense, not philosophy."

We drifted to a halt before a wide boulevard that drove back into the Temple Quarter. It was lined with great, fat-bellied iron pots, each of which hosted a thin sapling. The pots looked as if they could once have been used to boil sacrifices in some rougher, earlier age. Some were broken open by gnarled old roots that reached down into the pavers beneath, showing that great trees had once grown here.

Temples and priories and more anonymous buildings stood on each flank of the road. I realized this quarter was a small city in its own right. We'd walked past it on all four sides, without ever quite coming this close to it before. The Temple Quarter extended for blocks and blocks. From here, it seemed to have an endless depth.

"The Street of Horizons," the Dancing Mistress said. "So called, I'm told, because it runs forever."

"Or at least eleven blocks," I said, working the city-math out as we spoke.

"Yes, but can you see where it exits the quarter?"

I could not. Which really was the point. "Some old glamer?"

"That, or a very clever bit of architecture."

That was easy to answer. "If we walk this road running almost due east, we should exit the quarter once more."

"Of course. The architecture is not *that* clever."

I headed down the Street of Horizons. The Dancing Mistress followed close behind. She was letting me find my own way. If I could have smelled magic, I knew it would be reeking here like a building after a fire. Whatever the Lily Goddess had feared might be visible in some fashion. Surely the gods knew one another's spoor, even across the ocean. Their sight ran farther than that of men, whatever one thought of their wisdom.

That borderline blasphemy in mind, I found the temples crowded together like people in a market. *In a Copper Downs market,* I corrected myself. If they'd been crowded in the Kalimpuri fashion, they would have built literally one on top of the other. There were few common walls. Divine power apparently needed empty air to serve for insulation here in the chilly north.

Where most of the districts of Copper Downs had a style—reflecting either function, as in the warehouses down by the docks, or form, as in the counting houses along Redwallet Street and elsewhere in the financial areas—the temples enjoyed no unifying architecture. Each reflected the needs or nature of their gods. Gods being what they were, that meant the needs and nature of their worshippers.

The Street of Horizons was no longer abandoned, but it was still very quiet. Small groups of people shuffled to and from the demands of their religions. A man with a donkey cart wandered slowly in pursuit of what little trash was strewn on this road. Three young men with shaven heads led a protesting pig on a long leather leash to some sacrifice.

Little enough happened here. I wondered when these temples saw the bulk of their foot traffic. Dawn services? Was there a Petraean holy day? My readings under Mistress Danae had told stories of every possible combination of sacrament and dedication.

"How many people here worship regularly?" I asked.

"The priests complain of this often," she told me. "There will need to be a generation born without fear of this place before they see the crowds this street was built to host. People sidle in and out as they find the need, but in Copper Downs, the impulse to divinity is still a very private matter."

"As it is for your people," I said.

"We do not worship," the Dancing Mistress said.

"I know. You follow a path."

"Yes." She sounded somewhat miffed, as if I'd stolen a secret. "Worship requires a soul to hunger for the divine."

I doubted the distinction was so clear and simple, but I would not challenge her. Instead I kept walking, and wondered where the gods were. They did not come out to see me, whatever business they might have been about since their awakening.

If anyone in Copper Downs had recognized the taint of the Duke upon me, I might have thought it one of the gods. While I could not smell magic, they surely could.

Not this day, however.

We found the other end of the eleven blocks without incident. I felt no tickle nor tremble. Nothing. No gods, no ghosts, no in-between northern tulpas.

I was strangely disappointed. Whatever the Lily Goddess had hearkened to, it wasn't here. Of course, the coils of the Dancing Mistress' heart didn't twine through this most human of quarters in Copper Downs. Foreigners and nonhumans were to be found all over this city, but not in the Temple Quarter.

"Nothing," the Dancing Mistress said in that way she had of continuing conversations we had not actually been having.

"I might as well have been touring the bourses and looking at the corn bids."

"We did that yesterday," she said.

At that I had to laugh. Yet the lack of any response here meant we would next seek underground. My ghostly trail of victims would far more easily find me in the darkness below than they would in the busy daylight up here.

"Before we go Below," I told her, "I would like to make death offerings to the women of the Factor's court."

"That is not worship," she observed.

"I know. I do not mean it to be. I have laid my ghosts that way since you and Federo first showed me the rite of the two candles." *Or tried to lay them,* I thought.

We went looking for a wax chandler. The gods had said little enough to me. Perhaps my ghosts would say more. I wanted myself calm before I had to face them.

Half an hour later, the Dancing Mistress and I knelt together in a little grove of bay laurels in a plot of land near an old minehead incongruously located in the Velviere District. I carried lucifer matches with me, but was still quite glad that the sun was out. Autumn was at hand, but this was one of the pleasant days with which the Stone Coast could be blessed at the passing of summer.

I set out twelve black candles and twelve white. The Dancing Mistress had made no further comment at the purchase. I could not be sure how many women and girls had died in the Factor's house. Probably no one knew to tell me. This number felt right.

One by one I lit them. They burned fitfully in the little breeze, but the trees gave us sufficient shelter to keep them alight. The candles gleamed and spat. I did not have a speaking in mind, but words came to me unbidden.

"We all bent to the whims of a master we could not withstand," I said. "I meant to set myself free, thinking that would free us all." I passed my hands over the black and the white. The candles warmed my palms. "I am sorry for what became of you, each and every one."

The air swirled close. For a moment I thought the Lily Goddess was upon me, but it was just the wind rising and snatching away the flames. Then I realized I was done.

"When will we go before the Interim Council?" I asked her.

"Soon. Word will come, perhaps as early as tomorrow."

"I would take a good meal and rest my feet. We can go Below this afternoon or this evening, as you see best."

"Come," she said. "I know where to find stewed rabbits with corn and peppers."

I followed her to a meal I was more than pleased to eat.

At dusk we clambered the high wall that blocked the minehead and its tailings from the view of the wealthy who populated the Velviere District. Within the brambled, jumbled space we located the shaft entrance and descended Below by a long creaking ladder.

Once down, we didn't run as in the old days. We walked carefully with weapons loose in hand, coldfire pressed tight between our fingers. I understood this—we would not draw attention. It seemed a false economy. People saw best with their eyes. Most of what lived Below saw with noses and ears and stranger senses.

The Dancing Mistress did not lead with purpose, either. She murmured occasional warnings, guiding me onward.

I let my senses explore the dark. It was noisy here, in a way I had not remembered from the Below of my earlier days. Kalimpura was loud beneath the stones, but that was more a matter of Below there being a sewer system and thus well supplied with inlets serving to conduct sound. Given our climb down that ladder, we were a good fifty feet beneath the streets. Far beneath the sewers and into the mine galleries.

Old machines loomed, something else I had not encountered before. Rust and corrosion and the faint whiff of stale oil hung heavy in the air. My nose also found stone, of course, and standing water. Wood long gone to rot. Stray breezes. Flesh, but not nearby. My ears echoed with footfalls and odd clatters, but they were directionless phantoms. Threat was everywhere and nowhere.

I thought I had seen the Factor. Was he present in his persona as the Duke as well? The dead ruler had been more like an actor with two roles than a man with two homes. I was not even sure who knew of their commonality.

What of his agents? There had been other undying beneath the Duke's spell. I'd met two the day I slew him. Not to mention all the guards and functionaries.

We continued to move slowly. My sense of threat was almost overwhelming now. More than generalized dread—I was under attack. I let my pace fade and risked a whisper. "What is it?"

"I do not know," the Dancing Mistress answered quietly. The edge of fear in her voice chilled my blood.

"Not a ghost . . ." My words were cut off as something immediately before me shrieked with all the pain of a demon-culled soul.

I swung my blade wide even as my ears flooded with something hot and viscous. The edge caught on nothing. My hearing was blocked, which frightened me immensely. I opened my left hand with its small scoop of coldfire and nearly screamed.

The Dancing Mistress was sliding past me on my off side, away from my blade. She faced even farther left, as if she expected something to burst out of the dark there. Directly before me was a very tall imperfectly shaped man who had no skin. I saw bone and glistening fat and the strange marbled stripes of muscles. His eye sockets were empty, but even so his face was pointed directly at me.

Worst of all, my knife should have touched him.

I swung again. The knife passed through without intersecting his body. A bony muscle-wrapped hand caught me hard in the left temple.

Spinning back on my right heel, I had a moment to think how unfair this was, that he could hit me but I could not hit him, when the Dancing Mistress let fly a screeching cry of her own. All I saw between the shifting shadows and the tears of pain clouding my eyes was a leaping shape. Then I heard a horrid, tearing thump.

She'd attacked him bare-handed, I realized. This one could not be touched with weapons.

My hands lacked claws, but I could still use them well enough. I dropped my knife and charged head-down into the fight. When I hit, the feeling was like striking an open wound. Just grease and thick, slow blood, and nothing to grab on to.

My eyes were not filled with tears, I realized. I was being blinded by a flow of blood from my eyelids and nostrils. No sight, no smell, no hearing, except through a bubbling distance that did nothing to disguise the Dancing Mistress' shriek of enraged pain.

I head-butted again. This time something cracked. We had finally met one of the "worse things" the Dancing Mistress had promised me so long ago.

Strength, I prayed in a single syllable, then lunged once more. Blinded by darkness and blood, I clawed at the cold mess of this creature until my fingers snagged on bone. I threw my weight backwards and yanked hard as I could.

The piece I gripped stretched away, then snapped back. Our attacker gave another great shriek. I heard the Dancing Mistress' muffled shout of my name, then utter silence.

I stood with legs spread for a balanced stance, my hands high and ready for a strike.

Nothing.

Spitting blood, I listened with my mouth open. An old trick.

Nothing.

Carefully I lowered my left hand and touched my face. No blood. My hearing cleared with a faint popping noise. No blood there, either. Only my hands were sticky with the ichor of that shambling horror.

I listened until I ached.

Nothing.

The thing was gone, and the Dancing Mistress gone with it. *Or dead.*

My coldfire had been wiped out of my left hand with the fight, all but the faintest smear. I lowered myself to the ground and carefully felt across mossy stone until I found my blade. I then turned around and scraped back and forth in the dark until I found walls on both sides of me. Open space stretched in front of me.

There was *nothing* here.

Frustration boiled into anger. I opened my mouth to shriek, and nearly passed out. Lying on the stones gasping, I realized this was the feeling that came after a wound had bled too much. Yet I was whole.

The thing has forced my blood from me, then fed on it.

That realization made me retch. I'd prefer an honest slash to this rape.

Light flickered ahead. The pale gleam of coldfire in someone's hand.

Staggering to my feet, I held my blade behind me so it would not shine. I half closed my eyes for the same reason.

Whoever came moved slowly and breathed loudly. I waited patient as stone. They approached with care, until I could see they were human, or at least human shaped. My breathing was so shallow, it had virtually paused.

The stranger stopped two paces away. Summoning what little strength I had, I stepped so close, we could have kissed—and set my blade at his throat.

"Who are you?" I growled, ready to slit at a moment.

"H-have you seen a god here?"

By all the demons of far Avedega, I *knew* that voice. "Septio?" I whispered.

"Yes."

I could hear him getting angry. I could smell it. "That skinless freak was *yours?*"

He pushed the blade away. I did not fight. "What happened?" he demanded. "Who are you?"

"I am Green. And your . . . thing . . . has stolen away my Dancing Mistress." Just saying the words made me want to plunge my knife into his gut. I withheld my hand.

He must have heard my desire in my tone, for the bluff was gone from his voice when he answered. "Then she will be lucky if she dies quickly. An avatar of Blackblood has slipped our nooses and gone hunting."

That sounded horrifying. "What happens when it finds its prey?"

"Eventually it returns to the god."

"Break the Wheel!" I cursed. "How do we rescue her?"

His answer was chillingly simple. "We don't." Then: "Green. You do not sound well. Let us find a quiet place and talk about what it is that may be done."

"Qu-quiet, yes." I managed to put my knife away without stabbing my thigh. I very badly wanted to sit down, in safety.

She was *gone*. My greatest teacher was gone. A sick emptiness took everything good and right within me as I followed close behind this priest who might once have been my friend.

I kept enough sense of direction, even in my upset, to know that we were heading for the Temple Quarter. *Goddess, protect me from Your sisters and brothers here.*

Septio led me slowly to a colony of coldfire, for I could not walk fast. This time we both took plentiful swaths in hand. Somewhere in the darkness, we'd left behind the mine gallery with its corroded, bulking machines. Now the gleaming silver light showed a wealth of carvings. Faces and forms crowded the stone from the floor all the way up to and across the ceiling. The details of their features were wrapped in soft shadow, melting and flowing as we walked. Gnomons, for the dark-bound sundial of the underworld.

I let them distract me from the cracked well of my grief.

The Blood Fountain had originally been built much the same way. Kalimpura had entire temples in a similar style, buildings where every exposed face had been carved in a frenzied riot of detail.

I could not see why such a great effort would be made to line a tunnel few knew the existence of.

Eventually we found a tall, cold room lit by spitting gas lamps. Though it was at the level of the tunnel, the gas told me we were in the undercellar of some building of the Temple Quarter. How deep did the clever architecture go?

I found myself focusing on the smallest details as a distraction from my grief. This room had eight sides of equal length, making the floor an even octagon about twelve feet across. The corners where the sides met were relieved with little projections that rose the thirty feet to the ceiling to form a blunted vault. The walls were rimed with frost, as was the floor. A sigil was etched in marble beneath the frost.

Each wall held a doorway of blank stone. We had entered through the only opening. Septio stepped to the middle of the room. "Join me."

I did so. He shut his eyes, so I shut mine. I had the sudden sense of something larger and meaty close by us, though it did not have the blind, questing hunger of the skinned thing that had taken the Dancing Mistress. I clenched my fists and stood firm beside the priest, unready to surrender anything more.

His arm brushed mine. "Come."

The doors had moved. Stone blocked the path where our footprints disturbed the frost on the floor, and the opening now beckoned over virgin rime.

"Dread magic," I asked, "or a slowly rotating floor?"

Septio gave me a sour look. "Follow where the road leads, Green."

"I have spent too much time in a temple, and among practical women." The Dancing Mistress had been one, of course. The greatest of them. My eyes stung with the thought of her.

We passed through the darkness into a room almost as tall as the octagonal chamber, but longer, and thus relatively more narrow in aspect. This one was ranked by stands of dark candles, some deep brown beeswax. As we entered, the tapers flared to life to form a wave of light that reached the far end of the room and bloomed off the hammered silver mirror on that wall. The floor was littered with rugs and cushions and bolsters. A low table holding a few trays and bowls sat at the middle of the room amid the brightest candles.

"Come," said Septio. "Sit. Let us talk in a safe and peaceful place."

I watched the mirror as we moved to the center of the room. The reflection was delayed slightly, the way an echo might dally to follow after a noise. I had never known light to do that, and wondered what glamer was on the mirror. Or possibly on me.

"Below has not been good to me lately," I said as I sat beside the table. Something among the bowls had an interesting aroma. My body, starved for blood, began to hunger for it. I felt guilt at the hunger, as if my need were a betrayal of my lost mistress.

Septio tucked himself down next to me, not touching but still quite close, and reached for one of the bowls. "Try this."

"How will it help me find her?" I demanded. *Or her corpse.*

"Trust me in this. You need your strength, and we have time."

I did not trust him, but neither did I have much choice. Finely shredded meat in a very dark sauce. I lifted some with my fingers and tasted. Salty and rich, with a jolt of spice I would not have thought to find in Stone Coast cooking.

It was a balm to my thinned blood.

Dropping my veil, I began to eat. It was difficult not to make noises as I tore into the food. I felt like a beggar outside a bakery, driven half-mad by the scent and stuffing myself on the scraps before someone took the tray away.

After a few minutes, I slowed myself. There was no reason to lose control in front of this man, even if I did half-count him as a friend. "Now I have trusted you. Tell me, where is she?"

"I told you. With the avatar."

"And you said rescue was not possible for me. It happens I believe you, or I'd already be destroying this room looking for the way out to find her." An empty boast, though sitting in a decent amount of warmth and safety was doing much to restore me from the assault. "You led me to believe there might be other paths." I leaned so close that the warmth of his face mingled with mine. "Tell me now," I growled.

"That depends upon the god's aspect." Septio's voice was low to match mine. "Skinless is not a theopomp, so it will not lay her directly before the altar. She will be held awhile."

"Safely, or in pain and fear?"

"Green, what sort of god do we follow here?"

I exploded. "*Why?* Why do you honor such a cheap storybook villain? Life is difficult enough without mortifying yourself before a monster!"

"Do you know what we do here? Do you know why?"

"No," I admitted.

"Then do not criticize. The Sundering of Heaven was a stroke that has echoed across all of the world's time."

"You refer to theogenic dispersion." *Sundering of Heaven.* I despised his cant. The Temple of the Silver Lily seemed to have managed largely without the mummery so often associated with priests and gods. Simple description had been enough.

"Yes." Septio was surprised. "It is easier to talk of sundering, for most people."

I grabbed a lock of his brown, curling hair and yanked him close. "I am not *most people*. I will grant you that your god is a liver-eater worthy of your respect. Grant me that I know something of what I am doing."

"You have changed much during your time away, Girl," he breathed, then kissed me.

For one shocked moment I sat with his lips upon mine. Though he was clean-shaven, his face bristled. His presence was an electrick prickle on me.

Then I came to myself, pulled back, and landed an open-handed blow upon Septio's cheek. "I am not your harlot!" I shouted.

A long silence followed, which almost tilted into something more. Or less. "Now where *is* she?"

"W-we must see the Pater Primus ab-bout the Dancing Mistress," he finally said. "But I would know some things first."

"Will she be broken or consumed?"

"N-not until the theopomp takes her up."

"Who is the theopomp?"

His smile was crooked and bloody. "I am."

"You bastard," I hissed in Seliu.

"N-no, no." His hands fluttered like birds to draw a hawk from their nestlings. "There is a labyrinth. The avatar will be a while passing through it. I can do nothing until it emerges. With luck, she will not recall the journey."

"Why the focus on pain?" I asked again, distracted.

He sat up and dabbed at his face with a length of damask strewn on the floor. "You follow a southern god, yes?"

"Goddess."

"A women's temple?"

"Yes." I wondered where he was bound with this. I did not want him so close to the Lily Goddess, even with mere words. Not if there truly had been god-killers in this city sometime in the recent past.

"Does she take up the pain of birth? Of illness, or the death of a mother? The death of a child?"

"Well . . ." I had always supposed She must, but we never celebrated pain there except in the special way the Blades sometimes had of sharing love and hurt in the same moments. "Hopes and fears, yes."

"Your pain is as powerful as any prayer. Likewise the cripple, or the child who tumbles down a staircase, or a draft horse with a broken leg and the man with the sledgehammer not there yet to end it." He gasped, his breath shuddering. "Blackblood takes that in, along with the death cries of the prey in the field and the sheep in the pen, and much else that washes the world. My god's mercies are extreme, but they are mercies nonetheless."

"So death is his demesne?"

"No, not death. There are dust-dry temples tended by men wrapped in yards and yards of yellowing cloth who offer homage to what passes on the other side of life. Suffering is of this world. Death is of the next."

"They are almost the same," I protested.

"You have the right of it. Sometimes they *are* almost the same." His smile was sickening. "We celebrate pain as a way of celebrating life. When you can no longer feel the scourge, you are beyond this world."

I shook my head. "I suppose there is someone like him in Kalimpura, but I never passed within temples other than my own." *These priests are crazed,* I thought. Like one who lusts for the pain of the lash so much, she hurts and kills to feel it.

"Gods are rarely pleasant. Even the smiling queens of the harvest have the blood of a murdered king somewhere beneath the soil of their fields."

"We still possess a measure of grace."

"That is why men are greater than gods." Something in his voice caught at me. "We can know grace, and knowing grace, pass beyond. Even the gods themselves are not blessed with souls. When they die, it is forever."

"Neither is the Dancing Mistress so blessed." Though her people's paths mingled far beyond their lives. That gave me a trace of hope.

"No. Which is why I have not been so worried." He sighed. "She called you back from wherever you fled, did she not?"

Ah, to business. Finally. "To work against the bandit Choybalsan."

"I believe I understand her intent, though the details of her plan have not been made known to me."

"Whatever the plan was, it has failed." I stood and stretched. My body ached abominably. "I see nothing here, know nothing."

"That is because you are not looking at this problem through the correct lens." Septio's smile was small and tight. "The trouble belongs to the gods."

"I broke the Duke with my words. The power came from the path of the Dancing Mistress' people. Not human magic or the dreams of goddesses."

"You misunderstand me. Choybalsan is not a bandit chieftain coming with a thousand spears at his back. He is a god rising from the stones of the inland hills. The villages and steadings lost? Most are not burned. They join him."

"Why?"

"Because he is something other than this city. Copper Downs levies taxes, buys low, sells dear, and seduces away the children of the country for leagues about in all directions. What do the highland chiefs and headmen get for their trouble? Their life is like that of a flea which rides a dog. Choybalsan gives them power where they have had none since time out of memory."

He leaned close. "That magic of the Duke's. If you can channel it back, we can help the silent gods find their voices. Blackblood spawns avatars because the god himself is half aware. Likewise many of the other powers of this city. Those that have come to themselves scheme unseemly and poach on the rights and privileges of those who yet lie insensate."

So we came to the crux. He wanted his god empowered so the death gods and the hunting gods and whoever else from the divine squabble didn't make away piecemeal with Blackblood's supply of fear and pain.

The gods were like children fighting over cake.

Was this what the Lily Goddess had feared? An infection of *pettiness*? More likely the rising godhead of Choybalsan. If new gods of soil and stone could rise here, they could rise anywhere. Would some peasant cult from the distant rice paddies and mango plantations take Kalimpura by storm?

No wonder so many people despised the tulpas. They were afraid.

I realized I'd missed part of what Septio was saying. ". . . the Pater Primus. I think you must do it this way."

"I will have the Dancing Mistress back before I decide anything. Then I will speak with the Interim Council." I wanted very much to be quit of this city, but that was not a choice I could make. Not yet, before I could tell the Lily Temple something worthwhile. *Or sail west until I became a beggar at some distant dock, well away from the affairs of thrones and temples.* I pushed the thought aside. "There has been little of the Duke's magic here in Copper Downs, so we will go hunting Choybalsan. Under whose banner I do not care, for my sword will be my own."

That was a lie of sorts. Though I was on an errand for a goddess myself, I knew which banner I preferred. Kalimpura, wicked as it could be, lived in peace beneath the rule of dozens of smaller powers. The temples there were only a part of the balance. What Septio argued here was for placing the temples at the heart of the matter. More to the point, *his* temple.

I could not see how elevating the priests of a pain god to the seats of power was to anyone's good.

"Come," he said.

I let Septio take my hand and lead me toward the strange mirror. Once more, where I might have expected god magic, it was only a door—albeit a peculiar one. Beyond was a wooden staircase that folded around a shaft. The distant banging of gongs echoed.

Septio smiled at me in the dim light. I could see his teeth gleam. "We are timely."

Blackblood's sanctuary was nothing of what I might have expected from a pain god. Of a familiar formal design, it could have been any official building in Copper Downs. Pillars of black marble supported a vaulted ceiling on which the stars of some night sky foreign to the Stone Coast had been set in gleaming silver. Dark, narrow banners hung down in shadowed strips, much as they had in the palace. Low galleries behind each rank of pillars left and right hosted a series of stone couches, which might have been funerary platforms in a death house. Narrow curtained windows within the side galleries let in some light—*when had it become morning outside?* I wondered in a brief burst of worried fear—while gas lamps attached to the pillars hissed with the brightest fire. A pool between the pillars quivered like mud but showed a strange, malleable silver. The sanctuary smelled not of grave dust or funeral herbs, but mostly of the vinegar someone had recently used to clean the floors.

Neither altar nor throne stood at the far end, just a cluster of men in dark robes with cowls drawn up around their faces. Bareheaded young aspirants—in a brief moment of distraction, I wondered if they were so called here—circled the priests, banging gongs, shaking bells, and casting powders into the air.

More mummery, of the sort that irked me so. I checked the seating of my veil and trailed Septio toward his fellow priests.

One looked up at our approach. He lifted a hand. The leaping racket of the aspirants halted between one breath and the next, except for the faint ringing of the settling gongs. The other priests turned to stare.

They all wore masks woven from thin strips of leather, which covered their faces in ridges running from side to side. Again, mummery, but I had to admire the theater guising. At any distance, the robes would seem empty of all but shadows.

We worshipped the Lily Goddess bareheaded and barefaced, but perhaps these men felt a need to hide from their god. I knew I would if Blackblood had been my patron.

Septio stepped into their circle. He made a bow, which courtesy was returned by a series of nods from the masked priests. I tilted my own chin, which courtesy was returned not at all.

A lesser silver pool was set into the floor at their feet. This one shivered as the great one in the center of the hall had—except where it had been a strangely liquid silver showing nothing, an image was visible in this pool.

The god magic I had been expecting. I looked.

Skinless stood on cobbled stone before a whirling cloud of white dust. The Dancing Mistress lay curled on the ground beside it. I realized when I looked at her that the stones were flags, not cobbles. Skinless was very large.

The avatar seemed hesitant as well. Frightened, even.

I looked more closely at the dust. Or sand, perhaps, for it seemed I could spy coarseness. "What is it?" I asked quietly. "Salt?"

Septio made a small noise in his throat. "Yes."

"Why would the avatar of a pain god fear pain? Especially when his own priests embrace it?"

"Pain is still pain." Septio looked around at his fellow priests, then said something I did not follow. Their temple language, I assumed.

The one who had first acknowledged our coming nodded. Septio switched back to Petraean. "I must go bring the avatar to the god. The Pater Primus will pray for your teacher's release. Another sacrifice will be offered in her place. This should be sufficient."

"*Should* be?"

His eyes met mine with a cool amusement. "When are the doings of gods ever certain?"

Septio passed out of the circle into the shadows at the back of the hall. I remained with the priests, who continued to ignore me. Instead we all watched the pool. In time, the salt storm collapsed to a swirl of pale crystals on the ground. Without turning his head, the avatar reached behind and grasped the Dancing Mistress' ankle. He dragged her through the swirl to an iron door. There he banged his fist three times.

I was surprised to hear the echo of hammering from where Septio had just passed. None of the priests seemed troubled, so I held my tongue.

The door opened with a horrid creak I could hear all too readily. Of course, who would oil the hinges that closed such monsters out?

Visible in the pool, Septio stood in Skinless' way. His face was also masked with the horizontal leather strips, and he held a narrow iron rod high in one hand, where the avatar could see it. I realized the hook on the end was bone. Which made a kind of sense, since I had already learned at great cost that this thing could not be touched or turned by ordinary weapons.

What froze my heart was that Septio's other hand grasped the long blond hair of a nude boy who was covered with small red scabs. The boy's eyes were shut and his mouth hung open.

Tapping Skinless with the rod, Septio turned and walked out of the view. He dragged the boy with him. The avatar followed, dragging the Dancing Mistress. I heard the footfalls from the darkness beyond us.

The temple language echoed loudly. Septio made some prayer or address to Blackblood. The words were harsh to my ears, a tongue fit for pain. A great, slow syllable rumbled in reply, from a voice so deep, I felt the sound in my ribs and gut.

Around me, the priests sighed. Then there was silence.

I waited for whatever came next. The small pool was now so much dead silver, no different from the large one at the center of the sanctuary. The priests still stood as if expecting more.

After a while, Septio walked out of the darkness. His hands were empty— no iron rod, no Dancing Mistress, nothing. My fingers slipped down to the haft of my knife. *Where is she?*

I must have growled, for when Septio slipped off his mask, he seemed surprised. He turned the leather over nervously within his grasp before looking up at me. "Your teacher lives," he said quietly. "Can you find a healer of her people?"

"Yes. I would see her now."

"No." This was the one I had assumed to be the Pater Primus.

The other priests stepped away on business of their own as he stripped off his mask as well. Underneath was a slightly overfed face, skin shiny and pale in the northern fashion, his eyes hazel flecked with gold. Without the robes, he might just as easily have been a fruitier from the market.

"You are a great deal of trouble, young woman." His voice was ordinary, too. No hint of the god's nature possessed him now.

Keeping my veil in place, I answered, "The world is a great deal of trouble. I will see my teacher now."

"Our black moon sacrifice was taken up."

That did not seem to be an answer. I tried not to think about the boy, and what *taken up* might mean. "Where is she? Or shall I search for her myself?"

His hand twitched. "Do not go wandering in the shadows of this temple if you wish to leave as whole as you came in."

"Then bring her out to me."

"She cannot be moved yet," Septio said beside me.

"I will not let you see her in any case," the Pater Primus added. "Your path is different. I think you will have more dedication if you set your feet upon it now."

"You hold her hostage." My grip on the knife was firm, though in truth, I had no notion how to fight a temple full of priests. Especially as they'd inured themselves to pain.

"No. She will be bound over to Federo and the Interim Council, once she is ready to be moved."

This was his house. There was little I could do but seethe. "Then I will be away, to speed her escape from your dungeons." I itched to find the Tavernkeep and beg a healer of him. Later I might see if I could set fire to this temple.

The Pater Primus looked thoughtfully at Septio. "Is this one with us?"

"I will not be your enemy once my teacher is free." In truth I wasn't sure of that, but this was no moment to argue.

"She is with us," Septio added. "For reasons of her own, not just because her hand has been forced."

The Pater Primus turned back to me. "I hope you carry the old spells within you, girl, because one more blade in a woman's hand will be as one more stalk of wheat before the scythe."

"My blade reaches farther than you think," I snapped. Then, to Septio: "Show me the way out."

We walked back through the hall without further ceremony. "This is more than we have done for anyone before," Septio said.

"I suppose I should thank you, but gratitude is not in me now. Not with your Pater Primus holding the Dancing Mistress so close, like a child hoarding a festival toy." I thought on the boy again. "Besides that, we have traded life for life. I cannot feel so well about it."

Instead of turning into the gallery from which we had entered, Septio led me to a tall set of doors that seemed oddly familiar. I realized this was the black-faced temple that the Dancing Mistress and I had passed by.

"You do not understand. Once again, do not presume to judge."

We passed down the wide steps, which were made each too small for ordinary walking. That would cause the building to look larger, and make supplicants who approached uneasy. More clever architecture. Recognizing that the thread of my thoughts sought to turn away from guilt, I refused to distract myself. "You killed a child to retrieve the Dancing Mistress," I told him, letting my voice grow hot. "I, who have sworn a hundred silent oaths to stop the trafficking of children, allowed this to happen."

He paused at the bottom of the steps. "Which way will you find this healer?"

So much for an answer to my pain. I led him west up the Street of Horizons, following the quickest path out of the Temple Quarter and in the general direction of the Tavernkeep's quiet house.

The great room of the nameless tavern was empty, though I smelled Selistani cooking. I ignored Septio with the hardest set of my shoulders that I could muster. I would have preferred to ignore him with my knife.

Following the scent into the kitchen, I found Chowdry stirring something in a shallow sizzling pan, much in the Hanchu manner. He saw me and smiled shyly. "The master of the inn has found me decent seasonings in the market," he said in Seliu. "The meats are wrong here, but close enough." He took up a little bowl and flicked some food into it.

Possessed by a strong desire to purge even the memory of Septio's spiced meat from my mind, I tasted of what Chowdry had made. Goat, or possibly mutton, thin sliced and fried with sesame oil, chickpeas, red rice, and a heavy dusting of coriander. I closed my eyes and pretended for a moment I was in the refectory of the Temple of the Silver Lily.

When I opened them, Septio was also eating. I nearly dashed the bowl from his hands. He didn't *deserve* this shard of Selistan.

"Where is the inn master?" I demanded of Chowdry. My tone was far rougher than it should have been.

Chowdry dropped his eyes. "He is out, mistress. Meeting with the brewers, I think."

Which likely meant the Tavernkeep was not far away. I had no way of knowing where amid these surrounding blocks of breweries and malting houses he might be. "I require a healer of his people. For our Dancing Mistress."

The Selistani's eyes widened. "Has she come to harm?"

I did not realize Chowdry held any love for my teacher, but then, she had been kinder to him than I. "Terribly so. If the master returns without having spoken to me, tell him a healer is urgently needed at the temple of Blackblood."

Septio stirred at the mention of his god, for I had not made an effort to render the meaning of the name in Seliu. He set his bowl down.

"Our man is out," I told the priest. "I do not know where to look for him."

"Will you leave a note, so we can go about our business?"

"Two years this problem has been unfolding, and now you are in a hurry?" I turned back to Chowdry. "Is there paper and pen at the bar out front?"

He shrugged.

"Then tell him how urgent this is, and no mistake." As I turned away, I stopped. "Chowdry. I did not know you cooked so well. This fry is nicely done."

Another smile. "Who do you think fed *Chittachai* before you came aboard?" The memory of his lost ship chased the smile from Chowdry's face. The ghosts were visible in his eyes.

Not trusting myself to speak in that moment, I gave him the first few degrees of a bow, then left the kitchen for the great room. There was still no one about, but Septio and I searched beneath the counter until we found a tally book. I tore an empty page out of the back and wrote out what I could, taking care to emphasize the seriousness.

The Tavernkeep would not mistake the urgency, and I could only trust in the good faith of Blackblood's priests. Which would not last any great time, most likely, but at least so long as they thought they needed me.

You must summon the greatest healer of your people who can be found, I wrote in conclusion of the explanation I'd tried to make on the tally page. *Her soul-path may be badly damaged. Her body certainly is. Also I advise you to go with many strong friends. They are very difficult in the temple.*

Septio read past my shoulder. "We are sheltering you and her both from worse hurt," he told me.

"Your concern is a balm upon my heart."

Then, because I could not stand to sit and do nothing while she suffered, we went out on the fool's errand of finding the Tavernkeep somewhere in this quarter of the city.

We called at every brewery and loading dock within six blocks. I touched back at the tavern between efforts, as we crossed and recrossed the neighborhood. Wherever the Tavernkeep was, we could not locate him.

An hour or so before noon, as I was becoming almost violently frantic, Septio plucked at my elbow. "Look there," he said. "Is that your man?"

A pardine stalked along Gollymob Street. Not the Tavernkeep, but I knew their numbers were few enough. This one might have what I sought so desperately. I pushed after him, wishing I knew any words of their tongue.

He must have known I was behind, because he turned before I reached him. I stopped cold.

I had met only two of the Dancing Mistress' people in person. They favored robes or togas in the style of Petraeans, which allowed their tails to be free. I'd seen them wear sandals. Pardines seen in public were groomed sleek and clean, and seemed to be able to slip through the human life of this city like eels through a reef.

Not so this one.

He was even taller than the Tavernkeep, and broad-chested in a way that made me immediately think of some rangy tomcat on the prowl. He wore no robe, carried no sword, only a small satchel woven of tight-plaited leaves. The fur of his chest was matted into little shapes—squares, hexes, more irregular patches—each drawn up into a clasp that I recognized as knucklebone. The net of skin this exposed showed both the shifts of supple muscle and a goodly number of scars.

His eyes were feral, too, a deep liquid gold where the Dancing Mistress' were like water flowing on a summer day. His ears stood a bit larger and longer than hers, ragged-edged as if they'd been shredded by fighting.

Claws out, he flicked open one hand. A flower was crushed within. For a moment, I thought this another sending of the Lily Goddess, but it was an orchid. Likely one of the pale blossoms of the highest forests.

We studied one another. Where the Dancing Mistress flowed through the people of Copper Downs, the street avoided this one. Few stared, and no one tried to meet his eye, but everyone knew he was here.

"He is from the Blue Mountains," Septio said quietly. "Somewhere high in the ranges, where they still keep the older ways. Such a one rarely comes to the cities of men."

The pardine answered in the Dancing Mistress' language. I recognized the sounds, but could say nothing in reply. Perforce I used Petraean, though I doubted he spoke it. I made my words slow and clear.

"I have urgent need of a healer of your people. The Dancing Mistress is at the edge of life. Can you render aid, or do you know one who can?"

He stared at me a moment longer, unblinking. *This is like talking to a bullock,* I thought.

"She is the one who sits on the Interim Council?"

I could not keep the startlement from my face. His accent was a bit off, but his command of the language was perfectly clear. "Yes."

"I was told she had gone across the sea."

"She came back. Now she is in great pain, at risk of dying."

"Risk? We are all at certainty of dying." His face split open in what I knew had to be a smile, though several people passing by broke into a run. "Where is she?"

"The Algeficic Temple," said Septio.

"You will show me."

I was torn. I wanted to follow him, to see her over his shoulder as the Pater Primus would not let me go myself. I was certain I must still find the Tavernkeep, and pass the word among those of her people for whom this city was home.

"Will you go with this priest?" I asked.

"I find priests delightful," the pardine said. His voice was a deeper rumble than I'd heard before. His claws plucked at several bones knotted across his chest. "I keep my favorites very close by."

"Take him to the temple," I told Septio. "Once I find the Tavernkeep, I will go to the Textile Bourse on Lyme Street. Seek me there when you are done." I jabbed his gut with my finger. "Send word of whatever becomes of her, if you value any goodwill from me ever again."

Septio nodded, then looked up at the pardine.

"I am the Rectifier," the big cat said, then showed his teeth again.

It was just as good to be away from them. In the course of time, the Rectifier would become a great friend, and there was something of the rogue in him that I liked even then at the first, but I was so distracted in the moment of our meeting, I did not pay sufficient attention to his words. His friendship is like the friendship of fire to a man—it will burn a house down as readily as it will warm winter stew.

If not for his kindly nature, his killing ways would have made a terror of him.

As is so often the case, I eventually discovered the Tavernkeep where he belonged—in his tavern. I passed breathless through the front door for what must have been the dozenth time. He held my paper before him with a thoughtful expression.

"You are back!" I shouted. "We need a healer! Well, needed. I have found some help."

"I am pleased you located aid," the Tavernkeep said mildly. "I can seek more at need, but whom did you send?"

"Some great brute of your people. He is called the Rectifier."

The Tavernkeep's ears stood up tight, in a manner I recognized from arguments with the Dancing Mistress. "You sent the Rectifier into a *human temple*?"

I paused at his tone, and thought on what the huge pardine had said about the bones woven into the fur of his chest. Not that I had any great loyalty to the Pater Primus and his little band of finger-choppers, but I had not intended to send violence into their house, either. "Was that ill done?"

"Possibly." The Tavernkeep seemed divided between alarm and amusement. "It will be a day for them all to remember." He folded my note. "What is the nature of her injuries?"

"She was battered badly in a fight with a sending of the god Blackblood. It then dragged her some distance. I fear both the breaking of a hard combat lost, and damage to her soulpath for being taken into the depths of the Algeficic Temple."

He frowned. "I will fetch Healer and several others, that we might run together at need. Are you coming?"

"No." I hated saying that. "I am charged to go before the Interim Council, in part as a requirement by the priests before they will release the Dancing Mistress. If I go back to the temple, I will not have filled that commitment."

"Go, then. I will have what is needful to her within a few spans of minutes."

"Tavernkeep? . . ."

He paused in his busyness. "Yes?"

"Will the Rectifier hurt her more?"

"No. Yet his help may not be what she wishes for most."

I fled. Regret warred with shame in my heart. I should have stood by the Dancing Mistress. Could have. Except now I did the bidding of two deities. And what she wanted, of course. I had to hold on to that idea. This was what she wanted.

From the nameless tavern to Lyme Street was a quick enough walk. I passed out of the warehouses of the brewing district and through a few blocks of crowded houses before I made it onto the street. There had been tanneries there once, before they moved out to the eastern edge of Copper Downs. Some of the huge old buildings now held coach barns and stables. Others had been made into mercantiles for lumber and other goods that needed space.

Beyond them, Lyme Street was home to cobblers, tailors, and weavers, as well as to several felt works. The Textile Bourse, unlike many guild buildings either in this city or Kalimpura, was proudly close to its roots. I had not been within, and we had not passed by during our tours of recent days for fear of being called in, but the Dancing Mistress had pointed to it from a distance several times.

A facade of carved granite seemed intended to provide gravitas to the trade. The stairs were flanked by a statue of baled wool on one side, and a stone replica of a felting vat on the other. Someone had planted flowers in the vat, though now it was mostly weedy stems and dead leaves. The banner of Copper Downs hung from the roof, blocking the central windows—a copper shield in four parts, with a coronet and a ship. As I had been so carefully taught to read such symbols, more properly it was quarterly, in the first, on a field tenné a ducal coronet surmounting a ship on the sea proper; in the third, a field tenné; second and third, a field sanguine.

Somehow I was surprised they had not stricken the coronet.

A pair of guards stood before the entrance atop a half flight of steps. They wore the same raw leather as the fool at the treasury had, and each held a pike. As I walked up, one dipped his weapon to stop me.

"Ain't going in, boy. Especially not with that there mask on. In any case, they's busy."

I could hardly pick a fight here. "I am sent for."

"Now you're being sent away."

They both chuckled.

"Federo wishes to speak to me."

The chuckling stopped. The pikeman's eyes tightened. "And you are being certain you wish to speak to himself? Ain't no great treat, I don't reckon."

I thought of the certain pleasures of feeding *him* to Skinless, but held on to my rising irritation. "I won't know until I go in."

He took a step back and banged on a door featuring stained-glass images of the wonders of felt. An elderly, dry-faced clerk looked out.

The guard pointed at me. "This one say's 'e's for Federo."

The clerk looked me up and down. "I do not believe we sent for a boy as-sassin. Surely you belong on Lobscouse Street among the music halls."

I undid my veil and showed him the scars upon my cheeks.

"Perhaps I am wrong," the clerk said smoothly. "I see the rumors of your arrival did not overstate the case."

"Thank you," I told the guard sweetly.

The blacks were good enough for Kalimpura, where it seemed that there were as many modes of dress as there were people. Here where the costume was native to the stage, at least, I just looked strange. Veils were not in fashion especially, nor masks.

Now that I was in the Textile Bourse, there was little need for more secrecy. I tucked the veil away in my satchel as I followed the clerk through the doors.

The hallway within had once been grand. Today it was mostly crowded. Shelves and cabinets and desks were shoved in roughly squared arrays across the marble floor. Maps had been strung up over the portraits of long-dead bourse presidents. People trotted back and forth with papers in their hands, scratched with fountain pens, or met in little knots of two and three. Customs duties and the licenses of trade and guild had not stopped simply because a throne had fallen.

"As you see," the dry clerk said, "we are quite occupied. We find it efficacious to place the tax and fee work here, where public complaints can be met. Please, come with me."

I followed him through an irregular path threading across the room in twists and turns. The place was noisy, in a way that oddly reminded me of Below with its whispers and distant echoes. We mounted a grand staircase, now mostly a document repository, complete with little notes pinned to stacks of paper and ledgers. Once we'd cleared the wide turn that swept away from the tax floor, things were much more quiet.

The clerk paused at the top of the flight. "You are the girl, of course." His voice almost seemed to click. "I am Mr. Nast."

"My name is *Green*, Nast."

"And my name is *Mr.* Nast, Green." His smile was more of a mobile wrinkle on his face. "I expect we shall be the dearest of friends."

I could not help but laugh at that.

Mr. Nast led me down a hall of offices that overflowed with more people at their work. A few were women, but most were stout, older men. The walls here were stacked with paper as well. A large door at the end held another square of stained glass illustrating even more of the wonders of felt. An argument could be heard within.

Nast rapped sharply on the door.

"We are in confidential session!" shouted a voice.

"Sir," the old clerk called. "The girl Green is here."

Silence fell. Behind me, the bustle of the hall died. I looked back to see pale faces peeking out of doorways. A young woman stood with an armload of folders, hand covering her mouth.

"You may enter," the old clerk told me. "Best of luck, young lady."

I pushed open the door and stepped inside to finally meet Federo once more.

Five people were seated within. I scanned as I would facing any threat, eyes leaping to their weapons, the exits—for a moment I was a Lily Blade on the point of action. Then I met Federo's gaze, and I was once more just a girl beneath a pomegranate tree, waiting for my secret friend to return.

Those feelings swept over me like waves crossing a bar. They passed as quickly as they came, and once more I was fully and only myself.

Federo's yellow-brown hair was darker, except where it was shot through with gray. His face was seamed as well, as though he'd worn the years far more heavily than I. Even his eyes seemed to have faded.

For a long second, there was a hard look upon him; then his face split into a great smile. "Green!" he shouted, leaping up from the leather chair in which he'd been sitting. He raced around the table, saying in Seliu, "Welcome, welcome back," just before he collided to hug me close.

That felt real, at least, though I wondered at the passing hardness. When we pulled apart, I said in the same language, "I am honored to be in your home," using a formal register that emphasized his possession. Then, looking past him, "Do they know of all my deeds?"

"Only the least bit." His eyes flicked away like birds on the wing, giving his words the lie. "What is needed, nothing more."

My heart filled with sadness that he should begin our reunion with untruth. The Dancing Mistress had mistrusted something in him. I could already see why, if not what.

"Meet the Interim Council," he said in Petraean. Three of the four I did not recognize, but last was the Pater Primus of Blackblood's temple, dressed now in a formal cutaway with a bloodred waistcoat beneath. He now far more resembled a banker than a fruitier. Without his cowl I could see his hair was that rare and strange northern orange, blond alloyed with copper. He nodded slightly to acknowledge my recognition, but did not invite me to greet him.

Puzzled, I allowed Federo to lead.

"This is Loren Kohlmann," he said, pointing to a rotund gentleman with no hair on his head or eyebrows. Kohlmann was dressed in an anonymous gray suit, which could indicate any of the monied professions. Pale like the others, the man had dark eyes. His fat did not hang in folds, which suggested hidden muscle. "Loren speaks for the warehousemen and commodity brokers."

Federo then pointed to the man to Kohlmann's left, sandy-haired with the burnt-brown skin and rough leanness of a sailor, though he was also in a suit. I might have trusted the set of his eyes had I met him by a dock somewhere. "This is Captain Roberti Jeschonek. He speaks for the shipping trades, and those who work ashore in their behalf."

The next man was the Pater Primus, of course. "Yonder sits Stefan Mohanda. He represents the banks and bourses of Copper Downs." Mohanda nodded again, challenging me with his smile. Now I understood the masks and cowls, though I wondered why he had shown himself to me back in Blackblood's temple.

"Our last councilor is Mikkal Hiebert. He speaks for the carters, the laborers, and all the building trades." Hiebert grinned at me. Overdressed in brightly colored robes, he had the look of a man who enjoyed life far more than most.

"The Dancing Mistress speaks for those who are not Petraean by birth or tribe," Federo concluded.

I wanted to ask who spoke for the poor, for children, for women, for the tens of thousands of people in this city who had no voice in this room. I held my tongue, not being a fool. In their way, these proud northerners had reinvented the Courts of Kalimpura. I could not resist a twitting, though. "I am surprised that your renascent gods do not have a voice on the Interim Council."

Another shadow passed across Federo's face within an eye blink. "The Temple Quarter has ways of making its requirements known."

At least he managed not to look at Mohanda. Could this be what he was hiding? It would fit—a sending of Mohanda's god had come for me and the Dancing Mistress, then struck her down. This removed her from the situation and left me to rely on Federo. The man who had stolen me away in the beginning of my life.

"Have you yet received the story of what befell the Dancing Mistress this last night?" I was not above a hard look at the priest who hid himself as a banker.

"Word came this morning," Federo told me solemnly. "She was wounded saving you from attack in the Below, then a young priest took you both to safety. I have heard she recovers within the Algeficic Temple."

"Yes. That cult is well connected, it would seem."

Everyone laughed, including Mohanda. When the smiles had died, quickly enough, I pressed on to the true point. "I have been dragged back across the Storm Sea to aid you in your defense against a bandit in these hills. I have heard he is a man, I have heard he is a rising god. I have heard he burns all in his path. I have heard he takes farms and villages into his protection. I expect I'll soon hear he has fangs a yard long, but is also toothless." I looked around. "Have any of you *met* Choybalsan?"

They all turned to Federo. He appeared uncomfortable: genuinely so this time, not another lie folded a moment too late. "I have followed him through these hills in every season of the last two years. I have spoken with his lieutenants, even walked among his armies. He is often gone, always when I have come to treat with him."

It sounded idiotic to me. "How can a man roam the lands north of here for two years, complete with a fearsome army, and never come close to the city?"

Kohlmann cleared his throat. "Two years ago, his army was less than a dozen riders from the Karst Hills." He looked around. "Or so we were told. He burned a few stables and raided a manor house up in the Snowmarch River valley. A season later, he was on the road with two score younger sons who might otherwise have taken ship or joined some guard here in Copper Downs."

"The army, in the sense you mean it, is an artifact of this summer season," Jeschonek said gruffly. "He was first a raider, a rouser of unsatisfied country rabble. Now he has too many men and must find a city to house and feed them."

I looked back to Federo. The former dandy seemed so careworn. I wondered what plan he and the Pater Primus had in motion, and who would be betraying whom. Federo smiled. Fatigue was plainly upon him.

"You went looking for this man when he was riding with a dozen spears, bothering vineyards?" I asked.

"In fact, yes." He sighed. "That was the first season of this Council's rule. We'd heard of burnings out in the country, which seemed ill-omened, given how recently riot had ended here within Copper Downs. I went up to see, and came upon Syndic Alburth's manor an afternoon too late. So this trouble has been slipping my fingers from the first."

I decided to lay the problem bare. "You went to some expense to bring me back here where I never wanted to be. The Dancing Mistress is nearly dead of it." I drew my knife and slammed it flat onto the tabletop. "What is it you want me to *do*?"

"If I might," said Mohanda.

Federo waved him on.

"We think you may be in a position to judge whether Choybalsan is little more than a canny bandit chieftain, or whether he is in some fashion heir to the power that built and sustained our unlamented Duke." The secret priest pressed his hands on the table and leaned forward. "You might imagine this is of great interest in the Temple Quarter."

I'll bet.

Mohanda went on. "If the Duke's spells are broken and gone from the world, why have the gods not awoken fully and retaken their rightful—rather, the place they claim for themselves at the heart of this city's life? If the Duke's spells are still in the world, claimed and trammeled perhaps by an enterprising hilltop warlord who is still unfolding their powers, then the gods are at risk of being lost once more to long silence.

"As you are intimately familiar with the magic that had bound the Duke to this world, and you might recognize the scent or texture of it if you saw it on another man, well . . . You can imagine what value we could find in that."

I digested his words a moment. It seemed the path I might follow to pursue the Goddess' fears. Whatever could put a god to the silence of years, or rouse them again, was a powerful threat. A large step toward god-killing, which seemed to be a problem in Copper Downs as well.

As Septio had said, when a god dies, He is gone forever.

"How is it that I shall find this bandit when the leader of this council cannot?" I gave Federo my sweetest smile. "Old friend, I always thought you could winnow out anything. That was your main occupation for so many years."

"We have a priest," said Federo. "I believe you know him—Septio of the Algeficic Temple." I shot Mohanda a glance, but the man was smiling like a grandfather with his descendants before the solstice hearth. Federo went on: "He is clever and thoughtful. We would have the two of you travel together as ambassadors of one of our temples, asking to make terms with Choybalsan before he enters the city."

"He is known to be interested in gods," said Mohanda.

"I'd be, too, if I fancied myself one," muttered Kohlmann.

"We believe he will receive you," Federo finished smoothly.

"I am no priest," I told them. Which was not exactly true. There was small distance between an aspirant of the Lily Goddess and a priest. However, those people did not need to know my history, especially not the Pater Primus. "I will not be convincing."

"Follow this Septio," Mohanda urged. "Be his silent acolyte. His claim to speak for the temples will bear credibility because he is known widely as a priest of Blackblood. Your purpose will be to look and to listen."

"To see what may be seen of this vanished power." Federo, again.

"Why not send the Dancing Mistress, or another pardine?"

Federo shook his head. "Choybalsan slays them where he finds them. There is one rumor that does not seem to have its opposite being whispered alongside. The pardines of Copper Downs certainly believe it."

I retrieved my knife and studied the blade a moment. My eyes looked back at me from the murky reflection. Kohlmann was visible just above the point, as if I held the largest of swords underneath his jaw.

"If I go, and find nothing. Feel nothing . . ." I waved the knife for emphasis, and almost giggled to see Federo duck away from me. "Nothing is there. I can already say that. These past days, I could not taste it in the city. Locating more of it in some hill camp seems unlikely. When I return, will we then be quit?"

A complex web of glances passed around the room. "We will be quit," said Federo in their wake.

Good, I thought. I had no intention of running straight home, not until I understood the Goddess' fears a bit better, but I wanted to be free of the Interim Council. "Stand me a purse for my fare home, and a worthwhile consideration for my time. Give it to that man Nast outside. He would provide a receipt for his own grandmother, I am sure of it, and know years later on which hook he hung her. Make that thing happen, and give me your word that we've a sealed bargain. Then I will go looking for this wild goose of yours."

"Aye," ran around the room like a ripple.

"So recorded." Kohlmann scribbled in a tally book. "Five in favor and one not present, we carry the proposal."

"That was *it*?" The Courts of Kalimpura could take half a season to agree on whether the sun rose at dusk or dawn.

"You'll note there are no attorneys on this Interim Council," Jeschonek said dryly.

Mohanda's grin was positively feral. "Accidents will happen."

"So?" I demanded

Federo took my arm as if he planned to escort me into a grand ball. "So now we go tell Mr. Nast to write you a bond for fare and expenses for an amount we can both find satisfactory."

We stepped out in the hall. Several clerks stood there, looking through a stack of papers in one's hands, but at the sight of us, they moved off. Federo shut the door.

"Green," he said, his voice low. "I am sorry I do not have more time now. How is the Dancing Mistress?"

My face burned. "She might be dying, but I am ashamed to say I do not know."

He sighed. "It has been almost four months since I have heard from her. We disagreed, then she vanished. We had spoken of searching you out, and quarreled where we should not. I have been praying she had gone for you." His smile was crooked with sadness. "My prayers have been answered. She did not fall victim to Choybalsan's bandits. But her return is at such cost. What was she about?"

"The Dancing Mistress fears for the city." That was certainly true, though how much her concerns aligned with Federo's I could not say. Obviously they had been at odds over me.

"I am glad you are here." He made as if to embrace me, then changed his mind in the middle of the reach.

That, at least, seemed genuine. I wondered if the shadows and deceptions I glimpsed within him were just the product of being responsible for so much. As the Factor's man, he had had immense tasks, but not ultimate authority. Now he sat in the Duke's seat without the centuries of experience and adamantine confidence the old ruler had possessed.

"It will be good," I said. "I cannot but think this Choybalsan is a storm that will pass."

"We shall see," he answered grimly.

"Oh, yes."

As he called for Nast, I considered the Goddess' words. Federo and the Dancing Mistress were certainly entwined. Was it those coils of the heart she had warned us of? If my old teacher were to become distant and distrustful, she might perhaps betray this man and so lead him to a failure before the coming of the Bandit King.

I hoped that my role might be to reconcile them, and settle the confidence of the city's rulership.

Nast came. We made a chaffer about transport costs and guarantees and expenses. The old clerk finally wrote out a bond promising the cost of a cabin passage to Kalimpura as available from the three best ships in port the month I claimed it, plus triple that same value paid out as compensation for my services.

It did not seem to me to be so much money for the treasury of an entire city, even one in troubled times, but to see Nast and Federo argue, the terms of the bond might have been the last copper paisa to feed a starving family.

"I must go back to our session," Federo finally said. "I beg your indulgence. If you and Septio find some intelligence, do not hesitate to bring it straight to me. Ask here at the Textile Bourse. Nast and the privy clerks always know where I am to be found."

This time I did hug him. Something was wrong, some strange distance, but I thought now I knew what it might be. He returned my hug, stroked my hair, and murmured some vague apology before slipping back into the meeting room.

There was much running about thereafter. A scrivener with a good copperplate hand was made to come write out the final agreement on a length of vellum. Nast made me countersign the bond, which he gave me a receipt for. He then took the bond back and filed it with the bursary clerk to hold against a future payment demand, and gave me a receipt for *that*. I told him the papers might not survive my trip to the uplands, so he took the demand receipt and filed it with the council's privy clerk. I refused the last receipt, for I reckoned we had already made more paper than I'd ever have need for. Nast sniffed and slipped it into an inside pocket of his coat.

"Have a care, Mistress Green," he said. "I should not like to see you fail to return and thus be unable to reclaim your wealth from the coffers of this city."

That I did not even try to untangle. Instead I bowed. "I shall miss you as well, *Mr.* Nast."

The front door was not so hard to find, and so after resetting my veil, I showed myself out. Septio stood across the street, dressed as an ordinary working man and eating fried fish from a folded paper cone. Despite my manifold irritations, I smiled to see him and went to ask after the Dancing Mistress.

We ate fish together and walked slowly toward an ostlery on Shandy Legs, as that street was known. He told me what I sought to hear, though it did not all please me.

"I brought that great pardine brute to the temple." Septio took a large bite and gulped it down without much chewing. "We protect much there, as with any mysteries, but I was not so worried."

"More fool you," I told him quietly. "I was worried. Do you know what those bones were on his chest?"

"He said. Priests' knuckles." Septio grinned. I realized he was still as much an overgrown boy as he was a man. "I should like to see him try some tricks in our halls."

"Did he?"

"No. He looked at the large scrying pond and called up a shadowed forest." Despite his laughing demeanor, Septio grew very serious. "I have never seen an outsider do that. Even our priests have trouble with the pond."

"The long puddle of quicksilver at the middle of your sanctuary?"

"Uh . . . yes." He seemed surprised that I understood that secret.

"What of the Dancing Mistress?"

"When I took her from the god, I put her in the Hall of Masks. It is not so good a place for visitors, but also is sheltered from the . . . eccentricities, I should say, of the divine. She was in no position to respond."

"Why could I not go there?"

"I said, it is no place for visitors."

My hands began to tremble. "You took the Rectifier within."

"He is a spirit warrior of his people. And not human, besides. The eyeless faces would not trouble him. Even if they did, he would shed the disturbance as a teal sheds water."

Eyeless faces. "So what is her state?"

"Her injuries are not life threatening, though she should spend a week or two abed, the Rectifier says. He fears far more for the state of her soulpath. He told me to imagine a human whose spirit has been shredded and scattered. Then the Tavernkeep arrived with a healer of his people, and a little mob besides. They seemed ready to fight. Her wounds were treated, and she was bathed in the manner of their people."

I stopped walking, close enough to our destination that the smell of horses was rank in my nostrils. "I would see her before we set out on our journey."

"The Pater Primus has forbidden it."

The hair on my neck prickled. "He does not control me."

"No, no," Septio said. "He has sent word that the Dancing Mistress is to be kept under the protection of the Interim Council."

I did not like that much, but I did not see an easy way around it without looking like a fool or, worse, a child. I had accepted a task from the Interim Council. Having the Dancing Mistress recovering under Federo's watch might give them a chance to grow closer together, when their rift had been because of me. Following the path I already pursued was best for everyone.

Though it sounded good, I didn't really believe that. Something was still wrong here. In that moment, I couldn't say what with sufficient conviction to turn around and go back to the Textile Bourse with a demand to see her, and I was mistrustful of my suspicions.

Now I wish I had listened to myself, but at that time, I did not know my friends from my enemies. So I followed Septio into the ostlery and mounted a horse for distance for the first time in my life.

———

Whoever conceived of the horse as a form of transport must have been a man with no feet. Though I'd been educated in the details of harness and tack, presentation and points, and had sat atop a mincing mare trained within an inch of her life, that had all been at the Pomegranate Court, where the distance to be ridden was less than a stone's throw, and everything was for the sake of appearance.

The substance of being perched high on the bony back of a cantankerous nag with poor digestion and a desire to put its head down every time it rushed toward the bottom of a slope was quite different. I sat far too tall for my sense of balance. The horse paid no mind to my efforts at control. Even with the leather trousers and boots the ostler had provided me, the pressures of the saddle raised aches in muscles of which I had never before been aware.

Septio laughed to see me stagger bowlegged as I dismounted at the end of our first afternoon's ride. "My thighs shake a bit after riding over country," he said with a grin, "but you have the Vitus dance."

"If you hold still, I'll be happy to kill you," I growled.

Instead he unslung a blanket, then cleared some stones to lay it down. "Here. Lie flat a bit. I'll care for the horses."

I did as he said, and found myself most relieved not to be attempting the vertical for a while. My horse's head swung over me as Septio turned it away. I swear the wretched beast was laughing. The aches would pass, I knew, for every part of my body had ached at some time. I was not so sure about the smell.

Give me a ship, any time, or the two feet with which I had been born.

Septio pulled loose the bags we'd found waiting for us at the ostlery, then unsaddled the horses. Once they were freed of their burdens, he watered them, brushed them, then staked them out to crop at the thick grass that grew along the edge of the stand of trees in which we camped. A stream just between the boles explained why the grove was here, in a rising valley with mostly low bushes and scrub grass.

I continued to lie still as Septio arranged our camp and made a fire. He drew a small packet from his satchel and shook some powder over the sticks and bracken. When he set a lucifer match to it, the fire flared like a war among the insects.

"What is that?"

"Much the same stuff that is used in pistols," he told me. "Also festival crackers. It does not work so well when it is wet, but dry it is wonderful."

"I did not realize that people carried that about."

"Few do." Septio grinned. "An amusement among the temples, though it has serious uses as well."

He tended his fire a little while to make sure the flames were true. Once satisfied, he unpacked the saddlebags. I continued to watch him until he began wrestling with the problem of boiling some water.

Groaning, I sat up. "I will cook."

"That is not only a woman's duty." He looked down at the small pan before him.

"Dolt, I'm *good* at it. You manage the horrid beasts, I'll make dinner. We each have done our part that way, yes?"

He nodded.

Septio is not so bad, I thought a while later as I cut riverbank shallots into the developing stew. He was taking care of our situation.

"Tell me," I said. "What did you mean about the sacrifice being taken up?" This was not an issue I wanted to visit too closely, but I could not just let it go.

"When people are very sick or injured . . ." His voice was slow, thoughtful. "When they are in great pain, and there is only poppy to be given them by the healers at the Temple of Caddyce, sometimes a family will bring their father or son to the Algeficic Temple."

"Because of the pain?"

"Because of the pain. Instead of a suffering, a wasting of body and soul, it can become a sacrament. Some good may be found." He idly rearranged the firewood as he spoke, choosing his words with care. "As I told you, pain is part of life. A god such as Blackblood guards many doors for the people. Those who worship him, as well as those who pretend he does not exist. Even those who have never heard of him."

"So this man or boy suffers on your altar?"

"He suffers before the god arrives. Blackblood takes this up, takes him up. Sometimes . . ." Now I got a long, slow look, almost pleading. "Sometimes the pain is taken up, but the man or boy remains."

I felt a chill down my spine as the drawing dusk stole the light around us. "What becomes of him then?"

"He lives to serve the temple."

Ahh. Like the Bone Door on the alleyside of the temple of the Lily Goddess, only much more difficult to pass through. "As you did once," I said, my voice very soft. My heart flooded with pity for him.

"As I did once."

"Do you remember your family?"

"A small bit. Some recall more than others." Septio looked troubled. "If a fever is on the blood or brain, there may be little left of the former life. If it is the crab disease within the gut, the memories may remain complete as the seat of reason remains untouched."

"Most are taken up." I hated that idea. "How sad for them."

"No, no, you mistake me. Blackblood's priests? The Pater Primus, Tertio, all of us?" The sadness in his face deepened. "We are the sacrifices he rejected. We serve him in life because we were not wanted as part of his substance. Each of us seeks to find his way back to the god."

What a miserable theology, I thought. The victim blames himself because his pain was not good enough. "What of women who hurt? Or girls?"

"I d-don't know." Septio's voice was quite small. "They die in pain, I suppose."

That was quite enough of this conversation. I let it lapse only a little too late.

We were headed toward the Eirigene Pass. Our route was not up the Barley Road, which mostly followed the Greenbriar River as it ran through farming country, but another, higher trackway with little traffic. The soil was more sparse up here, and I knew from my studies that the conditions would be much harsher in the winter. The few steadings we saw were long abandoned.

"I do not wish to push through refugees," Septio said.

I stared at my horse, unwilling to mount, but just as unwilling to sit by this stream for the rest of my days. "What refugees? Copper Downs is not exactly overrun by the desperate."

"If Choybalsan has truly broken the Temple of Air, there will be villages' worth of farmers and servants on the move."

"Unless he's sworn them all, or given them tea and cakes." So much rumor, so little truth. This was an invasion of dust and shadows.

"I still think we are better served to find the place and follow his trail, than to swim against the tide he pushes before him."

"They do not teach rhetoric so much in your temple, do they?" I gave him a sly grin, then levered myself into my saddle. Or tried to, as the nag sidestepped just enough to drop me on my face in the dirt.

This time she definitely laughed.

"I will get you a block, and hold her bridle," Septio told me. "You need to be very firm with her today."

Though it was tempting to shout him down for condescending to me so, I could not afford such pride. Instead I stood mute and glowering at my miserable beast while Septio arranged things. I resolved that once I was asaddle, I would remain there all day. This in turn immediately made me regret the amount of tea I had just drunk.

We set out into a morning marked by mist on the stones above us, and a few furry goats on high. The place was pretty enough, and the air crisp, but so very northern a view that I felt a surge of homesickness for the sweltering fields of Selistan. This was a Stone Coast I had known only from Mistress Danae's books, for I had never left the Pomegranate Court to walk the high crags or upland meadows. Little engravings and bad poetry had told their story, but as a child might recount solstice gifts, with eccentric details and much missing of the point.

I reveled in the hundred shades of gray that made up the tumbled rocks amid the scraggly grass, and their mother cliffs above. Late flowers peeked pale as babies' eyes from thicker tufts. Sometimes a tree struggled away from the windbreak of its fellows, so a mighty giant could be little taller than I.

Small birds darted along the grass, juking and diving to catch the insects that fled before them. There were more goats. Occasionally the bones of a goat kill showed that something clawed and fanged kept a small kingdom here as well. When the trail ran close to the small river with its intermittent belt of trees, a different chorus of birds echoed from the shelter there.

The cliffs on both sides of us cut the sky into a ribbon of blue fabric from the loom of Mother Mooneyes. If a soul had a color, I imagined it might be that cerulean. Perhaps so many thought of paradise as lying somewhere above the air because we recognized the tint by instinct older than words.

That brought to mind a question that had slipped through my fingers more than a few times lately. "Septio." I pitched my voice firmly to carry from one dangerous nag to the other, without startling the whole valley. "There is a priestly question I would ask you."

"Perhaps I can answer," he said cautiously.

I did not know if his easy confidence and edged humor had been left behind within Copper Downs, or if last night's conversation about sacrifices weighed so heavily on him. Some good, solid theology of a more neutral sort might be the thing to bring him around.

"I have been thinking on theogenic dispersion," I said. "About how gods and men draw power from one another."

"Small questions. I doubt anyone has considered them before."

His tone was so serious that for a moment I believed him. Then I realized that the city had not kept all of the best of this man behind.

"Fool," I told him with affection. "I am serious."

Septio laughed. The sound gladdened my heart.

We rode on, my miserable nag ensuring that I was jostled and bruised as much as possible. I gathered my thoughts.

"As I have read the tale, the gods and goddesses were once far greater and more powerful. World-urges, Lacodemus called them. They made the races of man, and perhaps the other thinking creatures. Then the theogenic dispersion came upon them. Small fragments of their divinity were scattered through the plate of the world. Some of those fragments became the sliver of grace we all carry within us. Others became the gods and goddesses we know in this life."

He waited a moment to see if I was just pausing for breath. "A fair enough summation of what many believe."

"I have also read that gods and goddesses arise from the thoughts and deeds of men. This Choybalsan, for example, is feared in part because he aspires to godhood."

"Indeed." Septio was noncommittal.

"So I am told that the gods created man, and that man created the gods." I smiled. "The logic of this troubles me."

He laughed again. No mockery was in him, just delight. His grin was genuine, and warmed my heart. "Why can they not both be true? Is it that you suppose time has a beginning and an end, and so one must have come first?"

"Well . . . yes . . ."

"The world has no beginning and no end. The plate goes on forever beneath the path of the sun. Why should time be bounded when the world is not? It could be that man creates the gods, then in time, gods create man. Each returns the service to the other like a pair of players at the shuttle-net."

"That seems strange to me." I tried to tease out what it was that disturbed me about this logic. "A baby is born, a girl-child grows, a woman lives, a crone dies. Life comes from her loins and it begins again. This is a cycle, not a circle. Every plant and animal does the same. Everything in the world, except for gods."

"You were taught well, Green." His voice held real admiration. "Consider this: You say we all have a sliver of grace. What if it is the grace that flows through history, passing down the generations, and we and our gods are but seeds to carry it forward?"

That gave me much to chew on. Even though I had dwelt only in two lands, I had met sailors from a dozen more. Each had their own ideas about the soul's progress—the Wheel of the Selistani religions was quite different from the transit of the Petraean afterlife. They were not in profound contradiction, either. No one denied the soul. No one denied grace. Not even a dreadful, sanguinary pain god like Blackblood.

The day went on in idle chatter and difficult riding. The problem was not so much challenging horsewomanship as my challenging horse. I persevered.

That afternoon, the horses tired, we stopped just below the highest pass amid the last of the meadows. Smoke was visible in the northern sky beyond. Our little river was no more than a trickle up here, but there were pools. I spotted fish darting above their sandy floors, before darkness claimed such details, and wondered how their ancestors had come so far from the sea. Did they have small cold-hearted gods who spoke in voices of the tide?

I still ached, but today's ride had been better. I found myself aching in other ways, too, and eyeing Septio with a mix of appreciation and pity.

We built no fire as evening approached, for fear of showing a light. Septio explored a boulder field which had rolled down off the eastern cliffs until he found a crevice with no sign of recent occupation. There we set our blankets and ate a cold supper.

"The Temple of Air will be visible from beyond the crest of this pass," I told him. I'd read many maps in the Pomegranate Court. "This is the Giant's Wallow. It lets into a high valley that runs toward the east to join the Eirigene Pass."

"How far?"

"That I am not so sure." I looked at him, a pale blur in the starlight with the old moon yet unrisen. "I have never walked this land. Only seen it on a map as a bird soaring above a paper world."

"Well," said Septio, "either we will meet some of Choybalsan's men there, or we will find his trail." I could hear the pretense of confidence in his voice. "We shall approach from behind his line, a pair of unarmed religious wanderers, and ask for parley."

"Let us hope he gives it to us," I muttered.

Septio looked at me strangely. "We each have the protection of a god. You are marked by some southern power strange to me. I am Blackblood's man from the beginning to the end. We will don those brown robes tomorrow and style ourselves Brothers of the Empty Hilt."

"Who are they?" I liked something of the name.

"A jest, in truth." His voice was turned in embarrassment. "The acolytes of the Temple Quarter used to claim to be Brothers of the Empty Hilt, in the days before the Duke fell. That became a sort of password among us."

What would befall if this Choybalsan knew of the jest, I wondered, but that seemed to rank small among the sum of my fears.

After we had drawn off our boots, Septio preceded me into the rock cleft. We were to sleep close, both for warmth at this higher altitude, and because of the small space. He seemed so hot, and flinched when I moved to hug him.

"What is the matter?" I asked.

He would not answer, but I realized he was trembling. I ran my hands down his chest, and his trembling became nearly a fit. I do not know what possessed me—impishness, slyness, or a stirring of the love of the heart—but I touched his trousers and found him straining fit to burst his buttons.

"We should not—," he began, but I shushed him with a kiss.

I began to stroke him. "I am not accustomed to lying with men, but you delighted my heart and challenged my thoughts today."

"You for me as well," he whispered hoarsely, though by then his mind was elsewhere. We soon both reached that place.

Lying with a man did not hurt so much as I might have thought. The feeling of being filled with flesh was so different from the glass and leather and metal toys. So I rode him hard until we both were well spent.

Finally I lay wedged beside Septio. "You are my first b—man," I whispered.

"You are my first woman." Something in his voice grew very shy. "My first entry, in truth. I have only been the vessel, not the seed, within the temple rites."

We curled close then, wrapped ourselves in blankets, and slept through the hours of the night.

I awoke aching and sticky. Pretending not to see the way he strained for me anew, I slipped out of our little cave, threw a blanket over my shoulders, and wandered to the stream. The water was cold enough for pain, but it served to scrub me clean.

What was the point of that? I wondered, but I caught myself. Back at the Lily Temple after Samma and I had parted ways, I did not pretend so much at love of the heart with the older women. Instead I had treated the whole business as being of no consequence. Sex with Septio had been clumsy, to say the least, but also possessed of a sweetness I had not felt since Samma and I first began to slide our hands across one another in the dormitory.

"I do not need to push him aside," I told the fish in their pool. "There is also no need to cleave to him." The matter would play itself out.

Standing with the blanket open wide to fold around me, I turned to meet half a dozen grinning men. Three held crossbows.

It is very difficult to attack a man with a crossbow. Even an archer can be rushed, if you have the nerve. Men with blades may be met a dozen different ways. A crossbowman will have only one shot in a fight, but at arm's distance, that can well be fatal.

When one of the men began to open the laces of his trousers, I took my risk in hand. With a shriek, I leapt straight for the would-be rapist. I hurled my blanket at the two crossbowmen standing close to one another. Their shots were caught in the cloth as I had hoped. I took my first target down with a shoulder to the gut and a punch into his testicles.

The third bolt, however, tore a line of fire through the muscles of my bare ass.

I rolled forward to find myself unable to spring back to my feet. Another roll lent me the momentum to be up and moving toward our horses and my knife even as blades slipped free of their scabbards behind me.

Forty paces, uphill. I could easily outrun all those men, but the crossbowmen would have time to reset their cranks. I sprinted barefooted over gravel and raw, stubbled grass as Septio stumbled out of the cleft where we had been sleeping. His eyes widened, and he dived back into the shadows.

You'd better have a weapon in there, boy, I thought savagely.

I reached the horses and snatched free their hobbles. I would not fight from the back of one of those horrid beasts, even if my butt were not bleeding, but having the nasty animals stumbling about in ill-tempered panic served me better than it served the bandits.

Our saddles and gear were tucked in a cleft just beyond. I recovered my knife and turned to meet my attackers.

They were smarter than I'd hoped. The group had hung back to let the crossbowmen reset their weapons, and to laugh at their fallen comrade. When they saw that I had not taken up a bow of my own, the six spread out. Five trudged up the slope toward me. The last staggered groaning behind.

That was fine with me. I could catch my breath and climb a boulder or two. The height would slow them down. Well, if they bothered to climb. They could always shoot me off like a heron on a post.

I was forced to work with what was to hand.

Unfortunately, the muscles of my ass were giving up. I couldn't tell how large the wound was, but the backs of my thighs were sticky with blood. Climbing was far more difficult than it should have been.

Septio's head popped up from a gap in the rock. "Green."

"Get up here and fight." I turned so their clearest shot wouldn't be a second bolt in my butt.

That was a mistake, as I'd sat down unthinking. Very bad idea. I managed not to howl in pain, but was forced up into a very unstable crouch.

"I think these men are with Choybalsan," he said. "We should ask for him."

I could not believe my ears. "After the six of them have split *me* like a melon with their pustulent cocks, they might take *you* to him."

"Not if we make them respect us."

"A naked, bloody girl and a naked, sticky boy?"

He passed me a small paper packet. "Hold this, I'll light it. Then throw it at them."

I clutched his packet as a lucifer match flared. He touched it to the corner of the paper, which began to hiss and spark.

"*Throw* it," Septio said urgently. "*Now!*"

In midair, the packet burst in coiling red smoke, shot through with black veins.

Ah, I thought. *Fire powder.*

The sparking missile landed amid a stand of dried-out thistles, which resisted only moments before curling into fire themselves. The oncoming bandits yelped and scattered. A bolt whistled high to spang off the cliff face before rattling to a stop a few feet away on my boulder. The attackers regrouped about ten paces below me, just in front of the little flare-fire. Their grins were back.

"That didn't work," I said.

"I have more." Septio frowned and passed me a larger packet.

"We're going to amuse them to death?"

"Just throw it."

That packet sparked as the last one had. I tossed it right at the bandits. One of the bowmen grinned and caught it with his free hand, cocking his arm to throw it back at me.

This one went off like a granary explosion. A blinding flash erupted, followed by a solid thump, which I felt inside my chest more than heard. I closed my eyes, blinking away the glare just as a crossbow, hand and arm still attached, smacked into the stone above me. It slithered to rest nearby.

I grabbed up the bow, tugged the former owner's hand free, and set myself madly to cocking it. I happened to know where there was a bolt handy.

When I looked up again, four of them were down hard. One was on his knees throwing up. My would-be rapist staggered toward my boulder with murder in his eye. I sent him a crossbow bolt for his trouble. Not being practiced with the weapon, I missed his neck, but the shot to his cheek seemed to discourage him.

"They can have the damned fires out there for their funerary offering," I said, sliding down on my belly to where Septio had been hiding. I was in no way prepared to set my ass against the stone again. When I found my feet, I snapped at him, "We must go, now. That was enough noise and smoke to summon everyone within miles."

"You are welcome for saving your life."

I grabbed his face and kissed him. "Not now, foolish boy."

Septio had to wrap me around the hips in a sling of torn muslin before I could manage to tug on my blacks and riding trousers. My breasts ached a bit, but I bound them with more of the muslin. Over them I slipped into the robes we'd brought to wear as Brothers of the Empty Hilt. The horses had fled from the fire and the fighting, so we carried only water, our satchels, and my blade.

Two remained alive—the vomiting man and one who'd taken the brunt of the explosion. His eyelids were burnt off and his lips black. I gave him mercy as kindly as I could. The vomiting man had finished his business, but he had the shivers and would not talk. I gave him the mercy as well, but I let it hurt a bit. I wiped my blade on his cloak, then walked to the stream and cleaned it again there among the little fish.

When I stood again, I found Septio watching me. His face was drawn and pale.

"What?" I snapped.

"You killed them."

"Well, yes. They tried to kill me first." He was such an idiot. "Besides, *you* were the one carrying bombards in your satchel. What did you intend them for? Festival crackers?"

"No— I . . ." Septio's voice trailed off. "You made it so personal."

I began walking uphill, toward the crest of the pass. The muscles in my ass burned terribly, pulling me off my stride, but I kept moving. Out here I could scarcely retire to a couch and call for mulled wine until my body had healed itself.

I shouted over my shoulder at Septio, who trailed me by a dozen paces. "Death is always personal. How can you worship that bloodthirsty god and not understand that?"

He trotted to catch me. Presumably I seemed safer now. "People come to us already in pain. They ask to die, or be taken up."

"While these men were merely minding their business." I snorted. "I can see your point."

The Eirigene Pass was about fifty furlongs ahead of us, across the next valley. Except for the last of the fumes rising from before it, the morning was clear enough to see the alabaster ruins of the Temple of Air. A great dome had collapsed with the fire, and bodies were scattered down the stairs before it.

Then a dozen men on horseback pounded from behind the rocks immediately below. They shouted at us to lie flat or be slain.

The bandits were angry about the fate of their fellows. Not quite angry enough to kill us out of hand, but we took some good, solid kicks. When they began to strip off my robes and saw the blacks I wore beneath, a great discussion ensued.

Clearly they'd been set to search for me.

They were angry all over again when I would not sit astride one of the horses. Then they laughed at me once they understood why.

I wound up with my boots stripped off, making the ride slung over someone's saddlebags, which smelled of old cheese and moldering cloth. By craning my neck, I could see Septio. He seemed dazed as he swayed upright behind another bandit. The worst insult, in its own small way, was that our two faithless nags had come seeking the company of other horses, and now were being led riderless behind the column.

Our band took a trail that went downward through a ravine, rather than across to the ruins of the Temple of Air as I'd expected. That meant we would be joining the upper reaches of the Barley Road.

The ride was long and painful. I had not imagined I would be wishing so soon for my old saddle, but I did. Eventually, we passed through a series of camps, at first quite ragged and sparse, then in time more kempt and crowded together.

I heard thunder, too. A lightning storm seemed strange, given that my upside-down view of the sky showed clear blue troubled only by wisps of smoke.

The horse sidestepped to a halt. Rough hands dumped me over. I narrowly avoided striking my head on the ground. A redheaded man pulled me to my feet amid another echoing carronade of thunder as someone else led the panicked horses away.

Lightning sizzled down out of the clear sky to strike the ground about a hundred yards before me. It struck again and again, always in a circle that ringed a large tent of furs. After a moment, I recognized them as skins from the Dancing Mistress' people. My gut churned at that, and I found sympathy for Septio's reaction to my mercies of the blade.

It was a fence. A wall of electrick fire and deafening sound from the heavens. The cleared space extended around the circle in all directions, as Choybalsan's followers kept their distance.

"A god indeed," I said.

"Very good, for a priest," my fire-haired bandit growled. His Petraean was accented, but as a hillman's speech rather than a foreigner's.

"It takes no talent to see a miracle like this." No faith, either. This was godhood for the unbelieving. And a very expensive sort of magic. No wonder the Lily Goddess had been worried. Could a titanic come into the world again? Or were all divine births so explosive?

"In you go." I was pushed toward the lightning ring. Between my crossbow wound, the worn muscles, and the long ride, I could barely keep my feet. Septio staggered up beside me.

"Hey." I gave him a sidelong glance.

His eyes were unfocused. Blood trickled from his mouth.

I tried again. "What happened to you?"

Septio's lips moved, but he just popped a few carmine bubbles.

By the breaking of the Wheel, something was very wrong.

"Come on," I said. "To the tent. Either he'll kill us, or he'll let us off our feet."

My poor friend grunted, but he followed.

I did not even try to avoid the lightning. To what end? It belonged to Choybalsan; he could lift it or not as he pleased. Approaching the ring was a very strange thing even so. My mouth began to taste of metal. The hairs of my skin stood stiff. My head felt dull, while the air had a strange, empty, ringing quality.

We stumbled through the line, our strides so shortened by the ropes binding our ankles that we were almost hopping. Neither of us was struck down, though the thunder robbed me of my hearing. The tent was perched in the center of the circle, round with no ridge to speak of and a roof like a cap.

I pushed through the flap. Septio came so close behind me, he nearly knocked us both down.

A large black rock stood at the center of the space within, flanked by two poles. The rock appeared bubbled and burned—a fallen star. I'd never seen one, but one of Mistress Danae's books had contained a lengthy disquisition on the stones of heaven and how the gods must live in an iron house.

The walls were hung with horse blankets and a few ripped tapestries looted from some manor house. Likewise the floor of blankets and carpets with rushes strewn over them. A low backless seat was set before the stone.

We were alone in the house of the king who would be god. Or possibly the god who would be king.

Goddess, I prayed. *I do not ask You to deliver me, for that is my test. Nor for courage, as that is my test as well. Lend me what strength and wisdom You have to give.* Tears welled in my eyes. *Spare a measure of grace and mercy for Septio, if his god has not already cared for him.*

Federo stepped around me and looked me over carefully. For one strange moment, I imagined a rescue had come. Then I realized he was not wearing a suit, nor a decent set of robes, but the leather trews and thick felt vest of the bandits who rode in Choybalsan's train. Unlike them, he was unarmed.

He also appeared far less strained than he had back at the Textile Bourse.

I sagged in the face of such betrayal.

Then he took my chin in his hands and tipped my face up for inspection. That old, old insult brought me back to myself.

I snarled: "So you stand midwife at the birth of godhood?"

"Do not presume, Green," Federo said softly.

"Then where is he?"

Federo sat on the chair with his back to the skystone and spread his arms. "Choybalsan, the bandit chieftain."

Bound hand and foot, they had still left me the good, hard bones of my head. I hopped toward him with an angry roar and tried to butt him in the face. His moment of poise spoiled, Federo leapt up and tripped me. I fell forehead first into his plain little throne and smacked myself so hard I saw lightning all over again.

He bellowed incoherently as I rolled onto my back. My vision was doubled, but that was still enough to see Septio lurching toward Federo. The traitor sidestepped the priest, who staggered slowly around the altar, circling the tent and crying. Blood ran freely from his mouth now.

Federo began to laugh.

Enraged, I managed to bend nearly double, then lash a kick that took Federo off his feet. Bound and stunned, I had no follow-through. If my head had been more clear, I would have cursed every god ever born. Instead, I lay gasping while Septio waddled up to Federo and tried to lean over him.

The bandit-king held up a knife as my boy lover toppled. The point took Septio in the belly. A killing wound, but painful and slow. In the worst cases, the wounded might live for days while their belly dissolved into burning stench.

Federo pushed Septio away, then climbed to his feet. He took up a corner of carpet to wipe the blood and bile off his blade, his arm, and his vest. Septio began to retch.

"He is nothing." Federo leaned close. "Not like you. I shall let you watch him die." He stroked my hair. "Don't go far. I'll be back soon. You have kept something I need very badly, dear Emerald."

I watched him walk out of the tent. My head still reeling, I began to plot the most elaborate of deaths, slow agony that would give even Blackblood's priests pause. When my head had finally cleared enough for me to move, I crawled across the rugs to Septio.

He lay with his eyes closed. I could see he still breathed. The wound reeked of bile and shit. Which made sense. Federo's knife hand had angled *down* from the entry. That would mean a quicker death, at least.

"Septio," I whispered.

He did not stir.

"Septio."

Another slow, ragged breath.

"Septio!"

Still nothing.

I wriggled close and kissed the blood from his lips. He moaned a bit at that, but did not wake.

Pain might be his sacrament, but a gut wound was still a nasty death at the best of times. If he bled out quickly, he could die a little easier.

I raised my wrists behind my back, until my elbows stuck out. Throwing my shoulders back and forth, I tried to see how much clearance I could get on one side. My joints burned, but an errand of mercy needed doing.

Slowly I moved past him until my elbow was level with his ear. I raised it again and rocked myself hard to my right, trying to catch his head in the triangle formed by my bound arm and the side of my body.

It took me three attempts, sweating and crying, but finally I had Septio's head clutched close. I squeezed and rolled hard to my left. Not hard enough, for he cried out.

Once more.

"I am so sorry," I whispered, and thrashed with such strength that I broke his neck. Then I could not free myself. I lay there with his body clutched close and wept a long while.

Later I realized I could no longer hear thunder outside. The tent, quite dim when I had first entered, was now dark. My elbow was still caught around Septio's head. The smells of his death had long since eroded my senses. My body was so stiff and numb that I doubted I'd be able to move at all should Federo bother to free me.

Grief and betrayal warred in my head, so I fought them with the skirmishes of logic.

If Federo were a traitor, why send for me at all? He would have been safer with me forgotten across an ocean's distance. I could play no role in the affairs of the Stone Coast from Kalimpura.

If the Dancing Mistress knew Federo was a traitor, heir to the old Duke's magic, why did she not tell me at the first? Perhaps she had come across the sea despite him, to bring me back in hopes of finding some chink in his armor. I did not know whose wishes had prevailed, but I also did not think she had lied to me. Certainly she had not told all, but omission was not the same as deception.

We wouldn't have spent so much time casting about Copper Downs on our arrival if the Dancing Mistress had known with certainty where the rot was. In point of fact, *I* had asked that we not go straight to the Interim Council.

Finding who had played whom false was a skein not easily unraveled.

I worried instead at the reasons *anyone* would have had to come find me. That I had no love for Copper Downs would have been obvious to all who knew the truth of my life. No one could expect me to set myself at risk for the city. They could not have known, after all, that the Goddess would command me as She did.

Or that I would obey.

That made me laugh, and laughter made me cry. The grief slipped back in unawares and broke down the armies of my logic for a while. The one small comfort it brought was that the spasms of my arms slipped me free of Septio's head.

I would have kissed him again then, but my body would not move for all the money in King Pythos' vaults of legend. I had no sensation in my arms, and my legs were like blocks of wood shot through with ants. A corpse could hardly have felt much less.

On my other side, it was easy to lie and cry awhile longer. In time, I tired of that. My tears helped neither Septio, who was beyond them, nor myself.

Everything came back to what I had been told. Some piece of the Duke's magic was still missing. That I might be in possession of it seemed to be an idea fixed in the minds of both the Dancing Mistress and Federo. I was not magical. Not at all.

Unless it was similar to those splinters of grace scattered from the divine. Along with the balance of grace and evil that made up my soul, did I now carry a measure of the Duke's essence as well? How could that be? The magic belonged to the pardines.

Federo had wrapped himself in their skin and gone hunting in their countries. That chilled me all over again. Looking for the missing portion that would seal him to godhood?

All thoughts circled back to Federo and the Dancing Mistress. They were the two partners in the original conspiracy that shattered the intent of the Factor's training and set me on this path. A conspiracy to take the stolen magic from a once-human Duke and disperse it.

Surely the power could have settled in me. It had long since been grasped by a human hand, whatever the meaning and cost to the Dancing Mistress' people.

My imaginings chased themselves long into the deepest darkness. I did not realize I had slept until thunder woke me.

Federo had returned. The Dancing Mistress followed close behind him, bound hand and foot with silver chains and walking with her head bowed low.

The traitor lit small braziers all around the edge of the tent. He called men to come and take Septio away, along with some of the carpets. That business put a sour look upon Federo's face. He released our bonds, then ignored the Dancing Mistress and me completely while he set to cooking a small meal for himself, with tea and wine.

I did not know what he was about.

Neither did he, I realized in time.

Some small measure of hope stole into my drained courage with that thought. Whatever Federo's plan, it had either failed or he did not trust the outcome. Otherwise he would have stood over me gloating once more.

The whole while the Dancing Mistress chafed my wrists and ankles to try to bring them back to life. We took the measure of one another with silent looks. A deep, wounded sadness filled her, so that I wanted to fold her into my arms until it seeped away.

I did not know for certain what she saw in me, but there was plenty. Love denied, betrayal of my own, death on death on death.

Our eyes held a long time; then I made my mouth give her the words "I love you." Did I truly mean them? Even now, I cannot say. Back then, I thought I was going to die quite soon, and did not want to walk alone into the darkness.

She made a small kiss to the air. We both sighed. Then she set to kneading my arms, while I set to worrying more about Federo.

Eventually, he finished his meal and stood with an elaborated, false casualness. He perched upon his chair like a moody boy.

Whatever had taken hold within him over the years had slain the cheerful fop I'd once known. The old Federo was as dead as poor Septio. For all its raw power, the thunder rolling outside was the cheapest of stage tricks at the ragged end of a festival street. He had little left to threaten me with, having already taken my life. The actual dying would come soon enough.

I found I did not care so much what his game might be.

"Well," Federo finally said.

The Dancing Mistress hugged my shoulders where I lay in her lap. There was no illusion of safety, but I was comforted nonetheless.

There seemed no point in answering him. The Dancing Mistress remained silent as well, except for her ragged breathing. Much too loud for one of her kind.

He leaned forward. "You would never have me," he muttered. His eyes were tearful. "And I could never have had *you*."

The latter was presumably addressed to me. I smiled as sweetly as I was able to.

"You, girl, carry something I need. You, woman, hold the power to take it from her." His expression made my stomach lurch. "I shall tear it from both of you." He reached to one side, his back against the sky iron, and grabbed a long spear of the sort used by cavalrymen. It had been propped against one of the poles of the tent. The end was leaf-bladed.

Federo worked the spear around in his hand until the haft was mostly over his shoulder and the point directed at us. "A shred of the Duke still abides within you." He slid the spear closer until the tip rested against my calf. "We shall find a way to let him out."

He pushed slightly and tugged it sideways. The blade ripped open the leg of my trousers, leaving a deep cut in the skin beneath.

Sucking air between my teeth, I tried to fight a queasy rebellion within.

"I will cut them off you if you do not remove them," Federo said in a lazy voice.

It was nearly worth the trouble to let him slice away at me—I might die quicker—but I found I could not let go of life so readily. My fingers were still wooden as I loosened my pants and tried to draw them off.

Bending my legs to slip free burned as if I had been stung by a nest of hornets. I gave up the effort, gasping.

"You do not have to do this," the Dancing Mistress said quietly to me.

"Oh, she does!" roared Federo. A round of thunder rolled harsh outside. I realized it had been calm before, but not now.

Thunder, lightning . . . was he a storm god? I stared at one of the braziers and tried to frame my death prayer.

Braziers. I felt a cold shiver. Fire. I looked up at the Dancing Mistress. *Yes,* I mouthed. Then: *I have a plan.*

She seemed to understand my intention. That was sufficient. She helped me out of my pants—I swallowed a scream—before she went to work on my shirt.

"See, you know what I need." Federo's spear point settled against my back as the Dancing Mistress rolled me across her lap to free my arms.

The ant-bite pain was now everywhere. Which was good, I tried to tell myself. That meant I could feel all of my body. Nothing had gone dead from the ill-use.

What I felt was enough to make me wish some of it had. If Blackblood had been my patron god, he would have been drunk on sacrifice.

Soon enough, I was flat on my back on the floor, barely able to move. Well, I'd been there before. Never with an armed man leaning close, his face twisting with clotted emotion. "Keep that blessed point away from me," I growled.

"Oh, *this?*" He dragged the spearhead along my forearm, raising a welt.

The Dancing Mistress bent her face close to mine. I could see questions in her eyes. They warred with regret. I could not tell her, though. Federo seemed to hear perfectly well even above the sound of his thunder. I did not even want to *think* about my intentions, for fear the set of my body should give me away like a fighter signaling her next blow in a bout.

So I lifted my neck and kissed her.

She kissed me back.

Good, I thought. *Give him a show. Distract him.*

I tried to hug her, but my arms were like clubs. Mostly I beat them against her back. She clasped me close.

Federo moaned. I risked a glance. He was not the Federo I had known. Whatever the god within him might be, it had taken him as the crab disease sometimes took those with the tumors inside their heads. All the worst of him remained, while the worth of him was gone.

Then the spear caught me a scrape across the ribs. I resolved that he would die tonight, or I would die trying.

My hands had come back to life. They prickled much as if I had been sitting on them awhile, but they were no longer half-dead vessels of pain.

Legs, I needed my legs.

I crawled back up to nuzzle her face. "Oh, please," I moaned, "kiss my thighs." My voice would have had the Lily Blades falling out with laughter, but Federo just echoed the moan.

He was as the rankest of boys.

Facing Federo as I sprawled on the floor, I ran my tongue across my lips. Mistress Cherlise had shown me a number of such little bits of playacting which would arrest a man's attention.

The Dancing Mistress gripped my thighs hard and kissed me back and forth along the inner line of each leg, working down toward my knees. When she reset her grip to my calves and eased herself farther away, I nearly shrieked. Instead I rolled slightly to my left so Federo could see my right breast.

He wasn't looking anymore. His eyes were closed, his back arched in his chair as he stroked himself very hard. Outside, thunder rolled almost continuously.

Now, I resolved, before he begins to think again.

I shoved myself to my knees and crawled as best I could toward the door and the satchels that had been dropped there much earlier. Mine, and Septio's.

The Dancing Mistress rose to her feet to lean over Federo, occupying his vision a moment longer.

Catching at the strap of Septio's bag, I spilled it open. A pair of small bottles, some spare stockings, breadcrumbs, a box of lucifer matches.

And three more of those paper packets of fire powder.

I had no way to know if these were smokers or exploders. I prayed for the latter as I shoved one into the brazier by the door, then crawled as quickly as I could to my left.

Federo began to call out sharply. Lightning crackled out of sequence to the rhythms that had so recently matched him at his pleasures, but what cut him off was the spew of red and black.

It had not seemed so prodigious out in the open.

The tent filled with smoke and a dry, burning smell. Federo threw the spear aside and jumped up. The Dancing Mistress tackled him from behind. I rose up on my knees and cracked Federo on the temple with my two fists clenched together.

That stopped him completely.

The smoke had become horribly thick. It cloyed at my stomach. Outside, the lightning stuttered and died with Federo's fading consciousness. Nothing important seemed to have caught fire yet.

I was surprised to still be alive.

"Dress," the Dancing Mistress hissed. Federo had brought her to me naked except for her chains, but she was already tugging at the tapestries and cloths in search of something to wrap around herself.

My clothes were stiff. I ached at the thought of having to pull them over my unwieldy limbs. Yet there was some chance we might escape, and I could see no profit in running naked into the night. My boots were with our satchels, so I slipped them on, then walked limping back to Federo.

Gathering my breath, unwilling to apologize, I leapt in the air and brought my weight down heels-first upon his chest.

I expected a wet, splintering crunch. Possibly some blood. Certainly a rough cough, followed by the bellows breathing of a man at the edge of death.

Instead I slid off him as if he were made of marble.

I fell painfully to the floor. The Dancing Mistress picked me up. "He cannot be hurt so. It is the aspect of the god upon him."

"Federo would have had the decency to die," I said quietly. "This is Choybalsan and none other."

"Can you help me lift him?"

I did so, wondering how my blow to his head had affected him where the heels of my boots had not. Or was he like Skinless now, impervious to weapons but not to the hand?

We dragged him to the altar. She set about binding Choybalsan to the rough stone. Though we had little time, I had to know. I picked up the ridiculous spear, but could not drive it into his thigh. I stood close to him and pressed my thumbnail hard into the skin of his neck.

A red welt raised there as he stirred.

The Dancing Mistress was finishing her knots as Choybalsan came to himself. "Your death will be far worse now." He almost spat the words. Thunder renewed outside in a rapid roll.

I leaned close to his ear, remembering the old words. *"The life that is shared,"* I whispered in Seliu, *"goes on forever. The life that is hoarded is never lived at all."*

Nothing happened. This was how the death of the Duke had been completed, but the magic had hung in the balance longer than I thought possible. Sweat trembled on the tip of my nose.

Choybalsan just laughed. The braying shattered the moment. "You are so close to the secret, but you will never find it." He thrashed his shoulders against his bonds, but seemed more amused now than anything else. "Foolish Emerald. When I finally take your heart, you shall wish you'd let me kill you sweetly tonight."

Stumbling, I dragged another brazier close to him. The one by the flap, which spat red and black smoke, was too unhandy.

Amusement fled his face. "No fire!"

"I'm not going to burn you," I told him. I did not know what the other two packets held. If it was more smoke, he might suffocate. If it was another blast, so much the better. "Stop the lightning," I told the Dancing Mistress.

She boxed his ears, very hard. Choybalsan was stunned again. Outside the thunder rolled once more to silence.

"Now cut open the back of the tent."

The Dancing Mistress nodded, took up the long haft of his spear and stabbed at the tapestries until she was through them and into the skins of her people. She sawed back and forth for a minute or so, staying as far away as possible from the pelts. Finally she turned to me. "Done."

I threw the last two packets in the brazier next to Choybalsan's head. Then I stumbled toward my friend and lover. She shoved me through the ragged slit and followed me into the night. We ran across the open ground to the ring of burnt ground plowed by the lightning forks. The camp gleamed and guttered before us.

The tent exploded with a dull thump that hurt my ears. I stumbled and turned around, the Dancing Mistress catching at my arm. A fireball curled into the night air. It was already spreading to ragged tongues of flame. Part of the tent had collapsed. The rest was on fire.

All around us, a roar of voices erupted.

"Run," she said. We struggled through the crowd, which washed past us like the tide.

I have never understood how we survived the next few minutes. A storm of spears and swords glittered around. I am not so easy to overlook, unless I am hiding amid shadow. Given that I stumbled like a bandy-legged drunk in company with a pardine through that camp, we should have been bright as a tomato in an olive barrel.

Perhaps it was the hand of the Lily Goddess that covered us. She has never told me, and much has happened since to draw a veil over the moment.

We staggered into an area of fewer cook fires and more scrub. Both of us knew we must be full away from the bandit train before the hue and cry went up. I did not imagine we would live long, but I was willing to run as far as my weakened body would carry me.

In time, we found a stream. I dropped to my knees on round-stoned gravel to drink. The Dancing Mistress knelt beside me, looking as much like a hunting cat as I had ever seen her.

"Can you walk amid these wet rocks?" she asked.

"Of course—" I stopped. There was no *of course* about it. That I even still moved was amazing. Losing my footing in the dark seemed highly likely. "My apologies. I do not know."

"It will help your trail. They will not be so fast following you."

"Can you find me a good-sized stick?" I was ashamed to ask it, me who could leap from rooftop to rooftop like a bat on the wing. Still, such a thing might save my life.

She slipped away into the darkness. I could see lights swarming far behind us. Panic? Or the torches of an army setting out on the hunt?

I sat with my boots in the running stream and wondered how I might survive.

Though it seemed like an eternity, only a few minutes passed before the Dancing Mistress returned. She had a solid stick in one hand. A rabbit twitched broken-backed in the other.

Then it dawned on me she had said *your* trail. Not *our* trail. "Where are you going?"

"Higher into the hills." She handed me the stick and the rabbit. "It . . . it seems to me we must not be together. Whatever Federo wanted, he thought he could get from the intersection of the two of us. Moreover, I must carry word of all this to whatever is left of my people."

I wanted to cry. I wanted to kill her. I wanted to beg her to stay. I wanted to lie down in the creek and let the water race to take my life before the pursuing army caught me.

But I did none of those things. Instead, I said, "I will miss you."

The Dancing Mistress leaned close and kissed me, then passed her rough tongue across my face. "Follow the water. It will take you to the sea, and the city there. I will make a trail that may keep them after me awhile before they discover their error."

Then, before I could entrap her with either logic or love, she loped off into the darkness. I almost pitied any one of the enemy who met her this night, with her blood on the boil and god-killing still fresh on her fingertips.

This was what the Lily Goddess had feared. I had helped unleash a deicide, for the Dancing Mistress' love of me. Better that we had never set out at all.

Distant shouting reminded me I must be moving. As I clambered slowly down the creek, the surf was joined by the rolling thunder of a storm. I looked to see a hilltop behind me crowned with jagged streams of lightning.

So we had not killed him. Things would never be so easy.

For hours I crept. Twice I slipped and fell, the second time striking my kneecap so hard, I feared it broken. A wounded ass could be managed, at least for a while, but losing my knee would have been death.

The joint held, though. I kept going. Torches swarmed through the darkness behind me. Some passed in the distance to my left. They followed the Dancing Mistress. Watching that, I slipped again. This time I slid down a chute and over a drop into the darkness of empty air.

Water smacked me in the face as the irony of this death overwhelmed me. Losing my grip on my stick, I went down into cold. Twisting in the depths, I could not find the surface. No light guided me, though the burning pressure in my lungs urged me on. I flailed until my foot met something. There I kicked off hard.

Air came to me just as I finally lost control. So did my stick, which slapped me on the head to remind me how foolish I had been. The wood was thick and fairly light, and would float. For a very long while, I let it do the work while we spun in the pool at the bottom of the little falls.

No irony. Just more pain.

In time, I dragged myself over a shallow bar and into the current of the Greenbriar River. Once again, I let the stick do most of the work. The flow carried me away into the night, only sometimes forcing me to pause and crawl over rocks or sand or logs.

Somehow I managed not to further strike my head or knees.

Even more strangely, I seemed to sleep a bit. I could still see the new moon, her fingernail a little wider this night. Lilies floated on the water with me. Each one opened to show me a face, then closed again. Some were Mothers of the Lily Temple, others Mistresses of the Factor's house. A few I did not recognize.

Then I was drawn through another race of the current. Without taking my life, it spat me out into a much wider pool, where I was spun awhile until fetching up against the hull of a boat.

A small girl leaned over, then clicked her tongue. "Mama," she said, "there is a woman in the water."

I heard a muffled voice answer her.

"No, I think she is dead."

Opening my mouth, I tried to tell the child I was not dead. Not yet. The silly fool screamed to see my lips move, and fled the rail.

Her mother was there a moment later with a boat hook.

"I am not dead," I said, or tried to. Mostly, I gasped.

"Corinthia Anastasia," she shouted, "you are an idiot!"

Something darker than sleep finally claimed me as they pulled me aboard.

I woke with the sense that a great deal of time had passed. How much I could not say.

Corinthia Anastasia sat on a little chair eating fish from a bowl and kicking her heels. The odor made my stomach lurch. I watched the girl a moment. Pale curly hair, pale eyes, pale skin. A normal child living in the company of her family.

I wondered what that felt like.

Around me was the main room of a cottage. A decent-sized fireplace, two wall beds just beyond that. I could see a few pots in the rafters, and a loft as well. Clean enough, but there was little wealth here.

The girl saw me turn my head. "Awake this time?"

"Yes." I tried to puzzle out her question. "Have I been awake before?"

"No." She chewed slowly. "You been talking a lot in your sleep. Some furrin speak."

"I hope I did not bother you."

"No," she said. "I don't care. Some might say you was a witch, but Mama, she's too smart for that."

"Good." I tried to ignore the fish. My stomach was a clenched fist. It seemed unlikely to accept even a sip of juice right now—yet, strangely, I was hungry.

"You are the ugliest girl I ever seen," Corinthia Anastasia offered up.

I had to laugh at that, or try to. "You'll go far in life." Then I realized I was lying on my back. My buttocks mostly itched. As opposed to, say, pain.

How long have I been out?

What had become of the Dancing Mistress? Choybalsan? His army?

I tried to get up, but could not. My limbs had no strength. "Where is your mother? I need news of the world, and must find my way to Copper Downs."

"She says I am to tell you the world is still here, if'n you ask."

Panic peaked in my voice. "What about Copper Downs?"

"Still there, too, I guess." She grinned around her wooden spoon. "We ain't."

Arguing with her was not worth the trouble.

Eventually her mother returned. The woman was a larger version of her daughter, with filled-out curves and sun-darkened skin, wearing an orange dress of some coarse weave. Big farmer's boots stuck out below the hem. Under other circumstances, I might have found her attractive.

"The dock at Briarpool has been burned," she announced. "My boat with it. It was you that lot of swordspointers was after."

"Most likely," I said politely. "My apologies."

"They set fire to enough else, no surprise." Her tone was brusque, but regret tinged her voice. She sat on the little bed at about my waist and reached out to stroke my hair. When she spoke again, her voice was soft. "You've been badly used time and again, my sweet."

"Some was my own doing."

"You might have held the knife in your hand, but I wager others drove you to it."

"You could say that," I admitted.

"Foreign girl," she said. "From across some sea or another. I know what those out of the north look like, and you're not one of us. But you talk as if you just stepped from a doorway on Whitetop Street."

This woman had the authority of a temple Mother, but without the edges. I felt an irrational urge to trust her. "Someone in Copper Downs had the raising of me."

"You ever know any teaching Mistresses?" Her voice was even softer.

The question startled me. "Y-yes."

"I thought you might have that mark." Turning to the girl, she said, "Go out and find me some windfall nuts."

Corinthia Anastasia set the bowl of fish down and slowly stood up.

"And take your time about it!"

"Yes, Mama."

Moments later, we were alone.

"I was trained up in the Peach Court," she told me. "Perhaps twenty years before your time." She touched her own belly where it sloped out a bit beneath her breasts. "I was a very pretty girl. You have to be, to find yourself there, but when my monthly bleeding came, my body wanted to put on more weight than I could work off, no matter how they pushed me. In time, the Factor cut his losses and sold me to a manor well outside the city. Wouldn't do to have the world know they'd grown themselves a chunky girl."

I would have described her as maternal, but I knew that in the young woman she had been then, maternal was not the desired impression. "Here you are."

"Here I am. And I'm lucky they didn't ship me somewhere I'd never return from."

What happened at the manor? I wanted to ask, but this was her story. She would tell it as she saw fit. Or not. "I've been on a ship or two."

"Of course you have." She smoothed the covers over me. "You've been hurt bad. I've put what fluid in you I could, and dressed your wounds."

Wrapped in blankets, I hadn't thought how I was clothed. A simple cotton gown, from the feel of it. "Thank you."

"An army roams out there. Before, they were troublesome. Now they're angry."

"I didn't manage to kill their god."

A smile quirked her face. "That you even tried says much."

"Th-thank you." Catching her hand, I clasped it close. "I must get back to Copper Downs. I know Choybalsan's secret, or part of it." *And he knows some secret of mine that I do not.* Within whose heart had the Lily Goddess truly seen the danger?

It all made sense, if I believed the first principles. Federo had captured the Duke's magic. Or quite possibly the other way around. Perhaps the original conspiracy had contained a layer deeper than I'd ever known. Whatever, however, he was missing something. I was a part of it, key for a lock he hadn't yet found, rooted in the pardines from whom the power had originally been stolen. Which was why Choybalsan had been killing them indiscriminately.

In hopes *they* held the missing piece.

I knew his secret. More to the point, I knew he could be fought. If not killed, at least ground down. At least, I hoped so. The boundaries in that strange territory between man and god were unclear to me.

"I can show you the road right now if you wish," she told me. "You're not fit to walk. There's scouts and raiders up and down it already. The city's even sent out a few riders."

"Under what command?" Half a dozen major forces of guards and watchmen roamed the city, but Copper Downs had not maintained a standing army in centuries. There wasn't really anyone to fight.

Hadn't been, until now.

"They're raising the regiments. Old banners dangle in empty halls all over that city from other times."

"An army of grocer's boys and clerks is not likely to strike fear in anyone but themselves," I said. There was the problem, of course. How to defend the city.

Is it my *problem?*

"Give your body a few days." She squeezed my hands. "At the very least, wait until you can eat decently. Even healed of your wounds, you won't have any energy until you do."

"Might I have soup?" I asked, suddenly feeling shy. "Without fish, if possible?"

"I will make you some."

She rose from the bed and set an iron kettle near the fire. I let myself be eased by the bustle of her cooking and tried to think what I should do.

Go home to Selistan, of course. But I had not done what the Lily Goddess had set me to do. Choybalsan was loose, free. Whatever danger she saw had to be bound up in him. Certainly he had some tie to the coils of the Dancing Mistress' heart. He'd all but confessed to an old love for her. Besides that, his current rampage had written fear large across her.

There had been no major theogenies in recent history that I knew of. Gods and goddesses were a conservative lot. Jealous of one another's followers, craving prayer and sacrifice. They tended to prefer not to have new competition.

Some moved, coming with waves of migrants or travelers. Some were born, from time to time. Some died, even, of neglect or abuse or assassination. Wars among the gods were stuff of legend out of the deepest shadows of time. In many tales, such infighting was given as the reason for the fall of the titanics.

Did She fear the rising of a new god here, or did She fear one who would go to Her with sword in hand?

Federo had been a traveled man. Choybalsan knew the way to Kalimpura. And he'd known I was there, somewhere, carrying the missing fragment of his powers. I had stolen his measure of grace.

The Goddess had sent me to Copper Downs to keep him away from Kalimpura.

The only way I could go home was to end this threat. Stop the god-birth of Choybalsan, or slay him outright. Except killing a god did not seem a path back into the good graces of my own divine patron.

Thinking was giving me a headache. The woman brought me a simple corn soup with a few flecks of cress floating in it.

"Try this. If you want something with a bit more substance, I'll bring you bread."

"N-no. Thank you." I sipped at it. The smell was divine, but the taste was difficult in my mouth. A few swallows, and my gut felt full to bursting, as if I'd just eaten an entire solstice goose by myself.

"You are right," I told her. "I cannot leave yet."

"The city will not fall today, nor tomorrow," she answered. "They are not even trying to bring an army to the gates yet."

"Am I safe here? Are *you* safe with me here?"

"Yes, yes. I am not a fool."

"No. You have not given me your name, or asked for mine."

She answered with humor in her voice: "Your name is not needed. There cannot be two women on the Stone Coast with your face. My name does not matter."

I mulled that awhile, until sleep claimed me.

Awake but still weak, I had Corinthia Anastasia find me a piece of wood about the size of a good ham. "A whittling knife as well, please," I told her.

"I ain't allowed big knives."

"For *me*."

She went away awhile. In time, she came back with a chunk of softwood and a decent-sized blade.

I set to carving. I was bored, and still fuzzy in my thinking, and wanted to do something with my hands. Something specific.

It took me two days of working through most of the sunlit hours, but I created a crude version of Endurance's bell. I had to twist some scraps to make the rope for the clappers that hung on each side of the sounding cup. This one did not have nearly the tone of the bell Papa's ox had worn, but even this echo of my childhood reached into my soul and fed some hunger there.

The day after that, I was able to pull myself out of the bed and go walk through the orchards. Corinthia Anastasia trailed behind me, seemingly unconcerned, eating a green apple.

"I need to go to Copper Downs," I told her again.

"South of here."

"I know." This child was so very irritating. "I meant I shall set out."

"You ain't never been no prisoner in Mama's house."

"Here, let me explain this a different way." I resisted the urge to grab the girl by her curly hair and shake her. "Please tell your mother I would speak with her about my leaving very soon."

"All right." She grinned and tossed her half-eaten apple away. "All's you had to do was ask."

I was a bit weak when I returned to the cottage. Even so, I sat in one of the three chairs around the small rough-hewn table. I had spent far too much time abed. Especially given who—and what—was afoot out there.

Corinthia Anastasia's mother returned in time. This day she wore a well-patched dress, which had once been dark green velvet. She carried a bundle with her as she entered the cottage, and deposited it before me.

"You will need these soon."

I tugged at the folded cloth, a cheap print of trees in a reversing pattern. Inside were my blacks, repaired. "Oh." I looked back up at her. "Thank you."

"There was help," she said shortly. "Some in these hills are far more interested in speeding you on your way."

That implied there had been other options. I wondered who had been debating me, but as I did not expect an answer, I did not bother with the question. Instead I unfolded the clothing.

Not just repaired, but well repaired. Even my boots had been worked on. New soles and heels replaced what had been worn by fighting, fire, and too much time in water. I ran my fingers over the tightly sewn rents in the trousers, then looked back at Corinthia Anastasia's mother. "My thanks to whoever did this work."

"There are no names here."

Except the child, but there you were. "I understand. May I stay until the morning?"

Now something in her voice opened up again. "Of course, my girl. We will eat well tonight. A feast to send you off."

"I would prepare it for you, if you'd like." Suddenly I found myself shy.

She laughed. "Any woman of the Factor's courts can cook for kings and princes. Here I've been giving you corn soup and boiled grouse. I would be honored if you did so."

The afternoon passed into evening as we worked together. The cottage had no separate kitchen, just the fireplace with its pot hooks, and a little wrought-iron rack where I might set a bread pan. The pantry was better than I might have expected, especially among the spices. We sent Corinthia Anastasia out half a dozen times. She grew more willing as the scents of cookery multiplied.

Eventually I produced a braised rabbit in apples, baked into a butter crust. We had little nubbins of late lettuce from the garden, along with honeyed carrots and a boiled wine that I had carefully spiced by hand. I would have prepared our meal in the Selistani manner, but she had no spices for that, nor the right foodstuffs. Even so, I could have dined on the smells alone.

I was happy, in a simple, satisfied way. If I could ever find the knack of not killing people, I realized I might like to be a cook. Open a little cafe in Copper

Downs to serve Selistani food, or even better, a little cafe in Kalimpura to serve northern food. That scrap of dream distressed me, so I folded it away for another time.

Evening carried a chill. The woman and I went outside anyway, and shared a bench with blankets wrapped around us. Her thigh was pressed against mine for the warmth. Rested and well-fed, it was easy to imagine us as friends. Or lovers. I felt so safe that I did not even know where my knife was. In a sense, that relieved me.

Of course, it also worried me.

"I leave tomorrow," I told her.

"Be well on the road."

Somehow I had expected a protest. "Thank you for sheltering me."

"I am not ignorant of your identity." She paused, evidently choosing her words with care. "There are . . . versions . . . of your tale even in these hills. Especially in these hills." She gave me a long, slow look. "Do you know where you are?"

"No."

"Back when Copper Downs was a kingdom, before the Amphora Wars threw down the crowns of the Stone Coast, it was the custom of the city to bury the most important dead well away from the walls. I suppose they sought peace for their departed."

The Amphora Wars? How far into the past was she looking? I had not read of that conflict. The Ducal coronet reached back at least a thousand years, which meant any kingdom lay deeper in time than that. Thinking of the Factor, I said, "It also cut down on the ghosts in town, I imagine."

"You would not be wrong. There are long neglected tombs among these hills. Their inhabitants have not forgotten themselves, nor their city."

"You are a necromancer?"

"No, no." She smiled. "I speak with the dead—I do not summon them or bind them to my will. A necrolocutor, I suppose."

"With all that ancient wisdom, you live in a one-room cottage among the apples."

Snorting, she said, "Why do people always suppose the dead to be so wise, when the living are so foolish?"

I thought about that. Surely the wisdom of the ancestors was a truism. "I had assumed the grave taught patience, and lent perspective, if nothing else. For those who did not pass on along the Wheel, or wherever their gods sent them."

"Mostly it makes them angry."

"There are many I have sped out of this life. I . . . I cannot count the number anymore." I was thinking of the thieves Mother Shesturi's handle slew in the park. "If they are all angry at me, I must trail such distemper like a shooting star."

"You are a weapon, my girl. Made so by the hands of others. Wielded by your own will now."

"Mostly," I told her. "Mostly."

"You have a patron, yes? Patroness?"

"I do," I admitted.

"Yet your hand is not guided, your will is not bent. Was this true in the courts of the Factor?"

"Not at all. Nearly every moment was driven for me, and I in turn driven before the passing hours. I ran a race toward womanhood." I thought of Mistress Tirelle. The snap of her neck echoed still in my ears, when I let myself hear it. "I first killed there within the bluestone walls. Many more died because of me." A sob I had not known was coming escaped from me, though I tried hard to swallow it at the last second.

She put an arm across my shoulders and hugged me close beneath the blanket. "I told you, I have known who you were since the first. You are well thought of among the tombs of old, at least by those ghosts with any sense of the world as it is today."

"For sending so many to their deaths?"

"The city has its patrons. Its parents. Like any child, it journeys forward through time as they fall behind. You freed it."

"For Choybalsan," I said bitterly, hating the salt tears in my voice.

"Another step in the journey."

"I'm tired of killing people." Curled closer to her, I shuddered with a swallowed sob. "I'm tired of freeing cities."

"You want to go home?"

"Yes!" I shrieked at that, and cried into her shoulder for a while. When I finally found my voice, I stammered, breath heaving, "I have no home."

"Everyone comes home to the grave." She stroked my hair. "The lucky ones come home to their hearts while they still can."

I wept awhile longer. When I sat up again and found my eyes not so overwhelmed by tears, I asked her the question that had been hanging behind my tongue. "Do you know any who survived the fall of the Factor's house? Any g-girls? Or Mistresses?"

She gave me a long steady look. I could see the questions in her own eyes. Finally: "One called Danae lives among the tombs high in the hills. She is almost a shade herself, but has not yet given up to lie beneath the flowers."

"Mistress Danae?" Words leapt in my throat, to go see her, to speak to her, to ask after my younger self, but I held them. Something very wary was in this woman's tone.

"Just Danae, I think. It took her a season to trust me within a stone's throw. Even now we do not talk so much." Sighing, she continued, "I bring her food and blankets, and sometimes tell her of high places where she might find shelter or needful things. She has been used past the point of shattering her spirit."

"I would wish her well, but I will not disturb her peace."

"Peace it is. Strange and fragile, but something called her here. I will not let her be unseated from this resting place."

"Thank you." I leaned over to kiss her cheek. I knew from that brief taste of her that in a different time, this woman and I might have been great lovers and friends.

Morning brought the gift of a new veil. My old one was long gone.

"How did you know?" I asked with delight. This was a metal mesh, faced with black silk.

The woman smiled. "No one betrayed you, but the tombs have been watching."

I turned it back and forth, looking at the fine steel links, marveling at how light it was. "This is a grave good?"

"Yes. Freely given."

I boggled slightly at the dead making an offering, but was pleased enough. "Now if only I had a blade."

"I do not traffic in weapons," she said seriously, "but if you would like the use of my gray-handled boning knife, I will not object."

The kitchen tools hung near the fire from a wooden slat. I knew exactly which steel she spoke of. This blade was far smaller and lighter than the last two I'd carried, which had both been fighting weapons. Taking it down, I hefted the knife with an enemy in mind. I could fight well enough bare-handed, but others would not recognize the threat.

Is that why Skinless was immune to weapons but not to blows? Because no one here ever strengthens their hands hard enough to matter?

That question I put away for later consideration. The knife I put away for later use. The handle stuck out of my boot top and made me look the rogue, but the time for subtlety was past. Especially veiled and dressed in black.

Neckbreaker had seemed a good idea in Kalimpura. I was coming to understand how childish he was. Even so, he was a safer person to be than the girl Green.

I took up my veil and marveled at how well I could move, even with the raw seaming of scars about my body. I turned to my benefactress and her daughter. "There is much I owe you, but right now, my best thanks is my absence. I will head downhill and south, and forget that I ever knew this place."

Corinthia Anastasia darted toward me and hugged my waist hard. "Don't be stupid," she said earnestly.

Her mother smiled sadly. "Listen to my child."

With my knife and my little wooden bell, I walked out into the sunlit orchard and away from them. The city awaited me. Choybalsan, too, and the Lily Goddess in Her distant temple. For all my dallying with gods, it seemed strange that my greatest blessing had come from a lone woman and her child.

Though the tombs could not have been much more than a day's ride up the Barley Road from Copper Downs, it took me three days of walking to cover the distance. I traveled in the hills to the west, though they lessened with each furlong south. There were goat tracks aplenty, and odd mossy walls to shelter beside from time to time. Those could have been the remains of castles or cottages. I did not know, and did not care.

As I made my slow progress, I watched the road. Despite what I'd been told, it was largely empty. I did not know what the usual traffic here might be. Now there was only the occasional rider, always racing. They went both one way and the other.

Choybalsan's army might be called bandits, but truly they were farm boys and woodsmen dressed like rogues. There had never been enough people or trade in this empty country to support raiders. That meant they would campaign like farmers and woodcutters. Slowly and without precision.

I would have expected scouts, in any case. Whatever was he doing? My escape was more than a week old now. Unless they'd gone hunting the Dancing Mistress, they must fall upon the city soon. There would not be enough to eat up there, and frost was not far away in the higher hills.

Being ahead of them pleased me well enough.

Then I crossed a wooded shoulder of a hill and heard the noise of surf ahead.

Climbing away from the road, I found a good spreading oak. I scrambled up that tree to look south.

Copper Downs lay before me. The sea glinted beyond, showing an endless southern horizon. Choybalsan's army was drawn up in the open lands outside the city where the first few wayhouses and stables and shanties had been overwhelmed by several thousand men and horses. The lightning fence was not crackling just now, but surely this force had not come without their god-king before them in glorious array.

I had not arrived in advance of them. I had rested too long amid the orchards of the dead.

Brushing that aside as unworthy, I studied the army awhile. I looked as Mistress Tirelle had taught me. And saw with eyes of history, eyes sharpened by maps and mathematics. I was never an expert on the disposition and application of massed forces, but I knew more than a little of logistics. The Pomegranate Court had trained me in part to be a chatelaine. That is a job not much different from quartermaster, except for the uniform.

Here are the things I could determine:

They had been before the city at least three days. I was beyond crediting that an entire army had marched past me in the night unnoticed.

They had not come in a sweeping mass, or the roadway I'd been following would have been badly used in a manner I could have spotted even from a distance.

They had not fought since before arriving. The outlying buildings and small villages overrun by Choybalsan's bandits were still intact. No burning, no wrack. So no one had stood against them. Not in a body, at any rate.

That meant that some in and around the city had welcomed the army. Neither did anyone within sally out. The profusion of guards were largely patrolmen and gatekeepers, not trained to stand against massed force.

What was this army waiting for?

Perhaps Choybalsan was not here. In which case, I might not be too late.

Why would you conquer your own city?

That was when I knew where the bandit-king had gone. And why there was no lightning. Somewhere in the city, probably in the upper rooms of the Textile Bourse, Federo was offering the Interim Council the desperate bargain he would report having made with the perfidious Choybalsan.

He didn't *need* to conquer the city. He just needed to arrange a surrender to *himself*.

I sat amid some bayberry bushes and laughed quietly. Federo's arrogance had a surpassing cleverness that my soul was just dark enough to admire. At the same time, I wondered how it was he could put godhood on and off like a cloak. It seemed a most useful trick.

Had all the gods started that way? Was the Splintering nothing more than a metaphor for the way that the measures of grace and evil within any man could grow at the right touch?

Septio had said everything moved in a cycle.

Which in turn made me wonder who the Lily Goddess had once been.

My path led to the coast. I met the Quarry Highway with its small river along-side. A log tangle gave me a ford over the water. Sheer nerve took me across the broken pavers of the road. Close to the sea, I had to cross the East Road, but there I was able to crawl underneath the trackway following a flood channel meant to drain the north verge.

Here the stones of the city gave way to shale and gravel beaches. The littoral east of the city was too shallow for a harbor. Choybalsan's horsemen rode their circuit all the way to salt water. Some of the men, and most of the horses, seemed afraid of the sea, though a few riders raced whooping in the foamy edge of the water.

Clouds had rolled in to steal the warmth of the sunlight and replace it with a chilled gloom. I skulked among the low ridges with their sparse vegetation, cursing that I would have to go all the way back to the Greenbriar River and across before I found a decently unpatrolled way in. As I grumbled about my fruitless effort, I nearly fell into a muddy creek that had been invisible from farther inland.

That was odd. I should have seen it bridged at the East Road. I followed the water's lazy course alongside one of the graveled banks, staying low so I wouldn't be spotted by a horseman atop one of the ridges. The bank crooked west, as did the stream, until I found a stinking little pond choked with water lilies.

It trapped enough water to keep a busy stream flowing, but this pond had no *inflow*. I stared at the lilies awhile. They would grow in bad water. Some people said the plants even cleaned water, made it fresh again.

More to the point, the Goddess had sent me a dream of water lilies, when the Dancing Mistress and I had been imprisoned together beneath Her temple.

First I tied the wooden bell, muffled with some vines, to my waist. I did not want to lose it. While a good soaking was not ideal, water would not ruin it immediately. Then I hefted the boning knife and waded in. The pond had a muddy graveled floor, tangled with roots. My feet found broken junk and stones even through my boots. My nose found the refuse of a city. This was a drain for the water and blood of Copper Downs.

Standing still, I tried to locate a current. That was not so difficult. The flow seemed to originate from the gravel bank somewhat below the calm surface. I approached, the water growing first waist deep, then chest deep, then neck deep. I was in danger of being swallowed up before I met the end. With my free hand, I explored.

An outflow issued from an opening of worked stone.

Water never ran *up*. From this very low angle, the bank towered at least fifteen feet above my head.

Could there be a sewer tunnel underneath it? This entire stretch of twisting, angled banks and dunes might easily cover the ruins of some ancient quarter of Copper Downs.

The mine galleries beneath the city were certainly far older than the traditions of the people who lived above them now. Anything was possible.

Not admitting fear to myself—for I could not afford such a luxury as that—I took three great whooping breaths to puff up my chest and make my heart brave with quickened blood. I held my knife braced forward, ducked into the stinking water, and braced my free hand against the top lip of the outlet.

Pushing inward against the current was difficult. The roof of the drain remained obstinately level as I waddled at a crouch, while the floor was slick with some slime that threatened my footing and slowed my pace. I kept my free hand above me, hoping for some vault or rise where I might find air.

If this entire drain was filled with water, then that would be the last hope of my life.

Goddess. You showed me Your lilies. I do not believe You toy with me. We both fear what might be here. Help me on my way, that I might free all from the tyranny that comes.

Praying to the Lily Goddess from within a swirl of muddy water far across the sea did not seem likely to help me, but I needed to do something. Anything. My lungs stung. Reflex fought for breath, tempting my mouth to open despite the burden of water sealing it shut.

I could turn around, kick with the current, be back out among the lilies.

I could find blessed air and the light of day.

I could walk another path—surrender, even—and allow myself to be taken in.

I could feel the top of the drain suddenly curve upward.

Straightening my spine, I followed the rising stonework. My hand found air before my face, but a moment later, I was gasping in the dank, moldy air of Below. The familiar taste was as much a blessing as water in the desert.

After several deep choking breaths, I headed onward, looking to stand straight up. I could see nothing at all, for there was no coldfire here. My hands told me the sewer had a low vault. That must have ended at the outflow.

In order to breathe, I was forced to walk slightly bent at the knees and hips, with my head tilted backwards to keep my mouth above the water. The position was painful, but not excruciating. I had nowhere to go but forward.

My knife before me, I advanced.

I was forced to keep my feet in shuffling contact with the slimed bottom for fear of encountering a pit or a grate, or even just broken stones that might trip me and pull me under. The current seemed to become more powerful. I was cloaked in fear that slowly tinged with panic when I finally stumbled into a larger space where the air sussurated with echoes.

It took three attempts before I could lever myself out of the channel and up onto the walkway. I lay there stinking wet and gasping miserably awhile before realizing I could see. A faint glow interrupted by ridges of darkness presented itself to my eyes.

Coldfire. Over dressed stone.

Never in life had I been so glad for a revelation.

I stumbled shivering to my feet and pawed at the mossy stuff until I had a decent glowing lump in my hand. To hell with whatever might glimpse me coming. I would either kill it or recruit it to my cause.

With a few more deep satisfying breaths, I set out to find the part of the city I knew. My sense of direction had been unseated by the sewer tunnel, but logic told me that I had to be facing close to west. That I would work with, until I found something familiar here in the Below, or a surface exit that seemed safe enough for me to spy out from.

Away from the drains, I walked on damp stones beneath the city, wondering who might help me. Skinless could perhaps have been recruited to stand against Choybalsan, but Septio was dead. I would not even consider the matter of the Pater Primus. Him I could not trust the worth of a broken straw.

I had a friend or two here. Mother Iron, in her strange way. The Tavernkeep. Chowdry with him. They were not warriors. I considered seeking out the Rectifier. Anyone who killed priests and wore their remains openly wouldn't trifle to reckon with gods.

But he was one of the Dancing Mistress' people. I could not know their hearts. They seemed completely unable to oppose Choybalsan. Perhaps they could not fight their own magic. The pardines had done little enough against the Duke in his four centuries of rule, standing the whole time on their stolen power.

A vaulted arch loomed over me, a shaft of cloud-dimmed daylight spearing down from what seemed to be a street-side storm grate, though it opened to no drain. Where to go? Whom to seek help from?

The Factor.

I had seen his shade, that day. I was sure of it. He of all people had cause to hate and fear Choybalsan. Federo had stolen his very existence in order to become the bandit-king, the nascent god. Choybalsan was searching for the missing pieces—the keys, really—he thought I'd held. Surely the Factor's ghost was sustained by a shred of the same. Doubtless Choybalsan would attempt to extract that power from him just as he'd wished to extract it from me.

Whatever passions held the Factor here might serve my needs as well.

I stepped gingerly into the barred square of light at the center of the space. How did you call the dead? According to Lacodemus, with libations. I wished I'd asked the woman in the orchards what rite she offered. Perhaps that would not have helped. It had seemed she was harder pressed to quiet the voices in her high tombs than to set their ghosts to talking in the first place.

This would be done the old way. Warriors had poured wine into graves to speak with their dead, but I knew wine was only a signifier for blood. That was the Law of Similar Substitution, for those who pursued such things, and such exchanges always weakened the effect.

For a moment I marveled again at the education that had been forced upon me.

That same education suggested that I must not seek him as the Duke. As the Factor, he'd cared for me, in a strange way. As the Duke, I'd slain him, in a strange way. The form of this summoning certainly *would* matter.

I untied my bell from my waist. Crumpled wet vines slipped free from the clappers that dangled on each side of the hollow rounded cup. I set it at my feet, then opened a shallow slash on the inside of my left forearm with the boning knife. Setting down the knife, I took up the bell and swung it slowly so that it rang as if Endurance walked close behind me.

The sound brought tears to my eyes. A saltwater benediction could hardly lessen the power of the blood.

"Factor." There was no point in shouting. His shade would hear me or it would not. Blood dripped rapidly into the little square of sunlight to hiss slightly as it struck the mossy stones. The words flowed as they would. "Factor, I summon you. I, Green, whom you named Emerald, whose life you stole, call you forth." A chill shook my spine as I took a deep shuddering breath. "You called me in the broken yard of your house. Now I call you by that same bond."

I fell silent, though I continued to ring the bell. It clop, clop, clopped. The hair on my arms lifted. I began to feel as I had when I'd passed the lightning fence. With a rush of panic, I wondered if I had somehow summoned Choybalsan.

A scent of smoke met my nose. At my feet, the blood was curdling to black. A presence loomed at my back more dangerous than blades, more frightening than wounds.

There was not enough courage in the world for me to turn and look. I shivered, crying now, wishing I had done anything other than this summoning. My knees became soft, trembling fit to fold and swallow me to the floor. I considered casting myself on my knife.

A spray of water touched me from above. A single lily petal floated in the shaft of weak sunlight. It caught my eye, and my fear. The Goddess, I wondered, or some careless flower-seller in the street above?

Did it matter? Cycles and circles. They could be one and the same, after all. Miracles always worked best through the mechanism of the mundane.

Courage found me after all. Setting the bell down, I turned. The wooden clop continued to echo from within the surrounding darkness another moment or two before it faded.

The Factor stood there, grubby and grave-pale as I'd glimpsed him at the ruins of his house. He did not look like a ghost—no will-of-the-wisp or smoky aspect. He seemed as real as Mother Iron.

His eyes, though misted and dark, were not dead. The rest of him most certainly was, but laughter and tears and much more lived in that gaze. The opposite of how he'd appeared in life.

I felt an odd stab of hope at that.

"My prodigal Emerald returns to me at last," he said.

Hope, indeed. The old arrogance of power had not been washed out of him by death. With a laugh that I did not have to force from my lips, I replied, "I am Green, grown to myself, come to call you."

"I know who you are."

Even though I understood his perfidy, I felt a flash of sympathy for the pain that crossed his face.

"I know what you did to me," the Factor added.

"It was needful." I believed that, but I realized I believed it because I'd been told to.

"Truly?" Now his smile was sly. "Tell me. How many did I kill during my centuries on the throne? What wars did this city fight? Did coin shrink and the harbor traffic wither? Was there dread and fear upon the streets?"

His questions took me aback briefly. "How should I know? I was not given anything recent enough for me to understand such things. I was educated as . . . as . . ." My voice broke off as I realized the miserable truth. Softly, I continued. "I was educated as a woman of the time of your youth. Nothing was told to me of the world since you came to the throne."

"The long years are very lonely," the Factor said. "You would have reminded me of who I once was." His hand reached up as if to touch me, then dropped again. There was no noise as he moved, reminding me that he was not truly present.

A swell of bitter rage crested within me. His *loneliness* was the cause of all my own loss? "I would have recalled your youth until I withered with age. While you went on forever!"

"You will age with or without me." His voice was sad, his eyes watered with tears. "What is terrible about aging in a splendid palace with a great city ready to do your bidding?"

"You were a tyrant!" I tried to hang on to the old arguments, but really, they were nothing more than what I had been taught. What did any child know but what they had been told?

"I was a tyrant who brought peace and prosperity and quiet streets at night, and silenced gods so they could not meddle daily in the business of men." He sighed, though I wondered how someone with no breath could do so. Or speak, now that I thought upon it. "My crime, my tyranny, was not to rule, but to live beyond the years of ancestry and descent of entire families."

"Your crime," I growled, "was to strip power from a peaceful people and bind it to yourself."

"How peaceful were those people?" Now his face flared with passion to match my own. "Do you know of the last war this city did fight? Under me, as a living man? We battled the pardines. In their time, they were terrible hunters and raiders. Others followed them, thinking by their appearance that they were wise and powerful. The shared path they have instead of souls lent them a strength in this world that could not be matched. Over a thousand men were lost wrestling them down. I took what they used to wreak the death of farmers and children and traders, stripped it from them, and made peace for Copper Downs. I even made peace for *them*!"

I struggled against his logic. This man was the villain of centuries, yet to hear him tell it, he held the good of the city in his heart, and had delivered it.

He was right. Hundreds must have died in the riots that followed the fall of the Duke. There were still buildings, even entire blocks, burned out and not rebuilt. The sea trade had diminished. The city lived in fear.

As it had not under the Duke's rule.

A trick, a trap lay at the heart of this. I'd always known what it was. "You stole away the choices of generations. You stole away my choices. My freedom."

He laughed, bitter and hollow. "Freedom? To be a rice farmer's wife? You should be on your knees thanking me, *Green*, for saving you."

"That was my fate!"

Leaning close, the Factor said in that growling voice, "Then consider that I have changed your fate. You might rejoice in that if you were honest enough."

I took a breath and tried to fling his words away. I did not need his self-serving logic and the justification of his memories.

What I did need was him.

"We argue to no purpose," I finally said, collecting my thoughts. "You are what you are now—"

"What you made me," he interrupted.

"What you made yourself. You made *me*, after all." I gave him the sweet, nasty smile that I seemed to be perfecting. "You are what you are; I am what I am. Choybalsan will gut us both to set himself in your stead."

The Factor shook his head. "Oh, no. I was never a god."

"I do not think this one should be, either. He is too cruel and foolish."

"Did I make you to be a judge?"

I tried to stare him down, but that is impossible with a ghost. He did not blink. "No, but you made of me a person who is capable of judging, at need."

"You, who would kill gods, also have learned the ways of doing that?" His smile remained wicked. "My education must have been very deep, indeed."

"I l-learned that in the world. But to do what must be done, I need your help. Or at the least your advice."

The Factor spread his hands, like a greengrocer who has run out of turnips and must apologize. "You have only to ask."

Such a curious echo of Corinthia Anastasia's remark. It took me a moment to unravel that he meant for me to request his aid right at that moment. "Fine. Will you please help me save your city, and yourself, from this man who would be the god-king?"

"Yes."

He must fear Choybalsan far more desperately than I—he could not just board a ship, for example. The Factor made this sound so simple, so condescending, that for a moment I would have slain him all over again if I'd had such power.

A while later, I sat on a step. The Factor paced before me. He made no noise except when he spoke. I'd just finished telling him of the fight within Choybalsan's tent.

"What made you think you could harm a god?" he demanded.

"He looked like a man." I shrugged, feeling vaguely ashamed. "Besides, I have heard of god-killers here in Copper Downs. If they could do so, why not I?"

The Factor waved that off as inconsequential. "They were specialists from the Saffron Tower, passing through. One was not even human."

"Where did they fare next?"

"Selistan."

A stab of cold fear found my heart.

His malicious smile widened the wound. "Did someone go after you there?" he asked.

"I am no goddess," I told him. But I knew one. This killing was old news. Whoever they were, they had come and gone from Kalimpura long ago. Or so I devoutly hoped.

The Factor pushed the question. "Do you think you harmed him?"

"Only with the touch of my bare hands. I wish I'd thought to crush his chest while shoeless." I spread my fingers and looked at them. "Not until I reached Kalimpura did I learn to fight properly."

"You did well enough here," the Factor told me grudgingly.

I glanced up to see some distant emotion in those eyes. Had he been handsome once, four hundred years ago when he was a young man with a name and a future? "Perhaps," I said.

"Where is my part in this?"

"It is doubtful that I can bring him down weaponless," I admitted. "He is far more powerful than the largest man. I came back to the city looking for you, in hopes that you could raise the sendings and avatars that haunt the Below. Fighting Skinless taught me how they must be struck. Federo-as-Choybalsan is turning into one of them."

"Larval gods," he said with disgust. "Buds of the divine."

"Choybalsan is the get of no god." I added, "Except maybe you."

"I can promise you Federo had no touch of the divine. Whatever Choybalsan is, it uses him as a host. Much as those wasps that lay their eggs inside other insects. That is why he is so powerful. A sending is little more than the cyst of a dream, loosened from the divine mind." He was becoming angry again. "I spent much of my effort stamping them out, as a source of future trouble. He is a sending wrapped in a man."

"When he goes into town and plays the councilor, we see no lightning."

The Factor looked thoughtful. "The god may remain behind. Perhaps in that altar you mentioned."

I became excited. "In which case, we must attack Choybalsan at the Textile Bourse. He will be without his army, and lacking the full mantle of his powers!"

"Though I do not agree, neither am I ready to deny you." He renewed his pacing. "If I had Skinless, or something like it, we might be able to deal with the god. Have you ever seen dolphins kill a shark?"

"Uh . . . no."

"A shark of any size is more than a match for a lone dolphin. They are tough, powerful, and very dangerous. The dolphin cannot bite back. He has no swords in his mouth." The Factor grinned. All I could think of was the great dead-eyed monster that had nearly taken me when I first set out from Selistan. He continued: "Any one dolphin would fall before the shark like a child before a drunken guardsman. A dozen dolphins can surround a shark and batter him to death, moving too quickly for him to stop them."

"You want to surround Choybalsan with Skinless?"

"With sendings and avatars. The gods are stirring. I would prefer to lay them once more to quiet rest, but I would use their children for this before our argument can be ended by the deaths of all."

I nodded. He'd come to the same conclusion as I. "Then I will go above the stones and look for what friends I can. It may be of use to have a few arms in the corporeal world."

"As you will. But I cannot raise Skinless. The monster is too well kept within the Algeficic Temple. It roams sometimes, but it is not free like the older ones."

"The canny ones, whom you never caught," I said. "Mother Iron."

"Precisely." He looked irritated now.

I had my own problems with that temple. The god was a horror, and the Pater Primus a traitor, at the least. Still, they would no more profit by the coming of Choybalsan than anyone else. "I will do what I can."

He glanced over at the square of light admitted by the grate high in the ceiling. "It is a bit past the noon hour. If Federo is yet in the Textile Bourse, we must catch him today. Meet me at the Lyme Street cistern three fingers before the sun sets."

I actually knew where that was. Nodding, I opened my mouth to speak, but the Factor was gone. Gone as if he'd never been there in the first place.

Looking at my arm, I saw the long wound I'd made. I twirled the bell in my hand. A muffled clop sounded.

I followed the steps on which I sat, until I found an exit.

The stairs came up behind a set of public baths. A blessed good thing. It is difficult to persuade people to a cause when you are coated in drying sewage. I stepped out through a little closet. The steam was high, so these lower baths were in use. I stole to the first tub and slipped in, clothes and all, until I was completely under the near-scalding water.

Holding my breath, I scrubbed at my hair. A minute later, I came up gasping and began to search for my veil. I could not remember where I'd had it last.

At least I still held the knife and the bell.

"You are supposed to wash before you sit in here," said a man across from me. He was only a shadow through the curtains of steam.

I had company, too. My hand closed on the haft of the knife.

"The water has been terribly dirtied." I *knew* that voice. He continued: "I should call the attendants and have you beaten and thrown out."

Recognition dawned.

"Stefan Mohanda," I said. What in the name of all the gods was he doing *here*? "Or should I call you the Pater Primus?"

"Either is correct." He leaned forward, becoming a firmer silhouette as the stinking water sloshed back toward me with its scum of sewage, slime, and blood. "Though never both at once. The scrying mirror told me where to expect you. Now what have you done with my favorite priest?"

"Your fellow councilor laid open his gut and let him die."

"Federo? Never." The Pater Primus laughed grimly. "The god I could easily believe that of. Not the man. A pity about Septio. He was a good lad, with the ass of an angel."

He knew. *Everything.* My knife hand lay easy in the bath before me. I had not trained for water fighting, but I doubted very much this man had, either. His age and size would slow him.

Never let the enemy see your attack. That had been one of Mother Vajpai's first lessons. I stalled, talking to cover my small movements. "If you knew, why the charade of sending Septio with me up into the hills?"

"You asked to go." He sounded delighted. "You would bring yourself to him in the seat of his power. So much easier than abducting you from the city against your will. Surely you realize that you are very difficult to move unwilling."

I began to slide up out of the tub. "Then I will be on my way, and leave you—" Even as I spoke, I kicked off from the tiled wall beneath my feet, flinging myself at him. That was an attack I would not dare against a prepared enemy.

Mohanda, unfortunately for me, was prepared.

Unfortunately for him, he was also slow.

He raised himself up, thin robe dripping, something long and dark in his hand. For one horrified moment, I thought it was a crossbow. I crashed into that arm above the weapon, then slid my boning knife up into his armpit, letting the leverage of my sinking weight drive the blade farther.

A stupid blow, weak and wrong-angled, but it worked. Mohanda's arm nearly separated from his shoulder. He shrieked like a child as dark blood gushed from the gaping wound to flood down his body and into the tub. His panicked thrashing kept the blood pouring.

I snatched up his weapon. That was a short iron bar with a reversed barb at the top. Purely defensive—he'd expected me to attack. That meant he almost certainly had allies close by.

Flipping the bar around, I set the barb into the bouncing flab of his belly and smacked it hard with my other hand.

More foulness in the water as I tugged the bar free. I leaned close. "A pity about the Pater Primus. He was never a good man."

I tugged my knife from his body and, weapons in hand, tried to scrabble out of the tub, but I slipped. Mohanda clutched at my ankle. His eyes had already rolled upward, but his mouth moved. I bent close without setting my ear where he could spit a barb or some such.

"Blackblood . . ." That was all he said.

I kicked his head so that he slid into the water, then splashed quickly through the next pool as well as the one after that, rinsing as best I could. I felt badly soiled, far more so than I had wading through the drain Below. Climbing out of the second pool, I paused at the door. I was worried about priests on the other side. Or worse, a temple horror like Skinless.

It occurred to me that one way to kill a god was to kill his priests. *That* required little special training. Without prayer and ceremony, a god will atrophy. Time spun away with every moment for the divine as surely as it did for the human.

"Life is risk," I whispered, and kicked open the door to race into the next room.

The wood struck a man in the jaw, knocking him screaming to the floor. He'd been too close. His friend I caught with a cut across the face that did little more than loosen his nostrils, but also served to drive him back. Still moving fast, I took the third in the gut with my shoulder. The fourth grabbed at me hard, but I smacked him in the groin with the handle of Mohanda's weapon.

After that, it was a quick run for the stairs and through the upper baths, which were occupied as normal, at least until my bloody-handed appearance set people to a panic. I rushed with them out into the street.

I needed to reach the Tavernkeep's place quickly. Tucking my head down and sprinting, I looked for some place to climb unseen. Shouting echoed behind me. I took two corners hard, jumped onto an unattended cart, and from there rolled myself onto the flat roof of some portico. I tucked close against the building as the chase pounded by just below.

After a quick twenty count to let them get ahead, I wriggled to the end of the portico and dropped into the street between the cart and the building. A fat man in an apron over a denim shirt, wearing a straw boater, stared at me with a crate of something in his hands.

"Blessings on your house," I said in Seliu, then turned into the nearest alley.

Next it was a simple matter to gain the roofs two storeys up. I found a wooden water tank and cleaned myself thoroughly within, then broke the bottom. The flood would greatly trouble the people in the building below, but less so than drinking the water I'd fouled. I climbed down in the other end of the alley, stole a white shirt off a line, and quietly walked the rest of the way to the Tavernkeep's place.

When I found the tavern, Chowdry was in the main room serving something that smelled very much like home. The scent set my stomach to gurgling. Chowdry looked up and broke into a smile.

"Green, you are being alive!"

"Please," I replied in Seliu. "I must eat a little, and speak to the Tavernkeep at once."

"He is marketing." Chowdry looked around the room. A pair of pardines sat near the fireplace at table with a stoneware bowl and a scattering of flowers. One was the Rectifier, though I did not recognize the other. "You are knowing the Sentence, yes?"

The Sentence? "The Rectifier?"

"I say what his name means, I am thinking." Chowdry looked apologetic.

That fit. In a strange way.

"Please," I said. "Some curry."

He nodded, fidgeted through part of a bow, then ran back into the kitchen. I quickly stepped to the table.

The Rectifier looked up at me. "You should take trophies, you know." He gave me a feral smile. "I smell the killing on you."

"I cannot wear the knucklebones so elegantly as some." Taking a seat, I said to the other pardine, "I am Green. Known to this one a little, and known better to the Tavernkeep."

She returned my small nod. "You are known."

As was the manner of their people, she offered no name. She was rangy, perhaps the thinnest of them I'd seen, with tan fur that shaded almost white down her chest and belly. Neither she nor the Rectifier wore much in the way of clothing, unlike the city dwellers such as the Tavernkeep or the Dancing Mistress.

"You are in the midst of a battle?" the Rectifier asked politely.

"In a sense." I saw no point in coyness. "I seek to throw down the bandit-king who hunts your people near extinction. We hope to catch him before the end of the day, unawares and unprepared."

"You have an army?" the brown woman asked.

"No. But he is in the city today under guise, and does not have his army, either." My next words caught in my throat. I forced them out anyway. "I have fought him once already, with the Dancing Mistress beside me. We escaped with our lives. I believe I know how to fight him again."

The Rectifier grinned wider. "Where will this battle be, so that I might avoid the site at the proper time?"

"The Textile Bourse. Just before the sun downs." I laid my hands flat on the table. "I have an ally seeking help that can meet Choybalsan on his own terms. I am more concerned with whatever corporeal protection he has with him there. I will need to clear his shields before we can bear him down."

"So you wish to fight the city's own guards," the brown woman said. "After they beat you senseless and leave you in the cells beneath Penitent's Rest, what plan will you have then?"

"If we succeed, peace for Copper Downs and your people," I said promptly. "If we fail, I doubt we'll live to be arrested."

"Go raise your army of thugs," the Rectifier said. "We will think on this awhile."

Then Chowdry came with the curry: fish in masaman, coriander, and Hanchu parsley over steamed rice. It met my gut with a delicious rumble, and recalled me to the hot, wet air of Selistan. I said almost nothing as I ate. The pardines made no answer at all.

The food sufficed.

When I had cleaned my bowl dry, I stood and bowed. "Sometimes it is worth being on the side of the good."

"If only you know which side that is," the brown woman answered.

I nodded at them both and departed.

The crux of the problem came back to Skinless, and with it the seed of my solution. Mother Iron and the other sendings might well be able to mob and drive down Choybalsan, but Blackblood's avatar had the god's cruel strength. The avatar was almost an aspect, in truth. And Choybalsan was something more than a northern tulpa.

The god wore the man like a cloak.

I did not think that Blackblood would hold any use for me now. I had slain at least two of his priests, and perhaps more in the baths. His cult was not large. Of how much had I robbed him?

Sanity argued that even approaching the Algeficic Temple under these circumstances bordered on suicide.

My hopes for any success in the coming battle argued that I make the approach.

I wandered, going closer to the Temple Quarter in wide passages across city blocks as I tried to convince myself to do this thing. I prayed for guidance. The Lily Goddess was never so neat as to send me a sign at a time such as this, except for the blessing of my continued existence.

Septio could not advise me. The Dancing Mistress could not advise me. The Blade Mothers were not here.

In the end, I fell back on my oldest guides of all. What would Endurance have me do? What would my grandmother have me do?

That was when I knew I must find a way to make all this end decently. Whatever the cost to me. I could not let this city fall.

I found a quiet park a few blocks from the Temple Quarter. It wasn't much more than an unbuilt corner planted with elms and rhododendrons. A stele stood at the center of a little square of grass in commemoration of some long-vanished personage.

Drifting past it, I sat under the tree in the farthest corner. There I toyed with the bell. I wondered why I was carrying it now.

To remind you of what you lost, said a voice within my head. *Of what every child loses, even if they stay at their mother's hearth all the days of their life.*

That was said so clearly that I looked around, expecting to find someone close by. Conscience, I supposed. Or my Goddess finally answering me.

I still felt troubled, but less so. Comforted, even. Like a prayer, come the other way to feed my soul. Was this how it had been for the Temple Mother? To be a vessel, not for some priest's lust, but for the Goddess Herself?

Looking at the sky, I saw that I had lost all but my last hour. I needed to be afoot and quickly. Stepping out of the park, I trotted toward the Temple Quarter and the Street of Horizons. I would meet Blackblood in his own house and tell him of the deaths of his priests.

You killed the Pater Primus, the voice said, *but did he not conspire against his own god?*

The tall metal doors of the pain god's temple were drawn shut. There were no handles on the outside. Somehow, knocking did not seem to be the answer.

I stepped back and looked at the black-tiled face of the building. It was certainly climbable, but the rumor of war had put a number of people on this street looking for comfort or counsel. I did not wish to be quite so public as all that.

On the right, the temple nearly butted against a blocky tan building fronted by squat pillars, which looked older than everything around it. On the left, a slim gap separated Blackblood's temple from a white stucco wall topped with a gold-colored pediment.

Promising, that. I slipped within.

The shadows showed two brick walls facing one another over a trench of shattered glass, broken furniture, and other refuse. A very strange midden. That was an opening I could climb, though, and so I set my back against the neighboring wall and my hands and feet against Blackblood's wall to begin my ascent.

No wonder his sanctuary had lacked windows, I realized. Except for the roof, there was nowhere to *put* them. I had a bad moment with some iron gutters, but then I found myself staring from the outside at wide, short windows in the little hutch on the roof that was the clerestory.

I tried to recall the drop within. Thirty feet, even after accounting for the rise of the front steps from the street level. Banners hung there, so I had a way down.

On close inspection, the windows were hinged to open, perhaps against the summer heat. The wood was silvered and powdery with rot. No one had touched them with paint or glazing in my lifetime, at least. The problem would be prying one open without breaking the glass, or the ancient hinges making a horrendous noise.

With a silent apology to whatever cutler had originally made it, I slid the tip of my boning knife around the rim of one window. It caught hard in two places, so I moved to the next. I had to try four times before I found one that had not been frozen shut from the inside.

I worked very slowly to ease my chosen window out and up. The hinges resisted, then groaned and popped with a spray of rust. Silently cursing, I pulled the frame open past a right angle. I tucked the knife away, set the bell beside the opening, and propped the window with my left hand while I explored where to go next.

I crawled inward to a rafter spanning the gap formed by the interior of the clerestory. Below me, three men in street clothes argued next to the long pool of quicksilver.

Quietly I eased my bell in, then lowered the window behind me. When I looked down, the men were staring upward. One had a pistol in his hand; the other two were unarmed. I could see the question forming in their minds.

No time like the present. I tossed my bell toward the mercury and dropped knife-first onto the pistolier.

Thirty feet is a very long fall, especially toward an opponent who is no longer surprised by your appearance and has his weapon primed and ready. He discharged his pistol. Something slammed me hard in the left shoulder. I spun, forced into a tumble.

I landed on the priest but lost control of the boning knife. It skittered across the floor like a nervous chiurgeon. As I rolled over to fight him, my left arm gave way underneath my weight. Someone kicked me very hard in the wounded shoulder. I yelped, but swallowed it, and tried to curl into a ball. That earned me a pair of kicks to the spine. Then they decided to talk.

"By all the wounds of Martri, I think he's killed Sextio!"

That was punctuated by a kick so hard, I felt bile surge in my mouth. I tried to ease past the corner of the pain that had taken my shoulder.

Another voice: "No. This is that girl of Septio's again. Small wonder the Pater Primus is so afraid of this one."

"Well, and crap. If Sextio's dead, we're even shorter handed, with all the others Primus took."

"It will soon be over." That one walked away, calling over his shoulder, "Throw her to Skinless. Let the god take her up if he can. Everyone should have a last meal."

"I hate this," muttered the kicker. He grabbed my heels and began to drag me. My pain multiplied. Then he dropped my legs to step away a moment. I had some swift fever dream of freedom, until the bell fell on my chest. It was beaded with dollops of mercury.

I saw my face distorted by the curve of each little mirror. My body bumped over flooring and a few steps, while my shoulder grew cold. My appearance seemed to change, become in one bit of quicksilver a farmwife like that wretched woman Shar, back on Papa's farm. In another, I was a priestess standing before a glittering altar, my face tattooed with silver tears. In another, I wore a helmet of strange design and swung a sword that crackled with lightning.

On and on, like the faces in the lilies of my dream. I would become a hundred tiny imperfect copies of myself. Was this how the titanic gods and goddesses had felt when they splintered?

A slab of metal boomed close by. An iron door, some part of me realized. I looked up at the priest in his ill-fitted doublet with the pimple on his nose and murder in his eye. "You will all die," I told him.

"Everyone dies." He pushed me into a hole. I fell hard into darkness.

I awoke in deep night.

All is lost! I had not gone to our ambush even with my own little knife, let alone with Skinless.

Skinless. That name made the rest of my body as cold as my left arm. I knew it was there, for it pressed against me, but it might as well have been cleaved off by an angry girl with a boning knife.

Night, or a sacred labyrinth in a temple cellar where no one had bothered to set the gaslights burning.

Something was very, very close to me. Something that did not breathe. I tried to open my eyes, but they were already open.

Black, black as Below without coldfire. Black as a pain god's heart.

A snuffling noise. Dampness close to my face. A smell like meat in a sudden, overwhelming wave as if my nose had woken up.

"Skinless," I whispered. "You know me."

Which was a lie, of course. I'd fought him as he'd dragged away the Dancing Mistress. Nothing had been right since.

A huge pair of hands closed on me as if I were a poppet. A rough tongue licked at the blood on my left shoulder, granting me new agony in exchange. This time I let myself scream. Why not? Nothing was left to hide. Not here, at the end of things.

We moved. Whatever Skinless required a theopomp for, it did not seem to need Septio today.

"I took him into my arms the day before he died," I whispered. "Was he your friend?" My breath was ragged in my chest, though I could not say if this wave of pain was from my injured body or my wounded heart. "When death could be cheated no more, I gave him the gift of mercy."

My thoughts were clearing. Hours on the rack beneath the whip had granted me a certain perspective even when my mind was under assault. There was nothing of pleasure about this pain, but I'd met such intensity before and kept my head.

We raced, twisting and turning and occasionally jumping. Whatever the path to the god's bed, it was larger than the space that contained it.

Gods were always larger than the space that contained them.

No wonder Federo is mad beyond lunacy. Vessel for a god. Divine catamite.

I pitied him then, even his murdering madness. Did he crave his times in the city, when he could pretend normalcy even amid the scheming?

The Factor spoke up in my memory. "Peace," he said, "and prosperity and quiet streets at night, and silent gods who could not meddle daily in the business of men."

Peace filled this quiet darkness. I wondered if Blackblood should have been silent all these years. People knew pain regardless of the god. They would know more pain under Choybalsan. He had burned much, for all that his farmers and bandits worshipped him. Choybalsan would do anything.

By the time Skinless laid my body down again, my resolve had returned. It vanished momentarily in the renewed pain of weight on my shoulder, but I knew how to find myself amid suffering.

A light flickered, forcing me to shut my eyes a moment.

When I opened them again, Skinless was fumbling with a bit of smoldering punk, moving from bowl to bowl, lighting the crudest sorts of oil lamps. I found it odd to see this shambling horror stepping to the task like some chambermaid preparing for her lord's return.

The bell lay next to me, I realized. Most of the mercury was gone, but a few drops showed a throne on my other side. A small shadowed figure perched on the edge of the seat.

It took three tries, but I managed to force my head to turn the other way. My body possessed little strength.

In the guttering light of the lamps—which smelled like no oil I knew—I could see that the throne had been made of tiny skulls. Babies, perhaps, or monkeys. I could not tell. Blackblood sat on the edge, tapping his heels.

Where Skinless was a horror out of the depths of nightmare, the god was a child. He was robed, his head hairless. His eyes were filled with blood, as after a solid beating to the head. They glinted red in the flickering light of the lamps. Otherwise, he seemed almost normal.

"I see you have arisen." Amazingly, I managed to spit the words out without howling the pain that racked my body.

"To my surprise." He frowned. "Much has changed."

"Even in the last few hours." I had to stop, close my eyes, and let my heart race a moment. This would be a very inconvenient time for it to burst. *At least let me say my piece,* I prayed.

"You have seen my theopomp. Skinless smells him upon you."

"I t-told your servant. He died in my arms, after I gave him a mercy. Choybalsan had w-wounded him beyond healing."

The lights glittered with the tears that returned to my eyes.

Blackblood made a small noise. Then: "You are not one of mine."

"No. I follow a distant Goddess."

"Skinless smells Her upon you, too."

"Soon, oh god, there will be no more for you. We were to fight Choybalsan today."

He laughed. The sound was small, light, as the twittering of birds, yet it set all my joints to grating. I was lost in that wave of pain for a while.

When I focused again, the god looked pleased with himself.

"You do not understand time, little foreign girl. You are not of us. Your offering of pain is well enough done, but I cannot and will not take you up."

Several kinds of hope bloomed. "What of Choybalsan? Will you send Skinless to fight him, if it is not too late?"

Blackblood leaned toward me, then slipped from his throne to squat barely a handspan away. I would not have touched him even if I could move, but here he was.

"Why should I?" he whispered.

This was my moment. "To preserve yourself."

His eyes slid shut. He did not breathe, any more than Skinless did, but something rippled through the god's body. Without looking at me again, he spoke. "You value continued existence differently than I, because you do not understand time. There will always be pain. There will always be me, or something in my place no different."

"Even your priests have turned against you. The Pater Primus conspired with Choybalsan, and brought his brother priests along. You have little left. Is today the day you wish to die?" Then, thinking on what he had said, "Does Skinless miss its theopomp? Do *you* miss Septio?"

This time he giggled. Another wave of pain washed over me like the tide tugging at a body on the beach. "So asks the girl who claimed his life." His smile widened. I wished I had not looked within his mouth. "You claimed his seed, too." A pale hand stretched toward my belly. "I should not be so hard on myself, were I a woman in your condition."

My gut roiled in panic. He could not mean it so. Not me. Not here. Not now. *Not Septio.*

How could any woman be pregnant the very first time she ever lay with a man? Mistress Cherlise would have laughed to hear me say so. But it was too *soon* even to begin to suspect.

Unless the god had known from the beginning . . .

Blackblood brushed his fingers over my shoulder. The pain bloomed like one of his priests' bombards, then left me. "You will bring my theopomp's child to me in time. For now, go and do what seems best to you."

I somehow expected him to vanish as the Factor had, but he hopped back upon his throne and sulked. When Skinless took me up again, this time carrying me as if *I* were the baby, I began to cry.

Moments later, with no labyrinth in our way, we were in the upper hall. Priests scattered, shouting. A pistol cracked. Skinless ignored them all, until it reached the outer doors. My heart thrilled to see that it was still daylight outside.

The avatar turned and stared back at the cowering priests who had rebelled against its god. Hefting me to its shoulder as if it meant to burp me like an infant, it closed the doors with its other hand. I peered around, away from my view of the knobs of its spine and the muscle of its back.

Skinless pressed its palm against the doors until they smoked.

When we turned away, the doors were bulged and cracked and brazed shut. Within, the screaming began.

The screaming began as well on the Street of Horizons as people scattered in wild fear of my new protector.

Skinless loped through the city. I discovered that I once more clutched my ox bell. The boning knife was gone, and with it the lives that weapon had claimed, but this reconstructed memory clopped in time to its footfalls.

In daylight, I realized how tall Skinless truly was—twice the height of a normal man, and closer to three times my own. I also understood it carried me for speed. My pain had lifted, especially the shattering in my shoulder. Even the older aches, ghosts of prior wounds, were banished.

Such a gift the pain god had given me.

Thank you, I prayed.

A great pale eye ringed with muscle fibers and little folds of fat turned toward me a moment.

Its passage left a trail of shouting and fear, but no one tried to follow. I even saw some of the Interim Council's civil guards fleeing. Fewer people were about as we approached Lyme Street. The sun stood nearly at the appointed time when I glimpsed the Textile Bourse.

A mob roared before the temporary seat of government. Either the Factor or the Rectifier had done good work. Perhaps both of them.

Then I understood my error. He had said to meet at the cistern three fingers before the sun sets. The sort of powers the Factor could bring to this fight would likely not walk in daylight.

We would need to trap Choybalsan half an hour, perhaps longer, before our forces arrived. Even Skinless was not so powerful as all that.

It dropped me gently in front of him, then stood behind me with arms folded. The edges of the mob noticed the two of us. Their shouting trailed to uneasy silence.

I brandished the bell. That was foolish, but I had no weapon, and needed to raise a sign. "I am Green!" I shouted. "I am come to aid you in throwing down this bandit god-king out of the north."

Some people jeered. The Rectifier and the Tavernkeep stepped to the front of the press.

"Welcome," the pardine barbarian's voice boomed like an explosion in the street.

Bell held high, we advanced. With my hand on the rim of the sounding cup, it did not clop, but still it was my standard. I tried not to consider that I was stepping into an unwinnable fight with the unwanted burden of life just beginning to take root in my belly.

I tried not to think of children and what could happen to them in this world. I tried not to think at all. This was a time to stall for reinforcements, then fight.

The door to the Textile Bourse banged open. Nast, the old clerk, stepped out. Half a dozen guardsmen crowded around him and past him to fill the little landing at the top of the front steps.

They had pistols and crossbows in their hands, and swords across their backs. The council meant for there to be no rushing of their halls of state.

"The Interim Council takes notice of the fears of the people of Copper Downs." His voice was reedy with fatigue and stress, but it carried. I noticed Nast did not even read from the paper in his hand. "We are making favorable terms even now with the tribes who have come among us. Return to your homes, put away your fears, and await a new day of peace and prosperity. Any who leave now will be pardoned, their faces forgotten."

He looked around, his eyes widening at the sight of Skinless, then tightening once more when he saw me.

"Any who do not leave now," he continued, "are subject to the full terms of the Riot Decree. You have ten minutes to disperse."

I began pushing through the crowd toward the steps. Whatever had whipped them into a mob was fading. Too many edged away from Skinless, from the Textile Bourse, from so much trouble as all this had suddenly become.

When I gained the steps, Nast pointed me out to two crossbowmen. Though it made me itch as badly as any firevine leaf, I turned my back on them. If they shot me down now, the mob would re-form. Speaking out was my best protection.

"Copper Downs has been betrayed," I called.

A shuffling murmur answered me. The edges of the little mob had stopped bleeding men.

"An agent has been in our midst, working against us." This was not the moment to lay out my theories about how Federo had been possessed by the god. I prayed there might be a moment when such consideration mattered, but it did not seem likely.

"He has stood high in the halls of state, and made pretense of repelling our enemies, while secretly inviting them in." I drew another deep breath. "He has worked to quiet the gods before they can speak, and put the Temple Quarter to silent shame once more. He has allowed trade to be driven from the docks, employment to be lost from the factories and warehouses, and fear to run upon our streets."

"That's enough," said Nast quietly behind me. "Get along, Mistress Green, before you are pinned like a butterfly."

I turned back and gave him a steady look. "You will let all that he has done come to pass?"

"Before I permit the ruin of a war in my city?" Nast's words were brave, but his eyes were defeated. "Yes."

I faced the crowd once more. My shoulders itched worse now. "Do you want a war?"

"*No!*" Their voice was one, multiplied.

"We have not had a conflict in centuries. Why would Choybalsan bring us one now?" I glanced at the sun, which was already behind buildings, though it must yet be a finger above the horizon. "Why would Councilor Federo betray us to war?"

A pistol barked behind me. I dropped, though the ball had already whizzed past me and caught a man in advocate's robes straight in his chest. Another shot raised splinters of stone next to my head.

The mob rushed the stairs. I heaved myself over the side into the tangled, abandoned garden there, landing amid a thorny nest of roses.

This I would endure as well.

I clawed to my feet. A guardsman screamed as he flew over my head. Skinless loomed above me. I heard Nast's voice shouting, before the old clerk was cut off with a wet, breaking noise.

Down the street, more screaming began. The Factor and whomever he had summoned must be coming out of the cistern, I realized. Then lightning struck the peak of the Textile Bourse and began to dance there, and I knew the end of our plans had come.

We had hoped to take the man Federo without the god Choybalsan riding him. He was now greater than all of us.

The roof exploded. I saw him jump to the ruined peak almost directly over my head. Every window on Lyme Street shattered in a spray of glass as deadly as any pistol volley. His laughter must have echoed for furlongs.

So much for hope, I thought, and clutched at my belly to protect my baby from the fog of splinters shining orange in the sunset.

Skinless swept me up once more. The map of musculature and tendons that made up its body wept from a thousand small punctures. I tried to figure what that might mean, but it carried me away from the Textile Bourse so quickly, I could not catch up to the thought before the avatar set me down next to the Factor in the mouth of an alley.

The ghost was looking decidedly watery in the evening light. His apparent solidity underground did not hold up so well on the surface. He was also very angry. "So it has come to this."

I stood and tried to call the threads together. "There will never be a better chance than now." I spoke quickly, shouting over the rippling thunder. "We have as many forces as we can hope to summon, and Choybalsan is not surrounded by his army."

The Factor turned round slowly to look at his little group. Mother Iron, her cloak drawn tight around her face. The Thin Woodman of whom I'd been told. Three other corporeals I did not know, each demihuman and oddly shaped as the first two.

"You would kill this shark with five dolphins?" I demanded.

"And your naked wonder there."

I reached up to pat Skinless' thigh. "This is not mine, any more than they are yours."

"You have me." That was the Rectifier, bleeding from a dozen wounds.

The Tavernkeep stepped beside him. "Us as well." He was followed by Chowdry and the tan woman of his people whom I had met before.

I should have been warmed by this display, but mostly I was angry. Temper bubbled inside me, rising to color my thoughts and push reason aside. Choybalsan was defeating us merely by standing on a rooftop.

"We will join together in the Hunt," the Rectifier said behind me.

"Take up your spears." I looked around. "Do we have any pistols or crossbows? I want to get him off that high place so we can reach him."

"You won't hurt him with ranged weapons," said the Factor.

"I don't plan to hurt him. Let's make him angry enough to be stupid." Angry enough to match me, stupidity for stupidity. "I have faced him in a fight before, and beaten him down." *With the aid of the Dancing Mistress.* "If I distract him sufficiently now, draw him away from the height of his power, Skinless and Mother Iron and the rest can slay him." I took a deep breath, shaking. "But we need to get him *off the roof!*"

The pardines scattered, calling for the weapons I'd requested. The Rectifier and the tan woman bounded across Lyme Street and ran along the front of the line of buildings, out of Choybalsan's view. The Tavernkeep sprinted down the middle of the road, shoving past the fleeing crowd of citizens that were the remains of the earlier mob, along with whatever locals had had enough.

I sighted my finger at Choybalsan and wished that the Lily Goddess had granted me something more powerful than obligation.

Choybalsan turned and looked at me. His smile was visible even at my distance. I tasted metal in my mouth, and my hair began to prickle.

"Move, *now!*" I shouted, and ran for the street.

Light immediately behind me etched shadows in my vision. It came with a sizzling noise, like oil boiling, and was followed by a thunderclap that drove me painfully to my knees. My little wooden bell spun slowly on a cobble.

I could hear nothing. The shadows refused to be blinked away. Shaking my head, I rose to my feet. Someone pressed something into my hand. The Tavernkeep, I realized. I looked stupidly at the pistol he'd given me.

"I do not know how to use it," he said apologetically, though I could barely hear him.

I felt that metal taste again. "Get away! He's throwing lightning at anyone who comes near me." My best armor right now was the fact that Choybalsan still wanted something—the shred of the Duke's old power he believed I still held, that he required to complete his transformation.

How to turn that against him?

Lightning struck beside me again as the Tavernkeep sprinted away. This time, I had my eyes closed and my head bowed. My entire body felt as if it were smoldering, but I was neither blinded nor driven off my feet.

When I looked again, the Tavernkeep was picking himself up and staggering farther away. Skinless stood beside me once more, staring up at Choybalsan. Mother Iron stepped up to my other side.

The challenge would be clear enough. Now to bring him down.

I raised the clumsy pistol and aimed it at the god's feet, where he stood on a smoldering peak of the Textile Bourse's roof. The weapon barked and spat when I pulled the trigger. Stone spalled away from the facing well below him.

So much for accuracy. I was too far—pistols were never much good past a few dozen feet anyway. I threw the weapon aside.

Lightning continued to arc around Choybalsan. The roof smoked, and the thunder was deafening. Even in the face of such eye-bright violence, we had been wrong to flee the Textile Bourse before. I walked down the street. I would approach the god Choybalsan with upturned face and weaponless hands rather than cowering among the untended roses below his feet. My escort of avatars and sendings came with me.

I saw a crossbow bolt soar upward from near the foot of the building. It was a magnificent shot. Had Choybalsan been a man, he would have fallen with a wounded foot. As it was, he aimed lightning into the little garden of the building next door. Whichever of my allies had taken that shot did not fire again.

He had still not struck me down. Likewise he did not spend lightning on my escort. I stood in the street before the Textile Bourse, amid dropped weapons, pools of blood, charred wood, and the debris of a fleeing crowd. Spreading my arms wide, I called up to him.

"You wish to take your missing measure of grace from me!" I shouted. "Come down here and do so!"

Choybalsan jumped forty feet off the building to land flat on his heels in front of me. My escort was tense, ready to leap at him, but awaiting the word from me.

I held it back. The lightning had stopped.

"So you are ready to give up the last of my power." I could still see Federo, but he was filled with the overwhelming largeness of the god. His voice echoed in the bones of my chest, though to my ears he spoke as an ordinary man.

"You may try to take it from me."

"You must *give* it." His voice grew lower, as if rumbling through stones.

"No." So this was the point of contention. He had somehow hoped to use the Dancing Mistress to persuade me to this, back at the camp before we escaped. "I will not give you the last key to the locks of your power. Any more than I will give you my life."

Beside me, Skinless quivered. I nodded.

My allies fell upon the god. The Factor swept in, acting for the first time like a gibbering ghost of legend, followed by his trail of servant-shades.

Though I stood so close to their violence I could have reached a hand in like a trainer stopping a dog fight, I did not move back. I needed to see what happened next.

Lightning arced once more, but now it leapt from roofpeak to roofpeak down the length of Lyme Street. Sheets of sparks jumped across the width of the street. Balls of fire sizzled and rolled along the cobbles. The thunder became one rippling roar that faded as my hearing gave out.

This *was* like watching a pack of curs. These tulpas of the city hated the new god. They tore at him, butted him, grabbed him. Mother Iron's hands glowed red as she scored Choybalsan's skin with scorched furrows. The Thin Woodman rained blows upon him that would have cracked the bones of a mortal. One of their fellows, a shambling green mound that might have been the avatar of rot, extended a film of slime over Choybalsan's head. Skinless simply pounded him with giant naked fists.

The god subsided. He dropped to the pavement, first on his knees, then curled on his side. The lightning sizzled to a stop. Cool evening air blew across me in a sudden breeze. I thought the fight was over.

Skinless reached down to tear Choybalsan's arms off when the god rolled onto his back and opened his eyes. Now he showed wounds—not of this fight, though. Horrible burns that wept red and pale fluid.

I realized this damage had been inflicted when the Dancing Mistress and I had blown his tent apart. They seemed fresh even now, which made me pity Federo's agony, wherever he was beneath the wrappings of the god. He showed his true aspect.

We were winning. The god was down, and his powers were sloughing away. I actually smiled at the Factor, who stood on the other side of the fight with a grim expression on his spectral face.

When Skinless began to tug Choybalsan apart, the god flexed his muscles to shatter the avatar's forearms. It screamed, a thin, high keening like a frightened rabbit, and fell back. Choybalsan tucked forward and leapt to his feet. He grabbed at the shambling green thing and shredded it, scattering the bits. He broke the Thin Woodman in half and threw him over the rooftops toward the next block. He bore Mother Iron into a hug that made her wheeze like an overworked ship's kettle, then slammed her to the pavement so hard the cobbles shattered.

Finally, he turned to me. Lightning returned, dancing on the rooftops, setting the iron fences of the little garden beds aglow.

Despite my brave words earlier, I knew I could not fight him again. His divine aspect was full upon him.

How do I defeat a god? No priests were here to kill, and he had an army of worshippers outside the city. That was what they were here for—not to overrun the city, but to maintain the fervor of their newfound faith in Choybalsan.

He had prayer. I had anger. But my anger drove only me and those close by me to battle. The god had just struck down the most powerful beings I knew to throw at him.

What would Endurance do? What would my grandmother do?

Patience. They each in their way would have counseled patience.

His hand reached toward me. The fingers were smashed, I saw, held together by the main force of his will.

A series of questions flashed through my mind.

Why had the explosion hurt him? That was not a thing of my hands.

Why had the glass hurt Skinless, who could not be touched by weapons? *Because the glass had been hurled by a god.*

What god had set the fire and storm in Choybalsan's tent? The god that was him, his sliver of grace within me.

I dropped heavily to sit on the cobbles. "Stay your hand, Choybalsan. I shall release what you seek."

Even through the rolling thunder, he heard me. His hand drew back and a smile that was something of Federo crossed his ruined face.

A long, narrow shard of cobalt blue glass lay near me. I picked it up, moving with the deliberate pace of ritual while I tried to think past the next few seconds.

Such power as made Choybalsan a god now had first been stolen, or taken, from the Dancing Mistress' people. That was a power of woodlands and meadows and the turning of the world's life.

The Duke had held the power next. To hear the Factor speak, the Duke had thought himself a force for preservation, even renewal. He had never called lightnings or made war the way Choybalsan seemed all too ready to do.

Then I had snatched the power away and set it free. It was a cruel strength—the pardines hunted and had once made war; the Duke in turn had been ruthless in his rule—but that was the cruelty of the natural world. Not the deliberate goading and betrayals of Choybalsan. Even the Duke had been more like a farmer extinguishing weeds and scavengers among his crop.

Patience. The world was patient.

I slit my left forearm again with the glass, careful not to cut the vein. As the blood began to flow, I cast the glistening shard aside and took up my little wooden bell. I held it from the top this time and let the clappers swing as the blood fell on the stones. The bell echoed with its wooden clop as it had underground.

Goddess, I prayed, *send the least of Your servants to me. I offer up my own blood, and through me a part of the blood of the child within me, to carry the last measure of this grace which was never mine, out of my body and into Your servant.*

The gods in this place were silent, or were barely roused, but I knew that the Lily Goddess was fully clothed in Her power across the sea. However great or small She might be measured against Choybalsan, She attended me.

I rang the bell awhile, but nothing happened. No flash of light, no creaking of the Wheel, no manifestation in the street. Just me, a foolish girl with a little wooden bell, which I finally dropped.

"Thank you for your offering," Choybalsan said. Even gods could be sarcastic. He bent down to stroke his burned fingers in the blood.

That was when I realized the bell still echoed.

The god heard it, too. He glanced at my own bell, cast aside. He looked past me. Something changed in the set of his body.

Clutching closed the wound on my arm, I stood and turned.

Endurance walked slowly down Lyme Street. Though I knew him to be dead and gone, he approached with the steady pace I remembered from the first days of my life. His bell, his real bell, clopped in time with the fall of his feet.

My grandmother sat astride his back. She was wrapped in her cloak of bells. Except my grandmother was never so tall.

I looked carefully and saw a tail sweeping away from the hem of the cloak.

The Dancing Mistress.

I opened my mouth to cry gladly, then shut it again. A stream of pardines came out of alleys and side streets, so that in moments a crowd of her people followed behind—far more than I had ever seen. Dozens. Scores.

The three who had fought with me—the Rectifier, the Tavernkeep, and the tan woman—rose from their hiding places and stepped quickly to stand beside the ox. Chowdry followed them, drawn perhaps by the familiar costume my teacher wore.

What had she done?

What had *I* done?

The lightning died. Choybalsan stood tall, beside me now as the two of us stood together to meet the coming challenge.

The Dancing Mistress slipped off her cloak of bells. I saw this was not my grandmother's belled silk, that I had mistaken it so only because she was astride the ox. Endurance's eyes gleamed as he pitched his head toward me, ringing his bell again, but he did not seek to call me back.

She handed the silk to Chowdry. Though it seemed he could move only one arm, he took the cloth and gathered it close as best he could, before giving me a long look of mute appeal.

"Federo," the Dancing Mistress said.

"Choybalsan," the god corrected her.

She slid from the back of the ox and walked toward us. "You have something that does not belong to you. Something that was never meant for men."

"Whoever this power might once have belonged to, it is mine now." He flexed his ruined fingers, then pointed to a building down the street. A single bolt of lightning struck the roof, breaking off shattered bricks and smoldering splinters.

"That trick grows old," I found myself saying.

He looked at me with a set of his eyes that chilled my blood once again. "You are both here. Together you are the keys."

"No." The Dancing Mistress was at arm's length now. Her people had followed close behind, the ox Endurance with them.

I did not hear the wheezing bellows of his breath as I had always known them. That was when I understood that I had succeeded in reaching out to the divine. My measure of grace had spoken, my piece of the Duke's power. Endurance was not a sending so much as he was a calling.

A quiet, voiceless god of patience, if he survived long enough to grow as I understood that gods could do.

The Dancing Mistress went on: "There are no keys. You are a flawed vessel. Like a water crock into which someone has poured the red iron of the forge. You were never meant to hold this power."

The Factor stepped close. His shade flickered. I could see the pardines disturbed him. "Release the power, Federo," he said. "This has mastered you rather than you mastering it."

"No." Choybalsan began to quiver. I could taste metal in my mouth once more. "No, I will *not* let go!"

The Dancing Mistress' claws came out. "You cannot be touched by weapons, but I have a hundred of my kindred behind me. I assure you that we can lay claws on you until you are nothing but a ribbon of blood in the street."

Patience. Every time this dispute came to blows, somehow affairs grew worse. I had the habit of killing people, but this was both more and less than that.

We did not need to kill this god. We needed to persuade him to lay himself down.

"Please," I told the Dancing Mistress. "Please let me try."

I took Federo's hand as the god within him raised his other arm to call down more wrath. He tried to snatch it away, but somehow could not. Instead he turned to look at me.

"You came to claim me, thirteen years ago." I gripped his fingers close, as if he were Papa and holding tight could have saved me back then.

"That was the man Federo," he rumbled in the voice that made my ribs ache.

Ignoring him, I went on. "I hated you for it. You were kind enough, and spared me good words, and fed me better than I had ever eaten in my life. Sometimes, for a child, that can be enough."

His eyes held a distant, almost lopsided look. "You were a wise girl." I heard the man inside the god.

"Now I have come to claim you back. Whatever love you hold for *her*," and with that word I cast my eyes toward the Dancing Mistress, "whatever love you hold for me, let that be enough for you to follow me as I once followed you."

"I do not know how to let go," Federo whispered. Sparks crackled within the god's eyes. He shoved me away. I owe my life now to the fact that it was the man who pushed me and not the god, for I merely fell to the stones of the street instead of skittering half a block to the sound of shattering bones.

A stampede erupted. I curled tight as dozens of clawed feet pelted past me in a sudden burst of movement. For a panicked moment, I closed my eyes. I was too cowardly to face my death.

What came was not the shredding of my body, but the tearing noise of lightning slashing the air. I tasted metal yet again. All the hairs on my skin stood like spikes. Thunder clawed at my ears until only a heavy, smothering silence remained, though the stones beneath me carried the sound to my bones, echoing much as the god's voice had.

Goddess, I prayed, *a mercy on us all.*

I opened my eyes to see the divine Endurance standing over me, much as the ox had once done in my father's fields. Just beyond his front legs was a terrible roil of spark and flame and fur and claw. Pardines exploded under the stabbing bolts of lightning, flesh and blood and pelt shredding in arcs leading away from the violence.

My eyes were driven toward blindness from the glare, much as my ears had been from the noise. I capped my hand over my brows and tried to look only at feet.

That was bad enough. They clawed, fought, climbed. Skinless' great muscled legs passed my view. Lightning flashed and glared off the blood slicks on the cobbles. My whole body felt a bruising from the ripping electrick bolt, the buffeting of the wounded air.

Then there was no more. The lightning had stopped, along with everything else. Even in my deafness, I could sense that a hush had descended. I crawled out from beneath the ox, and with my right hand on his flank, got to my feet.

Carnage. Dead pardines everywhere. Skinless lay shattered, still as any anatomist's worktable project. Only Endurance and I stood.

The Dancing Mistress lay before me, coiled with Federo. She'd managed to bang his head into the cobbles sufficiently for reason to leave him. With his thoughts fled, the lightning had ceased.

It was indeed Federo. The aspect of the god had drained away.

The Rectifier loped up to me. He had a slender stone knife in his hand. I saw his triangular mouth flex as he said something to me that I could not yet hear; then he bent over to slice off Federo's fingers.

I launched myself at him, slipping on a slick of blood. Though my attack was wild, and he far, far larger, I took the Rectifier in the side of the leg and staggered him two paces away from Federo with the corpse yet unmutilated.

He whirled on me with the knife held low, then pulled his blow when he realized who his attacker was. The Rectifier bent, the knucklebones in his fur jiggling. He asked me a question. This time I heard his voice as if from a long, hollow tube.

Pointing at my ears, I tried to say, "Leave them be. I will see to them."

The Rectifier stood his ground, then tossed his head toward Federo. The meaning was clear enough. *You go first, then, and good luck to you.*

I looked to Endurance, then stepped over to my two fallen. The Dancing Mistress still breathed, though her ears were torn off and her face was a burned mess. I could not see that Federo still breathed.

The god had definitely left him. Where was Choybalsan? For a moment, I did not care.

Kneeling beside them, I wept to see their wounds. All of us seemed set one against the other as a matter of bloody, violent course.

The shake of Endurance's head, the clop-clop of his bell, brought me back. I turned to look up at my first friend in life, and I knew where the god had gone.

The ox was surrounded by the avatars and sendings from Below. Lightning danced in Endurance's eyes, illuminating a knowing squint I had never before seen.

Patience. I had called a god of patience. Who had no voice to rally armies and suborn priests. Who had no hands to direct the lightnings he might pull down from heaven. Who could stand quietly and watch over the angry spirit within him, centuries of human power and pardine loss compressed to the rumble of a ruminant's complex gut.

I had placed the greatest threat seen for generations into the tulpa born of my father's ox.

Even better, I had slain no gods.

Laughter bubbled up inside me. It roiled like the tide through rocks, spilling out through every part of my body, my soul, my voice. I fell beside the Dancing Mistress and Federo as the waves broke into tears. This could not be what the Goddess had meant for me, for all of us.

I slumped to a seat on the cobbles of the road and cried. My heart flooded into the world, tear by tear, sob by sob, and left nothing within my chest except a hollow beating. Finally I looked at the Dancing Mistress. Her eyes were open now. The left was filmy with the lightning burns that had scarred her face. The right looked at me with a tired curiosity.

I stared back at her and smiled, mouthing, *I think we won.*

The Rectifier knelt beside me again. "Can I take his fingers now?" the big pardine asked, tugging at my shoulder. "He is no longer using them."

"No!" I shouted. "Let Federo die decently."

"Death is never decent, human. We reclaim what is ours."

The Dancing Mistress' burned hand shot up to grasp the Rectifier's wrist. Her fingers were tight in his fur, shaking the stone knife he still held.

The Rectifier said something in the sibilant language of their people. She spat an answer, then turned to me. "I was . . . wrong. Do not . . . allow him . . ."

"Do not allow him what?"

"Do not let him . . . take it . . . back . . ."

Her eyes closed again as her hand fell to her side. I reached out to touch her lips—still breathing.

Thank you, Goddess.

When I looked up again, the Rectifier was slicing off Federo's fingers.

"No!" I shouted. I scrambled to my feet and tried to hit him, but he knocked me away and continued cutting. I scrambled around in the street among the bodies until I found a dropped spear. Hefting it, I ran toward the Rectifier.

This time he jumped up and grabbed the head as I rushed him. He was *fast*. I knew that, often as I'd sparred with the Dancing Mistress.

The Rectifier snapped the weapon out of my hands. I had to let go to avoid breaking my wrists. Then he came for me claws out. This time he was fighting for real.

"What are you taking back?" I shouted. I needed to change this game, for sparring with him would surely kill me.

He circled. His legs were nearly twice as long as mine, so matching me step for step, he covered twice as much ground. I received no answer.

I looked around for another weapon as I backed farther away. The Rectifier moved faster than I could track him, and launched a disemboweling kick. Sliding sideways to avoid the blow, I tripped and lost my balance. I went sprawling.

He rushed for a feet-down leap, as I had with Choybalsan in the tent. The dropped spear poked against my side. I rolled and grabbed it. The Rectifier overran where I had been, then spun on his heel to come back at me. I rolled again and turned the spear point-up.

He veered off once more.

Water dripped on my face. I scrambled to my feet, swatting it away. A sending from the Goddess. I circled back around the bodies of the Dancing Mistress and Federo.

The Rectifier wasn't going to let me take the time I needed. He came back again with a wide-handed swipe as he danced past me. No more crushing leaps to the chest. His claws took furrows of flesh out of my upper right arm.

The rush of pain nearly made me drop the spear.

Like Septio and the rest of Blackblood's priests, I knew what to do with pain. Shifting more of the weight of the weapon to my off hand, I used my right for balance. I thought I was about where I needed to be.

I was moving slowly. Too terribly slow. The Rectifier continued to dance like a leaf on a wind. He blurred in and out of my peripheral vision, moving behind me faster than I could turn, appearing on one side then the other.

"I take back what your people stole from mine," he said calmly.

Another open-handed attack. I parried with the spear and nearly lost the weapon once more.

He spun past me. His voice boomed behind me. "What the Dancing Mistress swore to help bring me to."

I snapped the spear butt backwards and ducked low. He sailed over my head, cursing as he struck the shaft and set it spinning loose from my grip. The Rectifier lost control of his leap in the same blow and landed hard on his belly. I jumped on his back, feet between his shoulders, and forced his jaw to the stone.

The crack was like the breaking of a tree.

His fur slipped beneath my feet, and I rolled forward onto my freshly wounded arm. I bellowed with my pain and came back to find myself in the street of wounded and their weapons.

The Rectifier rose, shaking off the blow, but he was not moving correctly now. I crabbed sideways, leery of my own pain, grabbing again for a weapon. The spear was gone, but I nearly tripped over a sword. The handle was big, the blade was too heavy, but I heaved it into my grip.

He wasn't in front of me. Instead, the big pardine charged toward Endurance. The Rectifier's pace wove as he ran. Skinless stepped in to block him, but he knocked the pain god's avatar aside with a mighty blow.

The ox did not even lower his horns. He stared at his attacker, lightning circling in those deep brown eyes, as the Rectifier leapt onto Endurance's shoulders like a hunting panther onto a kill.

I realized I was running, dragging the too-heavy sword behind. At the ox's bellow, I dropped the weapon and sprinted the last few steps to grab at the Rectifier's tail.

"Help me stop him!" I shouted. "Before he kills our new god!"

The Factor was at my side. Two of the city guards. Chowdry. A man in the plain suit of a clerk, marred by soot and burns. The Tavernkeep. A pardine I did not know. Mother Iron.

Our little mob clawed and clutched at the Rectifier. The knucklebones woven into his chest were toggles. His skin stretched. Hair tore, some popped free, others crackled with the last energies of their former owners.

Finally the Rectifier tumbled loose from Endurance. The ox bellowed again, then charged away into the darkness followed by his train of guardians. Little flowers bloomed where his blood dropped to the cobbles.

I stood aside as a dozen others bore the Rectifier to the ground. My lungs gasped for air so hard, I feared I would spew. My body shook as I placed my hands above my knees and leaned forward.

Finally I straightened and looked around.

The Rectifier was still down, blades and crossbows and pistols now keeping him there. The ox was gone, as were the rest of the divines and the ghosts. A small crowd of people surrounded us, the circle drawing closer as more and more streamed into Lyme Street.

"Anyone else?" I asked wearily.

The Tavernkeep stepped forward and took my arm. "I believe it is done."

"Good." I had no idea what he was talking about.

People pushed closer, except in a little lane where the tracks of the fleeing god left a stream of lilies blooming tall in the moonlight. These were not the survivors of the Interim Council. These were not priests and bankers. They were just people.

Questions flowed. Amid the buzz, I realized they were asking themselves, each other, me, what happened. Not fear, now, though there were dead and wounded aplenty already being borne off.

"Let me tell you a story," I said quietly. Somehow my voice echoed loud, pushing a ring of silence away from me. When I opened my mouth again, I spoke to a thousand listening ears. Swallows chirped as they circled overhead.

"Let me tell you a story," I repeated, "about a people who gave up their power long ago. A city man took it from them. Some agreed to this, but not all."

The silence held. I continued: "This man made himself prince of his city. He ruled for generations. There was peace, prosperity, a time of quiet. The gods fell silent, for the power was like a blanket to them. This took the soul of the people, for what are gods if not the sum of everyone who follows them? Choices fell away, as the power cared only for itself. Even so, the bargain was good for most.

"In time, some of the first people conspired with some of the city people to wrest the power back from the prince. The city would be free to be ruled and grow as it chose, to have gods once more. The people would have their souls restored and rediscover their might."

I paused again, but still the street was filled with listening ears.

"This theft went awry, or perhaps the power was stolen yet again. It came to rest in another. After centuries of replacing the habits of the gods of the city, the power thought itself a god. It rode the man it wore as worms might ride the heart of a dog. This new god would be feared in every land between the city center and the boundaries of the plate of the world.

"It wished to be a titanic reborn. It lacked only a last shard of the old power, a final measure of grace.

"Tonight this god has passed from the world, and taken the luckless man with it. In its place has been reborn a god of patience. The first god of this city come anew in more centuries than I know to count. This god is the ox Endurance. Voiceless, that the city might listen. Handless, that the city might not be quick to fight. Capable of drawing a plow deep in the soil, that the city might grow.

"Give a prayer to Endurance, for the soul of the man Federo. Give a prayer to Endurance, for the sake of the city in this tale. Give a prayer to Endurance, that he might bear you in your journey beyond death as he bore my grandmother so long ago."

I bowed my head. The crowd slowly dispersed without responding. No cheer. No catcalling. Just people talking quietly.

The wounded and the dead went with them, for tending. So did most of the mess in the street—souvenir-takers or just civic pride. Torches were set in front of the ruins of the Textile Bourse as some went in and others came out.

Eventually the Tavernkeep leaned close. "Come to my place," he said. "You must eat, and be warm awhile."

Chowdry held my arm as we followed the pardine through the city. The tavern was crowded to overflowing with the Tavernkeep's people—they held a remembrance for those lost, and discussions concerning those being cared for in the upstairs rooms.

A place was cleared, and some good Selistani curry set before me. The Tavernkeep sat with me a moment.

"Why are they not rising in anger?" I waved my spoon at the room.

"They followed the Dancing Mistress here to stop Choybalsan. Very few knew of her deeper purpose with the Rectifier."

"The conspiracy within the conspiracy," I muttered. Conspire to rid the city of the Duke and then conspire to reclaim his power.

"I do not think she had always intended that."

"I will miss her," I told him. "I would have loved to hear it from her lips."

"Are you leaving?" He seemed surprised.

"I . . . I don't know."

"Well, she is not dead. She lies in one of my rooms upstairs."

Shoving the curry aside, I nearly knocked over my chair in my haste to rise. "I will go see her."

A bustle erupted at the door. Two of the city guards pushed in, looking haggard. One had a bruise mottling his face. They brought Mr. Nast with them.

"Where is Mistress Green?" the clerk asked in his thin, severe voice.

"Here," I said. The Dancing Mistress waited upstairs while this piece of business bedeviled me.

His eyes caught mine across the room. "Begging your pardon, Mistress," he said, "but Captain Jeschonek would like to know what you plan to do about the army camped on the Barley Road. They've raised some bloody great fires out there."

"For the love of all that's holy," I began, then stopped myself. "What does Jeschonek want from me?"

"The captain says it was you that mislaid their god, it should be you that explains to them."

A thousand armed men on the verge of riot. I strongly considered telling him no. The Interim Council would have a difficult time winkling me out of this place where I was surrounded by dozens of the Dancing Mistress' people.

Still, I'd gone to a great deal of trouble to stop them from fighting. Starting it all over again seemed deeply pointless.

"Bring me Chowdry," I said to the Tavernkeep. "He's getting a promotion."

By the time I stumbled back across the room, the Selistani was at the door, looking worried.

"I have a new job for you," I told him. "The god Endurance has an army of worshippers outside the city. They will need a priest who speaks Seliu."

We went to calm a fractious force of farmers and hillmen and their bandit cousins, and tell them that their god had become an ox.

Anticipation

Some weeks later I rode up the Barley Road into the hills. Somehow I was once more upon a horse. Autumn was hard in the air, carrying a frosty edge that had me longing for the warm nights of Kalimpura. I wore many layers, but the cold contrived to bother me intensely.

I had no fear of bandits. The few still haunting the area were very afraid of me. Most of the countrymen had been listening to Chowdry. Endurance was already having an effect on both the Petraeans of Copper Downs and their rural cousins.

This day, I was bound for the high tombs and the half-wild orchards that spread out on the slopes below them. In one saddlebag, I carried spices and cookware for the cottage holder who had sheltered me. In the other, I had brought a few books and some warm winter clothing for Mistress Danae, should I be lucky enough to find her. Otherwise, I would leave them at the cottage. Paper and charcoals as well, for me to take up sketching again if time and energy permitted.

I held certain hopes for this day, of course. To learn more of anyone else who might have survived the Factor's house. To spread well-deserved thanks. To be away from Copper Downs for a while. Despite my destination, the dead did not interest me, not even those chattersome ancients in the high tombs.

The Rectifier was gone. None of his people would say exactly how he'd slipped their net, which meant they'd let him go. Which was too bad, in a way—I'd come to appreciate the old rogue. His purposes and mine had been somewhat in opposition at the end, but even I understood that our soulpaths were aligned.

The pain god's temple was shut for a time. A few half-trained acolytes and long-retired priests worked to restore substance to Blackblood.

Endurance had no temple yet, but the mineheads leading Below seemed a likely location. Chowdry was very busy. So were the priests recruited from the former army. I had sent letters to Kalimpura, to certain Courts and temples, and most especially to the Temple of the Silver Lily.

Nast paid me my bond, but I told him I had reasons to winter over. Instead of taking ship, I placed the money with the Tavernkeep. Him I trusted more than any bank, and I needed to stay awhile. Whoever my child was to be, her story would begin here in the shadow of my father's ox.

I vowed her first memory would not be, like mine, the celebration of a death. The silk the Dancing Mistress had worn into battle covered me quite nicely, and had nearly the right number of bells upon it. I did not know where she had gotten it, or why. There had been a sufficiency of sendings and divine manifestations that night for me to believe almost anything.

In the days since, I'd sewn a new bell at each dawn. The ancients here did not bury their dead in the sky as we had at home, but they were high in the hills, which seemed much the same to me. I patted my belly and the child hidden within as I rode into the day, the sum of my years singing a quiet song of death and life upon my shoulders.

My grandmother would have been proud of me.

I knew Endurance was.